AMERICAN SKY

AMERICAN SKY

A NOVEL

CAROLYN DASHER

LAKE UNION
PUBLISHING

Published by Lake Union Publishing, Seattle

www.apub.com

Amazon, the Amazon logo, and Lake Union Publishing are trademarks of Amazon.com, Inc., or its affiliates.

EU product safety contact:
Amazon Media EU S. à r.l.
38, avenue John F. Kennedy, L-1855 Luxembourg
amazonpublishing-gpsr@amazon.com

ISBN-13: 9781662526435 (paperback)
ISBN-13: 9781662526428 (digital)

Cover design by Mumtaz Mustafa
Cover image: © John De Bord, © Marcos Peralta / Shutterstock;
© NNehring / Getty; © Matilda Delves / ArcAngel

Interior image: © Denys / Adobe Stock

Printed in the United States of America

For Peter

1908–1943

CHAPTER 1

The kitchen air was thick with the sweet scent of plums, all lined up on the windowsill to ripen. Adele swiped the biggest one as she ran past. There was no one downstairs to tell her she couldn't. To tell her to slow down, to walk like a young lady. Her father and brothers were upstairs putting on their Sunday suits while her mother was pinning up Pauline's hair and buttoning her into her ivory silk wedding dress. Adele had been instructed to sit still and wait. She wasn't allowed to put on her own dress until the last minute; her mother wasn't taking any chances. She'd squirmed on the horsehair settee in the parlor for a quarter of an hour—watching the hand on the mantel clock judder forward one slow tick at a time—before deciding she could wait just as well out in the near barn.

The screen door thwapped shut behind her. She winced—if only she'd caught it before it slammed. "Adele!" her mother hollered, leaning out Pauline's window. "Get back in the house this instant!" Adele pretended not to hear. It was raining, on a wedding day, which had put all the grown-ups in a bad mood. Pauline had nearly cried at breakfast. "Don't," said their mother. "It'll swell your eyes up." Pauline had dabbed at her eyes with her napkin, eaten very little, then taken herself upstairs. Adele had been sent to do her sister's chores, plus her own. It had occurred to her as she swept the back steps that with Pauline gone, she'd have to sweep them tomorrow, and the next day, and every day after.

Another reason to hate Claude Demmings. As if it weren't bad enough that he was taking her sister away. The only way to escape the extra work would be to get married herself. And since she had no intention of ever doing that, she was in a pickle.

She raced past the untidy garden beds. Ugh. The squash. Another of Pauline's jobs. Now Adele would be the one to turn them and pick the slugs off. She ran on, past the chicken pen, the final outpost of her mother's territory, to the barns and cribs. Her father's domain.

Walking now, not minding the rain, she bit into the plum. Juice dripped down her chin. They wouldn't like that, but if she got herself into enough of a state, maybe they'd decide to call the whole thing off.

She chucked the pit, wiped her hands across the bib of her overalls as she entered the near barn, and came to a stop before the high wheeler. Still new enough that men from nearby ranches kept finding reasons to stop by. Adele had watched with pride as they circled it, running their hands along the fenders, inspecting the headlamps and the gasoline engine.

She hauled herself up into the seat, grasped the steering wheel with her sticky hands, and dropped so deep into pretending to drive that she didn't hear Pauline until she called out, "What are you doing up there? Mother's ready to tan you. You want Daddy in on that too?"

Adele took it as a good sign that her sister was still in her day dress. Maybe they'd arrive late enough to the church that Claude would just go away. She patted the seat, inviting Pauline up. "You must be joking. And get all greasy on my wedding day?"

"There's not a speck of grease up here. Daddy'd never allow it."

Pauline toed the footboard twice before deciding to trust it. She accepted the hand Adele offered ("Oh, sticky!") and pulled herself up onto the seat. "Why are you torturing Mother today?"

The barn smelled like gasoline and musty old hay, but Pauline smelled like lilacs. Adele snuggled close to her sister and took a big sniff. "Dellie, it's going to be all right. I'm only two miles away. We'll still see each other all the time. I promise."

Pauline stroked Adele's hair back from her forehead. As always, her sister's touch settled her mind. The notion of Pauline getting married grew a little less terrible, a little more tolerable. After several minutes, Pauline stopped. "Okay now?" Adele nodded.

"Good. Let's get you cleaned up at the pump. You can bring your dress to my room and we'll get ready together." Pauline placed each foot just so as she stepped down from the high wheeler.

"It itches," said Adele as she jumped down beside her sister.

"There are worse things than an itchy dress."

That was true. Pauline marrying Claude Demmings, for instance.

The next evening after supper, Adele washed and dried the dishes by herself. The plums on the windowsill had begun to wrinkle. She took another and went back out to the near barn. There was no need to run this time. Her mother had left her alone all day, hadn't even complained about her wearing John's hand-me-down overalls, because Adele had behaved herself at the wedding the day before. She'd washed her face and neck and even behind her ears, removing every trace of sticky plum juice. She'd worn the itchy dress without complaint, clutched Pauline's enormous bunch of flowers without fidgeting. And after it was all over, she'd kissed her sister sweetly. She wasn't sure how long her freedom would last, but she planned to savor every bit of it.

She devoured the fruit in two bites. She was always hungry, and growing much too tall, according to her mother, who seemed to think limiting Adele's portions at meals would remedy that. Adele wiped her hands on her overalls and slipped into the barn, intending to climb up on the high wheeler again. To pretend she was driving it around the ranch. When she was big enough, she hoped her father would let her. John and James didn't even have to ask. There was no point in asking for herself until she could reach the pedals. Besides, she had a more immediate request for her father.

No lantern light shone from the barn, and she'd expected to have it to herself. She heard a snuffle and looked up to see a shape—someone already sitting on the high wheeler seat. Her father passed a hand over his eyes and cleared his throat. "Hey, Dellie girl. Come to look at the truck?" She heard the smile in his voice. Certain things that her mother couldn't abide, such as Adele wearing her brother's overalls and taking an interest in machinery, her father found amusing.

"Yes, sir."

"Come on up, then."

She climbed up and sat next to him. There wasn't much space—her father was a big man. Wide across the shoulders, like one of his bulls. The cold from the metal seat seeped through Adele's overalls, and she shivered. He put an arm around her. "Missing your sister?"

"Yes, sir."

"Me too." His voice sounded raspy. He took a big breath and then let it out. "But it can't be helped. Natural order of things. You'll go and get married, too, someday."

Just over a year ago in the schoolyard, Adele *had* gotten married. Dickie Greer had tied a buttercup stem around her finger, and she'd kissed him, right on the lips, in front of everyone. Dickie had white-blond hair, pale gray eyes, and big front teeth. She thought his teeth made a nice match with her nose, which she'd gotten from her father. A nose that was angular and severe—a long sight from the cute button Pauline had inherited from their mother. Dickie had a purplish scar on his left temple, and he refused, even after the ceremony, to tell Adele how he'd gotten it. He was a boy of mystery.

Several other weddings immediately followed theirs. Then the boys galloped off on their pretend horses, shouting that supper had better be ready when they came home. Adele stood watching them fire their six-shooters at one another, pretend to fall down dead, and then leap back onto their horses. This was a game she usually joined. She was dismayed that Dickie had ridden off without calling for her to follow.

She saddled up her own pretend horse and galloped after Dickie. "Hey, husband," she shouted when she caught up to him.

Dickie wheeled around. "Adele, you can't be a cowboy."

She didn't see why not—she'd been a cowboy plenty of times. But since this was their wedding day, she humored him. "I'm a cowgirl!" He scowled. "We don't have any cowgirls in this game. You got to go back to the girls and get the meal ready."

"Cooking's boring," said Adele. "I'm gonna ride horses with you all."

But the boys, Dickie included, weren't having that. Every time Adele caught up with them, they rode off somewhere else. Every time she tried to talk to them, one said, "Wives got to stay in the house." Eventually Dickie took pity on her. "You could plant a garden or something if you don't want to cook."

Despite her mother's daily pestering, Adele had never thought of herself as on her way to becoming a grown lady. One who would be expected to cook, and sew, and garden, and play the piano.

Getting married, like Pauline had just done, seemed like locking yourself up in jail. She would never get married. But now was not the time to tell her father this. Not when she wanted to ask him for something so important.

Sitting still on the chilly truck seat was impossible. There was always an itch to scratch, a rhythm her fingers needed to tap out, some bug or pollen speck drifting past that demanded grabbing. She wriggled and scratched and tapped until her father said, "What's got into you, Dellie girl? Something on your mind?"

"Well, I'm turning twelve soon."

"Twelve! My goodness." It was the sort of thing he would say if he were teasing, but his voice sounded sad. So sad it almost made her stop talking. But he would never think to give her what she wanted on his own. She had to ask—it was the only way.

"John and James got steers when they were twelve." Her brothers had grain fed and sold them for beef, then used the profit to buy more steers and sold those too. James was on his third set and John was on his second.

"So they did."

Her father sighed, and an argument in her favor—because merely wanting something was never a good enough reason in the Clemson household—revealed itself to Adele.

"If I had a steer, I'd take such good care of it. And when it was fat enough, I'd sell it and buy two more. And before long, I'd have a whole bunch of steers. I'd earn my own money, see? Then I wouldn't have to go off and get married. Like Pauline. I could stay right here with you and earn my own keep."

"Oh, Dellie." His bulk shifted, and the truck seat trembled. In the dim, she worried he was about to laugh at her, but he was just fishing in his pocket for his pipe and tobacco. He passed the tobacco pouch for her to sniff. It smelled rich and loamy, with a hint of honey. She passed it back, and he tamped some into the pipe with his thumb. "You can't imagine it now, but you'll want to marry someone someday. It's just what happens when you grow up."

He lit the pipe and puffed. Adele waited, telling herself he'd most likely say no. It was silly to even hope.

"You really want your own steer?"

"Yes, sir. I really do."

He puffed again. "Your mother will have an absolute conniption."

Adele threw her arms around him and planted a kiss on his bristly cheek. He chuckled and said, "But you'll have to take good care of it *and* do all your chores. I don't want to hear any complaining about you not doing your share."

"I'll do everything she asks, Daddy. I promise."

Adele kept her word about the chores, and Pauline, for a time anyway, kept hers about visiting. She rode to the Clemson ranch a couple of times a week. Sometimes Adele and her mother rode to Pauline's. But then Pauline got too big to ride a horse. And then she had the first baby. A bald, bright-pink creature who fussed constantly and looked too much like Claude for Adele's taste. Pauline was tired and distracted, and just beneath her lilac smell lurked a hint of sour milk. Adele turned her attention to her steer. She fed it and watered it and combed it. She led it into the turnout pen every day and mucked out the holding pen. She talked to it and sang to it. Her father and brothers teased her, saying wasn't it the prettiest steer they ever saw. Adele didn't mind—it *was* the prettiest steer on the Clemson property.

She named it Beanie because it had a white patch on its flank in the shape of a kidney bean, and then she hardened her heart against it. Beanie was headed to market. To the dinner table. Once he was big enough, it would be wasteful to continue feeding him good grain.

When the time came to sell Beanie, Adele wanted to go along. But her father said they'd get a better price if she didn't. "They won't think he's as good as he is if they know a little girl raised him." She bristled at being called a little girl. She was almost as tall as her brother John, who was allowed to go along while Adele stayed home. Where her mother would badger her to work on her sewing. "I'm sorry, Dellie," said her father, "but it's the order of things. You want as much for him as you can get, don't you?"

She did. She stayed behind.

Her feelings were soothed somewhat when Beanie sold for more per weight than John's best steer did. She handed the money back to her father and asked for two more.

"Now, Adele, that's enough," said her mother.

Adele and her father started to protest. "No, Jim, I'm putting my foot down. Look at the state of her. Running around all day in overalls. Can't sew a straight seam. Useless in the kitchen. She's a young lady now, and she needs to behave like one."

When her father dipped his chin, Adele knew all was lost. He would defer to his wife. He usually did when it came to Adele and Pauline.

Just as her mother didn't interfere with his plans and instructions for James and John. Letting Adele raise Beanie had been an exception to the way things ran in the Clemson household. Her mother was not fond of exceptions.

Adele put her money in a cigar box and stashed it beneath her bed. Every now and then, especially if she'd had a bad day, she'd pull the box out, count the bills and the coins, and picture the calves they could buy.

The months that followed were full of bad days, and she frequently pulled the box from its hiding place. Adele had complained to her best friends, Susanna and Franny, about her domestic imprisonment, but they'd been more perplexed than sympathetic. Only the year before, Susanna and Franny used to ride over and play outside with her. They had jumped from the haymow into the unbaled hay below. They'd swung high and higher on the swing her father had hung from the barn rafters until the ropes went slack and they felt their stomachs drop. But lately Susanna and Franny just wanted to sit in the parlor with their ankles crossed and their skirts unmussed, comparing embroidery patterns.

They seemed to have crossed some border, invisible to Adele, and taken up residence in the world of Pauline and their mothers. Adele sensed her friends trying to drag her across the border too. She knew she ought to want to follow them. She ought to want to cook a good pot roast and sew a straight seam. To fill a hope chest with hemstitched linens and lacy underthings. To dream of marrying and setting up house.

She did still pine for Dickie Greer. His hair had darkened to the color of wet straw. He'd grown into his teeth at last. But Adele was a good three inches taller than he was, and he wouldn't even look at her. His cheeks remained smooth, but no doubt he'd turn pimply and sweaty and gangly any day, then grow into a man who would expect her to spend her life sewing and cooking. "Well, what else would he expect?" asked Susanna.

Susanna and Franny asked after James and John every time they came over. Wondering where Adele's brothers were. (Out working at whatever their father wanted them to do. Out driving the motor truck, stringing barbed wire, herding cattle.) Wondering what their favorite foods were. (Anything put before them—they were constantly ravenous, and their mother never limited *their* portions.) Wondering whether they'd be going to the spring dance. (Who knew? Adele certainly didn't plan to go herself. Dances didn't interest her.)

She began lighting out for the barn when she heard them coming up the drive. Let her mother entertain or shoo them off. "Your friends just left," said her mother as Adele crept in through the kitchen door. "They're probably not too far down the road. You'll catch them if you hurry."

Adele picked up a paring knife and started on the potatoes. "That's all right. I'd rather stay here."

Her mother sighed. "Suit yourself. And brighten up, young lady. No one likes a moper."

This was true. Adele didn't like them herself. But how was she supposed to keep from moping when a lifetime stretched out before her with nothing fun in it? How would her mother like it if someone told her she could never play the piano again?

"You should be proud of yourself, Adele." Her head snapped up. This was something new. "I mean it. I see how you've been trying. That apple pie you made last week was delicious. And your quilt is coming along beautifully. Granted, it's a simple pattern, but the blocks are uniform. And the colors are pretty."

She stopped peeling potatoes and stared at her mother, waiting for the "but."

"So we don't understand, your father and I, why you're hiding from your friends and acting gloomy."

"Well . . . ," Adele started, but her mother wasn't finished.

"It's not good for your features. All this frowning is going to carve lines in your face." Adele suddenly saw her path forward. Before her mother could offer her yet another jar of cold cream, she interrupted.

"I know just what you mean," she said.

Now it was her mother's turn to stare. "You do?"

"Yes. I don't want to ruin my features. I don't want," she lied, "to be an old maid. But it's hard to smile when the thing I want the most isn't allowed."

"Oh, Adele. Not that steer business again."

"Please, Mother. Listen for a moment. What if someone took your piano away? What if they told you that you could never, ever play music again?"

Mrs. Clemson's face paled. "Well, I don't see how . . . it's not the same thing. The piano is an appropriate pastime for young ladies. If you had only let me teach you—"

"But way back a long time ago, I bet the piano wasn't considered appropriate for young ladies to play. I mean, we have all these songs from Bach and Mozart, but we don't have any from lady composers from way back then." Her mother's eyes flashed. She loved making up her own tunes, just treble trills over left-hand chord progressions—nothing approaching Bach or Mozart—but Adele knew she was proud of them. "What if someone told you that you couldn't play your songs anymore? Wouldn't you mope?"

"I never mope," said her mother, returning to her chopping. But that evening after Adele had finished washing the supper dishes, she caught her parents whispering in the parlor. They hushed and drew apart when she entered the room. The next morning at breakfast, her father said, "Dellie, you still want two more steers?" Her mother ahem-ed loudly from over by the stove. "Same deal as before," he quickly added. "All your housework done. You're to help your mother when she needs you." Her mother ahem-ed again. "And you're to keep working on your hope chest."

Now was not the time to explain she'd never need one. She thanked her parents and dashed upstairs for the cigar box.

By the time war consumed Europe, Adele had four steers. By the time James and John and the other young men she knew were conscripted, she had six. Claude Demmings was conscripted, too, and Pauline moved back to the Clemson ranch, bringing her two young sons with her. She hadn't said anything, but Adele could see from the dark circles beneath Pauline's eyes and the swelling at her waistline that her sister was expecting a third.

With Pauline home and the boys gone, her mother let Adele escape the kitchen and help her father with the ranch work. She'd never been good with the horses, and she didn't enjoy repairing fences or herding cattle, but she had an aptitude for machinery. If the spark plugs in the motor trucks needed changing, Adele took care of it. If the belts on the baler needed replacing, she did that too. She handled the oil changes, the carburetor flushing, the tire patching.

"Dellie will look it over," her father said when any of the ranch hands reported a mechanical problem. Their eyes held respect for her now, rather than dismissal. That respect was something new for Adele, who never got it in the parlor or the kitchen. Her mother, after expressing pride in her quilt blocks, never again found much to admire about her sewing. When Adele was asked to display pieces of her scant hope chest for visiting ladies, they hmm-ed politely, said something bland about the fine quality of the fabric, then changed the subject. Usually to Pauline.

Pretty Pauline. Even though she was expecting, she took the time to curl her hair into ringlets. She tatted lace for her collars and cuffs, lace she managed to keep blindingly white. She kept her little boys clean and carried herself with a grace that most women in the family way couldn't manage.

After the ladies left, Mrs. Clemson would carry on for the rest of the day about how Adele wasn't doing herself any favors. And what did she need to be raising steers for anyway?

"Money," said Adele.

What did she need money for? Didn't her father provide her with everything she needed?

Adele agreed that he did, deciding not to mention that she was saving her money to buy a car of her very own. She wanted one desperately. Not a motor truck. Not a ranch-worthy vehicle. But an actual motorcar. For driving. As far from the house as she could get. So that she wouldn't have to hear her mother lament her unfortunate height and nose, her untidy hair, her insufficiently feminine wardrobe, her diminishing marital prospects.

"What marital prospects?" Adele asked one evening. "They're all in France."

"Not forever," said Mrs. Clemson. "They'll all be home before you know it. And they'll be looking for wives. So you'd best make yourself appealing. Clean the grease out from under your fingernails at the very least."

They didn't all come home. Adele scanned every issue of the newspaper, praying not to see James or John on the lists of the dead and injured. In August, INFANTRYMAN RICHARD C. GREER jumped off the page at her, and she was back in the schoolyard kissing Dickie on the lips, breathing in his cut-grass boy scent, whispering that if he told her how he'd gotten that scar, she'd keep his secret always. The grave would keep it now.

In September, a telegram arrived informing them that James had been gravely wounded. Another arrived a week later informing them that he had died. DEATH INSTANTANEOUS. HE DID NOT SUFFER.

Tall, quiet James, who had patiently allowed her to climb all over him when she was little. Who had carried her on his shoulders. Who had pushed her endlessly on the swing in the barn. How could they lie so blatantly about his death? How could they have shipped him across an ocean and put him in a trench in the first place? A righteous wail rose in Adele's chest, but Pauline put a hand on her shoulder, nodded toward their parents, and said, "Dellie, don't." Their father's face was slack, his eyes empty of outrage, of anything. Her mother's eyes were fixed on the carpet. To wail would be unseemly. They were Clemsons. They would bear their grief in silence.

There was no body to bury, no funeral, only the constant autumn work. There was Pauline's belly growing bigger by the day. There was, thank God, at last a letter from John, postmarked weeks before James's death. Impossible to know if he'd heard of his brother's passing. Impossible to know if he himself was alive this very moment. He had, he wrote, made a good friend, Charles Ector, from one county over. They played cards. Charles nearly always won, but John claimed he didn't mind. It was something to pass the time. They had created their own deck from three partials, discarded by others. They had painstakingly re-marked an extra three of diamonds to make it the eight of spades, which they'd lacked. Adele read and reread the letter, thinking that John wrote an awful lot about card games for someone who'd never cared for cards.

"It's because the rest is too horrible to write about," Pauline told her. "Claude says more than John, but not much. They're trying to spare us."

Pauline's first two children were born at her own home, but she was, it became clear to Adele, going to have this third baby in her childhood room. The doctor who had attended her previous births was now somewhere near the western front, practicing a very different sort of medicine. Mrs. Clemson stockpiled boiled cloths and fretted, "I suppose we'll have to call Mrs. Maggs." Mrs. Maggs tended to the poorer families. She delivered their babies and nursed their fevers and dosed their ailments with herbs she grew in her garden.

"Mrs. Maggs will do just fine, I'm sure," said Pauline. Adele didn't understand how her sister could be so calm about what lay ahead. "Well, I was there for James and John and you," said Pauline. "I had some idea about what was coming. And after two of my own, I have an even better one."

Adele had never witnessed a baby being born. Susanna's mother had had four babies after Susanna, and Susanna reported that she'd screamed loud enough to wake the dead each time. "And the sheets! I had to help Grannie wash the blood out of them, and I thought they'd never come clean again."

When Pauline's time came, Adele volunteered to fetch Mrs. Maggs, an errand she hoped would distract her from the ordeal that awaited her sister.

Mrs. Maggs, despite her wrinkles and gray hair, hopped up on the truck seat as if it were something she did every day. She said nothing about getting to ride in a motor truck, which was disappointing. Usually, people found it exciting. And their excitement gave Adele the opportunity to talk about the way the engine worked and how she'd tuned it up just the other day to make sure it was in perfect order for this very important errand.

Instead, Mrs. Maggs said, "Perfect weather for a birth. Not too hot, not too cold."

Adele, who couldn't see how the weather played into it at all, must have looked doubtful.

"Oh yes. Keeps the mother comfortable. As much as can be anyway. And we won't have to worry about the baby taking a chill. She's carrying nice and low—I saw her coming out of church a couple of weeks ago. I always say that's a good sign."

Adele, who had volunteered for this errand specifically to escape thinking about Pauline giving birth, realized she'd made a mistake. She gunned the engine. Faster meant a bumpier ride, but one that would end sooner.

"No need to rush," said Mrs. Maggs. "She's a bit on the small side, but she's had two good ones already. I pay attention, you know. She was back in church in no time at all with the first two. That's a good sign too. But you don't need me to tell you. Being her sister, you were there, I suppose."

"No, Mother said I shouldn't."

"Hmm. Mothers know best, I suppose, but I would have said different. Take away the mystery, is what I advise. Now you, you've got the frame for carrying a baby. Nice and tall—the baby will have plenty of room. You won't be as uncomfortable as some are. And you look strong. That's always a good sign. The ladies who spend time outdoors, who move around a bit, they tend to do better. Ah, here we are. And here's your good mama waiting at the door for us."

Six hours later, Adele, who, despite the encouragement of Mrs. Maggs, had remained firmly on the other side of the door from Pauline, had a new nephew. Her sister, who'd done a fair share of yelling for someone who knew what was coming, looked fresh and calm now. She handed the baby to her father and said, "His name is Jimmy. After James." Adele's father quickly passed the infant to Adele and mumbled that he needed to tend to something in the barn.

John came home in time for Christmas, his face thin, eyes haunted. He refused to say much about his time overseas. He refused to say what he knew, if anything, about James's death. Adele was dismayed at how easily they all papered over James's absence by refusing to speak of him. Mrs. Clemson no longer played his favorite songs in the evening. Silence replaced the stories about James hiding in the corncrib and falling asleep, breaking his arm jumping out of the haymow, teaching two of the herding dogs to run an obstacle course of rails and barrels he'd built one summer.

James and John had been only thirteen months apart. ("Your poor mother," said Mrs. Maggs.) Adele had grown up thinking of them as a unit—one was never far from the other. Sometimes they allowed her to play with them, but never as often as she liked. Just like everyone else, her brothers expected her to spend her time with Pauline, seven years her elder and every bit their mother's daughter in a way that Adele never would be. Now that Claude was home, easily startled by loud noises but otherwise whole and healthy, Pauline and her sons had moved back to their own house. It was just her and John now. Adele knew she couldn't fill James's place in John's heart, but she'd hoped they could remember him together.

She asked John to go with her to Oklahoma City so that when she bought her car, he could drive the motor truck back home. She'd decided on the Dodge Model 30, as opposed to the Model T. It was faster. And she liked the way it looked—sturdy and sporty at the same time—and that it had a full back seat. "I wonder what James would make of it," she said to John. "Me buying a car for myself. Do you remember when Daddy first let him drive the high wheeler and he—"

But John sighed. "I'm sorry, Dellie. I just can't."

They drove in silence the rest of the way. When they reached Broadway Avenue, John parked the truck and offered to accompany her into the dealership. Adele, smarting from his refusal to talk about James, told him that wouldn't be necessary. He could go on and take the truck home.

"They might not deal with you," he warned. "And then you'd be stuck here. I better come in too."

"If they won't deal with me, then they won't get my money. I guess you can wait, but I'm going in by myself."

She had worn a dress—not her best one, but close—and button-up calfskin boots that squeezed her toes. She'd marcelled her hair and pinched her cheeks. "Well, I hardly knew you!" said her mother when Adele came downstairs that morning. "You might make the effort more often."

Adele had made the effort because it was what men expected. John was right. They wouldn't want to deal with her, especially if they didn't like the look of her.

The shop smelled of new leather and Simoniz wax. Men with pomaded hair looked up, their eyes searching beyond her for a husband, a father, a brother. She clutched her leather wallet, ran a thumb over its smooth grain, reminded herself that she had good money to spend.

"Hello, Miss. You lost? Looking for the hotel down the street, perhaps?" The man who greeted her had a shiny bald head and avaricious eyes that went immediately to the wallet in her hands. She took this as a good sign.

"Actually, I'm looking for that," she said, pointing out the window to the gleaming Dodge Model 30 parked outside.

The bald man chewed his lip and regarded her with curiosity. His partner across the room, who was assisting two other men with their automotive needs, snapped, "Tell your husband he'll have to come in himself. We only deal with buyers directly."

"I am the buyer." Adele patted the wallet. The men across the room stopped talking about last year's Model T and stared at her.

The bald man said, "An automobile is a big responsibility. And a big purchase, Miss . . ."

"Clemson."

"Jim Clemson's daughter? I sold him a motor truck two years back."

"I know. I'm the one who changes the oil and the spark plugs on it."

The bald man extended a hand and introduced himself. Waves of angry disapproval and lemony pomade surged from the men across the room, threatening to swamp her. She was accustomed to sensing this disapproval from women. Men besides her father and brother usually just acted as if she didn't exist. Her salesman took her elbow and guided her toward the door, toward safety, murmuring, "Now the

Dodge Model 30 is a fine vehicle. Why don't we step outside and look it over? Right this way, Miss Clemson."

Adele slid out from beneath the Dodge and noted the slant of the sun's afternoon rays. She would be late to supper. Again. She dawdled in the near barn, putting away her tools. Maybe she ought to just stay outside until supper was over. That way she wouldn't have to listen to her mother's nightly account of everything wrong with her: her ragged nails, unstyled hair, and unfashionable wardrobe. And these were the things Adele could at least *do* something about—unlike her unfortunate height and the fact that she had her father's nose. The night before, John had defended her, saying Adele's nose made her look regal. Imposing. That men would think her handsome, if not pretty. Their mother had waved this off and said that if Adele would simply do something with her hair, pinch some color into her cheeks, direct some of her mechanical inclination to the sewing machine . . . Adele hated the sewing machine. She was beginning to hate suppertime too.

But she was hungry, so she stalked into the dining room, wearing John's old trousers, a grease streak over one eyebrow, and a scowl, only to find that they had company. John had invited Charles Ector, the card-playing soldier, to supper.

Her mother glared at her but said nothing, just passed Adele an insufficiently laden plate. John said, "Charles, this is my sister, Adele. The family mechanic." Mrs. Clemson let out a sharp puff of breath.

John continued, "Adele, Charles Ector. We met in France."

"I remember from the letters," said Adele. "You played a lot of cards. And what do you do now, Mr. Ector?" If she could get him talking, maybe she could focus on her dinner while making encouraging noises between bites of food.

"I'm in oil."

He was not, it seemed, inclined to elaborate. Adele, starving, looked mournfully at the forkful of pork roast that was halfway to her mouth.

John came to her rescue. "Charles is being modest. He's not just 'in' oil. He's on the verge of becoming one of the most successful wildcatters in northern Oklahoma."

"I don't care for that term," said Charles. "There's nothing wild about it. I use scientific methods to decide where to drill." He went on about the importance of soil samples, topographic maps, and geologic analysis while Adele cleaned her plate.

"But enough about all that," said Charles as she dabbed her mouth with her napkin. "I hear you bought a car."

Adele cut her eyes at John. Her brother looked strangely pleased with himself. "Oh, I didn't hear it from him," said Charles. "John only talks about cattle." Adele had noticed this herself. "Everyone else in the county is talking about it. A young lady walking into a dealership all by herself, buying her own car. It's all anyone can talk about. The girl who bought the Model T."

"It's a Dodge, actually," said Adele, and Mrs. Clemson huffed again.

"Even better. Superior horsepower. I'd love to see it."

She allowed herself to take a good look at Charles Ector. He was James's age, she recalled, her chest aching at the thought of her brother. He had a dark beard and dark eyes, and despite all his talk about maps and analyses, which sounded like desk work, he had a wind-reddened complexion. Good shoulders. Adele suddenly realized he was looking her over too. Her cheeks got hot. She ran a hand over her hair, wondering how mussed it was, but quickly gave up. She was what she was.

Mrs. Clemson's voice turned bright and cheerful. "I'm sure Adele would be happy to show you the car. After dessert, of course. No, Adele, you sit and entertain our guest. John will help me clear."

After the pound cake and peaches, they retired to the parlor, where Mrs. Clemson played them an interminable series of romantic ditties and Mr. Clemson puffed on his pipe and looked anywhere but at Adele.

John reached for a deck of cards, and Adele, before her mother could play yet another song or John could propose a game, stood and said, "Light's going. We'd better go have a look at the Dodge if you're still interested, Mr. Ector."

"Charles, please. And may I call you Adele?"

"Everyone does." She immediately regretted her sharp tone. "Yes, I'd like that."

The light was nearly gone, but he knew enough about cars to comment on the Dodge's floor-mounted gearshift and three-speed transmission. When he finished his inspection, they leaned against the car and watched the orange fade from the horizon. In the darkness, Charles said, "I'm sorry about James. We met at the cattle market once or twice. I liked him. He was easy to talk to."

"Yes, he was," agreed Adele, her voice shaky. "He loved books, you know. He read me *Treasure Island* one winter. And *Captains Courageous* the next. I didn't expect to like them, but the way he read them—well, it felt like I was part of the adventure."

"That sounds wonderful."

Adele's memories of James surged up inside her like floodwaters behind a dam. She opened the sluice gates and let them pour free. Charles listened. Someone, probably her mother, twitched the kitchen curtains aside and peered out. But no one called from the door to say that it was late, it was dark, that surely Charles ought to be heading out.

Adele told Charles everything she knew about James, and when she finished, Charles said, "Well, now I wish I'd known him even more. But at least I've gotten to know John. The war was good for that anyway. And I'm hoping I'll get to know you better too."

After seeing him off, Adele hesitated before entering the house. Her mother lay in wait on the other side of the door, ready to pounce and demand a full account of their conversation. Well, she'd just tell them all that she and Charles had talked about James. It was true, and it would shut them right up. But when she stepped, blinking, into the bright kitchen, they barely glanced at her. John dried the silverware, sorted it into the drawer. Her mother wiped down the drainboard. Neither of them said a word. "Well, good night," said Adele.

"Good night, dear," said her mother. Adele lingered, surprised to realize that she wanted them to ask. But John kept fiddling with the silverware, and her mother kept swiping away at the drainboard. Adele finally turned to go, but not before she caught John winking at their mother.

Never mind that her brother was a schemer. Adele liked Charles. She hadn't realized how isolated she'd become. Susanna and Franny had houses and babies and husbands. Like Pauline, they had disappeared into secret domestic worlds of their own.

Spinsterhood had been easy to choose at age eleven. Before she understood the loneliness it would entail. Now Charles came to supper several times a week. They took drives and had picnics and sat in the Clemson parlor listening to Mrs. Clemson play her most romantic repertoire.

"I don't sew," Adele told him one afternoon as they drove out to see a piece of land he'd recently acquired and intended to drill on.

"I don't care," said Charles.

"I can make a pot roast with potatoes, but not much else. Well, there was a pie once. Apple. That was years ago, though," said Adele as they tramped through the brush to a creek bed he wanted to show her.

"Yes, your mother has mentioned the pie. More than once. See that scum along the edge of the water there? A lot of men would just drill right there."

Adele dipped a finger into the scum and sniffed it—oil. "But not you."

"Not right off, anyway."

"Because you're waiting for the soil samples to come back." The other wildcatters sneered at Charles's deliberations, his fascination with scientific methods. They accused him of wasting good money and time when anyone could see there was oil right underfoot.

Adele asked whether it bothered him, and Charles laughed. "I spent a year in a trench, every day swearing that if I made it out, I'd make my own decisions. Not listen to the foolish old bastards who put me there. Life's too short to worry about what other people think. But you already know that, don't you?"

He took her hand and pulled her toward him and kissed her. The week before he had asked her to marry him. Adele, who'd wanted to say yes immediately, had only allowed herself to say she'd consider it. In the meantime, she was sampling Charles, doing her own analysis of what it would be like to be his wife.

She pushed back from him. "I like wearing trousers."

"I know. You're wearing them right now. Surprisingly fetching." He pulled her toward him again and kissed her neck, whispering, "I already have a cook. I don't care whether you ever sew a stitch. Say yes, Adele. I promise you won't be sorry."

Adele wanted the wedding as soon as possible. She was eager to sleep with Charles, but, because her virtue was the one thing about her that the women in town had never questioned, she was waiting for her wedding night. When Susanna had rushed down the aisle, everyone whispered that she must be in the family way. Susanna's baby had come "early" and yet entered the world with a full head of hair and a good half pound on any of Pauline's babies. Adele, who already knew that women laughed at her—laughter underlaid with more than a little envy given Charles Ector's bank balance—didn't want them whispering that she'd forced him down the aisle.

To speed things up, she vetted her mother's plans based on how fast they could be implemented. No, she wouldn't wait for a full trousseau to be sewn. Mrs. Clemson insisted on sewing a new nightgown for

Adele. Adele insisted it be a simple one, with as few frills and tucks as possible. No, she wouldn't wait for roses to come into season; hyacinths would suit her just fine. Yes, she'd allow the making of a travel suit and a wedding dress, but only of the simplest patterns. Mrs. Clemson stitched Valenciennes lace onto the bodice of the dress while Adele was out. Ripping it off and refinishing the dress with simple satin edging, Adele's preference, would have only caused delay. There were worse things than an itchy dress.

Standing at the front of the church, she resisted pulling at the lace around her neck. She wished the preacher, who rattled on about wifely duties, would get to the vows. The sooner the ceremony concluded, the sooner she could change into the comfortable serge travel suit. She took a deep breath and eased her grip on the flowers so as not to crush the stems and release their juice. She'd never successfully kept a pair of gloves clean for more than a day. But on this, her wedding day, she was determined to at least get through the ceremony without staining them. At last, the preacher ran out of things to say about wives submitting to their husbands. He turned to Charles and asked if he promised to love, honor, and cherish Adele.

"I do," Charles answered firmly.

Then the preacher turned to Adele and asked if she promised to love, honor, and obey Charles. Adele flinched. Why hadn't she thought about the vows? She'd watched Pauline promise to obey Claude Demmings. No doubt her mother had promised to obey her father. And yet Adele had witnessed both her sister and her mother disagreeing with their husbands and doing what they pleased. What was the point of this promise if everyone felt free to ignore it? She herself planned to ignore it, but even so, it seemed an unfair thing to ask. Did Charles expect her obedience? She widened her eyes at him. He winked and shook his head. The preacher ahem-ed.

"I do," said Adele. Then she whispered, softly so that only Charles could hear, "Except for that third thing."

They exchanged wedding bands, were pronounced man and wife, and Adele rushed her new husband up the aisle and out into the fresh air, where she could breathe again.

It was a relief to change into the travel suit, to free herself from the itchy lace and constraining stays of her wedding dress. Her gloves, she was proud to see, were still spotless. As she climbed into the passenger seat, someone in the crowd murmured, "See, she's already coming around." The engine turned over once and died. Adele sprang out of the car, ignoring the groan of disapproval from the crowd—she'd show them *coming around*. She tossed her gloves on the ground, lifted the hood, fiddled with this and then that, turned the crank, and instructed Charles to engage the choke, slowly this time. The car rumbled to life. She hopped back in the passenger seat and waved goodbye, leaving her gloves where they lay.

Changing out of the travel suit and into her new nightgown—"It doesn't suit you at all," said Charles. "Let's take it off."—brought even greater relief: letting her body, finally, have what it craved.

The night before, her mother had dithered on about the physical aspects of marital duty without ever managing to say exactly what those physical aspects entailed. Pauline, several days earlier, had been only somewhat more forthcoming when she told Adele, "It hurts at first, but you get used to it." Adele had seen plenty of animals engage in the "physical aspects of marital duty." None of them seemed too out of sorts about it. She had also, years ago, discovered certain rewarding ways of touching herself. She was delighted, on her wedding night, to find that Charles knew these ways of touching too.

"How did you know how to do that?" asked Adele, once she got her breath back.

He turned pink. His eyes flitted about the room, looking anywhere but at her. *Ah,* she thought. *He's done this before.* When he cleared his throat, she realized he was about to tell her the truth, as he always did. And also, that she didn't want to know it. She put her fingers over his lips and whispered, "Never mind. It doesn't matter."

They honeymooned at the Grand Canyon, admiring the view during the day and each other's bodies during the night. Adele wanted to write to Pauline that their getaway had been "painless in every way." But that wasn't something ladies talked about—not even sisters—and she thought it might come off as bragging. Sometimes good things happened and you couldn't share them with everyone. Which was a nice balance, she supposed, to all the negative things you were never supposed to share with anyone. This was the other wonderful thing about her marriage—she felt she could say anything to Charles. And she did.

"Pauline told me it would hurt," she whispered one night.

He whispered back, "Guess Pauline doesn't know everything, does she?"

Despite the fact that Adele and Charles frequently and happily fulfilled the physical aspects of their marital duty, every month she bled. Charles seemed unfazed by this. But Adele's mother was always dropping by, finding a reason to peek at the laundry pail, and lecturing Adele about "allowing" and "submitting," about spending more time sitting still and less time rattling around in automobiles, which, her mother insisted, could not possibly be good for—and here her voice dropped to a strained whisper—"the womb." Adele ought to spend more time with Pauline, who was expecting again. Mrs. Clemson was certain that this time Pauline would have a girl. She seemed equally certain that her elder daughter's condition might spread, as if by contagion, to her younger child.

But before Adele could catch anything from Pauline, her sister's baby arrived too early, stillborn.

Pauline retreated to her bed, refusing to see anyone at all. Not Adele. Not her mother. Not even her children. Adele did her best to help out. Her inability to cook or sew meant she was tasked with minding her nephews while Mrs. Clemson and Claude's mother battled over the management of Pauline's household. "Oh, had you already beaten the carpets? I'd no idea. There was so much dust in them still." "Oh, is that blancmange you're making? I would have thought a beef broth more restorative." The brightness of their eyes and smiles did nothing to conceal the war they waged. Claude Demmings kept well out of the way. Adele followed suit.

She had, at the insistence of her mother, allowed Dr. Sawyer to examine her. He reeked of gin, and his hands shook. After the examination he'd thwapped her on the thigh as if she were a horse and pronounced her "sound." She hated him. If she was so "sound," why wasn't she carrying a child? Obviously because she wasn't womanly enough, motherly enough.

Occasionally, rarely, she wondered if maybe Charles was the problem, not her. On the final night of their honeymoon, a loud sob from her husband had startled her awake. "Charles?" His eyes were open, glazed with terror, but he didn't see her. He hunched into a ball next to her, shaking, weeping. Adele wrapped herself around him and whispered, over and over, "It's all right. I'm here. It's all right." Until the shaking subsided and he gave a final moan and closed his eyes.

In the morning, she'd wanted to ask him about it, but something in his manner told her not to mention it. That they could talk about anything and everything except for that. It happened again a few weeks later, and every few weeks after that, especially if anyone had mentioned the war. Perhaps this break in Charles's mind had broken his ability to father a child too. Or maybe the two of them combined to create a mutual defect, something that made them unsuitable for raising children. If Pauline had been her usual self, Adele might have worked up the courage to ask her. Even though Pauline didn't know everything.

To distract herself from these worries, Adele took long drives. Finding herself out near the lake one day, she decided to drop in on Mrs. Maggs, who knew more than Dr. Sawyer ever would. She might have some idea about how to fix Pauline.

"You've just got to let her do her grieving," said Mrs. Maggs, who hadn't stopped weeding her garden when Adele drove up. "Some things can't be rushed. Why shouldn't she lie in bed and cry? Makes all the sense in the world to me."

"There's nothing you can do?"

"Oh, I'll stop over. If they let me in—Mrs. Demmings probably won't—I'll give her a little something. Not medicine—there's no medicine for this. Just tea. Something warm. Something that might give her a bit of hope. Or it might not. I make no promises."

Mrs. Maggs pushed herself up from the dirt and looked Adele up and down. "And what about you?"

"Me?"

"Oh, I see. You came out here just for your sister. Been married a year now, that right?"

"A little over."

"Mm-hmm. Well, I wouldn't worry."

"Who says I'm worried?"

"Well, don't be. Sometimes things just take a while. Go on about your business and be patient."

Patience was not one of Adele's virtues. She drove off wishing Mrs. Maggs had offered *her* some tea. Something warm. Something that might give her a bit of hope.

Pauline got up from her bed and started eating again, just in time to attend John's wedding. A few months later, both she and John's bride let the family know they were expecting. Mrs. Clemson could barely contain her delight. She darted like a dragonfly between their households. Adele pretended to be relieved, but she was stung by how quickly her mother discarded her.

And then one month she didn't bleed. If Charles noticed, he didn't mention it. Adele said nothing about it to him or to her mother. She carefully counted the days, trying hard not to hope. Another month passed and she still hadn't bled. She thought about waiting a third but couldn't bear the idea of keeping the news from Charles any longer.

Adele was tall, but Charles was even taller. He picked her up and swung her around and then, sheepish and concerned, set her gently back on her feet. "Are you all right? Did I hurt you?"

"Of course you didn't. I'm perfectly fine. Don't coddle me, Charles. You know I can't stand that."

"I'll try, but I can't promise I'll succeed. I'll be worrying about you every day."

"Nonsense. Women do this all the time." But they both knew of women who hadn't lived through it. And the ghost of Pauline's lost baby hovered between them. "Mrs. Maggs says I should keep moving." She wasn't going to be put to bed. Not like Pauline, who had been told she must rest and do nothing to harm the child she carried now.

He chuckled. "I can't imagine stopping you."

The next day Adele drove out to the Clemson property. She barely managed to say she had "good news" before her mother embraced her. "Oh, Adele! I knew it would happen! I just knew it! How are you feeling, dear? Any sickness? Tiredness?"

Adele had felt neither of these things yet, but suddenly she tasted acid on the back of her tongue. Her mother brought a basin just in time. She rubbed Adele's back and cooed that it was all "perfectly natural" and would go away in time. Adele should eat plain foods and get plenty of rest, and do or not do a whole list of other things that she couldn't take in because she was heaving over the basin again.

She was sick for weeks. Five months in, the nausea faded, only to be replaced by heartburn, swollen ankles, and utter exhaustion. She felt colonized by some invading force. Why had she wanted this so much? Why had Pauline and Susanna never told her about any of this?

By her seventh month she could no longer slide beneath cars, nor could she easily bend over an open hood. "It's just a temporary condition," Charles reminded her. But it felt endless to Adele. She drove to visit Pauline often, watched her sister closely for signs so that she would know them herself when her own time came. Pauline appeared perfectly serene, propped up on the pillows in her bedroom. She sewed and knitted and directed her household as if she were a queen on an upholstered throne. "Don't worry, Dellie," she said. "It will all go fine. You'll see."

But it hadn't gone fine for Pauline the last time, thought Adele as her baby kicked and tumbled inside her. She placed a hand on her belly. This child—she hoped it would be a boy, because a boy would have more freedom in the world—despite having caused her so much discomfort, had already burrowed itself into her heart. She understood now why Pauline hadn't gotten out of bed for months after losing her fourth baby.

Adele was in the nursery. She had removed the motor from the sewing machine her mother had insisted on giving her and was working out how to rig it up to the cradle so that it would rock automatically. She was so absorbed in the problem that she didn't hear John knocking. She didn't hear him open the door and climb the stairs. She didn't hear him until he was behind her saying, "Dellie," in a strange choked voice that told her everything he had come to say before he spoke the horrible words. Pauline was gone. The new baby too.

On the day of the funeral, Mrs. Clemson urged Adele to stay home, preferably in bed, but Adele refused. She refused Charles's umbrella too. She stood in the weather, rain soaking her hat, mixing with the tears that ran down her cheeks, and watched them lower her sister and the baby, in their shared casket, into the earth, while her own baby turned somersaults inside her.

No one would tell her what happened.

"Best not to dwell on it," said Mrs. Clemson.

"Dr. Sawyer did all he could," said Mrs. Demmings. Claude nodded along with his mother.

Adele's father couldn't speak Pauline's name at all. He seemed suddenly old, so much smaller than he'd been only a year before. John ran the ranch now. Adele was relieved when Penny, John's wife, delivered a healthy girl and sprang back to her sturdy farm-girl feet within a week.

As her own time approached, Adele grew huge and clumsy. Her mother stopped in daily, bringing her broths and marrows to strengthen her blood. Adele, who once would have darted out the back door to avoid her, was too slow and ponderous to escape. Her thoughts were jumbled and contradictory. She dreaded her mother's visits but she also dreaded the prospect of an afternoon passing without her mother stopping by. She dreaded the baby staying inside her too long, growing larger and more difficult to expel. But she dreaded the day the baby decided to enter the world.

What if the child lived and she died? How would Charles manage it? Adele couldn't see any way but to let her own mother raise the child. This thought was sufficiently terrifying that she drank the broths and ate the marrows. She had to make sure her blood was strong.

Her mother was there, watching as Adele dutifully sipped her latest concoction, when she winced at the first pain. Mrs. Clemson sprang up, alert. "It's nothing," said Adele. "Just a twinge." She'd had these occasionally—a feeling that the muscles deep within her were stretched to capacity and wanted to snap back to their customary places. She kept sipping, had almost finished the bowl—an accomplishment, as there wasn't nearly enough salt in the broth—when she felt her insides twist and clench. She dropped the spoon and clutched her belly. Mrs. Clemson ordered the cook to fetch Dr. Sawyer.

"Get Charles," said Adele as her mother helped her up the stairs.

"Don't worry, dear. We'll get him when it's time. Doctor first."

"I want him now," said Adele, sharply, because the pain had struck again.

"Plenty of time, plenty of time. Don't worry, dear. You sit here while I fix the bed." Her mother led her to a chair. Adele suffered the next pains in silence as her mother stripped the bed and remade it with older sheets. Her water broke as her mother helped her stand. Mrs. Clemson squeezed her hand and said, "Good girl!" because she hadn't ruined the sheets? Because she was following instructions? Adele suspected it might be both.

When Dr. Sawyer arrived, Adele flashed back to him thwapping her on the thigh. He leaned over her, probing her belly, his breath smelling strongly of peppermint, and, beneath that, juniper from the gin. His hands moved downward, beneath her nightgown, probing, probing. Her mother politely turned away and looked out the window. Adele, trying to ignore the doctor's fingers, cast around the room for something else to focus on. Dr. Sawyer's battered leather bag sat at the foot of the bed, partially open, revealing the tongs of an enormous set of forceps. Had he used those on her sister? Had he pushed them inside Pauline and torn her apart with them?

"I want Charles!"

The doctor removed his fingers just as Charles burst through the door. Warm tears of relief slid down her cheeks. "I'm here," he said. "I'm here." He rushed to her side and took her face in his hands. "I'm here," he whispered.

"Get him out," Adele whispered back. As the doctor was the only other man in the room, there was no mistaking whom she meant.

"Adele, you need—"

"He killed Pauline! Get him out!"

Dr. Sawyer drew himself up and opened his mouth to protest, but Charles stopped him with a look, then turned back to her. "Adele, you shouldn't say such things."

Why not? She was sure it was true. But she could see from their appalled expressions that they wouldn't listen to her. No, they would treat her like a child, certain they knew best. They would ignore anything she said today, and maybe for the rest of her life. She sobbed. The pain struck again, and she doubled up and wailed. "I want him out! I want Mrs. Maggs! Not him! Not him!"

Charles's eyes had the panicked look of a steer realizing what the gun was for. He turned to Adele's mother and said, "Who on earth is Mrs. Maggs?"

Dr. Sawyer fished in his bag. Charles caught sight of the forceps, and his eyes widened further. "Mrs. Clemson, who is Mrs. Maggs?"

"The old widow down by the lake. She delivered Pauline's third."

"A fraud is what Mrs. Maggs is," said Dr. Sawyer. "No medical training." He found what he was looking for and extracted it from the bag—a dark-brown glass bottle. Adele pressed her lips tightly together—she wouldn't take any of his medicine, not willingly anyway. But he tipped the bottle toward his own lips. Seeing the disapproval in Mrs. Clemson's eyes, the doctor said, "Purely medicinal. Steadies the hands."

"Get out," ordered Charles.

"Under the circumstances—" Dr. Sawyer began.

"Oh, Charles, you mustn't—" said Mrs. Clemson.

"Out! Now!" Charles pointed at the door. The doctor shrugged and said, "Suit yourselves," then stalked through it.

Adele lay back in the bed and let another pain course through her. It involved her whole body now. Without Dr. Sawyer there, she felt free to give it her full attention. As if from a great distance she heard Charles open a window and yell out to one of his workers to fetch Mrs. Maggs.

After it was all over, after Mrs. Maggs had changed the linens and dressed Adele in a clean nightgown, after Charles had come back in and kissed her and held the baby, after she'd been clucked over by her mother, Adele lifted the baby from the cradle, laid it on her bed, and unwrapped it. Once she had confirmed with her own eyes what they had all told her, that the baby was indeed female, she sighed, bundled her daughter back up in the blanket, and held her close. Georgeanne regarded her calmly.

"Oh well," said Adele. "You're a good-size baby, anyway."

She put her nose to the faintly pulsing soft spot atop her daughter's head, breathed in her fresh daisy scent. Already she loved her ferociously. Had her own mother felt this way about her babies? It was difficult to imagine. Someone, probably Mrs. Clemson, had clipped a pink silk rose to the baby's sparse swatch of hair. Adele gently removed it and chucked it into a corner. "We won't be having any of this nonsense. At the very least, I promise you that."

"You forget," Pauline had told her when Adele once asked her why any woman would get herself in the family way again once they knew how painful it was to give birth.

Adele pressed her sister: "You were screaming."

"Oh, that must have been Jimmy crowning. You can see even now he has such an enormous head." This was true. Adele wondered how she could have missed the horrifying geometry problem posed by her nephew's head. Then Pauline had taken hold of Adele's hands, and Adele felt her sister's peace course through her. "Don't worry, Dellie. It'll all be fine when it happens. Look at me. I'm not worried."

This discussion had taken place less than a month before Pauline went to her final childbed. Pauline had forgotten. Pauline hadn't worried. And look where it had gotten her. Adele would never forget. Even now, nearly six months later, she could smell the iron tang of her blood, the ripe, embarrassing fumes of her own shit—no one had ever said anything about that part, and she very much doubted any of them had forgotten—and, strongest of all, the stink of her own fear.

She bundled Georgeanne into the apple crate nest—a plush swirl of blankets padding the wooden slats. Georgeanne smiled up at her, as if she already knew what being placed in the apple crate meant. "That's right, George. We're going on a little drive." The baby loved nothing more than a ride in anything motorized. She gurgled and cooed and, if the ride lasted long enough, drifted into a sound sleep, her cupid lips pursed with pleasure.

When they reached Mrs. Maggs's place, Mrs. Maggs held out her arms and said, "Oh, this one's a peach, isn't she." Adele surrendered her baby and watched with pride as Mrs. Maggs traced George's perfect nose—a button like Pauline's and Mrs. Clemson's—as she gently probed the top of George's head, as she unwrapped and kissed George's sweet pea toes.

Her baby *was* a peach, and she ought to want another one. Both her mother and Mrs. Maggs had praised her after the delivery. Told her how well she'd done. What an easy birth it had been. How it would be even easier the second time around. No one had mentioned the loss of Pauline's baby. The loss of Pauline herself.

"Aren't you sweet to bring her out for a visit. Come in and have some coffee and tell me all about her."

George kicked against her blankets. "A strong one too. Just like her mother." Mrs. Maggs handed George back to Adele and lit the kerosene lamps in her dark kitchen. She set the water to boil and then regarded Adele. "You're looking healthy."

"Thank you. I believe I am."

Mrs. Maggs peered at her some more. "Sometimes when ladies bring their babies to see me, they're really coming for themselves, because something's ailing them."

"Oh. No, I'm not ailing," said Adele.

"No. I can see that. And not expecting again either. I'd see it round your eyes if you were."

Some panic must have flashed across Adele's face, because Mrs. Maggs nodded. "Ah." Then: "She's eating well? You weaning her yet?"

"Oh yes. I mean, to the eating well. Not the weaning."

"Rare for a woman to get with child again before weaning. Not impossible, but rare."

Mrs. Maggs set a cup of coffee before her. Adele blew on it, then sipped. It was bitter, mostly chicory. She would remember to bring a bag of coffee with her the next time she came out. "And what about after weaning?" Adele asked.

She prepared herself for a talking-to about how George wouldn't be a baby forever, how Adele would want another child before she knew it. But Mrs. Maggs just said, "Drink your coffee, and then we'll go out to the garden. I'll show you what you need. Nothing's foolproof, mind. But then, you're no fool."

Adele dressed George in trousers most days. Dresses were for church and company. And thanks to Mrs. Clemson, George had a closetful of the frilly, impractical things. Adele's mother was always measuring George and asking her to try things on, two activities Adele had hated when she was a girl. But George didn't seem to mind. She twirled her ruffled skirts and giggled. When her grandmother presented her with a choice of fabric, she inevitably chose the floweriest, most-likely-to-show-a-stain pastel option. Mrs. Clemson was delighted with her granddaughter. Her only complaint was that George would not stop growing. "Just like you," her mother said accusingly, as if Adele had any control over her daughter's height.

Though she secretly believed she might. *Let her be tall,* Adele thought as she spooned hearty servings onto her daughter's plate, remembering how often she'd risen hungry from her mother's table.

She could work herself into a state thinking about all that. But then George would climb into her lap and put her sweet, soft arms around Adele's neck, and Adele's mind and nerves would calm. "She has what Pauline had," Adele said to Charles one night. "Somehow she just settles you."

Charles admitted that he had felt it too. "But I haven't had much experience with children," he said. "I thought it was just her being little that did it."

"I don't think so," said Adele.

Charles reached for her and kissed her neck. "We could find out. Do an experiment. Have another one."

He'd begun hinting at this. Making it clear he wanted another child. They weren't careful with their lovemaking, and she was eager for it still. Surely by now he must know a baby would not be coming. George was nearly six, after all. Despite the way he was kissing her neck, she stiffened.

He drew back. "Adele?"

She felt the tears starting—she hated to cry in front of anyone, but she especially hated to cry in front of Charles.

"Oh, honey." He folded her into his arms and pressed her between them.

He wasn't Pauline or George, but the pressing calmed her enough for her to whisper, "I can't, Charles."

"I know it took a while the first time. And it might take a while again. Once you stop drinking your . . . well, you know."

This surprised her. She had thought her herb garden was of little interest to him. She'd assumed he never noticed the teas she brewed and drank. Men weren't supposed to know about these things.

Charles sighed and said, "You hate gardening, but you're religious about tending that patch near the kitchen door. And there was a . . . woman . . . in France. A woman I met during the war, who—" Already Adele wanted to cover her ears. "I asked her how she kept from . . . you know." He turned bright red from the collar up and began to stammer.

It wasn't just that she didn't want to hear about the woman—she hoped it had been only one—in France. It was that talking about the war meant he'd have the dreams. He'd wake up shaking and sweating, and she would hold him until the terror subsided, saying, "Oh, honey, it's okay. It's just fine. I'm right here. I'm right here with you. I'm right here. Always." In the morning, he'd seem his normal self, and they would not speak of it.

She didn't want to speak of this. She was the one shaking now, remembering the forceps protruding from Dr. Sawyer's leather bag, the smell of blood and shit and fear, her sister's casket descending into the muddy trench. Mrs. Maggs had, the year before, been lowered into her own deep hole in the dirt. No new midwife had taken her place, and no new doctor had arrived to compete with Dr. Sawyer. Even if one had, Adele wouldn't have taken her chances with him.

Charles would love her less if she told him. It was a miracle that he had ever loved her at all. She was odd. People talked about her. They laughed about her. She could tolerate the laughter—she laughed right back. It was their pity she couldn't bear. Pity for strange Adele Ector, not woman enough to bear more children.

She hated the way her body shook. The way she was powerless to stop it. Charles pressed her tightly and whispered, "It doesn't matter." A sob escaped her. She clapped a hand over her mouth. He held on to her and said, "Oh, honey, it's okay. It's just fine. I'm right here. I'm right here with you. Right here. Always."

When Adele's mother brought George pink satin hair ribbons, George bounced up and down with glee. "For her first day of school," said Mrs. Clemson. How could George be old enough to go off to school? Adele fussed and fussed tying and retying the ribbons until the bows looked relatively similar in size. *What a waste of time,* she thought, and then, seeing George's smile in the mirror, she felt an increasingly familiar pang of guilt. "Oh, Adele," said her mother. "They're just ribbons. What's the harm?"

The harm was that George was going out into the world. Where she'd meet more girls in ruffles and bows, and boys who wanted her to stay in the house and pretend to cook while they galloped around the schoolyard on their pretend horses. She couldn't prevent this from happening. All she could do was try to counter it with her own example.

On Saturdays, she led George on tramps across the Ector property, took her down to creek beds to search for crawdads. She drove her to the Clemson ranch and tried to get her interested in the steers. "When you're older, you can raise one," said Adele.

George looked appalled. "Why?"

"For the experience of learning to take care of an animal. And to earn money," said Adele.

George blinked her golden-hazel eyes—eyes just like Pauline's—and said nothing. She was a polite child—too polite, Adele often thought. Rather than say she wasn't interested in learning to take care of a steer or selling one for money, she just kept quiet. Had Adele taught her to do that? She didn't think so, but George had certainly picked it up somewhere.

Possibly from her new friend, Helen. Adele was hearing quite a bit about her these days. Thanks to Helen, George had asked for patent leather shoes. Impractical *and* uncomfortable, and thus, an utterly ridiculous request. But George kept pestering until Charles said, "Maybe for your birthday." Men were weak.

They tramped back through the long grass, George wearing a chain of oxeye daisies she'd woven while Adele poked around in the shallows, turning over rocks and hoping to flush out a crawdad. Her daughter skipped alongside her and asked if she could have an embroidery hoop for her birthday instead of the shoes. "And some floss," she added.

Adele planned to get George a bicycle for her seventh birthday. Something she would have dearly loved as a girl. "What for?" asked Adele.

"For cross-stitch. Helen has one."

"Oh, I'll bet she does."

"Lots of girls at school do."

"Hmm."

"It's about time I learned to sew, don't you think?"

Adele most assuredly did not. But the longing in her daughter's eyes stopped her from saying so. She was the wrong mother for her daughter. Any other woman would do better—would be the mother George clearly wanted. A mother like Adele's, who enjoyed curling her little girl's hair, who knew how to tie ribbons and do cross-stitch.

Adele sighed. "Let's go home. I need to tune up your father's truck before he drives down to Wichita Falls this week anyway."

"Ford!" whooped Georgeanne. She bounded ahead of Adele, punctuating each leap by singing, "Model! Teeee! Pickup!" The fragile daisy chain fell to the ground, but George didn't notice. She glanced back at Adele. "Can I help?"

CHAPTER 2

"*May* I?" her mother corrected.

"*May.* I. Help!" Georgeanne sang as she bounded ahead. She knew her mother would say yes. Her mother liked it when she did boy things.

"Yes," said Adele. "You may." George leaped up and spun in the air. If she'd had on a dress, it would have belled out and swirled around her knees in the prettiest way. But the happy note in her mother's voice was nearly as satisfying.

Her mother had seemed glum down by the creek. George was scared of crawdads, with their shiny beetley bodies and their claws. "Much too small to hurt you," said Adele. "You'd barely feel a pinch." Why would she want to feel any pinch at all? Why would she want to get her feet muddy wading around in the creek hunting for the things in the first place? "They're good eating," said Adele. "If you can get enough of them." George fervently hoped they never would.

The truck was also shiny and beetley, yet far less scary than a crawdad. George had gotten a glimpse of its insides the week before, and she was eager to see them again.

Her mother was always taking things apart, then putting them back together. The kitchen table, much to the cook's dismay, was regularly spread with gears and belts and hardware, lined up just so atop a layer of newspaper. "Don't touch," said Adele whenever George approached the table. She'd clasp her hands behind her back and study the pieces.

It was like looking at a puzzle. Sometimes she could guess which ones fit together; sometimes she couldn't. Her mother always knew.

"I'm afraid we're not doing anything very exciting today," Adele said when they entered the garage. "We'll start with the tires." She held up the tire gauge, round like a clock with a little nozzle poking out of its side. She twisted the nozzle onto another thingy that stuck out of the tire ("A valve," said Adele), then tapped the face of the gauge. "What's that number?"

"Thirty," said George. She could count all the way to one hundred now. Miss Parry claimed that if you could count to one hundred, you could count all the way to one thousand, but George hadn't tried it yet.

"Very good. Thirty. Now see these ticks between thirty and forty?"

"Yes, ma'am."

"Each tick stands for a number. Thirty-one, thirty-two, all the way to . . ."

"Forty!"

"That's right. What tick is the needle on?"

"Thirty . . ." George counted twice. It was important to get this right. ". . . four?"

"That's right. Thirty-four. And that's good. We want every tire to be at thirty-two or more—but not too much more. Thirty-four is just fine."

George was allowed to check the other tires herself and call out the numbers to her mother. She was allowed to empty the dirty gas from the sediment bulb and to help top off the oil. She was allowed to stand on an upturned apple crate and watch her mother point out the cam shaft, the fan belt, and the cylinders. She was allowed to touch anything she wanted to touch.

"Wait till I tell Helen," she said as they put away the tools.

"Hmm," said Adele. "Let's wash up and go see what your father's up to."

Her mother didn't seem to like Helen. She kept suggesting that George play with the boys instead. That she run around and stretch her legs and fill her lungs during recess. Which showed how little her mother knew about school. George had begun to wonder if she might be wrong about other things too.

Before starting school, George hadn't spent much time with children other than her cousins. Aunt Pauline's boys were older and mostly ignored her. Uncle John's kids were her age or younger and wanted her to help muck out stalls and tend livestock. George was about as interested in cattle as she was in crawdads.

Her first morning at school, she'd stood frozen in the schoolyard, overwhelmed by the mass of children chattering and whooping and swirling past her. It was a relief when Miss Parry rang the bell, and they all shushed and filed inside. It took most of the morning for her heart to stop thudding, and she only half listened to Miss Parry. Mostly she stared at the head of the boy sitting in front of her. His hair dripped with so much pomade that it darkened his collar.

Many of her classmates knew each other already. After lunch they clustered in groups behind the schoolhouse. George and a few stragglers circled the clusters, sizing them up, seeking out gaps they might step into. George was just getting up the nerve to edge up to a knot of girls when the pomade boy, a straggler like herself, darted up to her and shouted, "Your mother wears pants!" then darted away again.

This was baffling. George wore pants herself most of the time at home. Her mother had even asked whether she wanted to wear them to school, but something in her granny's face made George say, "No, thank you. I'd like to wear a dress." As soon as she entered the schoolyard, she knew she'd chosen correctly.

The straggler who yelled at her joined a group of boys, who all turned and taunted her. "Pants! Pants! Your mother wears pants!"

The girls gawped. One of them cackled, and the others joined in. George's ears burned. Her throat got thick and tight, the way it did when she was about to cry.

She turned and ran. She was a fast runner. Faster than every one of those girls, and most of the boys, too, she'd bet. She raced around the corner of the building.

The yard in front of the schoolhouse belonged to the older kids. Big girls—George guessed they were ten or twelve years old—stood in their own circles. Older boys played catch nearby. None of them spared her a glance. She felt . . . not exactly safe, but invisible, which came close. Keeping her eyes on the ground, she slowed to a stroll, pretended to hunt for something in the weeds.

As she passed a clump of bushes, she heard snuffling. She peered into the thicket, and there, deep inside, crouched a girl her own age. The girl's nose ran with snot; her cheeks were red and wet with tears. She pressed her hands tight across her forehead, as if she had a headache. "Hey," said George, easing between the branches. "Hey, what's wrong?"

The girl startled and dropped her hands to her sides. The pale-blond hair just above her forehead had been sheared to an uneven bristly patch that stuck straight up from her scalp like a boot brush.

"Oh!" said George. The girl cried harder.

George crept closer to her. "Hey, don't cry. Maybe we can paste it down with some water."

"I already tri-i-ied that," sobbed the girl. "It just pops back up."

George crept close enough to reach out a hand. She wanted to touch the top of the bristles. The girl jerked away. "Just let me see. I can't make it any worse." She licked her palm and slicked back the bristles, but they did indeed pop right back up. She slicked them forward. They popped up again.

"See!" she wailed. This girl wasn't afraid of being called a crybaby. George scooted closer.

"I'm Georgeanne. What's your name?"

"Helen."

She put her arms around Helen and squeezed. "It's going to be all right, Helen. There, there, now. There, there." This was what Adele did whenever George got upset about something. It seemed to work on

Helen too. She quieted down. George loosened her hold, but Helen put her hands on George's arms and said, "A little more. Please?"

"Sure."

Helen's breath slowed as George hugged her, and after a bit her shoulders went slack. George loosened her hold again, and Helen allowed it this time. She wiped her eyes and nose on her sleeve.

"What happened?" asked George.

"My little brother got hold of the scissors and snuck up behind me yesterday. Mama tanned him—he could have put out my eye! I almost wish he had. Then she would have had to let me stay home. You got any little brothers at your house?"

"Nope." She had asked, more than once, for a little sister and had been told no. The answer hadn't changed when she'd said a brother would be fine too.

"Well, lucky you. I've got two, and I hope I never get another." Helen swiped at the bristles. "What am I going to do?"

"Stay here. I'll be right back," said George. She pushed out of the bushes and ran to the back of the schoolhouse. The boys were playing mumblety-peg in the shade. She saw the one she wanted—his head gleamed in the sun. "Hey, you!" she shouted. "Hey, Pomade Boy!" He flinched, and the other boys hooted. Then they sang out, "Hey, Pomade Boy!"

This time she darted up to him. "What'd you do? Use the whole jar?" He stiffened and blinked furiously, fighting tears. *Serves him right,* she thought as she swiped her hand across the top of his head, raking his hair with her fingers to get as much of the goop as she could. "Yuck!" she shouted. Then she ran off before anyone could start up again about Adele wearing pants.

Back in the thicket, she crouched next to Helen. "If this isn't enough, I know where we can get more," she said as she plastered down the bristles. Maybe half of them stayed flat, so her hair didn't look all that much better. But when Miss Parry rang the bell, Helen marched back into the schoolroom with her head high.

After a few weeks, Helen's bristles grew into bangs and the taunting about George's mother wearing pants died down. The boys left the two of them alone, and the other girls allowed them into their circle.

By Thanksgiving time, George had learned to read short words and add single digits. She had learned that hair ribbons weren't just for special occasions, that other mothers actually liked ruffly dresses, and that other girls were learning to sew. And, after bragging to Helen about helping her mother work on the truck, she learned that her fascination with cars was considered odd. "But that's all right," said Helen. "We just won't tell anyone else."

Instead of the cross-stitch hoop and floss she'd asked for, George received a bicycle for her birthday.

"Can I take it apart?"

"*May* I take it apart, and no," said Adele. "It's for riding."

Riding a bicycle sounded hard. George wanted no part of it. She wheeled the bike into the garage and ignored it. Every sunny weekend she prayed that Adele had forgotten its existence, but her mother was relentless.

George straddled the thing and put one foot on a pedal. "I've got you," said Adele. "Go on, other foot up." George did as she was told. A ladybug landed in the middle of the handlebars and crawled toward her right hand. She watched it, fascinated. Would it climb onto her? Would its tiny legs tickle when it did?

"You've got to pedal." Her mother waggled the bike. The spotted insect raised its orange wings, and George saw that it had plain, more delicate wings beneath the fancy ones. It launched into the air and whirred past her ear.

"Do ladybugs have engines?"

"No. Come on, now. You've got to try."

"Then how do they go?"

"The same way birds and other bugs go—with their wings. Stop stalling and pedal."

She pedaled, frequently glancing back to make sure her mother hadn't let go of the seat.

"You'll never get anywhere if you keep looking behind you," said Adele.

"I don't want to get anywhere." This wasn't true. She yearned to fly off with the ladybug. Which would be much more fun than riding a bicycle. She pedaled slowly, swiveling her head, looking for the ladybug. Maybe it would come back. A metallic whine filled the air. A crop duster buzzed low along the horizon. George put both feet on the ground to watch it. "Mother, does that airplane have an engine?"

"Of course. Anything that makes that sound has an engine."

"Is it bigger than the truck's engine?"

"I suppose so. But I've never seen an airplane engine."

"Is someone driving it?"

"There's a pilot flying it. Come on, now. Feet up."

The plane turned, and George saw the pilot's head. She willed him to look at her and wave, but he steered away from them, flew off out of view. She wanted to ask how he told the plane to turn, but her mother waggled the bike again. George sighed and put her feet back in place. The pilot didn't have to pedal. Lucky him.

"Maybe you should just let her take it apart," she overheard her father say one night. She couldn't catch her mother's muffled response.

The following Saturday, Adele said, "Let's make a deal. Today you look straight ahead—no looking back at me—and pedal your very hardest. And if you do that three times, you can use my tools and do what you like with the bicycle."

"Really?" asked George.

"Really."

On the second try, George made it halfway down the driveway, pedaling hard, before she realized Adele no longer huffed behind her. She stopped pedaling. The bike wobbled. "Mother?"

"Pedal!" yelled her mother from much too far behind her. She steered into the azaleas and let the bike fall.

"That was great, George! You did it!"

"You let go of me!"

"Of course I did. That's how you learn to ride. And you did it!"

Her mother, that traitor, beamed at her.

"Come on, now. One more time. That was our deal."

She sighed. Most of the time it was easier to give in and do whatever it was her mother wanted.

"I'll hold you up to get you started."

Fine, thought George. *I'll just fall over as soon as she lets go. Then I'll be done.* But she didn't fall over. She kept on pedaling down the long driveway. Wobbly at first, but steadier as she went. This time, she didn't steer into the bushes. She pumped the pedals faster and felt the wind on her face and the joy of making a machine do what she wanted it to do. As she neared the end of the drive, she coasted until the bike slowed, then dragged her feet until it stopped. She walked the bike back to her still-beaming mother. "*Now* can I take it apart?"

"Yes, George. Now you *may* take it apart. Or you could ride it some more. Wasn't that fun?"

George just glared at her and wheeled the bike into the garage. She heard the crop duster again, buzzing over the neighboring property. A machine that flew—what a thrilling idea.

She took the bike apart and reassembled it, repeatedly. Occasionally she rode it, but mostly she treated it as a mechanical experiment, adding and removing parts, playing with the gear configuration and the brake rods. Over the next several years, she did the same with any other machinery her parents allowed her to mess with.

She never mentioned this hobby to the girls at school. Only Helen knew. "That's fine, George," Helen said. "I mean, it isn't surprising, considering your mother. But we've got to do something about your fingernails."

Helen rubbed her thumbs across George's nails. Each cuticle was rimmed with a thin, dark line of motor oil. No matter how hard George scrubbed, she could never get them to look clean like Helen's.

She was fretting about the state of her nails, and the fact that she'd worn a skirt with no pockets where she could hide her hands, as she and Helen, now both fifteen, strolled the fairgrounds looking for boys they knew. "Or might want to know," Helen added. George was terrified of unknown boys, and even of some she knew, but she trailed in Helen's perfumed wake, trying to look game and keeping her hands out of sight.

An engine roared above them. The plane buzzed low over the crowd. "Oh!" said Helen. "A barnstormer! The boys will be over at the airfield. Let's go!"

At the airfield, the boys had no attention to spare for girls. George had none to spare for them either. Not with the plane rocketing high above them, corkscrewing down into a dive, then pulling its nose up and climbing again.

The barnstormer flew figure eights and loop-de-loops. George felt as if she herself were at the controls, sending the plane higher and higher, tracing beautiful curves in the sky. All too soon, the plane landed and taxied to a stop in the middle of the field. The pilot climbed out and pulled off his leather cap and goggles. The crowd gasped to see a cascade of dark hair tumble down. The boys hooted and whistled as the lady pilot took a bow. Then she pulled a lipstick from her pocket and applied a touch-up.

She wasn't as tall as George—other than Adele, George never saw women who were—but as the pilot strode toward the crowd, she gave the impression of towering over everyone else. There was nothing soft or retreating or . . . ladylike . . . about her posture, and yet, she seemed every inch a lady. It was only her clothing—jodhpurs and a man's leather jacket—that had fooled everyone into believing she was a man. She began signing autographs. George had nothing for her to sign but pushed toward her anyway.

"Georgeanne, where are you going?" asked Helen.

"To meet the pilot."

Watching the plane as it spiraled and swooped above the crowd, George wished she were up in the sky, commanding the machine herself. Despite having Adele for a mother, she had immediately written off this longing as impossible, simply because she had the misfortune to be female. But this pilot's very existence said otherwise. She wasn't exactly sure what she'd say when she reached the front of the line—she only knew she had to meet this lady pilot. Some of the boys also wanted to meet her, so Helen didn't argue.

While they waited their turn, a mechanic checked over the plane. Once he was satisfied, he set up a signboard. Airplane Rides $3. George regretted the funnel cake she'd bought earlier. She was twenty-five cents short. "Helen, do you have a quarter?"

Helen was too busy tossing her hair for Frank Bridlemile to respond.

"What do you want a quarter for?" asked Frank, turning his attention to George.

"Really, George." Helen scowled at her. "You can't possibly be hungry again. Not after all that funnel cake."

"I'm not," she lied. She was always hungry, which was embarrassing. Almost as embarrassing as being too tall. "I need it for that." She waved a hand toward the Airplane Rides $3 sign and quickly wished she hadn't. Three dollars was a fortune. Especially these days. Especially for some of the boys standing around Helen. George understood that recent years had been brutal for certain families in a way they hadn't been for hers and for Helen's. Adele insisted George and Helen must always bear this in mind but never, ever speak it aloud. Asking for a quarter, along with admitting she had purchased food from a stand, rather than bringing a biscuit from home, was basically speaking aloud what should have remained unspoken.

Frank's family didn't have much—George suspected he'd be lucky to find a lonesome dime in his pocket. So she didn't take offense when he said, "You'd have to pay *me* to go up in that plane with a woman flying it."

"Georgeanne Ector, you can't be serious," said Helen.

"I'm completely serious."

Frank's attention settled on her now. "Wowza, George. Hey, you know, you have the strangest eyes."

Helen's own eyes narrowed. She stepped smoothly between George and Frank and pressed a quarter into George's hand.

Up close, the plane, made of wood and cable, seemed like nothing that ought to fly.

"It looks like a toy," George immediately regretted saying.

"Best toy I ever played with. Never underestimate a Jenny. They're stronger than they look. I'm Florence," the pilot said as she shook George's hand. Florence looked like someone who ought to be sunning herself poolside in Hollywood, not bundling her beautiful wavy hair into a leather helmet. "Climb on up."

The mechanic set a stepladder next to the wing. George stepped up and craned her head to see inside the rear cockpit. It had a polished wooden dash pocked with black gauges. In the center, a compass held pride of place. Some of the other gauges were self-explanatory: altitude, airspeed. Others mysterious.

"What's a Victometer?" asked George.

"That's my tach," said the pilot. "Place your right foot here. You're climbing in the front."

"What's a tach?" George surprised herself by asking. "And what's that one just above it? And that one over to the right? Do you steer with that stick?"

Florence guided George into the front cockpit. It had no instruments, except for a baseball bat–looking stick, just like the one in the rear cockpit. George wanted nothing more than to try it out. She folded her hands in her lap and surveyed the crowd until she spotted Helen. Helen fluttered her eyelids as Frank whispered something in her ear. It must have been very loud over there, because Helen stood on tiptoe and tilted her head, as if to catch every word. Florence fired up the Jenny, and then it was loud in the plane too. The engine whined and roared, making George tingle from her toes to her scalp.

"Keep your mouth closed till we're off the ground," yelled the pilot as she maneuvered the plane across the field. "Unless you want bugs in your teeth."

George, afraid of saying something else stupid, had planned to keep her mouth shut anyway. She was grateful for the helmet that kept her hair from blowing across her face, and for the goggles that allowed her to keep her eyes open as they sped into the wind. Her stomach lurched only a little as the wheels left the ground. The Jenny lifted, dipped slightly back toward the earth, then went up, up, up until George couldn't help it: she had to bare her teeth in an enormous smile, bugs be damned.

The sky above her was blue and cloudless. Below her lay the patchwork quilt of northern Oklahoma. Red and brown earth with hints of green and more quicksilver lakes than she would have imagined. She watched the shadow of the plane as it moved across the red dirt far below them, waving her arm and grinning as her shadow did the same.

Her chest hummed with the vibrations of the motor; she felt like she had a chorus inside her, holding a long, low note in unison. Her face and arms stung, raw in the wind, sharply defined. "You don't know where you begin and end," Adele used to say when, in the midst of her childhood growth spurts, George knocked over furniture and stumbled into doorjambs. Well, today she knew. Up in the air, the wind picking out her outline against the sky, she knew exactly where she began and ended.

"I can tell you like it up here," Florence yelled. "I better introduce you to Stu when we land."

George didn't want to land. Ever.

"Stick around," said Florence as George reluctantly climbed down, dazed and glassy eyed.

George viewed the string of people lined up for flights with dismay. There was no way Helen would wait until all of them got their fifteen minutes in the air. Here she came now, marching toward the plane, Frank still in tow.

A florid, paunchy man ignored Florence's instructions about where to put his feet as he climbed into the plane. His wife urged him to reconsider, but he just set his mouth in a grim line and clung to the wing.

Finally, a man in a coverall emerged from the hangar and strode toward the Jenny. "Sir," he said. "You just climb on back down and start again, now." Hearing a male voice freed the paunchy man to obey, and at last he made it into the plane. Then the man in the coverall clasped Florence's waist, spun her around, and gave her a long kiss. "Hello, darlin'!"

"Stu! About time you showed your face. Hey, this is . . . Miss? What's your name again?"

"Georgeanne Ector." She pretended not to notice Helen's alarmed expression.

"Miss Ector needs flying lessons. I told her you might be able to help her out."

Frank whistled long and low. Helen looked as if she might explode.

"Well, I do love to help a young lady out." Stu winked at George.

"Does he ever," said Florence. "You let me know if he tries to get *too* helpful."

George giggled. The airfield, she already understood, was its own universe. One where certain customs and rules were looser. She felt herself loosening, felt like she had just come home.

"Mother, guess what?"

"Good afternoon to you too."

"Hello, Mother," said George. She was supposed to ask how her mother's day had been, and then Adele would ask about hers, but today she couldn't wait. "I've decided something. I don't want a car for my birthday."

Adele had been talking about getting her a car for nearly a year. A car of her own would be fun to tinker with, George supposed, but she was already allowed to tinker with her parents' car. Also—and she could never ever admit this to anyone because it was a spoiled way of thinking—the notion of owning a car bored her. Lately, almost everything bored her. Nothing merited her time and attention. She felt antsy and unsettled. She'd confessed these feelings to Helen and had been relieved to learn that her best friend felt this way too. She wasn't the only one being a moper—something Adele could not abide.

Adele's expression indicated that she was far from surprised by the news that George didn't want a car. "We've been over this, Georgeanne. A car is independence. For you and for me. I can't be driving you all over creation these next few years, and, believe it or not, you will actually want to leave this house someday."

Independence was a big theme with George's mother. She was always telling stories—others told them too—about what an independent young woman she'd been. George knew she disappointed her mother in this regard. She wasn't bold. She didn't flout convention. When Helen successfully lobbied the school board for permission to take science with the boys rather than homemaking with the girls, suddenly Adele turned into Helen's biggest fan. She constantly talked about Helen's willingness to fight for what she wanted, Helen's refusal to settle for less than. Helen, Helen, Helen. George pointed out that Helen didn't care a fig about science—she just wanted to be the only girl in a roomful of boys. "Be that as it may," said Adele, "she wanted *something*, and she went out and got it."

Despite her boredom, George *did* want things. She wanted to take apart and reassemble the engine of her grandfather's Ford. She wanted to go out to the derricks with her father and the engineers and look over the machinery. Her parents forbade both of these things. The Ford was on its last legs. The engineers would find her distracting. But now—now she wanted something that she thought might make her mother happy.

"I do want to leave the house," said George. "I want," she said, delighting in how surprised her mother was about to be, "an airplane."

Her mother stared at her. "A what?"

George's confidence faltered. "An airplane," she said, softer this time. Her mother gazed at the ceiling and frowned, no doubt remembering the bicycle that George had refused to ride. She had to make her see that this was different. "We saw a barnstormer today. Her name is Florence, and—"

"The barnstormer was a woman?"

"Yes."

"Here in Garfield County. A woman barnstormer."

"Yes!" Adele, who had always encouraged her to do anything boys did, was clearly skeptical about the idea of a female pilot. "She took me up in her plane. It's a Jenny—"

"Look, George, I know you don't want a car, but this is a little much, expecting me to believe—"

"It's true! I bet she's still at the airfield. Let's go! I'll introduce you. She could take you up in her plane." She wasn't even certain Florence would remember her. Florence probably saw fifty starstruck girls a week. But the dream that had revved her pulse all afternoon was stalling out in the face of Adele's disbelief. "Please," George urged, tugging at her mother's sleeve. "Please, Mother. Come meet her."

The crowd at the airfield had thinned as folks headed home for supper. On the field, the mechanic hefted the AIRPLANE RIDES $3 sign and carried it into the hangar.

"Georgeanne Ector, did you pay three dollars for an airplane ride?"

"Yes." She didn't regret one penny of it. She only regretted that they'd arrived too late. The Jenny was nowhere to be seen. What if Florence had flown off to do a show somewhere else?

"Maybe she's in the hangar," said George, but she doubted it. Florence was such a force; George was certain she'd sense it if she were nearby. Something buzzed in the distance—a dot on the horizon, growing larger as it approached. The buzzing built to a roar as the small plane descended.

The Jenny taxied to a stop, and a young man climbed down from the front cockpit. "That's not a woman," said Adele.

"The pilot sits in back," said George.

"That's not a woman either," Adele said. But it was Florence all right, swinging out onto the wing spar and then hopping down to the grass below. She strode toward the hangar, pulling off her helmet as she went, setting her long wavy hair free. Adele's eyes widened. From the back of her throat came a startled squeak.

"Florence!" George called out.

The pilot turned. "Miss Ector. You're back." She looked at Adele, taking in her trousers, and smiled. "You must be Miss Ector's mother." She held out her hand.

"Adele," her mother croaked, gawping at Florence.

"Florence. Looks like we might have a pilot in training on our hands here." Florence nodded at George.

Her mother cleared her throat and grinned. "Looks like we just might."

"She wants an airplane, of all things," Adele said that night at dinner. "Can you believe it?"

Her father, smiling, admitted he could not.

"Can't be bothered with a car," said Adele. "No, sir. It has to be a vehicle that will leave the ground, apparently."

Even with her mother's backing, George wasn't sure she'd get the plane. She knew, from talk at the dinner table, that oil prices had been soft since the start of the Depression. "Fortunately, I pulled most of our funds out of the market before the crash," her father had said. He'd been able to keep his crews intact and his wells pumping when other oilmen couldn't.

"And I don't spend half as much on you and your mother as most men I know spend on their wives and daughters," he told George two months later when he presented her with the papers for a secondhand Taylor J-2.

George hadn't been so delighted with a birthday present since she'd received her own set of socket wrenches when she turned twelve. She couldn't believe her luck. A plane, flying lessons to go with it, and the uncustomary warmth of her mother's approval. "My daughter," Adele said, to anyone who would listen, "the would-be aviatrix."

She spent her first lesson mostly on the ground. Stu made her check every cable and wire, every fastening mechanism, the condition of the belly of the plane, the tire pressure. He startled when she asked what PSI they wanted to see. His jaw went slack when she took the gauge from him and attached it to the valve. When they checked the fluids, she surprised him again by knowing where to look before he told her.

"Hey, kid, if you're as good with this plane in the air as you are on the ground, this'll be a snap. Up you go."

He didn't help her into the front cockpit, which was a relief. George had never spent time in such close proximity to any man besides her father. Stu was younger than her father, and, with his Clark Gable mustache, much more handsome. It had been thrilling to surprise him with her knowledge of tools and engine components.

Away from the airfield, she daydreamed about him swinging her around and kissing her the way he'd kissed Florence. He was two inches shorter than George, but somehow in the daydream this didn't matter. At the airfield, she dreaded that he might somehow guess at her fantasies. "Focus on the plane," she told herself sternly. "Think about flying, and that's all."

"He's so handsome," said Helen when George stopped by her house. "Is he married?"

George had no idea if Stu and Florence were married.

"Well, does he wear a ring?" asked Helen. She hadn't thought to look. Helen sighed. "You're hopeless, Georgeanne." She always used George's full name when she was exasperated with her. "Now, tell me what you think about this dress. Frank's taking me to the dance next weekend."

The dress was perfect. Helen's sunshiny blond hair was perfect. She wasn't too tall. She had a boy who wanted to take her to movies and dances. Compared to Helen, George felt hopeless indeed.

As Stu tightened the rudder attachments before her next lesson, George examined his hands. No ring. "Is Florence around?" she asked. She hadn't seen her in over a week.

"She's doing a string of shows in Texas. Here." He handed her the wrench. "I keep forgetting you can do this yourself. I never know when she'll blow through, but she always does."

His rueful smile told George everything she needed to know about how Stu felt about Florence. She couldn't blame him. Florence was glamorous and bold. When she wasn't flying, she wore her long dark hair down and wavy. Or tied up in a silk scarf. Her lips were always siren red. "My signature color," she told George once as she swiped on a fresh coat. Florence walked as if everyone were watching and she expected nothing less than their full attention.

George, despite Adele's constant admonition to stand up straight, slouched when she walked, trying to minimize her height. Her hair wouldn't hold enough curl on the left and held too much curl on the right. Whenever she tried on Helen's pink lipstick, she felt like a child playing dress-up. No wonder Stu only had eyes for Florence. No wonder he called her kid. To him, that's all she was.

One morning before Stu arrived at the airfield, she spotted a golden tube on the flight office desk. She peeked outside. No sign of Florence's Jenny. George pocketed the lipstick. She'd try it out when she got home and return it to the desk the next day. No one would be the wiser. Certainly not Florence, who might not blow through again for weeks.

Her hand went to the smooth metal tube in her pocket repeatedly as she ran through the preflight checklist. Stu trusted her to do most of it herself now. Just as he let her handle the controls almost entirely herself while they were in the air.

"You're a natural, kid," he shouted as she banked the plane after takeoff.

"A natural," she repeated in front of her mirror that afternoon as she tried on the red lipstick and rolled her lips together. Her eyes looked brighter. Her unruly hair looked tamer. She felt pretty. There was only a nub left in the tube. Maybe Florence had left it behind on purpose. Maybe she'd never miss it. George slipped it into the drawer of her vanity.

She ventured downstairs, holding her breath, waiting for her mother's judgment. Her parents had never forbidden makeup, but her mother rarely wore any herself. "Well, look at you. Don't you look nice," Adele said, and George exhaled.

"How'd you get to be so grown up?" asked her father at dinner that night. It was funny, George thought, that wearing lipstick—more than flying an airplane—made her seem grown up. "It suits you," he said.

"That's a good color on you," said Helen the next day. "Did you get it at Woolworth's?"

Before she could answer, Frank joined them on the porch. "Wowza, George!"

"Georgeanne was just leaving," said Helen.

George's shoulders slumped. Frank was funny and kind. He never made her feel like a third wheel, even if Helen sometimes did. He was an inch taller than her, a rare thing among boys her age, and thin as a rail. He had dark spaniel eyes, and when he looked at her, her stomach did a little flip.

Helen's mother didn't approve of Frank. The Bridlemiles lived a step up—and only a small one—from hand to mouth. But George saw why Helen liked him. And why she wanted him all to herself. Helen could shoo her off, but she couldn't shoo away the fact of Frank's "wowza."

George squared her shoulders and rose to her full height. "I'll see you two later," she said airily. Descending the steps of the Cramer porch, she did her best imitation of Florence's walk.

Stu wanted Florence. Frank wanted Helen. Somewhere in Enid, Oklahoma, there had to be a boy who'd want her. Finding him was the challenge. The rule that a girl had to date boys who were taller left George with only a handful of possibilities. Like Frank, many of them already had girlfriends. One was the Pomade Boy who had teased

George when she was little. He teased her still, asking her how the air was up there. Asking her how she could tell whether she was flying or walking, because no one else could. He didn't say a word about the red lipstick, though. "Stunned into silence," said Helen. "For once."

Mel Carson, a varsity starting linebacker, seemed like a possibility. "You two would look good walking down the hall together," agreed Helen. "Frank's on the team. I'll get him to introduce you." George doubted Mel would care much about Frank's recommendation, but a few days later, Helen reported that Frank had arranged a double date for them on Saturday. "Frank wants to see *Stagecoach*. Then we'll go for ice cream after. Wear your blue dress with the Swiss dots. And that lipstick."

George did as she was told. Frank drove his father's car. He picked up Helen first, then Mel. George waited for them on the porch. Helen wouldn't approve of that—she'd cautioned George about appearing overeager. But George couldn't bear to sit inside with her parents, who were obviously dying to assess Mel Carson. Their invisible antennae quivered, telegraphing questions and exclamations back and forth at one another. Height aside, George had barely assessed him herself. She didn't want to hear her mother's opinion until she had formed her own. Adele's opinions tended to be big and weighty, and George's often collapsed in the face of them.

When Frank pulled up, she dashed down the steps, calling out, "Bye!" She'd closed the car door before her parents made it out onto the porch. "Goodness." Helen scowled. "Where's the fire, Georgeanne?"

George knew better than to explain her parents' antennae on a first date. She ignored Helen's irritation and spoke to Frank instead. "Thank you for picking me up."

"Sure thing. Mel, George, you know each other, right?"

"The girl who flies airplanes," said Mel. His neutral tone yielded no hints as to whether he was impressed or put off. He must not be too put off, she supposed, since he'd agreed to this double date.

"That's right. Seven more hours of solo time and I'll have my private license."

"Well, that sounds nice," said Mel.

"Frank wants to see *Stagecoach*. That okay with you, Mel?" asked Helen.

"Sure. That sounds nice," said Mel.

"Don't pretend you don't want to watch John Wayne for two hours, Hel," teased Frank. Helen and George laughed, and, after a beat, Mel joined in.

George was grateful for the enforced quiet of the theater. Mel, beyond agreeing that things sounded nice, didn't contribute much in the way of conversation. George sympathized. Talking with people she'd just met wasn't always easy, but at least she tried. Her mind ran through everything she knew about him—not much, it turned out—or might ask him. *What's your favorite class?* seemed like a question that only a grind would ask. *What do you like to do besides play football?* sounded like something her father would ask. While Frank and Helen chattered away in the front, the air in the back seat thickened with awkward silence. Maybe Mel was struggling to think of things to ask her too. She glanced over at him. His expression was placid; he didn't appear to be thinking anything at all. At the ice cream parlor, careful to keep the desperation out of her voice, she asked what his favorite flavor was.

"Oh, pretty much anything." He didn't ask about hers.

George envied the ease of Frank and Helen's banter. They had fun together. They tried to include George and Mel in their fun, but the strain in Helen's eyes showed that it was heavy going.

Back at the Ector house, Mel walked George to the door. She hoped he wouldn't try to kiss her. Not with Helen and Frank watching from the car. Then again, if he didn't try to kiss her, that would only confirm what a disappointing date she'd been. Oh well. At least now she'd *been* on a date. She'd be better prepared for the next one. She knew which dress to wear. She had the lipstick. She just needed to memorize some questions and a few interesting anecdotes. She was already combing through her personal history, searching for possibilities, when Mel leaned in and pecked her on the cheek.

"That was fun," he said. "Want to go out again next Saturday?"

The peck on the cheek felt exactly right. Not too much, but more than nothing. "Yes," said George. "That sounds nice."

Just like that, she had a boyfriend. Someone who held her hand in the hallway between classes. Who took her to dances and the movies. In exchange, George enrolled in a secret extra class, one with an endless homework assignment of thinking up topics to discuss and stories to tell. Mel's responses were always kind, although they never did much to move the conversation into new territory.

She'd been nervous the first time they parked. She'd never kissed a boy before, only seen it done in movies. Those movie kisses appeared deceptively simple: a man and woman pressed their lips together for longer than seemed necessary. She could tell something else was going on, but it was impossible to suss out the mechanics of it. "Tongues, George," said Helen. "They're using their tongues."

This information was both unhelpful and slightly terrifying. Using their tongues for what? George, already feeling like a baby, didn't ask Helen to elaborate.

Mel parked near the lake. He turned off the car and slid to the middle of the front seat. George scooted toward him, praying she wouldn't make a fool of herself. He put his arm behind her and pecked her on the cheek again. She turned and pecked him back. Then they pecked on the lips. Mel put his other arm around her and pulled her toward him. He put his lips on hers again and then opened his, and George thought, *Aha! Tongues!* She didn't need specific instructions. She knew what to do, and so, apparently, did Mel.

As they kissed, George pressed close, mashing her breasts against his chest. She wished she could press right through his clothing. She wished his hands, which remained locked against her back, would move to her front. Her insides felt electric. She could have kissed him all night, but eventually he pulled back. "It's nearly eleven thirty. Better get you home."

After that night, they necked at the end of every date. Once or twice, all they did was neck. She looked forward to parking, to the cessation of talking. To the desire—always unfulfilled—to lie down, strip off her clothes and his, too, to feel his hands wander her body and touch her somewhere, anywhere, besides the center of her back.

"Maybe he's being a gentleman?" suggested Helen when George confided in her about Mel's well-behaved hands. But the doubt in Helen's tone confirmed that she thought it was odd.

Eventually, Adele insisted that Mel come in for a glass of tea and a slice of pie. She wore a dress for the occasion, without George even having to ask. Mel shook her father's hand and said yes, ma'am and no, sir to her parents' questions. He bolted the pie and gulped down the tea. "Thank you. That was nice." At last, after a stilted half hour in the Ector parlor (*What do you like to do besides play football, Mel?*), her father released them, saying, "Well, we should let you two get on with your evening."

"Thanks for doing that," George said after they'd made their escape.

"Oh, sure. It was nice," said Mel. "Your parents are nice." He sounded surprised. George wondered if he might suggest she meet his parents, too, but he didn't.

She and Helen ran into Mrs. Carson, Mel's mother, in Woolworth's the next week. George was hunting a replacement for the depleted red lipstick, and Helen was spritzing herself with the cologne sampler when Mrs. Carson approached the cosmetics counter.

"Hello, Helen," she said.

"Hello, Mrs. Carson," said Helen. Helen's and Mel's mothers were second or third cousins, which meant Mel and Helen were distantly related. "So distantly it doesn't really count," emphasized Helen. George supposed that was why Mrs. Carson greeted Helen first.

"How is your mother doing these days?"

"She's just fine, thank you, ma'am. This is my friend, Georgeanne Ector. She's Mel's—" But Mrs. Carson's gaze locked on to Helen in a way that erased George entirely.

"And your brother? I heard he had scarlet fever."

"Oh, he's fully recovered. I'll tell him you asked. This is—"

"No loss of eyesight?"

"Not that we've noticed."

"Well, I'm relieved to hear it. I'll say a prayer for him."

"Thank you, ma'am," said Helen as Mrs. Carson walked away.

"That was rude!" Helen whispered to George once the woman was out of earshot.

"Maybe she was in a hurry," said George, eager to find a reason beyond herself for being rendered invisible.

"Maybe," said Helen. But there was that doubtful tone again.

That night on the way to the lake, George told Mel she'd seen his mother at Woolworth's.

"Yeah. She mentioned that."

"Oh. It seemed like she didn't really notice me."

"How could anyone not notice you?" He slid toward her on the seat.

"Maybe you should introduce me to your folks soon," suggested George.

"Okay, that sounds nice."

Then they stopped talking and necked until it was time to drive George back home.

On the drive, she told him the news she'd been saving. "I got my private pilot's license! That means I can fly with passengers. I could take you up sometime."

"Oh, I don't know."

"It's really fun. I'd love to take you."

"Well, that sounds nice. I guess."

His lack of enthusiasm left her deflated. Besides Stu and her parents, no one seemed excited for her. Helen certainly wasn't interested in going up in George's plane. "No offense, Georgeanne, but I'd prefer to keep my feet on solid ground." Evidently Mel felt the same.

"Hey, George," he said. She turned toward him in surprise. Mel never initiated conversation. "How long do you plan to keep flying?"

"What do you mean?"

"Well, now that you've gotten your license, you've shown everyone you know how to fly. So I thought, well, maybe you'd gotten it out of your system."

"Gotten it out of my system?"

"I mean, you'll have to stop someday. You can't fly once you get married. Or . . . engaged."

It wasn't okay to get angry at a boy unless he did something terrible, like kissing another girl. Otherwise, a girl was supposed to smile, say something bland, and smooth over any rough patches in the conversation. No one had ever explained this to her, but deep inside she knew this was how it worked.

Mel must have known it worked that way too. His smug tone and expression declared his confidence that she'd agree with anything he said. Because that's what she was supposed to do. Her heart pounded. Heat flooded her face. All the "supposed tos" inside her dissolved in the acid of her anger. "Then I'll never get married. Or engaged."

He looked stunned. "Yeah. I guess not."

She couldn't believe that only moments ago she'd wanted them both to take off their clothes. To do exactly what, she wasn't certain. But she'd trusted, after the experience with the kissing, that they'd figure it out. Now she wanted to get as far away from him as possible.

Yet here she was, stuck on a back road for another half hour while he drove her home.

"Aw, George. Don't cry, now. I didn't mean to make you sad."

If only she could make lightning come out of her eyes instead of tears. She wasn't sad. She was furious. "Just take me home." She put her face in her hands and didn't look up until they reached her house. As soon as he braked, she bolted out of the car, not even bothering to slam the door shut behind her. She raced up the steps and into the house with a roar.

"George!" Adele tossed aside the latest issue of *Popular Mechanics* and rushed toward her. "Oh, honey, what is it?" George flung herself into her mother's arms and sobbed.

Adele stroked her hair back from her forehead, the way she had when George was little. George wished she were little again so she could curl up in her mother's lap.

"What happened? Did he . . ."

George snorted through her tears. Mel was a coward. Too cowardly to go up in her plane. Too cowardly to introduce her to his mother. Too cowardly to do more than kiss her, even though she'd given him every indication that he could.

"No. Nothing like that." She sniffled and pulled away.

"Then what?"

"He asked me when I planned to stop flying."

"He *what?*"

"He asked me when I thought I'd get it out of my system."

Adele's lips whitened. Her fierce eyes narrowed. "You told him never, I hope."

"He said I had to stop before I got married."

Adele took her by the shoulders and gave her a shake. "You listen close, now. You're a teenage girl with an airplane. People believe we spoil you—and they aren't wrong—not entirely anyway. But your instructor says you're very good."

George was appalled. Everyone—even her mother—thought she was spoiled. Worse, her parents had been checking up on her.

"Don't look at me like that. I pay the bill, and I like to know what I'm getting for my money. Stuart says you're one of the best students he's ever taught. You have talent. Pretty much everyone gets some sort of talent, but almost no one gets the opportunity you have. Don't you dare waste it, Georgeanne Ector. No matter what anyone else says."

In the hallway at school, she batted away Mel's hand. When he found the nerve to call her again, she told him she was busy. "I'm flying all weekend. I want to get my commercial license too. And a couple of endorsements." He never called again. She dated other boys occasionally. When they parked, she found she missed Mel's restraint. It was up to her to make sure things didn't go too far, even when she was tempted to let them.

If things went too far, word would get around. It was bad enough that they talked about her being rich and spoiled. It was bad enough that they disapproved of her flying. She wasn't going to have them talking about how she went fast in the back seat of a car too.

After graduation, she enrolled in the women's college outside Oklahoma City. She wasn't especially excited about it, but she wanted to get out of Enid and couldn't think of what else to do. She had hoped Helen would go with her, but Helen and Frank had gotten engaged, and Helen said she didn't see the point. Not when she had a wedding and a trousseau to arrange. Besides, Frank wasn't going to college, and Helen didn't believe a wife should have more education than her husband.

At the college, George felt more awkward than ever. The other students were all so petite, their waists and feet so tiny. George had always believed herself to be slender, but she felt like a burly giant among these girls. She didn't care for studying, which meant she didn't fit in with the grinds. And she hated the homemaking classes that made up the nonacademic portion of the curriculum. The other girls already knew how to sew and cook. George caught them looking at her with pity or derision when she couldn't do the simplest things. She lasted until Thanksgiving break before telling the dean she wouldn't return.

Her father came to collect her. George ran down the dormitory stairs as soon as the Nash pulled up. "Hello, Georgie!" He beamed, and her fears that he disapproved of her not sticking it out disappeared. Reaching the car, she noticed the deep shadows beneath his eyes. "Ah, just trouble sleeping now and then. Nothing to worry about, Georgie." He insisted on taking her suitcase and putting it in the trunk himself, a simple action that left him winded.

"Not your cup of tea," he said as they drove away.

"No, sir. Not by a long shot."

"Well, you'll find something that is. I've been thinking it's time to show you more about the business. And you have your flying, of course."

At home, when he shed his overcoat, she was shocked to see how gaunt he'd become.

"It's this business in Europe," whispered Adele. "It . . . keeps him awake." Hitler had invaded Poland the year before, then marched on, invading one country after another.

"I'm just fine, honey," said her father when she expressed concern. "Don't you worry about me. How's the flying going? How's the plane?"

"It's great, Dad. You know I love the plane." She was racking up hours and qualifications for her commercial license and an aeronautics endorsement. She'd learned how to do a lazy eight. She was practicing her tailslide. When she wasn't flying, she sat with her father in his study, listening to him explain the accounts.

In the evenings, she tried to soothe Helen. Helen's parents refused to pay for a wedding until she turned twenty *and* Frank found a decent job. "They say nineteen is too young. And they refuse to say what they mean by decent." Helen's mother had even suggested that she and her so-distant-it-didn't-really-count cousin, Mel, might hit it off. "As if I'd waste a minute of my time with that numbskull. Oh. Sorry, George."

Despite her full days, George felt herself stagnating in Enid. Everyone in town knew who she was, or thought they did. That too-tall girl with the airplane and the indulgent parents. She dreamed of flying bigger planes to bigger places. She dreamed of meeting people—ideally some of them would be young and male—who respected her for her talent.

Then Japan bombed Pearl Harbor, and Stu enlisted in the Civilian Pilot Training Program, leaving George without an instructor.

"I wish I could sign up too," she told her parents.

"I don't know, George," said Adele. "If there's one advantage to being a woman, this might be it."

Months later, when the telegram boy knocked on the door of the Ector house, she assumed the message was for her father. They always were. But this time, the boy said, "Telegram for G. P. Ector."

George gave him a nickel and tore open the message. She read it through once and thought, *At last.* She read it through again to make sure they understood she was female, that they actually wanted female pilots. They did. She was to reply by telegram to confirm her interest.

She showed the message to her mother, who blanched. "I suppose you'll go."

"If they'll take me. The planes will be bigger than my J-2. Heavier. They'll have instruments I haven't seen before."

Adele waved a hand as if none of that mattered. "They'll take you, George. They'd be fools not to." She blinked rapidly. George realized she was trying not to cry.

"I thought you'd be happy for me."

"Oh, George. I'm proud that they asked you. But war does terrible things to people. You have no idea."

This from the woman who'd always pushed her to be independent, to do what the boys did, to be bold and walk tall. The tears in her mother's eyes were more proof that the world was coming apart at the seams. The only hopeful thing in it was the telegram in her hand.

"I'll be just fine, Mother. Don't you worry about me."

CHAPTER 3

Her world had grown small. Well, no, Adele realized, it had just never been big. When she was a child, the world had been made up of the Clemson ranch, her parents, James and John and Pauline. Then she married Charles, and they split off, forming a planet all their own. One that doubled in size the day that George appeared on it. Her childhood planet became a moon, circling them. But unlike the real moon, it shrank, year by year. Now it was barely a speck in the sky.

A pale-green mass had cleaved away from that moon when James died in his trench. Half of what remained splintered to nothing after Pauline passed. Claude Demmings waited a suitable interval, then remarried. He took his new wife and his sons to Arkansas, leaving Adele with a single photograph: three boys lined up in the suits they'd worn to their mother's funeral (now snug at the shoulders and short at the ankles), Pauline's button nose in the center of each tight-lipped face.

Several years later, her father caught a cough. First the barking took his voice, then his ability to eat. His bull's frame withered. He refused even the smallest sips of broth, speeding himself toward his final choking breath but never managing to outrun his suffering. Six months later, Adele's mother complained of a headache, lay down in her bed, and never rose from it again.

The Clemson ranch went to John. He'd been running it anyway, continuing the modernization begun by their father. He'd built up the herd to several hundred head and had plans for more. Then the drought hit. The Clemson pastureland was halved, and two years later, halved again, along with the herd. The remaining cattle choked on dust. He sold the ranch for next to nothing and, like so many others, lit out for California.

His letters, with their descriptions of orange groves and palm canyons and vast stretches of sand along an endless ocean, made her chest ache. She couldn't picture John in those places. She sensed the time coming when she'd no longer be able to picture him at all. Just as she could no longer easily call up Pauline's face, or James's. In the depths of her memory, her parents walked and talked as their younger selves. Not the broken-down invalids of their last years, when Adele had been the one bringing marrows and broths and soothing fevered brows.

And now George was leaving, could not wait to go. To form a world all her own—one much bigger and brighter, one that Adele was destined someday to circle. *The natural order of things,* she heard her father say. *No one likes a moper,* her mother chimed in. Adele cleared her throat and straightened her spine. Tallying her losses would never alter their sum.

George darted past her. "I'm going to see if Helen wants to drive up to Oklahoma City with me. I need a train schedule. Interviews are in Washington, DC."

She blew out of the house, taking every bit of fresh air with her. A sniff confirmed it: the room smelled musty, stale. During the drought, they'd kept the windows shut for months on end—a fruitless attempt to keep out the dust. *Enough of that,* thought Adele. She strode from room to room, opening windows, letting in the crisp fall air. She saved Charles's office for last.

"Come in," he said to her knock. He was always home these days. She knew he trusted the site foremen, but she also knew it wasn't wise for the boss to so rarely make himself seen.

"I'm airing out the house," she said. "And George is off to the city with Helen. The telegram came this morning." Charles blinked hurt from his eyes, and Adele's throat tightened. George should have told him herself about the telegram—the one they'd all been expecting for so long. But lately, George went out of her way to keep things to herself. If Adele hadn't been standing near the door when the message arrived, she'd have been left in the dark too. She turned toward the windows, fought back tears as she opened them one by one. The last window stuck. She smacked the butt of her hand hard against its sash until it gave way. Charles came up behind her, wrapped his arms around her, pressed his chest to her back, his rib cage sharp against her shoulder blades.

"She'll be okay, Dellie. They won't send her overseas."

"We don't know that. There are American girls flying in England as we speak."

"That's not what this . . . Women's Airforce Service Pilot program is recruiting for. You saw the article in the paper. They want girls to transport planes mostly."

"And train artillery gunners."

"That too. But I'm sure they have a safe way of doing that. It's training, after all. They won't let gunners actually shoot at girls flying planes."

They let boys die in trenches. They sent the ones who survived home to have nightmares for the rest of their lives. Who could say what else they might allow?

Charles gave her a final squeeze and released her. "I'm thinking about taking out a lease on the Greer property."

"Haven't they already drilled that piece of land?" She turned and followed him to the desk.

"Not all of it." He pointed to the topo map he'd been studying when she came in. "Only the southern half. But look at these depressions up in this quarter. And here."

Adele only pretended to look. The map didn't interest her. What interested her was the topography of Charles's hand. The way the skin between his knuckles and wrist matched the dull gray of the map background. The bulging dark veins traveling over the sunken flesh.

The bony hills of his knuckles, each riven by its own valley. His face was gray too. Lately when he climbed the stairs, he'd pause at the top and huff. His ankles swelled over the tops of his shoes. The cook prepared his favorite meals, but even so, Charles mostly rearranged the food on his plate and then retreated to his study. Suddenly it occurred to her that he spent all his time at home because driving out to the wells and checking on the crews was too exhausting.

And now he wanted to discuss leasing rights with her. Lately he wanted to talk over every business notion that crossed his mind. How had she been so slow to catch on? He was preparing her, making sure she could run things herself. Or at least understand what properties they held, in case she wanted to sell.

She slapped her hand down on the map, and he jumped.

"Stop it!"

"Stop what?" If he was so innocent, why was he blushing like a little boy caught dipping his finger in cake icing?

"Stop trying to teach me the business. You are not dying!"

He put a gray hand over hers and squeezed. "Dellie. We're all dying."

She shook him off. "Not anytime soon. Not without a fight."

Dr. Lattimer said it was Charles's heart. He prescribed digitalis and regular elevation of the feet. "And no smoking," said Dr. Lattimer, stubbing out his own cigarette to emphasize the point.

"I don't smoke," said Charles.

"Good. Don't start. Some doctors might disagree, but in my opinion, it revs up the heart, and yours doesn't need any extra rev. Take a walk every morning and a nap every afternoon. Sound advice for everyone. But especially for a man your age."

"He's barely forty-eight," said Adele.

"Exactly," said Dr. Lattimer. He tapped another Lucky from the packet, dismissing them.

Charles took the pills. He walked and napped. His color improved. His appetite returned. He still huffed a bit after walking up the stairs, and his ankles still swelled more than Adele would have liked. But he began driving out to the drilling sites again. She went with him, not because she was worried, but because he was right: she needed to learn the business. She needed to accustom the foremen to her presence. To see which ones looked her in the eye when they answered her questions and which ones looked over her shoulder.

She sat with him in his study, too, going over lease agreements and oil-in-place estimates, reviewing payroll and equipment expenses. She didn't particularly enjoy this desk work, but it provided some distraction from George and her all-too-evident eagerness to leave.

George was always running off to the airfield or to Helen's. When she was home, she found a reason to exit any room Adele entered. Recently, she'd begun driving out with Frank Bridlemile in the evenings. Adele wondered how Helen felt about these outings, but George never held still long enough for her to ask. Some days Adele felt like a hunter, creeping up on her daughter, hoping to snare her into conversation, into closeness.

At the dinner table, George stared into the distance. Dreaming of flight training, Adele supposed. A world Adele couldn't imagine and would never be part of. If only they could go back to the days when Adele could do something simple like jack up the car and George's eyes would widen with awe. The evenings when George would scoot right up next to her on the sofa so that they could study the diagrams in *Popular Mechanics* together.

There must have been a last time that George climbed into her lap. A last time she'd carried George somewhere. A last time they'd leaned over an open hood together. So many lasts, none of them marked with the least bit of fanfare. *No one likes a moper,* she heard her mother say.

She did her best to stay occupied, to maintain a sense of dignity as she let her daughter go. The Packard didn't need a thing done to it, but she decided to change into her coverall anyway and poke around under the hood. Reaching the top of the stairs, she smelled the orange-peel-and-vanilla scent of Shalimar. George had taken to wearing perfume lately. Adele suspected this had something to do with Frank Bridlemile.

George's bedroom door was open. She stood at the foot of her bed, arms crossed, frowning at the outfits she'd spread out. A couple of utility dresses. A tailored blouse and a pleated skirt. Light wool trousers and a twinset.

"Deciding what to pack?" asked Adele.

George looked up and smiled so warmly that Adele's heart turned over like a newly tuned engine.

"Oh, I'll take pretty much everything," said George.

The engine died. Of course, she thought, because George didn't expect to return home again anytime soon.

"I'm trying to decide what to wear for my first day of training."

Already? She had weeks to figure that out. George hadn't consulted her about what to wear for her trip to Washington, DC. Adele didn't expect her daughter to consult her about her wardrobe for her first day in Sweetwater either. But George hadn't shooed her out of the bedroom. Maybe that was an invitation.

"Those trousers look nice," said Adele. "With that twinset."

George smirked. "Oh, Mother, you always think trousers are nice."

When was the fanfare-less last time her daughter had wanted her advice on anything? *The natural order of things,* she heard her father say.

Why did this natural order of things have to sting so much? "Wear what you like," she said as she closed George's door behind her.

The week before Thanksgiving, Adele stood beneath the green-striped awning of the market, thumbing through her ration coupons, as if shuffling them might make them multiply. She'd decided to bypass the turkeys this year—too scrawny and too pricey—and make do with a couple of chickens instead.

"Hello, Adele." Bess Cramer, Helen's mother, approached, canted to one side to counterbalance the heavy basket on her opposite arm. Her hair, once golden like Helen's, had faint gray streaks in it now, but her eyes remained bright and lively. And friendlier than most women's. Adele didn't spend much time socializing with other women in town, but she felt she and Bess shared a sense of practicality.

"Hello, Bess. You must be in the thick of it. The holidays *and* a wedding." She wasn't going to pass up this chance to confirm that Helen and Frank were still engaged.

"Well," said Bess, setting down her basket and leaning in, "just between us, we've decided to wait on the wedding. Frank's shipping out soon, and we don't want Helen rushing into anything because of the war. It won't hurt them to wait. Not that Helen sees it that way. She's simply livid."

Helen was a girl who didn't hear no easily. No doubt she was raising quite a fuss. "Well, you're probably right about the waiting."

"And Georgeanne? When does she leave?"

"In the new year. She'd go tomorrow if she could."

"I envy you the calm house you're about to have."

"Hmm." Adele imagined the hours in Charles's study, reviewing derrick maintenance schedules. The days that would pass while she waited for the mailman to deliver a letter from George. She pictured the Cramer household, bustling with Helen's two younger brothers. Boys still young enough to need some mothering, whether they knew it or not. Plus, the commotion an outraged Helen would add.

Adele had never regretted having just one child, but she envied Bess her not-so-calm house.

"Not that it's the same, but Helen wants to do her little part too," Bess went on. "She's signed up with the Red Cross to help organize assistance for soldiers' families. We're hoping it takes her mind off Frank."

Adele winced, thinking about her plan to "make do" with two chickens rather than a single turkey. She would still buy two, she decided, and take one and a basket of dry goods to a family in need. Then she would call Helen and find out how else she could help. She would escape her too-calm house. She would make her world a little bigger.

CHAPTER 4

Vivian tugged her wagon down the sandy street. Only a handful of roads in Hahira, Georgia, were paved by 1929, and Oak Street wasn't one of them. Her wagon wasn't a Radio Flyer—even if they'd had that kind of money, the Shaws wouldn't have spent it on a toy—but a crate her brothers had sawed down and bolted to two axles. A gift for her seventh birthday. They'd painted the sides red and attached a leather tow strap. The metal wheels refused to turn on the sand. Vivian dragged the wagon behind her like a sled, hauling a heavy basket of peaches to her aunt's house. At least she didn't have to lug the basket of fruit all the way there in her arms. Carrying it up Aunt Clelia's steep front steps was enough of a job.

She paused in the cool shade of the porch, panting a little, basket at her feet, and listened through the screen door. Voices—Aunt Clelia and Rosemary, her lodger—carried from the kitchen.

"Where is that child?" demanded Aunt Clelia. "Never around when you want her and always underfoot when you don't."

"Bless her heart," said Rosemary.

"Vivvy's heart's been blessed so much, she should be walking around beneath a halo."

Rosemary said something about Vivian's "poor mother" and blessed her heart too. Rosemary hated to let anyone's heart go unblessed.

"Poor nothing," said Clelia. "Don't get me wrong—my sister has had her trials. Husband couldn't catch a nickel if you glued it to his palm. Forever chasing after some scheme. The boys have always been a handful. And she's never gotten over losing the two between Walter and Elizabeth. But she got Mama's house because *she's* the one with a family to raise. Even though we all know it's Elizabeth who's raising Vivvy."

This wasn't the first time Vivian had heard women whispering about her mother. Clara Shaw didn't dote and she didn't coddle. She rarely scolded. Or did the motherish things Vivian observed at her friends' houses. She left Vivian's mothering to her oldest daughter, Elizabeth.

"Bless her heart. That Elizabeth is just a girl herself," said Rosemary. "No wonder Vivvy runs wild. You can't tell where the dirt ends and the young'un begins."

Vivian looked down at her bare feet, gray past the ankles and suddenly itchy. She rubbed the arch of one foot against her calf, unable to recall the last time Elizabeth had made her bathe.

Except for the part about her being dirty, she hadn't learned anything new from eavesdropping on Rosemary and Aunt Clelia. It didn't bother her that they thought her father was a no-account. He was mostly gone—a traveling salesman—toting a new case of samples whenever he blew back into Hahira. It didn't bother her that Clelia was upset about her mother getting Grammy's house. Clelia had a perfectly fine house of her own—smaller, but plenty of room for herself and Rosemary—that Old Man Suttle had left her. He'd died shortly after their honeymoon. Just went to bed one night and never woke up again. Now there was a notion that bothered Vivian. What bothered her even more was anyone thinking Elizabeth wasn't doing a good job.

When Vivian felt scared about going to bed and not waking up again, it was Elizabeth who hugged her. Their mother was busy turning the squash patch, trellising the beans, or pruning the peach trees. When Vivian got hungry, their mother was busy digging sweet potatoes or weeding the corn, so it was Elizabeth who rustled up something to eat. Whenever Vivian put herself in her mother's path, between her and her pruning shears, between her and the strawberry bed, between her and anything at all, her mother shooed her away, saying, "Go ask your sister." Vivian adored Elizabeth.

Aunt Clelia reared up on the other side of the screen door. "There you are! Why didn't you knock? Bring those on in here." Vivian hoisted the basket to her chest—her arms barely wrapped around it—and stumbled after her aunt into the kitchen.

"Well, look what the cat dragged in," said Rosemary. Vivian had seen the disgusting things her mother's tabby dragged in—when Rosemary's back was turned, she stuck out her tongue at her. Aunt Clelia thwapped her on the top of her head.

Because Aunt Clelia had done it, Vivian had to look meek and sorrowful. If anyone at school had done it, she would have thwapped them back, and better. Her brothers had taught her how to throw a punch just last week. She'd only tried it on their open palms so far, and on a bolster in the parlor. She was itching for a chance to try it on a kid.

Vivian lingered in the kitchen, hopeful. Sometimes Aunt Clelia gave her a penny. It seemed that today would not be one of those times. "Go on. Scat. We don't have time to entertain you. We've got to peel and pickle all of these."

She slunk down the porch steps and towed the wagon back onto the hot sand of Oak Street. Elizabeth was off with her girlfriends. Since she turned twelve, Elizabeth spent a lot of time giggling with her friends and rag curling her hair. Vivian decided to go find her brothers and ask them how to oil the wagon wheels. Phil Jr. and Walter helped fill the family cash jar by tinkering with bicycles, cars, and tractors for whatever anyone could afford to pay. Not much, usually. Anytime she wanted, they let her lie down on the creeper and slide under the cars. Just the other day, they had promised to show her how to use a socket wrench. She skipped ahead, jerking the wagon along behind her, no longer thinking about a bath.

The smell of bacon woke Vivian when the sky had barely paled. Her mother was probably already out in the garden, yanking any weeds bold enough to sprout overnight, deadheading spent flowers, and cutting the best ones for Elizabeth's wedding bouquet.

How good of Elizabeth to cook a real breakfast on the morning of her wedding. The next time Vivian wanted bacon, she'd have to fry it herself. But that was all right. She was eleven now. Able to fend for herself. She dressed quickly, then peeked inside the chifforobe. Her new dress, with its tatted Peter Pan collar and its gored skirt, pale blue like the morning sky, swayed on its hanger. Her mother was a talented seamstress. She usually only deployed her talents for paying customers, but she'd sewn Vivian this dress for her sister's wedding. She'd sewn Elizabeth's dress too. Peach satin, cut on the bias. "Wear it while you can," Clara had sniffed during a fitting, casting a grim glance at Elizabeth's waist.

"Some women *want* babies," said Aunt Clelia. "The majority, seems like."

"Wanting and not having any choice in the matter are two different things," retorted Clara. "Some of us would give our eyeteeth to still be able to wear a bias cut. Babies put an end to that."

"I want lots of babies," said Elizabeth, peering over her shoulder at her reflection. She vamped to see how the satin clung. "For the record, I've got *plenty* of time to wear dresses like this."

"I should hope so," said Clelia and Clara at the same time.

Vivian hoped to wear a bias-cut satin dress herself someday. She'd never given a thought to whether she wanted babies. She didn't own a doll, found her friends' dolls not just boring but inconvenient. Why burden yourself with a toy you just carried around, a toy that didn't *do* anything? Give her a bicycle any day.

The custardy smell of scrambled eggs reached her. Time to head downstairs. In the parlor she drew up short. The room was free of its usual clutter. The cushions plump and recently fluffed. The floor free of grit. A lace doily graced the back of the wing chair. She heard a glug

glug glug from the kitchen. The sharp tang of pine oil now vied with the smell of fried bacon. It could mean only one thing: her father was expected.

Sure enough, before she set a foot in the kitchen, her mother waved her back with the mop. "Your plate's on the back porch. Go around the outside."

"Is Daddy coming home?"

"Of course. He'd never miss Elizabeth's wedding."

Vivian wasn't so sure. Phillip Shaw had missed many special occasions. Most of her birthdays, a fair number of Christmases. But her mother always knew when he was coming—somehow he got word to her. Vivian took in the line of pound cakes cooling on the counter, the peaches simmering on the stove, a chicken seasoned and trussed and ready for the oven. Her mother must have been up all night. Not just to prepare for Elizabeth's wedding, which would be held in the backyard at 3 p.m., but because Phillip Shaw was expected. What Clara Shaw never did for others, wouldn't even have done for wedding guests—beating the carpets, roasting a chicken, mopping the floors—she happily did for him.

Elizabeth was already on the back porch, crumbling bacon into her grits. "Daddy's coming," she said.

"I heard." Vivian tucked into her breakfast. "Wonder for how long." As long as he stayed, she'd get a breakfast like this every day. Her mother would be cheerful. She might even ask about Vivian's days and care about her answers. Might hover and chide and kiss her cheek and smooth her hair.

"Don't get your hopes up, Viv."

Phillip Shaw, wearing a slick-elbowed suit and a barely pressed shirt, arrived just ahead of the preacher.

"Sweet Vee, the sweet pea! How's my baby girl?" The last time he'd come, Vivian had thrown herself into his arms and he'd spun her around. Today, mindful of her new dress and the dignity of her eleven years, she held herself like a lady, and he kissed the top of her head. "All grown up, I see. Heading down the aisle herself before we know it, eh, Clara?"

Clara smiled, purely agreeable now that her husband had returned.

Elizabeth descended the stairs in her peach satin as the preacher stepped in with Aunt Clelia. They all gawped. "Oh, my, my," said Phillip at last. "Isn't she a beauty, Clara?" He took Clara's hand, and the hardness left her eyes. She looked almost as young and beautiful as Elizabeth.

Clelia undid the clasp of her pocketbook and drew out a string of pearls. She fastened them around Elizabeth's swanlike neck. Vivian sucked in her breath. The pearls glowed against the peach satin, against her sister's rosy skin. Elizabeth kissed Clelia. "They're beautiful. Thank you."

"Are those Mother's?" asked Clara, a grasping note in her voice.

"Not anymore. Now they are Elizabeth's."

Clelia fished in her handbag again and pulled out a gold necklace. "And this is for Vivian." It was the first piece of jewelry Vivian had ever received. A round locket the size of a nickel with a tiny starburst diamond chip set in its center, strung on a thin chain.

"Really for me?"

"Really for you, provided you remember your manners."

"Thank you, Aunt Clelia." Vivian latched the clasp behind her neck and traced a finger around the diamond chip. She had a new dress, a beautiful sister, and a gold locket. Her mother was, mostly, happy. Her father was home and might even stay for a while.

But when she raised her eyes from the locket, she saw her father's cheeks had flushed. His glance veered from Elizabeth to the door. Duty and desire battled openly across his face. Her mother scowled at Clelia as if to say, "Now look what you've done."

He would leave, sooner rather than later. And when he did, her mother would sink back into herself, retreat to her garden beds.

Elizabeth cleared her throat. The preacher stepped forward, holding his Bible before him like a shield, and said, "The groom's ready. Shall we begin?"

Vivian worked after school in her brothers' repair yard, fixing cars and bikes. Now that she was sixteen, she'd also begun working on being more of a proper girl. A girl that boys like Bobby Broussard would want to ask out.

Bobby Broussard had the use of his brother's car—a Hudson Terraplane. As he drove her home from the cinema, Vivian listened to the engine. It never pinged or rattled, just hummed evenly along. She wanted to try out the Electric Hand gearshift, to lift the hood and inspect the engine, even though it was only six cylinders. That sort of thing wouldn't do, so she restrained herself except to say, during a lull in Bobby's conversation, "It sure drives smooth, doesn't it?"

He agreed that it did, then said, "Let's park." She had an hour until curfew, and there was nothing else to do in Hahira, Georgia. Besides, Vivian liked the combination of fear and longing, resistance and surrender, that parking entailed. The Hudson had a large, comfortable back seat. They spent their hour there engaged in battle over the territory of her body, Bobby saying, "Please, baby, c'mon, please," and Vivian intercepting his hands, saying, "No, Bobby," with decreasing frequency as the minutes ticked past. The battlefront had expanded steadily over the weeks they'd been seeing each other, Vivian breathlessly and strategically conceding small bits of territory along the way.

When they finally pulled up to her house, fifteen minutes past curfew and a light blazing in the kitchen, Bobby rewarded her most recent concession by offering her his pin. Vivian dutifully displayed it for her mother in the bright kitchen after the Hudson had pulled away and the yelling had stopped.

Clara Shaw ran a finger along the edges of the small diamond-shaped pin. Vivian held her breath. Perhaps she had finally captured her mother's attention. Clara handed it back without meeting Vivian's eyes and said, "You better go talk to your sister tomorrow."

The next day, Vivian found her sister pinning little Henry's just-washed diapers to the line. "Mama sent me," she said.

"She called," said Elizabeth. "Did she send anything?"

Elizabeth lived only three blocks from them, but their mother rarely walked the distance, preferring to send Vivian instead. This time with an offering of cold roast chicken.

"She's too good to me," said Elizabeth. "Set it on the kitchen table, would you? I'm nearly done out here."

When Elizabeth entered the kitchen, she went straight to the percolator and poured two cups. Vivian, who was never offered coffee at home, sat up straight in her chair, cultivating a womanly posture as she sipped hers. Elizabeth smoothed her skirt beneath her rear as she sat down. She looked like an overexposed photograph of her former self. Her husband and baby and housework had leached the color and definition from her features. She'd been Queen Bee in Hahira's Honey Days parade her senior year of high school. Now she looked just like all the other housewives in town: tired.

"Mama says you're pinned and that I should speak frankly to you about things. Back when I was your age, she sent me to Aunt Clelia, who either wouldn't say what she knew or didn't know anything, so a lot of good that did me."

"You don't have to."

"Know it all already, do you?" Elizabeth raised her eyebrows. They needed plucking. "Then you won't mind hearing it anyway."

As it turned out, she didn't know it all, though she suspected much of it. "You have to be firm with them," said Elizabeth, as if Bobby were an entire army, not just one teenage boy. "They'll push and push and push, but they depend on us to draw the line and hold it."

Vivian had drawn plenty of lines, then erased them and drawn them elsewhere, then erased those too. Perhaps this showed on her face, because Elizabeth said, "Don't repeat this to anyone, hear? Just use your hands. Your mouth too—they like that a lot. It keeps them away from the other."

Then Elizabeth cut her a slice of pound cake, gave her sugar for the coffee she'd stopped drinking, and talked about the baby until Vivian's cheeks cooled.

It was Bobby Broussard who drove her out to the Valdosta airfield to see the barnstormers, but he wasn't the one who drove her home. Even though it was broad daylight, he acted surprised when she wouldn't climb into the back seat with him before they headed to the airfield. Vivian said he'd invited her to see a show, and a show was what she expected to see. Bobby had gotten lazy of late about treating her to milkshakes and burgers and the cinema. After she began following Elizabeth's advice, he rushed her into that back seat as quickly and as frequently as possible.

She'd begun sussing out other prospects in Hahira. But the pickings were slim, and she suspected Bobby had told most of them what she was willing to get up to in a back seat. A day at the Valdosta airfield suggested expanded possibilities.

She'd never seen barnstormers before, and her expectations for the entertainment were modest. But she knew there'd be a crowd of young men there—men who lacked notions about her. She hated being so mercenary about it, but that's how a girl had to think. She didn't want to follow in the footsteps of her mother or her sister, worn out and chained to some grown-up version of Bobby Broussard. She didn't want to spend the rest of her life in Hahira. Valdosta wasn't that far away, wasn't even that much of a step up, but it was a start.

Even though it featured three planes, it wasn't, she would later learn, much of an air show. There were no wing walkers, no one hanging from his teeth by a strap attached to the wheel axle, no one shinnying up a flagpole mounted to the top of the fuselage, no parachutists floating down in jellyfish-like formations. Just three planes, flying wingtip to wingtip, taking turns flying upside down, then playing what looked like leapfrog with one another. One plane dipping low, almost to the ground, while the others, though parallel to it, took turns leaping "over" it. Then the planes shot straight up in the air, stalled, plummeted down-down-down until she was sure they were done for, then shot skyward again. Vivian's heart was an engine, stalling and racing and shooting toward the heavens.

Bobby pulled at her arm—*C'mon, baby, please.* She swatted him off and threaded her way through the crowd, ignoring the interested glances of the men, until she reached the rope that kept the crowd back from the airfield. She strained against it, gasping as the three planes came in for a coordinated landing, one rolling straight on ahead, the other two peeling off in opposite directions. The straight-on-ahead plane made right for her. The crowd shrank back, but Vivian leaned forward, would have snapped the rope if she could have, she so longed to put her hand on the side of that airplane. It slowed and came to a full stop about fifty feet from her. Who would have thought wood and canvas could combine into something so magnificent?

Vivian had left her house that day feeling pretty magnificent herself. She had on her best summer dress. She'd curled her hair, rifled through her mother's vanity until she found the right shade of lipstick, and then ducked out the front door before her brothers could stop her.

The pilot climbed down from the plane, peeled off his goggles, made a perfunctory bow to the crowd, and then strode over to Vivian.

She allowed him to take her hand and kiss it. Still bent low over her hand, he raised his eyes to hers and said, "I'll bet you'd like a ride."

Not, *Would you like a ride?* Louis Korman, she would quickly learn, didn't ask questions. He made statements. He gave commands. After he'd walked Vivian around the plane (a Jenny, he said, bragging about its liquid-cooled V-8), after he'd told her he liked tall girls—the taller the better—after he'd leaned her up against the side of the hangar and kissed her, tapped her locket and said, "Pretty, like you," after he'd bought her dinner and scrounged up a car in which to drive her home, he said, "Come back tomorrow and we'll take that ride. I'm here for four days." Vivian, who had already been scheming about which of the cars in the repair yard she could borrow with the least resistance from her brothers, said she would.

The next day, they flew over Titusville and Quitman and even Waycross and the Okefenokee. Below them farms and towns stretched out to the horizon. A horizon that kept opening up, endlessly expanding ahead of her. The sky was cloudless. Vast. She leaned forward in her seat. Trained her eyes to the ever-shifting edge of the blue. A person could go on forever up here. A person could end up very far from Hahira, Georgia.

They dropped closer to the earth, hedgehopping over fields and ponds. "This looks like a good spot," Louis said. Vivian's shoulders jumped—she'd forgotten he sat behind her. In her mind, she was, without doing a thing, flying the plane herself. He brought the Jenny down in a clearing near a lake. From a compartment she hadn't noticed, he produced a blanket and a picnic.

"Where are we?" asked Vivian.

"Hell if I know, sweetheart."

"This has got to be somebody's land."

"Don't worry. As long as we don't scare any livestock or plow through the crops, the farmers generally take these little visits as a compliment." Louis snapped open the blanket, spread it on the ground, patted it. "C'mon, sweetheart. I won't bite." He waited until they'd eaten the sandwiches to kiss her. He was older than Bobby Broussard, but younger than her brothers, which seemed just the right age. He knew how to kiss a girl. How to put his arms around her in a way that felt natural and safe, like he knew what he was about. He smelled of tobacco and ham sandwiches and RC Cola, and before long his hands found their way beneath her skirt, and Vivian liked this better than when Bobby's hands went beneath her skirt. Even so, she blocked them with her own. Louis retreated. "Whatever you say, sweetheart." No *C'mon, baby, please* for him. He rolled away from her, flipped open a silver lighter, and lit up a cigarette. She stared up at the sky, thinking, while he smoked.

"How long did it take you to learn how to fly?" she asked, running her locket back and forth along its chain.

"Not as long as you'd think. You just have to pay attention and believe you can do it, that's all."

He flicked his cigarette aside, and Vivian, who, despite the golden glamour of the day, was still in a rather mercenary frame of mind, rolled atop him, kissed him hard, returned his hands to the place where they'd left off. "Well, well," he said, once she let him up for air. "Didn't take you long to change your mind."

"Maybe I still need convincing."

"You seem pretty convinced to me." She could hardly blame him for thinking so, seeing as she was unbuckling his belt.

"Maybe I'd like to learn how to fly an airplane."

"Maybe that can be arranged."

She levered herself back, hovered over him. "That can definitely be arranged."

"Definitely." Louis pulled her back down. His arms were strong and warm and certain. "Definitely that can be arranged."

It didn't take as long as she'd thought it would, losing her virginity. She just had to pay attention and believe she could do it, that was all.

But flying took longer to learn than Louis had let on. It would certainly, Vivian realized during her first training flight, take longer than his remaining two days in Valdosta. Especially since Louis made her spend so much time oiling the rocker arms and checking the antifreeze, the oil level, the cables, the fuel drains, and the air in the tires. All of this before he allowed her to climb into the front cockpit, which didn't even have any instruments. "We'll get to those," said Louis. But Vivian could tell they wouldn't get to them before he left.

Which was why, on the morning he was scheduled to depart, she arrived at the Valdosta airfield carrying an old cardboard suitcase she'd begged off Aunt Clelia. She knew there was a good chance Louis would send her back home. Knew from the way his face clouded over that he was strongly considering it. But in the end, he said, "I guess it won't hurt having a pretty girl sell tickets."

That was fine with her. Selling tickets was the least she was willing to do in exchange for learning to fly.

The pilot who lived nearby stayed behind. Which left three men and now Vivian. Louis and Chance Durham each owned a surplus Jenny from the Great War. They were in perfect agreement on the type of show they wanted to fly—no spinning by the teeth from canvas straps, no wing walking; they left all the aerobatics to the aircraft—and that allowed them to tolerate the mismatch in their personalities. Chance Durham had what Vivian's mother called the black dog. He rarely smiled—and never at her. His every expression and gesture made it clear he wasn't happy about her joining their crew. "She'll have to wear a better dress than that," he said, "if you expect ticket sales to cover the cost of hauling her around with us."

"It'll be fine," said Louis. "You'll see."

"Her dress seems nice enough." This was from Bob Quigley, the mechanic, who more than earned his keep by maintaining the Jennys and smoothing over the occasional disagreement between Louis and Durham. He gave the impression of being wiser than the pilots. Which might have been true, or might have just been the effect of his wire-rimmed spectacles.

"She's too tall," said Durham. Like Louis, he was on the shorter side. "She'll scare off the ticket buyers."

"They'll be able to find her in the crowd," said Quigley. "Besides, she's strong enough to help me with the planes." Quigley was the tiebreaker. Vivian stayed.

Durham did what he could to make her want to leave. She found her only pair of stockings, which she'd hung to dry in a shared hotel bathroom, laddered from thigh to toe. There was no affording another pair, so Vivian took a grease pencil and drew seams down the backs of her legs. Durham gave himself away by taking her by the shoulders, spinning her around, and smudging her calf with his finger. "Look at this," he said to Louis. "What kind of a show are we running here?"

"Vivvy, what happened to your stockings?" asked Louis.

She rubbed a spit-coated finger over the smears, furious that she'd need to redraw her seams.

"Vivian?"

"Someone wrecked them. Someone who doesn't want me around."

Durham snorted, and Louis said, "Now, Vivvy, you were probably just careless with them. You do leave your things lying around."

They toured all over the South. When she wasn't selling tickets or avoiding Durham or helping Quigley, who was thrilled to have a spare hand, she was learning to smoke and learning to fly and learning what Louis liked in bed. Variety, it turned out, was what Louis liked. There were other girls at other airfields. Glamorous in their scarves and sundresses. Eager to be leaned up against hangar walls and kissed. As long as she got her regular flying lessons, Vivian pretended not to notice.

Sometimes they joined forces with other barnstorming troupes. Outside Knoxville, they teamed up with a group that included a female pilot. Ethel Blankenship was petite and curvaceous and unafraid to stand on the fuselage of her plane while her copilot took the controls. "My God, I could never do that," Vivian told her over dinner.

"Gutless," scoffed Durham.

"Can you do it?" Ethel challenged him.

"Rather have you walking on planes than flying them," said Durham.

"I'll take that as a no." Ethel turned to Vivian. "Louis says you're learning to fly."

Vivian admitted she was. What she didn't admit was how challenging it had become to get Louis to take her up.

He often had "business to take care of." The business usually being a girl. He was taking care of business elsewhere that very evening, which meant Vivian, after washing up in the shared hotel bathroom, made her way back to an otherwise empty room.

"You look lonesome, Shaw." Durham loomed up out of nowhere in the dim corridor. "You lonesome? Need some company?"

Before she could answer that she certainly didn't want his, he pushed her, sent her stumbling down the hallway. Vivian kept herself upright, but barely, and Durham advanced, ready to push her again.

A door swung open. Ethel Blankenship emerged from her room. Durham stepped back, dropped his arms to his sides. "Everything all right out here?" asked Ethel.

Vivian's pulse pounded. She felt ashamed for being caught in the hallway with Durham. What if Ethel thought she'd encouraged him? "Yes," she said, walking purposefully to her own door. "Everything's just fine."

"Well, good night, then," said Ethel, a dismissal pointedly directed at Durham. Vivian got herself on the other side of her door and locked it quickly. Put her ear against it and listened to Durham's boots thud back down the hallway.

As soon as she had the hours to fly solo, she took enough from the cashbox to cover her bus fare back to Hahira. Louis had slept elsewhere again, and it was nearly dawn. She grease penciled on her seams, put on her best dress, and, with a twinge of guilt, pocketed his silver lighter, telling herself he shouldn't have left it behind. He shouldn't have left *her* behind. She was carrying Aunt Clelia's cardboard suitcase through the hotel lobby when someone said, "Leaving us?"

Quigley sat next to the cold fireplace, puffing a Lucky and blowing smoke rings. "Didn't mean to frighten you," he said.

"I'm not scared."

"Don't mean to offend either. I'm sorry to see you go."

"It was fun. But I think it's time."

"Yeah, I've been thinking about cutting out too," he said. "Heading back north. I've spent enough time down south." Vivian, who was headed farther south, only bade him goodbye.

Back home, her brothers refused to speak to her. Her mother barred the door. Elizabeth clutched her newest baby to her chest and said, "You can't stay here. Henry would have a fit. Impressionable children, and all." None of this surprised Vivian. It was what a girl who ran off with a man and returned without a wedding ring had to expect. She'd been fooling herself, hoping for better. Aunt Clelia let her in. "Against my better judgment," she said. "And only because I believe in redemption."

Planes filled the sky over Hahira now. The USAAF had, almost overnight, built an air force training base on the old Davis Plantation. They named it Moody after a downed pilot, laid down airstrips, put up barracks, and brought in air cadets for training.

From one of these cadets, Vivian heard a rumor that female pilots would be recruited for war service. The cadet had laughed this off—the idea was ridiculous as far as he was concerned. But Vivian had latched on to it as salvation. If it was true, it offered a change of horizon, a chance to go somewhere—anywhere—else. If it was true, she needed all the flying time she could get. Which meant she needed a way to get to the Valdosta airfield. Which meant that she needed Bobby Broussard's car.

After Pearl Harbor, Bobby Broussard and his older brother had bused off to basic training, leaving the Hudson sitting idle. Mrs. Broussard never drove it. Bobby had told Vivian, more than once, that his mother didn't approve of women driving cars. No one needed to tell her that Mrs. Broussard didn't approve of *her*. No doubt all the upstanding, churchgoing sons of Hahira had been warned away from her by their mothers. She'd never been introduced to Mrs. Broussard, but she hoped that, with Bobby safely out of reach, the woman would talk to her.

Vivian rounded the corner and spied Mrs. Broussard pruning roses in the front bed. She gave no sign that she'd noticed Vivian, yet quite suddenly she dashed into the house. The crocheted panel over the door window still swayed as Vivian knocked.

No steps approached. No one called out for her to wait a moment. The crocheted panel stilled. Vivian peered through its stitches just in time to see Mrs. Broussard duck down behind a wing chair.

She rapped louder.

"Mrs. Broussard, please. I really need to talk to you."

She knocked again. No sound came from the parlor. She turned to go. A flutter in the window across the street caught her eye. White sheer curtains being twitched aside. Grace Thorpe was watching. Grace had a party line and was always looking for news to share over it. Vivian turned back to the Broussard door. She knocked again.

"It's not about Bobby, if that's what you're worried about." Vivian raised her voice, making sure Grace could hear. "Nothing to do with Bobby at all!" She turned and waved toward Grace's window. "Hello, Mrs. Thorpe! Do you know if Mrs. Broussard is home?"

Mrs. Broussard rose up from behind the wing chair, deploying her handkerchief before her like a white flag, as if she'd just been hunting for it, not hiding. She trotted to the door and opened it just a crack, hissed for Vivian to hush.

A crack was all Vivian needed. She held up the ration tickets. Aunt Clelia was always going on about the temptations of sugar, as if it had been cast out of heaven with Lucifer himself and now its sole purpose was to lure innocent people into his clutches. Mrs. Broussard's lush figure suggested she viewed sugar more fondly than Aunt Clelia did. It suggested she might be willing to make a trade.

"A month of sugar," Vivian said. "In exchange for Bobby's gas coupons and the use of the Hudson."

"You said this had nothing to do with Bobby."

"This is between you and me," said Vivian. "But I suppose I could make it about Bobby." She cut a glance at Grace Thorpe's window. "Do you think he'd appreciate a letter? I'm not much for writing generally, but I could make an exception. For Bobby."

Mrs. Broussard squeezed the door closed. Vivian stuck her foot in the diminishing gap. "Butter," she said. "I heard the market's getting a delivery tomorrow. I'll stand in line for you." The door opened, and Mrs. Broussard snatched the ration coupons from Vivian's hand.

"Bring the butter by tomorrow and I'll give you the keys."

Vivian kept to the shady side of the street as she walked back to Aunt Clelia's. She caressed the *LK* on Louis's lighter as she strolled, wishing she could afford cigarettes. She'd come close to selling the lighter twice—so that she could offer something to Aunt Clelia for her keep. But she missed Louis. Keeping the lighter felt like keeping a little piece of him.

She took the long way home. This late in the day, Clelia and Rosemary were usually bickering about supper. What to cook and how much of it. Vivian felt keenly that she was another mouth for her aunt to feed and took small portions. She kept the daybed on the back porch made up, her things stowed and out of the way. She tried to make herself as inconspicuous as possible. Rosemary hadn't complained about her presence, but she also hadn't blessed Vivian's heart lately.

Aunt Clelia, despite her belief in redemption, would find the loss of her butter ration hard to forgive. It was Vivian's job to stand in line—sometimes for hours—for scarce goods at the market. If she was lucky, she'd get a quarter pound of butter tomorrow, and Aunt Clelia would be furious to learn Vivian had given it away. But that couldn't be helped.

She'd just claim that the market had run out before she reached the front of the line. She didn't like lying to her aunt, but it was necessary to get the use of a car. Now that her brother Phil had shipped out, leaving Walter and his flat feet behind, Vivian had finagled a job at the repair yard. Walter wouldn't pay her much, but it would be enough for some flying time.

Happy with her plan, she approached Aunt Clelia's house. The lights had not yet been lit. She assumed that meant Clelia had, today anyway, won the ongoing battle she and Rosemary fought over when to turn on the parlor lights. Rosemary would have lit up the house like the sun. Clelia was always following her around, switching things off. She claimed to prefer kerosene lamps to electric. Rosemary called her an old-fashioned stick-in-the-mud. Clelia maintained that just because something was "modern" didn't make it better.

It was odd, thought Vivian, that not even a kerosene lamp glowed through the parlor window. The ladies liked to sew before suppertime. She skipped the squeaky tread on the porch steps and paused in front of the screen door, listening, a childhood habit she'd never broken. She heard a sigh.

She horseshoed her hands against the screen and peered into the house. She saw a shape on the sofa. Someone, too large to be either Clelia or Rosemary, was just inside. Did they have company? And why had they left this visitor sitting in the dark? Vivian's skin prickled.

The shape on the settee rocked and emitted a low moan, as if in pain. Maybe Clelia and Rosemary had gone to get the doctor. But wouldn't one of them have stayed behind to help tend this poor soul?

Another moan, louder this time. This person needed help. She yanked open the screen door and rushed into the parlor. The shape split, its halves springing apart, taking the forms of her aunt and Rosemary. Vivian stopped midstride.

"Aunt Clelia?"

"Rosemary had . . . a little speck of . . . ummm—" Her aunt's voice quavered to silence. She reached for her sewing basket and rummaged in it, pretending to hunt for something.

"Yes!" said Rosemary. "In my eye. An eyelash, most likely. Thank you, Clelia, for helping me get it out. I feel much better now." She dabbed at her eye with her handkerchief.

"Then why on earth didn't you light a lamp?" asked Vivian. She turned and busied herself with the glass chimney of the nearest kerosene lamp, spun the flint on her lighter, and set the flame to the wick. She eased the chimney back into the metal clips slowly, giving them plenty of time to gather themselves. By the time she turned around, they had scooted to opposite ends of the settee. Rosemary still fussed with her handkerchief. Clelia clutched her embroidery hoop in one hand, but no needle in the other. She wore her sternest expression. "You're supposed to be eating at Elizabeth's. We weren't expecting you."

Elizabeth had called earlier to report that "Henry said it would be all right" if Vivian joined them for dinner. This hadn't seemed like much of an invitation, and Vivian had decided she'd rather dine on a small portion of food at Clelia's than a full serving of righteous judgment from her sister's husband.

"Funny how things turn out different than we'd expect," said Vivian, smiling brightly at the pair on the sofa. "I'll get supper started." She headed for the kitchen. The butter wouldn't be a problem after all.

Thanks to her older brothers, Vivian felt at ease around men and machines. She understood the unwritten rules. Out at the airfield she wore no makeup, kept her hair pulled up in a tight knot, dressed in her brothers' baggy pants and jackets and an old pair of work boots. She tried to blend in, to be one of the boys.

She sold the gold locket to buy fuel. She traded her repair and maintenance skills for flight time. If the field manager decided the floor needed sweeping and who better than Vivian to do it, she swept the floor without complaining that she was the one who'd swept it last. And would no doubt be the one who swept it next. She did whatever it took to get time in a plane.

The telegram she'd been waiting for arrived that autumn.

IF INTERESTED IN ENTERING WOMENS AIRFORCE
SERVICE PILOTS TRAINING CONTACT . . .

Vivian begged Elizabeth for the bus fare to Washington, DC.

"Mama would have my hide. You know she doesn't approve of you flying."

"Mama will never approve of anything I do. Not after Louis."

Elizabeth shushed her and tipped her head toward Henry Jr., as if the very mention of Louis might corrupt her little boy.

"There're lots of pilots around here now," said Vivian, "just over at Moody. Four hundred of them, I heard the other day. I was there for my physical. The flight surgeon said they're bringing more every week." These cadets were not warmly welcomed in Hahira, given the stir they caused among the town's young ladies.

Elizabeth set her mouth in a hard line.

"I find pilots so dashing, don't you? There's something about a man in an airplane that's just . . . irresistible."

Elizabeth reached for her pocketbook.

Entering Jacqueline Cochran's office, Vivian tried not to flinch as Cochran, seated behind an immaculate walnut desk, looked her up and down. She felt the age and shabbiness of her best skirt and blouse and hurried to sit so she could hide her cracked leather pumps beneath Cochran's desk.

"How did you learn to fly, Miss Shaw?"

"A barnstormer taught me."

"Ah. Was he local or just passing through?"

"Passing through. But in town long enough to get me started."

"I've met my share of barnstormers, Miss Shaw. In fact, a number of the girls in this program got their start on the circuit. In my experience, and I'm sure these other girls would agree, barnstormers are a parsimonious lot. They don't generally give out lessons for free. But I suppose you had your looks going for you."

"I paid for my lessons," said Vivian.

Cochran eyed the frayed cuffs of Vivian's blouse. She launched into a speech about virtuous behavior being the foundation of the Women's Airforce Service Pilots program and how its representatives must remain above reproach.

Vivian, during Cochran's infrequent pauses, supplied a series of dutiful "Yes, ma'ams."

"Your accent," said Cochran, slipping for an educational moment into her own. "You from north Florida?"

Vivian, whose cheeks had remained cool during the speech about virtue, felt the heat rise in them now. "Near there. Hahira, Georgia."

Cochran said nothing, but her quick blink told Vivian she recognized the town. "Well," Cochran said at last, "war has a way of mixing people up, allowing them to transcend their origins." Her north Florida accent had vanished so completely that Vivian wondered if she'd imagined it. Cochran extended her hand across the desk. "Take good advantage of this opportunity, Miss Shaw. Who knows how far you'll go?"

CHAPTER 5

As George took a seat in the flight surgeon's waiting room, a straw-haired boy with more freckles than she'd ever seen on one face jeered, "The ladies' is down the hall, darlin'."

"You'd know," a familiar voice replied. Frank Bridlemile crossed the room and sat down beside her. "Hey, George."

"Hey, Frank."

"Helen said I might see you here. It's been what? Three days now?"

"Yep." Three days watching the nurse lead one man after another back to the exam room while she sat uncalled. When she complained, the nurse had nodded sympathetically. "Sorry, hon. The major insists we prioritize the fighting men. He says the war depends upon it."

George had considered driving down to Texas or up to Kansas, but who knew if the flight surgeons there would feel any differently. She'd decided to wait him out, and now here was Frank, waiting with her.

"Well, you're still two steps ahead of me," he said. "You already know how to fly."

"If I can do it, you can."

"Sure hope you're right. Rather be up in the air than an infantry grunt."

"Bridlemile," called the nurse.

Frank stood. "Hey, you want to get a Coke afterward?"

Helen wouldn't like that, but then again, everyone knew that Frank and Helen were a serious item, and having a soda with Frank shouldn't make their relationship any less serious. "Sure. Sounds fun," she said.

"Okay, I'll meet you outside after."

She watched the windowpaned sun patch creep across the floor. She watched Frank stalk back through the waiting room. He didn't look her way, but the set of his jaw told her he hadn't passed. She watched men come and go through the door behind the nurse's desk until only she remained. She recalled Florence, striding across the airfield in her jodhpurs and goggles, dazzling Adele. Florence wouldn't sit politely in a chair for days on end, hoping someone would reward her good behavior by calling her name.

George stood and smoothed her skirt and hair, checked the seams of her stockings—her last pair, donned now only for special occasions—and took ten deliberate steps to the door behind the nurse's desk. The nurse pretended absorption in her paperwork. George rapped lightly on the door, then harder, and when there was still no response, she cracked it open and peeked through. A trail of cigarette smoke drifted down the hallway. She followed it and found the flight surgeon, Major Halloran, at his desk, annotating a file.

"Excuse me," said George.

"Miss Ector." He didn't look up. "Is there something I can do for you?"

"Yes. I need my Form 64 physical."

"That exam is for pilots. If you need medical attention, you should see Dr. Lattimer."

George extended the telegram to him, hating the way her hand shook. He took a long time reading it. Then he stubbed out his cigarette and said, "Well, this is nonsense as far as I'm concerned, but since you insist. The exam room is next door. Strip down. You'll find a gown in the cabinet."

She changed into the thin gown, folded her clothing into a neat pile, and perched on the metal exam table. She hopped back down, tucked her underwear and stockings beneath her skirt and blouse, and scooted back up onto the table. The cold steel raised goose bumps on her dangling legs. The men had to undress, too, she told herself. Not long ago, Frank had been here, wearing only a scratchy gown. A flip in her belly as she imagined him sitting in this exact spot.

The door swung open. Halloran strode in, looking down at a clipboard rather than at her. The nurse followed. "Step down," he said. He took her height and weight, had her read the eye chart.

"Sit back on the table." He clamped a hand beneath her jaw and shone a light into each eye. Impossible not to blink. He peered into her ears, then her mouth, pressing against her teeth as if she were a horse he was thinking of buying. Like Dr. Lattimer, he smelled of cigarettes, but with something gamy underneath. His face was inches from hers. She tried not to breathe, made herself sit perfectly still, refused to flinch from him.

He tapped her knees and flexed her ankles, listened to her heart and lungs through the itchy gown, then told her to lie down. He drew a small sheet over her lower half and pushed up the gown. She stiffened. He prodded at her, the way she'd seen her mother poke at a chicken carcass at the market. Then he pressed harder, digging his fingers into her belly, first one spot, then another. She fought to keep her breathing steady.

His fingers marched lower, pausing at the border of her pubic hair. She clenched her teeth and stared at the nurse, whose calm eyes said that this was okay.

"Bend your knees," said Halloran.

She hesitated.

"I can't complete this exam without confirming that you're actually a girl."

The nurse moved to his shoulder. "I can look, Doctor." Halloran started to speak but then closed his mouth and stepped back. The nurse took a quick glance beneath the sheet, patting George's foot as she did. "All good," she said.

"Any history of VD?" asked Halloran.

George's jaw was so tight, she could hardly ask what he meant. "Venereal disease."

"I don't know what that is," she whispered.

He gave a skeptical snort and told her to get dressed. He held the door for the nurse and followed her out of the room.

"What about my paperwork?" asked George.

"I'll take care of it."

Passing his office on her way out, she saw him close a file and lock it in his cabinet. It looked just the same as all the other folders, and George wasn't sure how she knew it was hers, but she did. "Dr. Halloran!"

"Major Halloran," he said. "And I'll thank you to address me in a tone befitting an officer."

"Major Halloran, I need that form to get to Washington or I won't be able to fly. Sir."

"You're Adele Ector's daughter, aren't you?"

"Yes."

He tapped a cigarette from its pack and lit it. "I knew her back when she was still Adele Clemson. You probably can't knit. Much less can vegetables. Not much of an asset on the home front, are you? Is that why you want to go off and fly airplanes?"

She thought of Mel, of his assumption that she'd stop flying if they got engaged. Of how she'd longed for him to touch her bare skin, the same skin Halloran had just touched with his nicotine-stained fingers. She would never let these men keep her from flying.

"I want to fly airplanes because I'm good at it." Her voice rose in pitch. "Women can fly planes from factories to the air bases. And that frees up more men to fight."

He took a drag, gestured with the cigarette at her shaking hands. "Women are too emotional to be trusted with airplanes."

She clenched her fists, lowered her tone, spoke as unemotionally as she could. "General Arnold doesn't think so. Which is why he set up this program."

"Got his head turned by that femme fatale." He picked a speck of tobacco from his teeth. "Jacqueline Cochran."

She had endured his icy fingers, his rancid smell, his contempt. There was no way she was leaving without her form. "Give me my paperwork."

"I didn't quite catch that, Miss Ector."

"Major Halloran, would you please give me my paperwork? Sir." Halloran had known her name. He knew she was Charles Ector's daughter. She'd seen the way people stood straighter when her father's name was mentioned, the way men listened when he spoke. She didn't want to have to go running to him, but if she had to, she would.

Perhaps Halloran had reached the same conclusion, because he unlocked the cabinet, pulled out her file, and dropped it on his desk. "Obviously this is the only way to get you out of my office."

She snatched up the folder and fled before he could change his mind. "Good for you, dear," whispered the nurse as George rushed past her. Then she was outside, and it was done. She scanned the form to make sure it was complete, that it was signed, that she had passed. It was and she had. She hugged the file to her chest.

She found Frank leaning up against the side of the building, digging the toe of his boot into the dust. Seeing her, he straightened and grinned. "Well, at least someone passed today. Good for you, George!"

"Oh, Frank. What was—well, I shouldn't ask."

"No, it's okay. Turns out I'm colorblind. No flying for me."

"I'm sorry."

"Yeah, well, someone's gotta march. Anyway, I promised you a Coke."

"Oh, you don't have to do that."

"I know I don't have to—I want to. C'mon, say yes. It'll cheer me up."

She opened her mouth to say, "Let's get Helen too," but what came out was, "Sure, let's go."

Helen's mother, determined to avoid a war wedding, insisted that if Helen wanted to see Frank, she'd do so in her own parlor, where Mrs. Cramer could keep an eye on things. Every night at 10 p.m., Mrs. Cramer shooed Frank out. And every night at 10 p.m., George applied fresh lipstick and dabbed Shalimar on her wrists, trying not to think about Helen. Moments later she slipped out the front door and into his car. Frank drove them out into the countryside, to this lake or that creek. They lay on the warm hood of the car, listening to the engine tick, and talked for hours.

Her own mother caught her at the front door one night and clutched her arm. "I don't know what this is all about, George, but it can't be anything good."

"We're just friends," said George. "He just needs someone to talk to. He can't burden Helen with all his worries."

"I don't see why not. And you make sure that he doesn't burden you with any *worries*, either, hear?"

George yanked free of her mother's grasp. "Don't be crude, Mother. We're just talking."

"Maybe you should spend more time talking to Helen and less time talking to her boyfriend."

But George was already in Frank's car, shutting the door on her mother's voice, wishing she could shut the door on the guilt that dogged her.

The night Frank finally leaned over and kissed her, George kissed him back. This went on for longer than she meant to allow before she gathered herself enough to say, simply, "Helen."

"Georgeanne"—he traced a finger along her collarbone—"let's not do that."

"Do what?"

"Bring Helen into it."

And even though George knew there was no way to keep Helen out of it, that Helen was already very much in it, she kissed him again.

On the nights that followed, neither of them spoke much at all.

Peeling off her girdle took so long, they didn't bother with taking off much else. The pain took her by surprise, shook her from her want. But Frank went slow. The pain subsided. Her want reared up stronger. The skirt bunched around her waist was nothing. The armrest jammed against her head was nothing. The tingling in her arm, pinned between him and the seat back, was nothing. There was only the weight of him, the rush of his breath on her neck, the urgent need to press closer, closer, closer. When they finished, all she wanted was to start again.

Had he done this with Helen, she wondered as he wiped her belly with his shirt. It seemed unlikely, with Mrs. Cramer standing watch. George felt a flash of triumph, quickly dampened by guilt. But Frank was right. They had so little time left. Why bring Helen into it at all?

Frank bused out, and a week later, George kissed her parents goodbye at the train station, doing her best to ignore her mother's teary eyes and her father's labored breathing. The guilt she felt at leaving her parents behind was outweighed by her relief to be leaving Enid. Not just for the opportunity to fly, but because Helen's tragic heroine-in-mourning act had become unbearable. "He hasn't even reached the action yet," George said to Helen.

"Georgeanne Ector, I can't believe you. You sound as if you wish he had!" Helen dabbed at her eyes with a handkerchief. George rubbed Helen's back and murmured some pap about how Frank needed her to stay strong, and tried not to picture Frank holding Helen the way he'd held her.

In Washington, DC, in the waiting room outside Jacqueline Cochran's office, George found more women crying—women walking out, rattled speechless. Not all of them—just the softer-looking ones.

The interview began before George even settled herself into the plain wooden chair facing Jacqueline Cochran's polished desk. "Miss Ector. I have not received your Form 64 results."

George produced the brown folder. "I brought them myself."

"That's quite unusual," said Cochran, setting the file to one side and staring intently at George. As she hadn't asked a question, George offered no answer, just sat receiving the full bore of Cochran's gaze. "The standard procedure is that the flight surgeon sends it in. That way we can be certain it hasn't been tampered with."

"I assure you, I haven't tampered with it, ma'am. I'll take another physical if necessary," said George.

"I'm interested to know, Miss Ector, why you deviated from the standard procedure."

"He was going to lock it up in a cabinet," said George. "He wasn't going to send it at all."

"And why was that?"

There was no way that George was going to say Halloran didn't think she was qualified. There was no way she was going to put that idea into Cochran's head.

"I couldn't say, ma'am."

"You couldn't say?"

"No, ma'am."

"Did Major"—Cochran flipped open the brown folder—"Halloran perhaps not think women fit for this sort of duty?"

Cochran stared at George, smiling slightly. George recognized the smile as an invitation to complain about Halloran. She smiled back. Cochran was perfectly coiffed. Perfectly made up. The files on her desk were perfectly stacked and aligned. The seams of her blouse were perfectly pressed. Instinct told George that this was no accident, that Cochran did not make, nor did she accept, excuses for anything less than perfection, that Cochran was allergic to complaints of any sort, no matter how valid. Jacqueline Cochran hadn't gotten where she was by complaining about men trying to stop her.

"I couldn't say, ma'am."

Cochran flicked the folder closed and extended her perfectly manicured hand across the desk to George. "Welcome to the WASP training program, Miss Ector. You'll report to Sweetwater in January."

1943–1945

CHAPTER 6

Standing in her third line of the morning, Vivian felt like a hayseed. Most of the other pilots arrived in Sweetwater wearing the latest utility suits. Their impressive shoulder pads and belted waists lent them a confidence she envied. Vivian had hemmed up her skirt to fashionable knee length and carefully pressed her outfit, but nothing could hide the fact that her blouse was nearly sheer from repeated washings.

As the line snaked forward, she daydreamed about the new clothes she'd buy with her first paycheck. A utility suit of her own. Maybe some trousers and a twinset. But first she'd have to pay back Elizabeth, who'd lent her the bus fare to this stark, flat piece of Texas.

Finally, she reached the front of the line and stated her size. The airman made a note of it, handed her a paper chit, and told her she'd trade it in for two zoot suits later that afternoon. She could hardly wait. Once they were all dressed in their uniforms, she'd look the same as everyone else.

The pilots filed into an auditorium for Jacqueline Cochran's welcome address. Tomorrow they'd begin training. No more Piper Cubs. They would get to fly real planes here. They would get to serve their country while doing it. And they would be watched.

Cochran made that point from the stage after she welcomed them to Avenger Field. "You will be watched. You will be judged. Fair or not, the judgment will be harsher and quicker than if you were men. If that troubles you, go home and roll bandages, knit socks, plant a victory garden. Get yourself a factory job building armaments. There are plenty of honorable ways to serve your country."

But Vivian believed, and she could tell Cochran did, too, that some ways were more honorable than others.

"Not all of you will qualify. Close to thirty-three percent of our female trainees wash out. The same rate applies for the men, by the way, so if you happen to be one of the unlucky ones, don't let anyone tell you it's because you're a woman. It won't even mean you're not a good pilot—just that you're not quite good enough for our purposes."

The pilot next to her squished her plush shoulder pad against Vivian's arm and whispered, "Enough chatter. When can we fly?" She smelled like Evening in Paris, the perfume Elizabeth wore. "I'm Marian Fontana. I met your sister earlier."

Confused by the familiar scent, Vivian turned and scanned the auditorium, then shook her head. "Oh, my sister's not—"

Jacqueline Cochran paused and trained her disapproving gaze in their direction, like a teacher hushing schoolgirls. Vivian shifted away from Marian Fontana, hoping she'd take the hint and stop whispering.

"People will be waiting for you to fail," continued Cochran. "And if you don't fail, they'll be waiting for you to demonstrate a lack of femininity. Which is why you will take great care with your appearance. You will keep your clothing clean and pressed. You will keep your hair neatly combed. You will keep your faces well made up. You will learn to drill with precision. You will attend ground school for the same number of hours as your male counterparts and master the same concepts. You will receive the same in-flight training. And you will never—no matter what—make any public complaint that might draw critical eyes to this program, that might allow anyone to suggest that women can't handle the training, that women can't fly for their country."

After they applauded Cochran's speech, Vivian introduced herself to Fontana. As they joined another line, she explained that her sister was nowhere near Sweetwater and never would be.

"There she is," Fontana said, pointing out a tall woman well ahead of them in line. "You're telling me you two aren't related?" The woman bent to accept a form and then rose to her full height again. Perhaps she felt herself being watched, because she turned and looked straight at Vivian. They were both a head taller than the pilots between them, which gave them a clear view. They stared at one another for a moment, and then the woman smiled a big red-lipsticked grin. Vivian smiled back, feeling like she was looking at herself in a mirror. She gave a mock salute. The woman laughed and saluted back. Then the line swept her around a corner and out of sight.

Vivian didn't see her again until the chow line, where, once again, she was up ahead, out of reach.

Some of the girls near Vivian had already picked up their zoot suits. "They're men's sizes," said Joyce Elliot. She shook hers out and kicked at the legs, "walking" the oversize suit back and forth. Fontana howled. They'd need to roll the legs and arms and cinch the waist high or they'd trip all over themselves. "So much for keeping a neat appearance," said Elliot.

"I packed a sewing kit," said Susan Dubarry, a serious, dimpled girl from Ohio. "Maybe we can hem the legs." After some prodding, Dubarry confessed that she'd also packed a tool kit and a book of engine schematics, just in case they might come in handy.

"Wow," said Elliot. "Were you a Girl Scout or something?"

Dubarry's eyes widened. "Weren't you?"

Elliot smirked, but Fontana said, "I was. How about you, Vivvy?"

The Shaws couldn't have afforded the dues, but Vivian was spared from answering when a Wellesley girl said, "Fontana. Sounds Italian. Are you from New York?" Fontana was by far the most stylishly dressed pilot there. The Wellesley girls had been sniffing around her all morning, trying to figure her out.

"Philadelphia," said Fontana. "We're Catholic, but otherwise pretty Main Line." The Wellesley girls nodded as if this sentence made perfect sense. Vivian caught Dubarry's eye and was relieved to see her shrug.

She and Fontana sat down at a table with a girl from Radcliffe, who asked if they were interested in sailing as well, "or only ships that fly." Fontana rolled her eyes. Before Vivian could answer, the Radcliffe girl looked her over and said, "Never mind, let's just talk planes."

Vivian talked planes with the Radcliffe girl. She talked planes with a ranch girl from Kansas and another from outside Sacramento. The pilots fit one of two types. First, there were the girls who'd grown up on farms, where the family or someone nearby could afford a crop duster. They'd learned to fly the duster, then moved on to Piper Cubs. The second type kept horses and wore pearls. They'd learned to fly Daddy's plane, usually a Taylor or a Fairchild.

She'd expected the two types would keep a wary distance from one another, the way the farm girls and town girls had at her high school. But they all seemed absolutely delighted to talk to any other girl who loved flying—regardless of where she came from. As the day wore on, Vivian relaxed about her wardrobe.

At last, she collected her zoot suits and was directed to the barracks. The women clumped together outside, shifting from one sore foot to another, waiting for their bunk assignments. Vivian searched the crowd for her look-alike. The pilots behind her jostled her back. "Hey, watch it," muttered Fontana. Then the tall woman appeared beside Vivian, asking, "Mind if I stand here?"

"Be my guest." Now well practiced in the preliminaries, she offered, "I'm Vivian Shaw. Hahira, Georgia. No college. No crop-dusting."

"Georgeanne Ector. Enid, Oklahoma. No crop-dusting. Tried college. Didn't care for it. You can call me George." She smiled, her lipstick as vivid as ever. She wore a twinset and tiny diamonds in her earlobes, and she tugged at the neck of her sweater as if it itched. She caught Vivian noticing. "My mother told me to wear this. I hate it. Wish I'd worn a blouse like you. I can't wait to change into my zoot suit."

The next obvious question, the question everyone asked that day, was *How did you learn to fly?* But neither Vivian nor George asked it. Neither of them said anything more for the moment. The women around them practically vibrated with exhaustion. But George exuded a sense of peace, and Vivian found herself breathing easier beside her.

More women pressed forward, pushing Vivian against George. "Sorry," she said, pulling back. She'd been about to say that maybe they'd be assigned to the same bay. But then she recalled her goodbye with Elizabeth—how Elizabeth had tsk-ed that she hoped Vivian wouldn't "come back *like that*." This, no doubt, was due to Vivian opening her big mouth and hinting to Elizabeth that something about Aunt Clelia and Rosemary's friendship seemed a tad . . . unusual.

She didn't want George to think she was *like that*. She didn't want to frighten her away. It was a rare thing finding someone you knew you were meant to find, someone you knew right off that you'd be friends with. Why did people only talk about lightning bolts in the romantic sense? She stood next to George and savored the aftereffects of the strike.

Vivian and George whispered to one another in the chow line, between flight school classes, while waiting their turns for the Link Trainer. They murmured in their cots at night until Elliot and Fontana pleaded with them to just hush already. But they had too much to explain to each other. Their families. Their hometowns. How they'd learned to fly. When George told Vivian about the female barnstormer and the way her heart had opened up during her first flight, Vivian understood. When she told Vivian about the racy atmosphere of the hangars outside Enid, Vivian, thinking of the airfields she'd visited with Louis, wasn't surprised at all.

It was pitch dark out—cloud covered and starless—when Vivian told George about Louis. She was soaking wet and freezing, clutching a Stearman mooring rope as fierce winds tried to rip the plane off the ground and send it tumbling across the field. The siren had blared, and the women had zipped into their zoot suits and stumbled out into the night. Vivian had wrapped a scarf over her mouth and nose to keep out the grit and pulled on her gloves, having learned from the first couple of storms that her hands would be raw and bleeding from the ropes by the time the storm passed over.

She told George about the picnic and how she'd cajoled flying lessons from Louis and the suitcase from Aunt Clelia. How she ran off with Louis and took money from the cashbox to get back home. "Because what you said about your heart opening up? I know that feeling. I had to have it too. And Louis was the only way I was going to get it."

George didn't respond. Vivian wondered if she'd spoken loudly enough. Perhaps with the wind and the scarf over her mouth, George hadn't heard her. That was probably for the best. It was a story she should never tell anyone, even George. George not hearing her was far preferable to George having been shocked into silence. Far preferable to George requesting a new bunkmate and avoiding her in the chow line.

Then George's voice cut through the wind, saying something about a girl named Helen and a boy named Frank. The howling gale made it difficult for Vivian to follow, but in the end, she understood. When the winds died down at last, they shook out their aching arms, peeled off their gloves, and blew on their palms. They leaned toward one another for warmth as they made their way back to the barracks. George put an arm around Vivian's shoulders, and that feeling of peace coursed through Vivian again. She had offered up her worst secret and kept her friend.

CHAPTER 7

George collected two letters at mail call—one from her mother and one from Helen. She and Frank had agreed not to write, and she chided herself weekly for wishing he would anyway. During their last week together in Enid, her stomach had been a wreck, roiled by fears of getting pregnant and of Helen finding out about them. She and Frank had shifted back to just talking. Mostly.

She tossed Helen's letter in her footlocker, where it joined a clutch of unopened envelopes. There was a limit, apparently, to how good a friend she could be. She could give up Frank, but she couldn't bring herself to read and reply to Helen's letters.

She slit open the envelope from her mother. Adele wrote that she was glad George was making friends—George had told her about Vivian—and warned her not to let friendship distract her from the reason she was in Texas to begin with. She managed, with only her penmanship, to imbue the word Texas with Oklahoman disapproval.

George pulled out a sheet of stationery and began to write, telling her mother she needn't worry. That simply not washing out wasn't good enough for her. That she intended to be the best in her class. But the words seemed too boastful. She balled up the paper and tossed it. She was too tired to write a decent letter.

Reveille was at six, but if she wanted any time in the john before she fell in to march to the mess hall, she had to wake up by five. Six girls to a bay and two bays to a john meant zero privacy. She'd never spent so much time in close quarters with other women. It felt like being surrounded by a crowd of Florences, fascinating and frazzling at the same time.

It was easier to face these Florences alongside Vivian. Sometimes she secretly pretended they were sisters; she loved it when people assumed they were related. She liked that Vivian was quieter than most of the others. She was serious and diligent. "I don't have a choice," Vivian told her. "They don't want me at home." Vivian rarely received letters.

Shoulder to shoulder, they marched to mess. To class. To the flight simulator. All the while, George tried not to stare too hard at the class ahead of theirs: experienced trainees who wore their zoot suits with easy grace, women who no longer had to log hours in the hot, stale, cramped Link training simulator. Women who flew solo runs. Who had priority for the bigger, more powerful AT-6s and C-78s. If she didn't wash out, she would be one of them soon.

The first washout of their class was Claire McNamara. George liked Claire, who was suntanned and cheerful and full of encouragement for anyone struggling with the course material. But Claire herself had struggled to dismantle and reassemble the Ranger engine. And then, on her first flight with the instructor, she'd bottomed out on the landing. The instructor had neglected to turn off his radio, and everyone in the control tower heard him yelling that she was "no pilot, and never would be."

Claire returned to the bay in tears, packed her bag, and by chow time boarded a bus to wherever she'd come from.

"Did you see the speed of that crosswind this morning?" asked Vivian as they stood in the chow line.

"I know," said George. "I'm glad I didn't get called to go up today. It could have been me."

"You're better than she was," said Vivian.

George hoped so. All she knew for sure was that she was a good mechanic. On the day they'd dismantled and reassembled the Ranger engines, she'd intentionally claimed a spot on the opposite side of the bay from Vivian. She wanted no distractions. The temptation to check her friend's progress and compare it to her own would have wrecked her concentration. The bay was silent and tense. Hours of no sound except for the occasional ping of a dropped screw.

George dropped nothing. She worked methodically, laying out her hardware and parts as her mother had taught her. Once she'd tightened the final spark plug, she surveyed the room. Vivian and Elliot, at adjacent engines, were neck and neck, and George could tell they knew it. She checked twice to make sure she hadn't missed any parts or hardware, then raised her hand to alert the instructor that she'd finished. The other women sighed. Vivian's eyes were full of envy when she looked up. Then she raised her own hand, seconds before Elliot's shot up.

George gave her a thumbs-up sign. She wanted Vivian to do well—just slightly less well than she herself did. She drilled herself on meteorology and Morse code, memorized control panel diagrams, and checked the flight list daily for her name. She still hadn't been called for her first flight.

If she was better than Claire McNamara, then why had Claire been called so early? Claire had pretended not to care that she was one of the first called, but she'd flounced all the way to the hangar. "You're looking for rhyme and reason in the armed forces?" asked Vivian. "I bet they draw names out of a hat."

If that was the case, then Vivian's name was drawn the next day. Vivian didn't flounce as she headed off, but George's insides twisted up all the same. Why had she been passed over again? Maybe they'd already decided she'd never cut it as a pilot.

She didn't mention her fears in her letters home. Her mother would only label them nonsense and not waste any time on reassurance. Instead, George wrote:

> Studying hard. Still waiting for my first flight. Have you heard any news about any of the Enid boys?

Adele replied with no news of any Enid boys, but plenty about Helen.

> She's got the Keywanettes putting together care packages for the boys overseas. She's got everyone— except me, of course—knitting socks for them. Quite a force, our Helen.

George tucked the letter away in her textbook. She spent her minimal unscheduled time studying for her ground school courses. But it was a beautiful day, and she found it hard to focus. Girls sunbathed outside the barracks, pretending to study as they watched the sky. Both for Avenger Field planes (scrutinized as potential competition) and for any male-piloted aircraft that might stray over Sweetwater. Cochran had banned all flyovers and unscheduled landings at Avenger Field. Whenever an unknown plane ventured through Sweetwater airspace, each girl imagined the trespassing male pilot might notice her among the other sunbathers and find some way to get in touch.

Easier said than done, but some managed it. George wasn't sure how. Cochran had the place pretty much on lockdown, which only fed everyone's war-fevered desire to meet men. George was pretty sure Susan Dubarry was seeing one of the flight instructors. Which was forbidden, not to mention a conflict of interest, but no one was about to rat Susan out, let alone rat out the man whose clipboard might hold their fate.

"Hey, Ector, since when do you pull your nose out of a book? You expecting a flyboy?" Fontana and Elliot peered at her over the tops of their meteorology textbooks, which they'd been using to fan themselves as they basked in the premature spring heat.

"Nah," Elliot said, smiling. She had perfect pearly-white teeth and a naturally happy disposition, which meant she often showed them off. "She's watching for Shaw, I bet. Didn't Shaw go up today?"

"Missing your twin?" Fontana asked.

George, who as an only child lacked experience in this sort of banter, wondered if her ears were as red as they felt.

"Honestly," said Fontana. "It took me a week to sort you two out."

"You been up yet, Ector?" asked Elliot.

"No," said George, unable to keep the wistfulness out of her voice.

"Me neither," said Elliot. "Fontana went yesterday."

"The instructor yelled at me the entire time," said Fontana. "I've never been so nervous in my life—not even my first time flying solo. I almost forgot my sweep checks before I did my chandelle. I would have washed out for sure if I hadn't remembered in time."

"At least you had a good landing," said Elliot. "Our turn will come," she added.

George thought about everything she'd have to remember up in the air. It wasn't like Enid, where, if she made a mistake, she'd probably only hurt herself. Here the planes were so thick in the air, they sometimes had to land at other bases.

"Speaking of chandelles," said Elliot. "Look up." A PT-19 overhead banked into a 180-degree turn.

"Beautiful," said Fontana. "I bet that instructor's not yelling."

"You think that's Shaw?" asked Elliot.

"Don't know," said George. "Could be anyone, I guess." But somehow, she knew it had to be Vivian, executing that perfect 180-degree right chandelle. The sunbathers applauded, and then, as the pilot executed a snap roll, they leaped up and whooped and waved.

"Oh, he's yelling now," said Elliot. George's pride in her friend curdled to fear. An instructor would never have authorized that snap roll. If that was Vivian, she'd wash out for showing off.

George kept her ears open as she went through the chow line, listening for whispers of "washed out," "sent home." She nearly dropped her tray in relief when Vivian shouted, "Ector! Over here!"

"God, I wouldn't dare," said Vivian when George told her about the snap roll. "Maybe it was Anderson. She's pretty full of herself after her perfect performance on the Link." Vivian's own flight had been uneventful. "But"—she winked—"you would have liked my chandelle too."

Back in the barracks, they heard Anderson was gone. Washed out for the snap roll.

When George climbed into the cockpit for her own first flight, her hands trembled. But by the time she started the engine, the routine of the preflight checklist had steadied her. Her takeoff was textbook, her flight uneventful, her instructor, if not impressed, at least not disappointed. A few days later, Jenssen washed out for sloppy stick and rudder technique. LaFollette washed out for suffering air sickness on a particularly turbulent day. Worst of all, Fontana washed out for a rough landing.

Back in the bay, Fontana crammed her beautiful clothing into her trunk. Vivian tried to help, but Fontana batted her hands away. "I can do it. I'm not a child."

"We just want to help," said George.

"Well, you can't." Fontana whipped out the door without saying goodbye, leaving her zoot suits on the bunk.

A week later, she wrote to Vivian, apologizing. "I don't know what came over me."

But George knew. She thought of Helen's letters, arriving with less frequency, and still unanswered. Letters likely full of news and worries about Frank. Worries only a fiancée was entitled to. George recognized envy when she saw it.

CHAPTER 8

The heap of pole beans on Harriet Mayes's countertop filled the kitchen with the scent of spring grass. Adele breathed deeply, tried to settle her nerves. It was just a canning lesson. She had done far more difficult things than canning beans.

Harriet's blue enamel stovetop gleamed. The Ectors' cook had taken a job at a gunpowder factory outside Pryor. For the first time in her life, Adele found herself responsible for her own kitchen. She cooked the same three meals in rotation and did her best to tidy up afterward, but her stovetop would never look like Harriet's. Why was a garage so much easier to keep clean than a kitchen?

"First we'll wash, trim, and cut these," Harriet said. "I like mine two knuckles long." She pressed her thumb to the second knuckle of her index finger, as if Adele might not understand. Adele took another breath and strove for patience. Back in their school days, Harriet had struggled with the simplest subjects. She'd dropped out before graduation to get married. All she was good for, Adele had thought at the time. Harriet—like a number of women Adele had previously dismissed—had proven her wrong.

Adele and Helen had driven all over the county urging women to collect scrap metal, to knit socks, to roll bandages. They organized marketing schedules so that women could take turns standing in lines and buying for each other. They collected dry goods for needier families and war widows.

Adele had been so busy knocking on other women's doors that she was surprised one evening to find Harriet Mayes standing on her own doorstep. Harriet was out preaching the virtues of growing a victory garden. Adele recalled weeding her mother's garden beds, picking the slugs off the squash, carting bucketloads of water from the well during dry spells. Even tending her little herb patch, blessedly no longer needed, had been a chore done out of necessity. She politely declined.

But Harriet had persisted, and now Adele had three rows of beans, three rows of squash, plus tomatoes, corn, and potatoes. "No point in growing all of that if you don't can it," admonished Harriet when Adele invited her over to show off her weed-free furrows.

So Adele stood in Harriet's pristine kitchen, slicing beans and listening to Harriet's plans to spread the canning gospel further. "Plenty of ladies can hot-water can, but pressure canning is another thing entirely," said Harriet. "With beans, you have to use pressure or you'll give someone botulism. You should buy a good pressure canner. Then teach someone else and lend it out, and then they can teach someone else and lend it out again. Meanwhile, I'll do the same with mine. No sense in everybody buying their own."

Adele appreciated Harriet's tact in not mentioning that while the two of them could afford pressure canners—Adele planned to buy two if she could find them—many others could not.

She also appreciated Harriet not mentioning that Adele had sliced only half as many beans as she had. The doorbell rang, and Harriet excused herself. Adele chopped faster, hoping to catch up before she returned.

Her hands stopped when a boy's voice piped, "Western Union!" Telegrams were a dicey business these days. Adele set the knife on the counter and moved toward the parlor. "No, ma'am, you keep that," said the boy.

Adele rushed to the front door. It hung wide open, daylight framing Harriet, who stood rigid, a dime in one hand and a telegram in the other. Unopened. Four black stars on the outside.

Even Harriet could do the math. Two sons overseas plus one four-star telegram meant one more stone in the graveyard, one less chair at the table. The only unsolved variable was which son wouldn't be coming home.

Adele brushed past Harriet and ran after the telegram boy, shouting. She wasn't nearly as fast as she used to be, and he was on a bicycle, but at last he heard her and turned back. Adele pushed a quarter at him. "Go to Merchant's Bank and tell Paul Mayes to come home. Tell him right away. Understand?"

"Yes, ma'am."

Back at the house, Harriet still stood in the doorway, staring at the unopened telegram in her hand. She blinked at Adele and said, "Well, we should get back to it."

"Harriet, no."

"Those beans aren't going to can themselves. And they're cut now—they'll just go bad if we don't do something with them."

Adele led Harriet to a chair in the parlor and gently lowered her into it. She took the dime and the telegram and set them on the credenza. "Where does Paul keep the whiskey?"

"Right under there." Harriet pointed to the credenza cabinet.

"I'll be right back," said Adele. In the kitchen, she poured the dregs of the coffee from the percolator into a cup. It was tepid, but she doubted Harriet would care. She sloshed in a good dose of whiskey and then delivered it to Harriet. "Drink this."

"Oh, I don't need anything."

Harriet rose. Adele put a hand on her shoulder and gently pushed her back down. "I won't do any more canning until you get this all down." Paul would arrive soon. He would make Harriet see sense.

Harriet drained the cup, gave a polite cough, and blinked again at Adele, who wondered about supplying her with a second dose. "I sent the telegram boy to get Paul."

Harriet ignored this. She stood, swaying slightly. "The important thing to know about pressure canning is that you have to keep the pressure steady at ten pounds."

"I'll be sure to do that. Paul will be here soon, though. Once he gets here, I'll take all the beans home with me and get someone else to teach me."

Harriet snorted. "Who? Bess Cramer?" She leaned toward Adele and whispered, "I heard she reuses her lids."

Adele had no idea what to say to this.

"I won't have these beans go to waste." Harriet stalked back to the kitchen, and Adele trailed behind her, thinking that surely the telegram boy must have reached the bank by now. Surely Paul must be on his way home. She'd go along with this canning business until he got here and then leave the two of them to their grief.

They finished the chopping and still no Paul. Harriet sterilized the jars and lids and rings, and still no Paul. They filled the jars, leaving, per Harriet's instructions, "just a finger width of headspace" at the top, set them in the canner, and hovered over the gauge, making sure the pressure stayed steady at ten pounds.

They'd finished three batches by the time Paul Mayes finally walked in. He went straight to Harriet and put his arms around her. "Where is it?" he asked Adele.

"On the credenza. She hasn't opened it yet." She wanted to apologize for the sparkling countertop, the jars of olive drab beans in neat ranks atop it.

"I had a war bonds meeting down in Edmond," said Paul over Harriet's shoulder. "They told me as soon as I got back to the bank. Thank you for staying with her." Then he spoke into Harriet's ear. "Honey, let's go sit down. Let's read it together."

"I don't have time to sit down. There's too much to do," insisted Harriet. Her breath must have still carried a hint of whiskey, because Paul looked a question at Adele.

"I gave her a little something. It didn't take."

"We can read it after I finish those socks," said Harriet. "I promised that girl Helen I'd get her another pair by tomorrow."

"I'll take them," said Adele. She was desperate to escape the wave of heartache about to crash down on Harriet and Paul. To run as far from it as she could.

"You can't knit," scoffed Harriet.

"Helen will finish them. Paul, do you know where they are?"

"The basket by the wing chair."

Adele kept her steps deliberate as she approached the basket, hiding her hurry to leave. "I'll bring a casserole by tomorrow." She cringed at the insufficiency of this offer. "I'm so sorry."

She took the knitting basket directly to the Cramer house and was met at the door by a panicked Bess. "Have you seen Helen?"

"No, I was just bringing her—"

"She left a note. She's run off to San Diego. But she's never been farther than Dallas, and I just can't imagine . . . When I saw you drive up, I thought she might have run to you instead."

Adele was flattered. Helen struck her as thoroughly self-sufficient. She possessed a natural authority that made even older women sit up and listen. She quickly found the simplest way to cut through any organizational complexity. To Helen, nothing was impossible—she seemed incapable of hearing the word no.

A word the Cramers had deployed repeatedly when it came to Frank Bridlemile. Who, Helen had told Adele just last week, had finished basic training and had been sent to San Diego, where he was preparing to ship out to the Pacific.

She managed to say something soothing to Bess, but Adele wasn't worried about Helen. And now she was considerably less worried about George. All those nights George went driving off with Frank, she'd feared her daughter might make a life-changing mistake. What if she got pregnant. Got married. Ended up stuck in Enid, unable to fly. Adele had been too cowardly to say these things outright to her daughter.

Her daughter who, in every letter home, asked whether Adele had news of any Enid boys. Adele knew exactly which Enid boy George meant. She filled her own letters with news about Helen instead.

But, she decided, as she drove back home to Charles, she wouldn't write George with this particular Helen-related news item. Let Helen share it herself. Adele intended to keep well out of the mess these young people were determined to make.

CHAPTER 9

By late spring, George and the other pilots in her class were flying solo. They'd worked their way up from the PT-19s and BT-13s to the AT-6s. George especially loved flying the AT-6. The plane knew what she wanted it to do almost before she did, its every reaction silky and precise. It sliced cleanly through the air—didn't rattle her teeth like the BT-13. She never wanted her AT-6 flights to end.

With the nimbostratus layer beneath her, she felt like she was gliding over a wooly gray carpet. Beneath the clouds, steady rain fell. Above them, all was dry and clear. She wanted to stay up forever, sailing high above the troubles of the hidden earth below.

"All planes must land, Ector," said Captain Patterson, "including this one." She'd almost forgotten the instructor was there, the cockpit was so spacious and her attention so entirely on the controls.

If he hadn't had a say in what and when she flew next, George would have circled once more over Sweetwater. She guided the plane into its descent and, at just the right moment, locked the tailwheel for landing.

Down at Avenger Field, it was pouring. The slog to the barracks would leave the hems of her zoot suit heavy with mud. Her other suit was already in that condition, and she didn't know how she'd find time to wash them before lights-out at ten, given that everyone else was in the same boat and all the sinks would be in use.

"Might as well climb down and take your medicine, Ector. Just like everybody else," said Elliot, who had just disembarked from her own flight and was already up to her ankles in Sweetwater mud.

"Will it never stop?" George pulled off her goggles.

"Oh, sure. We'll be back to complaining about the heat and choking on dust before you know it."

"It's sending all the scorpions inside," said George. "Check your boots before you put them on." Elliot was from San Jose, California, where there were no scorpions or roaches, and, according to Elliot, even mosquitoes were in short supply.

"Jesus, Ector. I don't know how anyone can stand living in this sort of place."

"We'll be through in a month." She mentally crossed her fingers, made a wish. Any one of them could still wash out. "Maybe you'll get assigned somewhere in California."

As she reached the barracks, she saw Vivian in the shelter of the eaves, laughing with a woman in full WASP uniform: khaki pants, white blouse, bomber jacket with a USAAF patch on the shoulder. Vivian spotted them and called out, "Ector! Elliot! Come meet Ethel Blankenship."

George dragged her mud-heavy boots over to them and shook Blankenship's hand.

"Ethel and I met on the barnstorming circuit," said Vivian. Jealousy spiked in George. Blankenship had more in common with Vivian than George ever would. "She does the sweetest inverted flat spin you ever saw."

"On purpose?" joked Elliot.

Blankenship bowed with a flourish. "Whatever brings in the crowds, right?"

"Ethel was two classes back from us. She's ferrying a B-17 to Barksdale but doesn't have to be there until tomorrow, so she stopped over."

"And now that I'm here, I remember why I was so ready to leave. They could at least put some planks down over all this mud," said Blankenship.

"Don't hold your breath," said George, liking Blankenship in spite of herself.

"Oh, I won't. Hey, I'm heading over to Love Field tonight to look up an airman I used to fly with. Why don't you girls come along? I've got plenty of friends in Dallas. I can get someone to fly you back before morning. If my guy's not there, I'll fly you back myself."

"I'd love to get out of here for a night," said Vivian. "Come on, George, what do you say?"

George wanted to go with Vivian and Blankenship so that she could assess the degree of friendship between them. But if she didn't wash out her zoot suits, she'd be grounded for not maintaining a neat and feminine appearance. "I've got two filthy zoot suits. I have to get them clean tonight."

"Me too," said Elliot. But Vivian ignored Elliot, George noticed. Perhaps the jealousy cut both ways.

"Come on, George. Say yes. It'll be fun!" urged Vivian.

"Seriously. Shearer will ground me."

"Oh, go on, Ector," said Elliot. "I'll wash out one of your suits tonight if you wash out one of mine tomorrow."

"Sure you don't mind?"

"I'll mind later when I'm dealing with a sink full of mud, but you should go, Ector. Really. You can owe me."

It was a short hop to Love Field and a quick jeep ride to the bar where Blankenship expected to find her guy. George felt giddy wearing real civilian clothing, walking alongside Blankenship in her crisp uniform. In a month, if everything went well, she'd be wearing her own uniform, striding proudly down sidewalks between ferrying assignments. Meeting her own guy in her own familiar watering holes.

Just outside the bar, a circle of male pilots doubled over, braying at a joke George was pretty sure she didn't want to hear. They straightened as George and her friends approached, and leered at Blankenship.

"I love a woman in uniform!"

Blankenship stiffened. The women picked up their pace.

"Hey, baby, tell your friends to sign up too. A woman's place is in the Army now."

"A woman's place is in my flight suit."

"Come on, sweetheart, Uncle Sam wants you to keep this flyboy warm tonight."

Blankenship hurried George and Vivian into the bar and deposited them at a table. She fanned at her red face and said, "Wait here. I'll get us a round."

"They've got nerve," said George when Blankenship rejoined them. "Talking to us like that."

"No kidding. I know they were drunk, but you'd think we weren't all on the same side," said Vivian.

Blankenship sighed. "You've been locked up in Cochran's convent, so I guess you haven't heard the tall tales going around."

George and Vivian shook their heads. "Well, they're really about the WAACs, but no one on the outside can tell a WAAC from a WASP from a WAVE. We're all the same to them—women wearing uniforms."

"They sell WAAC uniforms, or something close enough, at the JCPenney in Enid," said George. "Anyone can buy them."

"Yes," said Vivian. "The victory girls that hung around Moody liked to dress up in them."

"Which only feeds the fire," said Blankenship. "Because the rumor is that the WAACs and the WASPs were recruited to boost soldier morale. And that we were all issued . . ." She dropped her voice: "Rubbers, just like the enlisted boys, so that we could do the job properly. And that the only sort of women who would sign up are women who, well, who lack a certain degree of self-control, let's say."

Vivian paled, and George's beer tasted suddenly sour. Blankenship went on, revealing another rumor: that WAACs were being shipped home from northern Africa because they were pregnant. She'd met one who'd been stationed over there, and it was all baloney. "But the story's just too good, I guess, so everyone's decided it must be true."

George had hoped for an evening of dancing, of feeling a man's arms around her, maybe even kissing a soldier in a dark corner of the bar. But now every man in the room seemed to be leering at them. She and Vivian hunched over the table and nursed their beers.

Blankenship found her guy and lost herself in dancing and beer, but not before she found a friend to fly them back to Sweetwater. "You kidding?" he said. "Who wouldn't kill for approval to land at Avenger Field. Sign me up!" On the short hop back, she thought about the rumors going around, the assumptions people in Enid must be making about why she'd signed up for the WASP.

She thought about how Ethel, dancing with her guy, had indeed appeared to be up for it. At least with that guy. She remembered the times she'd been up for it herself. Once a girl was up for it, people assumed she always was. Probably even their friendly pilot, deep down inside, thought she and Vivian were up for it. Probably he'd tell the story about flying some WASPs back to Sweetwater, and his friends would laugh knowingly. Just thinking about it made her queasy. The atmosphere in the plane became awkward, quiet except for Vivian clicking her lighter open and closed. George scanned the moonlit ground below for landmarks, ticking off the miles until they returned to the safety of Cochran's convent.

Fewer and fewer pilots washed out as the training progressed. George and the remaining women had each completed ground school and logged thirty-eight hot, claustrophobic hours in the Link flight simulator. They'd each logged one hundred and eighty flying hours in a combination of PT-19s, BT-13s, and the more advanced AT-6s and C-78s. Soon they'd graduate and disperse, moving on to their official assignments.

"I hope we get posted together," George said to Vivian.

"Me too. But if we don't, we'll manage to meet up."

"Right." George thought about how easy it had been for Blankenship to stop in at Avenger Field. Earning their wings would also earn them a level of independence—bounded by all sorts of regulations, naturally, but with far more latitude than they currently possessed.

But first they had to make it through their night flights. Two or three planes went out each night, with two pilots and one instructor in each plane. One pilot flew the long leg out, and the other flew back, each navigating by instrumentation only, with the instructor evaluating their performance. George wanted to fly with Vivian. She wanted Vivian to see her handle the controls, show her what she could do. But Vivian drew Elliot, and George drew Dubarry.

Vivian and Elliot went up on the first night. George watched their C-78 head north and then bank northwest. The bay felt empty without her friends. She wondered where she'd be sleeping in a month, assuming she passed her night flight. There was talk of WASPs testing drones at Liberty Field in Georgia. There was ferrying to be done from bases in California, Michigan, Massachusetts, and Delaware to pretty much everywhere else. There was artillery target towing in North Carolina. She fell asleep hoping she wouldn't get the drone assignment. She wanted to fly the plane she was in, not ride in one plane while flying another one by remote control.

At morning mess the day after their night flight, Vivian and Elliot clinked their coffee cups together, then dipped into extravagant curtsies as George and the other pilots from their bay cheered. "It's strange to fly without any landmarks," said Vivian. "All those little towns we've learned are just scattered lights on the ground. Trust your instruments and you'll do great."

"Patterson tried to get us to land at Midland," said Elliot. "Watch out for that trick."

George felt nervous and out of sorts about her upcoming flight. Vivian's completed test had opened a gulf between them. Now Vivian and Elliot were virtually guaranteed to pass. If something went wrong, if George and Dubarry botched the navigation or, God forbid, even the routine preflight check, then she'd wash out. The gulf between herself and Vivian would be permanent, uncrossable.

She found Dubarry studying nav charts in the common room. "They flew north, then northwest last night," said Dubarry. "But we should expect them to mix it up."

"Did Patterson tell you that?" Everyone knew Dubarry was seeing Patterson on the sly. They were discreet, and Patterson made sure he was never Dubarry's evaluator, but George wondered if he might have dropped a few hints about what to expect.

Dubarry's dimples disappeared. "Nobody told me anything. I'm thinking for myself, Ector. You should too."

But she couldn't stop herself. "Shaw and Elliot went up with Patterson last night. They said he tried to trick them into landing at Midland."

"If he did, I'm glad they didn't fall for it."

The flint in Dubarry's stare brought George up short. "Sorry, Dubarry, I just . . ."

Dubarry softened. "We're all scared of washing out." She rotated the chart so they could both read it. "All we can do is study up, so come on."

George and Dubarry's weather briefing noted clouds well above their planned flight altitude. "Might get choppy here and there," the briefer said, "but nothing you girls can't handle." George loved him for that.

Dubarry took the controls on the way out. The clouds above them blocked the moonlight. The scattered patches of lights on the ground told George nothing. Her internal gyroscope sensed the plane tilting. "Dube!" she hissed.

"Just straightening it out," whispered Dubarry.

George peered ahead and saw what Dubarry meant: an enormous cloud bank sloped up in the distance. Dubarry read it as the horizon and had adjusted the plane accordingly. George sensed the sudden alertness of the instructor seated behind them. She checked the altimeter. Dubarry was taking them too high, up into the territory the briefer had told them to avoid. "It's not the horizon," George whispered, hoping the instructor wouldn't hear but that Dubarry would. "It's clouds." Dubarry checked the altimeter and returned the plane to a safe altitude, and everyone in the cockpit breathed easier.

When it came time for George to bring them back to Avenger Field, the clouds had dropped to their planned flight altitude. She tried taking the plane higher, but the cumulonimbus column was endless. At last she flew out of it, saw a scattering of stars. Before she could pick out any particular constellation, they flew into the next cumulonimbus column. This one threw them around like a toddler tossing a beanbag.

Her palms were sweaty on the controls. She stared out into the dark, searching for some patch of light, some star or planet, something to fly by while she tried to handle the bucking plane.

"Trust your instruments," she heard Vivian say.

Right. There was no point in looking out the windshield. There'd be nothing to see. All the information she needed was on the dash in front of her. She trained her eyes to her instruments, gripped the controls, and prayed.

CHAPTER 10

Vivian dreamed of ack-ack exploding around her plane as she navigated a night sky, dodging spotlights, heading for safety. The explosions came closer, or at least grew louder, until a great, percussive crack rocked her ship, spinning her off course. She bolted up, fully awake, grateful to find herself in her bunk, in the stifling bay. A cool breeze snuck through the window, raising goose bumps on her sweat-damp arms. Raindrops plunked into the soft dirt outside the barracks. The window lit up, and the bay shook again with a crash of thunder.

"Wow," said Elliot. "Glad we went up last night. What are you doing?"

"Getting dressed," said Vivian. "Think I'll go out to the control tower."

Elliot said, "I've flown with Ector three times now. Never seen anything rattle her."

Vivian gestured at the puddle forming beneath the open window. "Want me to close that before I go?"

"No, I'd rather mop up later and have the air now. Unless you want me to come with you?"

But Vivian was already out the door, tying a scarf over her hair, racing through the pelting rain to the tallest structure at Avenger Field. At the door to the tower, she nearly collided with another form. Both of them had their eyes on the ground, trying to dodge the puddles.

"Jesus, Shaw, what are you doing out here at this hour?" It was Patterson, pale in the light from the doorway.

"Couldn't sleep," said Vivian.

"Yeah, me either."

Hamblett was in charge of the control tower that night. "We're not putting on a show here," he said when they slipped inside. Then, perhaps seeing the misery in Patterson's face, he relented and gestured to an unoccupied spot. "You can stand over there. Don't touch anything. Don't say anything."

Vivian and Patterson stood silent and dripping in their appointed place. She wanted to ask which direction the storm was moving. She wanted to ask if they'd had radio contact with the C-78s. Patterson massaged the nape of his neck and sighed. A gesture she'd seen before, usually when she or another pilot had done something verging on stupid during a practice flight. His very own distress signal.

From a distance, the dots on the radar display meant nothing to her. She edged closer, but Patterson put a hand on her shoulder and pulled her back.

If only Hamblett would say something reassuring. If only the storm would move through quickly and leave the sky above Avenger Field clear. But the storm, if her old-fashioned counting of seconds between lightning flashes and thunderclaps meant anything, sat directly over them, not moving at all.

As if to confirm her suspicions, Hamblett finally spoke up. "We've got two fronts pushing against each other. Sort of thing that sparks twisters. Not that we could see one coming tonight."

Vivian checked the time: 0348 hours. About an hour before daylight. The planes should come in soon. None of the controllers spoke. Patterson massaged his neck.

"Aren't they in range for radio contact yet?" she asked.

Hamblett glared at her. "Another word and you're out."

He murmured something to one of the controllers. Something about landing at Abilene or Midland if they could get clearance.

The radio crackled. "Avenger Tower, this is JIG VICTOR-36 requesting clearance to land. Repeat, Avenger Tower, this is JIG VICTOR-36 requesting clearance to land."

"Where are they?" said Hamblett.

"Sir, I don't have them," said one controller.

"Paulson?" asked Hamblett.

"Sir, I don't have them either."

Hamblett picked up a headset. "JIG VICTOR-36, this is Avenger Tower. You do not have clearance. Repeat, you do not have clearance."

Patterson nudged Vivian, and mouthed, "Ector?" But the garbled voice on the radio, further dampened by the rain spattering against the control tower windows, could have belonged to anyone. Vivian shrugged.

Hamblett darted from display to display. "They're not up there," he said. "They've gotten themselves lost. Paulson, put a call in to Midland. Tell them to radio JIG VICTOR-36. See if they can land there."

"JIG VICTOR-36, this is Avenger Tower. We don't have you. Repeat: we do not have you. Check your location and report back."

"JIG VICTOR-36, this is Avenger Tower. Repeat: check your location and report back immediately."

"JIG VICTOR-36, this is Avenger Tower. Repeat: check your location and report back immediately."

Hamblett seemed destined to repeat those two sentences forever with no response. Patterson was mumbling now, just behind Vivian's ear. She thought he might be saying the rosary. She wished she knew it, too, so that she could chant it along with him.

"JIG VICTOR-36, this is Avenger—"

"Sir, Midland reports a ship down two miles south of base. Responders on their way."

"Shit!" said Hamblett. "Shit, shit, shit. What are you looking at me for? Get your eyes on those screens and fucking find me my other plane!"

"Yes, sir!" Paulson and the other controllers snapped their eyes back to the radar displays.

Hamblett paced behind his controllers. Patterson's rosary went up a notch in volume. Vivian tapped his elbow, but he didn't notice. Hamblett, however, did. "Patterson. Shaw. Get out of my tower."

"But, sir—" started Vivian.

"Now."

Patterson didn't look capable of navigating the stairs. Vivian wished she could get him a chair, though she suspected he'd refuse it. "I'll go, sir. Right away. But please let Captain Patterson stay. He won't be in your way. And he'll stop . . . he'll be quiet. Right, Captain?"

Patterson managed to nod.

Hamblett said, "If this is your idea of going right away, Shaw, you obviously don't know the meaning of right away."

"Yes, sir." Vivian staggered down the stairs and out into the rain. Just because a plane went down didn't mean it was George's plane. And just because a plane went down, didn't mean the crew had been harmed. She'd seen pilots walk away from terrible landings, even from crashes. George and Dubarry were probably just fine. She leaned against the wall of the control tower, pressed her ear to the siding, hoping the sound from inside might carry through the structure, but all she could hear was rain snicking into mud.

She slogged back to the barracks, not bothering with her rain scarf. A light shone in the common room. Elliot was up. She shifted something out of sight beneath the table, then, recognizing Vivian, brought her hand back up, set her silver flask on the table. "Well?" asked Elliot.

"One plane down near Midland. No contact from the other one."

"Here." Elliot pushed the flask toward Vivian.

"I thought you got rid of your stash."

"Ask me no questions, I'll tell you no lies. Go on. I got it out for you, after all."

Vivian took it, twisted open the top, then pushed it away. "I might need to go out there."

"Where? To Midland Field? For what, Shaw?"

Vivian choked back a sob. "Someone has to take her home."

Because that was how it worked. The female pilots were technically civilians. If they died in training, the USAAF didn't put them in a flag-draped casket and ship them home. The other WASPs chipped in for a coffin, for transportation, and one of them accompanied the body, returned the dead pilot to her family.

Elliot leaned across the table toward Vivian, her breath sweet with whiskey. "Look, Shaw, I think you're a little bit like me. Every now and then, you fudge a rule. Just a little bit, just here and there." Elliot waggled the flask. "But not Ector. She follows every. Single. Rule. All the rules. All the time. And that's what's going to get her plane back down safe tonight."

The sky was lighter now, the raindrops smaller, the thunder fainter. The storm was moving on, and the sun was rising. Another day was about to start. She and Elliot stared out the window into the distance, wishing a plane into view. A face loomed up outside the window, and they jumped.

"Captain Patterson!" Vivian raised the sash, and Elliot swished the flask behind her back.

"They're safe, Shaw. Landed at Big Spring. They're arranging transport back this afternoon."

Vivian started to tremble. "And the other plane?" asked Vivian, embarrassed at how her voice shook, thinking of Aisling and Gardner and Captain Shearer, the instructor who had gone up with them.

Patterson shook his head. "Hamblett wouldn't say outright, but I could tell. They didn't make it."

Vivian leaned heavily against Elliot, who, still trying to hide her flask, nearly toppled over from the unexpected weight. "Sit down, Shaw." Patterson used his captain voice. "Sit down and have some of whatever it is I don't see in Elliot's right hand."

Vivian obeyed, and Elliot said, "Sir, it was only—"

"Since I don't see anything, I don't need anything explained to me. And I'm sure the sergeant won't need anything explained to him at barracks inspection this afternoon. Because there won't be anything for him to see, either, will there be, Elliot?"

"No, sir."

Patterson nodded at Vivian, who had steadied after a slug of whiskey. "Make her eat something," he said to Elliot, before he disappeared.

The sun eased over the horizon, and the birdsong gathered strength. The women sipped their whiskey and waited for reveille.

CHAPTER 11

Adele drove down for graduation, but George's father didn't accompany her. In the front row of the auditorium, she stirred the hot, dusty Sweetwater air with the church fan she'd wisely stashed in her pocketbook. From the stage, George could practically see her mother thinking, *My daughter the aviatrix.*

George held her breath while Jacqueline Cochran, elegant as always, pinned wings on the collar of her crisp white blouse. Cochran moved down the line and did the same for Vivian. George wished Vivian had someone in the audience celebrating her too.

"I suppose it was too far for your people to travel," said Adele as she shook Vivian's hand.

"Yes, ma'am," said Vivian. She didn't sound bothered, but George wished her mother hadn't said anything. Vivian's family disapproved of her flying, and, from the sound of it, pretty much everything else she did.

Adele took them both for chicken-fried steak at the Blue Bonnet Hotel to celebrate. What with the long drive back to Enid, George had expected her mother to stay another night at the Blue Bonnet, but her mother said, "I just can't leave your father for that long."

"Is it his heart again?" asked George, her own doubling its pace. Before she left home, her father's color had returned. But she recalled his labored breathing from the day she left. He'd written her that he couldn't come to her graduation because he had to iron out a new lease deal. The war effort required oil, and he was pumping as much as he could. But now she understood it wasn't just patriotism that had kept him away. "I should go with you, Mother," she said. "I'll request leave."

Adele dismissed this with a wave of her hand. "You'll do no such thing. He'll be fine. You do what you came here to do."

"But I—"

"This is important, Georgeanne. You keep at it, no matter what. Hear?"

When she and Vivian got back to the base, they found their fellow graduates clustered around the assignment board.

Women called out their postings: "Delaware!" "California!" "Liberty Field!" George squeezed Vivian's hand.

"Camp Davis!" shouted Elliot.

They threaded their way through the knot of women. George scanned the list and then flung her arms around Vivian. With Elliot and Dubarry and twenty-odd other women whom George recognized as the best fliers in their class, she and Vivian were heading for coastal North Carolina, where they'd tow targets for antiaircraft artillery training.

"Days off at the beach!" cheered George. She'd get to see the ocean for the first time.

"What's a day off?" joked Vivian.

"Hey, girls!" Dubarry beamed at them. "Don and I are getting married after mess tonight. Will you come?"

It took George a moment to connect "Don" with Captain Patterson, but Vivian got it right away. "Of course we will! Best wishes, Dubarry! Or should we call you Patterson now?"

"Not for another three hours, officially. But if you want to start practicing, that's fine with me."

"I guess you'll be flying back here as often as they'll let you," said George.

"Well, I would, but they're transferring him to California in two weeks. The brass likes to keep married couples far apart."

After the ceremony, the pilots hooted and cheered as the newlyweds sped off to the Blue Bonnet on Patterson's motorcycle. "Lucky Susan," said Vivian.

"No kidding," said Elliot. "But hey, we're all about to be done with Cochran's convent."

George remembered how sexy she'd found the atmosphere at the Enid airfield. Maybe it was the swaggering confidence of the pilots. Maybe it was that they all felt godlike, daring to travel so far above the ground. Maybe she'd find some of that at Camp Davis.

"Well, we'll certainly find men," said Elliot.

"And real planes to fly," said Vivian. "No more training flights!"

They stayed up all night, talking about the men and planes that awaited them. The Camp Davis contingent was particularly excited. The base was so big, it had four movie theaters and two Officers' Clubs. Even a roller rink!

And they'd arrive in style: General Arnold himself was sending a plane to deliver them right into the arms of those handsome pilots just waiting to escort them to movies and take them dancing at the Officers' Club.

CHAPTER 12

Stepping off the plane into the humid, pine-scented air of Camp Davis took Vivian right back to Hahira. "Wow," said George. "It's hot."

"Wait until August," said Vivian. A group of male pilots stood on the tarmac. Lieutenants, captains, majors—Vivian had the insignia down now. But no colonel. The CO must be busy.

The men escorted them to their barracks, helped them hang blinds on the windows and tack up aircraft diagrams on the bare walls. A few introduced themselves, but mostly they worked silently while the women unpacked. Elliot tried to goose things along, suggesting that they all head to the Officers' Club for a beer—"and maybe some dancing." The men shot uncomfortable glances at one another, mumbled excuses, and slinked away.

"What's that about?" demanded Elliot.

"That," said an unknown female voice—its feathery pitch unmistakably civilian—"is an exemplification of gentlemanliness. Beer and dancing at the Officers' Club, my word!" Vivian turned toward the voice and found its owner: a woman wearing a loose floral dress with tatting at the collar and sleeves. She fluttered a church fan that her red face and wilting hair wave indicated was no match for the sticky heat. "They promised me air-conditioning," she said, the first of many times she'd voice this complaint.

Vivian laughed. "Welcome to the armed forces, ma'am."

"Oh, but I am the one welcoming you, dear." Vivian cut her eyes at George. Their first day at Camp Davis wasn't turning out as expected. There'd been no tour of the base, no welcome speech by the CO, and now, no beer and dancing.

"You'll want to go into Wilmington and get some nice things. Dust ruffles for the beds, some floor mats. I have the bus schedule in my room." The woman looked as if her postdebutante days hadn't panned out quite as she'd expected.

"You have a room here?" Elliot was the only one of them with a functioning tongue. The rest just stared, mouths slightly agape, as a trickle of sweat carved a trail through the woman's face powder.

"Of course I do," said the woman. Then her eyes snapped in awareness. "Oh, you have not been informed. I am Mrs. Mellon." And when this didn't alter their perplexed expressions: "Your housemother."

"It's Cochran's convent all over again," Vivian whispered to George, who cursed under her breath.

"Now, I may not be able to fly airplanes, but I can help you get this place spruced up. And I think you'll find I'm not a *terrible* stickler when it comes to the rules. But don't tell Colonel Stephenson!"

"Rules?" said Elliot.

"Well, I can see they've told you nothing. I shouldn't be surprised, considering the mix-up with the air-conditioning. The rules. Two main ones, really, and they make a little rhyme, so they're easy to remember: *Lights-out at ten, no fraternizing with men.*"

Colonel Stephenson needn't have bothered with his rule, thought Vivian. The men must have been under orders to move them into their barracks. After that, they wanted nothing to do with the female pilots. At the airfield, they edged the women out of the ready room. When the CO bothered to make an appearance, he either ignored them or made a point of saying they should go home and knit for the troops. Worse, he assigned them to dull, low tracking missions in light aircraft. When the women groused, he told them he wasn't about to risk his better planes to the inferior capabilities of substandard pilots.

Vivian still showed up at the field every morning, hoping to draw a decent plane, but some of the other pilots from Sweetwater stopped bothering. George included.

"Come on, George. You'll be late." Vivian rocked her friend's shoulder.

George groaned and pulled the blanket over her head. "What's the point?"

"The point is to get out there and fly. Come on."

George hauled herself upright and swung her feet over the edge of her bunk. "This isn't flying. We're just being sent to our corner to play with toys." They'd both been assigned to PT-19s all week, the same models they'd flown early on during training.

"For now," said Vivian. "Besides, what are you going to do otherwise? Sit here and chat with Mrs. Mellon all day?"

George groaned again and flopped backward across the bed.

"Well, I'm going." Vivian couldn't see how avoiding the airfield would win them any points in the long run. The CO was delighted to let the women stay in the barracks; if they didn't show up to fly, he'd have a legitimate reason to send them home. Vivian didn't feel like she had a home to go back to. She couldn't recall the last letter she'd gotten from her sister. Her mother never wrote, and her father hadn't spoken to her since she ran off with Louis. George's parents wrote her all the time. They'd be thrilled to have her back.

Fine for George, thought Vivian as she stalked toward the hangar. But everything was fine for George. She had nice parents. She had nice clothes. She was beautiful. Despite talk of their resemblance, George was much prettier than Vivian would ever be. And, Vivian reminded herself, George was kind. She never acted like having money mattered, but she never pretended it didn't, a difficult balance to strike. But nowhere near as difficult as being poor.

Inside the hangar, the cicada scritching of socket wrenches relaxed her. She checked the assignment board, saw SHAW V on it, and immediately perked up. She'd drawn an A-24. Wait until she told George. That would get her out of bed.

Unless it was a joke.

She surveyed the men nearby for signs of laughter. But the pilots were inspecting the planes they'd been assigned, the mechanics were engaged in repair work, and no one paid her any mind. She scanned the hangar again and saw a familiar face: Quigley squinting through his wire-rimmed glasses at the hydraulics on a BT-13.

She'd known it was only a matter of time before she ran into Louis or Durham or Quigley. This, she'd learned early on at Avenger Field, was one of the more interesting aspects of military life: it jumbled everyone up so that you were bound to run into people from your past. She was glad it was Quigley and not Louis or Durham.

But would he be glad to see her? He might begrudge the barnstorming money she'd taken from the cashbox. He might, like so many of the other men in the hangar, feel she was trespassing into male territory. *May as well find out now,* she thought. "If I remember correctly," she said to his sweat-damp back, "you said you were done with the South."

He turned with a smile. "Aw, well, you know . . . Met a girl . . ."

"That happens," said Vivian. "Or so I hear."

"V. Shaw. I hoped it was you when I saw the board this morning. Look at you!"

Vivian straightened and saluted.

"Nice uniforms they give you girls."

"Beats the men's extra-large flight suits we trained in, that's for sure."

She didn't want to get him in trouble—she felt the eyes of the other pilots on them. "Let me buy you a beer later at the O Club," she offered.

"Nah, not a member of that club." He pointed to the staff sergeant stripes on his sleeve. "But there's a place just off base. The Knotty Pine."

"This isn't the sort of place you should come on your own," said Quigley, as if Vivian couldn't tell that just from walking in the door. She was hesitant to be there even with a man. Several victory girls paused their trolling for soldiers to glare at her. "The pilots keep mostly to the O Club, and the other mechanics to the NCO Club, so this seemed like a good place to catch up."

He'd been on leave her first week at the base, seeing his girl, and hadn't heard from Louis or any of the barnstorming crew since the start of the war. He assumed they were all flying, doing their part, just as he was doing his. She could tell it rankled that he couldn't serve as a pilot. His limp and nearsightedness doomed him to dealing with planes on the ground. "Thanks for not ratting me out," she said. "When I left. Sorry about the cashbox."

Quigley shrugged. "Figured you'd earned it. I know how Louis is when it comes to girls." He asked her about her WASP training and how she found Camp Davis so far. "It's a shame the way they've shut you girls out."

She told him which planes they were used to flying, and he whistled. "But listen," he said, "it's not some superstitious fear of women messing up the planes—well, for a few of them, maybe it is. It's that these guys, the older ones anyway, they didn't get the plum jobs overseas. These target-towing runs are all they've got left. They're worried you girls are going to replace them and they'll be reassigned to infantry. A lot of them have asked the colonel for transfers out."

"More flight time for us, then," she said.

"They'll come around," said Quigley. "Some of them anyway."

CHAPTER 13

George waited until Vivian left to pull her mother's letter from underneath her pillow and reread it.

> He's not well enough to write you himself, or he would. Now I know you're thinking you should come home. But don't. He wants you to stay and do your job. He's so proud of you.

Not once in the letter did her mother explicitly say that her father was dying, and yet every word said exactly that. Her father was dying, and here she was next to a mosquito-infested swamp, dodging a housemother, reduced to flying inconsequential planes for inconsequential reasons.

In her head, she made this point to Adele, who responded that the planes must not be too inconsequential or they would have been melted down for scrap. And that no one—not even the armed forces—allocated fuel for anything unimportant these days.

In her head, George argued that she should see her father, and Adele looked at her with such searing disappointment that it drove her from her bed. She dressed and wrote a letter to her father and hurried out to mail it before heading to the airfield. He wanted her to fly, and so she would fly. No matter what sort of plane they put her in. She'd show the men at Camp Davis with every maneuver what she could do, and would keep on showing them until they could no longer refuse to see it.

The Officers' Club was just as bad as the airfield. "Why do we bother to come here?" complained Elliot. "The bartenders freeze us out, and the drinks are mostly water."

"Wishful thinking," said George.

"It beats the Knotty Pine," said Vivian.

A group of them had ventured into the Officers' Club after convincing themselves that the male pilots had been kinder that day. Talk of transfers had died down. But no real sense of welcome had followed.

George had given up hope of dancing and camaraderie with the men. She tried to ignore the salacious commentary, growing louder by the minute, coming from the tables nearby.

"I know," shouted a young lieutenant. "Inspection time! Line 'em up against the back wall. We'll start a pool—which one'll be the first to go home pregnant?" The men roared.

"She looks ripe," the lieutenant said, pointing at Gries, a plump and extremely pretty WASP. Gries never missed church on Sunday mornings and sometimes even went back in the evening. She'd been nursing a Coca-Cola and staring at the clock above the bar. She was only at the bar because George had begged her to come. Now her mouth fell open in a shocked O.

George, who'd spent the afternoon in an A-24 with Gries and learned that her fiancé was missing in action in France, exploded. "Shame on all of you!" she said. "Pumping yourselves up at our expense. Cowards! All of you!"

A moment of silent shock, and then the jeering began.

"Settle down, sweetheart. We're only teasing."

"Must be that time of the month."

"Come on, we're just having fun. Give us a smile."

George wanted to stand her ground, but Gries had tears in her eyes, and George's own throat was dangerously tight. She wasn't about to cry in front of these men. They already believed she was weak and overly emotional, and thus unfit to do her job. She took Gries by the elbow and guided her toward the door.

"Awww, now they're leaving."

"No! Anything but that!"

"Don't go, ladies! We were only teasing!"

"Whassamatter, can't take a joke?"

The other women followed. George wanted to tell them to go back, to insist, by force of their presence, that the men accept them. But that strategy hadn't worked yet, and she didn't have much hope that it ever would.

"Good for you, George," said Vivian as they swatted through the mosquitoes escorting them back to the barracks.

"Not that it'll do any good," fumed George. She was glad of the dark. She didn't want Vivian and the others to see the tears on her cheeks.

"I don't know, George," said Susan Patterson. "I'm going to send a letter. It's time Jacqueline Cochran knew what was going on down here."

George doubted that Patterson's letter would do anything but get Patterson reassigned somewhere less prestigious. She remembered all too well Cochran's no-complaints policy. But it must have been a good letter, because Cochran flew in a few weeks later and ushered herself into Col. Stephenson's office. The next day, the colonel announced a change to the flight assignments. He had determined, having now given the matter sufficient study, that the WASPs were ready to begin their target-towing training. He emphasized that the training could not—would not—be rushed. Until he believed they were ready, they'd be paired up with male pilots to train.

George was elated. Now she'd show them what she could do. She couldn't wait to try target towing. While she flew, an airman in the back of her plane would spool out a long target cable. The Ack Acks—the artillerymen down below—would try to hit it. The Ack Acks were supposed to feed coordinates into target directors, rather than aiming their 90 mm guns by eye. But they found the target directors slow and frustrating and often eyeballed the target instead. The artillery rounds were live, even in practice, and no matter how skilled her flying, a pilot might take shrapnel in the tail of her ship.

After a few runs, most of the male pilots looked at the women with new respect. But there were a few—George dodged them—who took the opportunity of time alone in a cockpit with a woman to "accidentally" brush a hand across her breasts, her thighs. These men soon had their favorites among the WASPs—women George assumed didn't thwart their advances, women who now drank with the male pilots at the O Club. "Hey," said Diana Rasmussen when Susan Patterson sneered at her one day, "I'm the one flying the A-26. I'm getting more target-towing missions than you are. And I'm not sleeping with anyone to do it either."

"I don't believe that for one minute," Vivian said. Neither did George.

George's final training flight was with Simpson. Simpson wasn't handsy, just stingy about sharing the controls. Conditions were choppy, and during the worst patches of turbulence, her flying had elicited appreciative grunts from Simpson. She'd executed a flawless landing. The next time she flew, she'd be in charge of the ship.

She was ready. She'd done her night training with the Ack Acks firing up at her, diving low into "enemy" fire, live shells whistling inches from her aircraft.

As she entered the hangar, she heard, "I'm married, for God's sake!" It was Patterson, red-faced with rage, hissing at an amused O'Leary.

"Me too, sweetheart. You wanna fly today or not?"

Patterson only needed one more training run too. Unfortunately, she'd been assigned O'Leary: very handsy, but happy to share the controls. For a price.

George whirled around and said, "Hey, Simpson, Patterson needs her last training run. Why don't you take it?"

O'Leary's amusement turned to fury. "I'm the one on the roster."

"Yeah, but she doesn't want to fly with you. And we all know why."

Simpson looked from Patterson to O'Leary, his reluctance to take Patterson up vacillating with his evident dislike of O'Leary.

"I never laid a hand," insisted O'Leary. "Whiny little bitches."

Simpson turned and began walking back to the airstrip. "Well," he called over his shoulder to Patterson, "are you coming?"

"Liar!" O'Leary shouted after them. "Whatever she says to you, she's a liar!" And then to George: "All of you are just a bunch of whiny, lying, little . . ." But George had already walked away.

Still shaky with adrenaline, she entered the barracks in no mood to deal with Mrs. Mellon. The housemother had planted herself in the doorway, like a spider waiting for a particularly delicious fly.

"Oh, Georgeanne, dear . . ."

"Hello, Mrs. Mellon. Goodbye, Mrs. Mellon. Have to be somewhere." She and Vivian had planned to spend the rest of the day at the beach, but George wanted to shave her legs first. She loved the ocean. The breeze cut the humidity and kept the mosquitoes at bay. The crashing waves drowned out their conversation, which meant they could talk freely there, away from the barracks and Mrs. Mellon.

"Yes, dear. You do. Just not where you think you have to be." Mrs. Mellon sounded even more melodramatic than usual. "Oh, you poor girl. Your father . . ."

She knew as soon as she heard the word "father." She shivered, suddenly ice cold.

"Sit down, dear," said Mrs. Mellon. "You're in shock, naturally. Sit down right here."

George lowered her trembling body onto a chair. *I should be crying,* she thought. *Why aren't I crying?* Mrs. Mellon pulled her close, clasped George to her damp, un-air-conditioned bosom until the shivering subsided and George managed to say, "My mother. Did my mother call?"

"No, dear. Someone else. Let me think . . . Helen. Yes, that was her name."

George hadn't gone home. And now her father was dead and her mother was alone. No, not alone. Helen was there. Capable, competent Helen, making the necessary phone calls. George's tears came at last. She leaned into Mrs. Mellon's softness and cried and let herself be held.

George waited for nearly an hour before the CO would see her. An hour of pacing and trying to think of anything to keep her tears from starting up again. She had expected him to belittle her for requesting bereavement leave, to say something about women not taking their service obligations seriously. But he brightened as she spoke.

"Request granted, Miss Ector. Go. Stay as long as you feel you need to. Still have a mother? Then she'll need you. Consider that before you come back. Sullivan!"

Col. Stephenson's aide trotted in. "Sir?"

"Miss Ector requires unlimited bereavement leave. Take care of the paperwork."

"Unlimited, sir?"

"That's what I said. Unlimited for her and any lady pilot friend she wants to bring along. Take two or three, Miss Ector. Hell, take the whole bunch."

A wave of heat rose in her. She tried to keep the quaver out of her voice when she requested a plane.

Col. Stephenson snorted. "Denied. And dismissed."

"Maybe it's for the best," Vivian told her later. "I'm not sure those old things would make it to Oklahoma."

"I guess I'll get the train out of Wilmington."

"Let's talk to Quigley. He'll get someone to fly you. Us. I'll go with you, George."

"No, Vivvy. You stay here. I don't want to give that man the satisfaction of taking any more of you away."

Quigley knew just the pilot to fly Georgeanne to Enid. "Tom Rutledge. He's heading back to Walker today. He can make a stop at Vance."

Georgeanne braced herself for Tom Rutledge to resent the tear-streaked female cargo foisted upon him, but as she approached the plane, he held out his hand. "You must be Ector. I'm Rutledge. I'm real sorry to hear about your father."

Once they were airborne, he said, "Those A-24s sure have seen better days." George explained that they were mostly planes that had been retired from the South Pacific because they weren't fit for actual combat. The tires were worn, the instruments faulty. "They fill them with ninety octane instead of one hundred," said George. "Which means the carburetors are always watery." She didn't mention that some of the WASPs suspected male pilots of sabotaging their planes, and that the mechanics—not Quigley, of course—saved the best spare parts for the ships flown by men.

Instead, she asked Rutledge what he liked to fly. And he asked her the same. They talked about Oklahoma, and Kansas, where he was from. "Hoping to pop in and see the folks before I fly out tomorrow."

"Oh, I'm keeping you away from your family. I wish you'd said no when Quigley asked you to take me."

"I don't." His eyes sparkled as he grinned at her.

After they landed, he walked her to the hangar. "Will someone come get you? How will you get home?"

George teared up again at the mention of home. How could she have allowed this sandy-haired man and his sparkling eyes to distract her? "You're off duty now. Go home to your folks. I can fend for myself."

"I don't doubt it," said Tom. "That's just my natural chivalry kicking in. I'd tell you to have a good visit home, but you won't, under the circumstances."

"It was good of you to bring me," said George. "Thank you. There's my friend, Helen, to pick me up."

"Good, I'm glad you've got a ride."

"Yes, well. Goodbye." But George didn't move toward Helen's car.

"Goodbye, Georgeanne." He stepped back, then stopped. "This isn't the appropriate time to ask this, but I'm going to ask it anyway."

"So much for natural chivalry," said George.

"Right. Screw chivalry. Once you're back at Camp Davis, once you're . . . settled, could I give you a call? Fly in sometime?"

Helen leaned on her horn. George said, "Maybe I'll fly to you instead."

It bordered on obscene the way Helen's belly pressed against the steering wheel. "Look at me," said Helen. "Another week and I won't be able to reach the pedals. Oh, George, I'm so sorry about your dad. He was a good man."

She'd been thinking about Tom Rutledge, how handsome he looked in his flight suit, how well he handled the controls, and how he said he'd call her. Because this was so much easier than thinking of her mother waiting for her, alone, without George's father. And then, seeing Helen—more to the point, seeing Helen's belly press against the steering wheel—George thought only of Frank Bridlemile and the nights before he bused off to basic, before she went to Avenger Field. "Helen, what happened?"

"What do you mean? You do know about the birds and the bees, don't you?"

"Is it Frank's?"

"Georgeanne Ector! What do you take me for? Of course it's Frank's. I went out to San Diego to meet him before he shipped out, and we got married. I wrote you all about it, but I guess you never get my letters. We wanted to keep it quiet till he got home, then maybe have a small reception or something, but, well, we got lucky right off the bat."

"Congratulations," said George.

"Huh. You don't sound happy for me at all."

"Oh, I am, Helen, of course I am. I'm just surprised, that's all. My mother never mentioned it either."

Helen gunned the engine. "Sometimes a woman likes to have a secret or two. Don't you agree?"

They didn't say much the rest of the ride. George hurried out of the car when they finally reached her house.

"No one," said Adele, arching her brows, "is discussing it." She meant Helen's pregnancy. "Supposedly they're married."

"Knowing Helen, I'm sure they are."

"You can't be sure of anything these days, except that people make terrible decisions when they think their lives are at stake."

"Well," said Adele, when it was all over, "no one can say we did that wrong." Which was, George realized, the goal in places like Enid—not necessarily to do things right, but, no matter the cost, to avoid doing them wrong. The visitation and service had gone well. The covered dishes and floral arrangements had been logged in the book provided by the funeral home. Adele and George had dressed and comported themselves in the fashion expected of them. They had appeared sad but hadn't allowed themselves to collapse into open, unseemly grief. When the rites of Charles Ector's passing had concluded, mother and daughter had opened a box of black-edged Crane's and tackled the thank-you notes, which took three days. Charles had been widely well regarded.

After she signed her name to the final one—to Helen's family for a majestic wreath of lilies and blazing star—George said to her mother, "Maybe I should stay."

"Nonsense, Georgeanne. You've got a job to do, and everyone needs you to do it."

Her mother looked gaunt, pale. At meals she ate just enough that George couldn't claim she wasn't eating. But she certainly wasn't getting enough. She insisted she was sleeping well, but the creaking floorboards told George she paced all night. "But, Mother, you—"

"Don't 'But, Mother' me. I will not have you in this house, shirking your duty to your country. I'm not my usual self, I admit it. But I'll get past it. Clemsons always get past things. You will, too, if you just keep getting up every day and doing your job."

CHAPTER 14

After her father's funeral, George wrote letters every day. Vivian assumed they were all to Adele until one Saturday, a dreamy-eyed George introduced her to Tom Rutledge. He was tall and golden haired. He and George gleamed in the autumn sun. On her off days, George flew to him. On his off days, he flew to her.

Vivian found herself at loose ends. If she kept to the barracks, Mrs. Mellon buzzed around her like a perfumed gnat. At the airfield, O'Leary was always in her path, taking any opportunity for a grope.

She spent her free time with Quigley and Elliot, mostly at the Knotty Pine, where the drinks weren't watered down. Vivian found that she enjoyed a strong drink very much. One drink and she was as beautiful as George. And just as good a pilot. "You *are* just as good a pilot," said Quigley. Two drinks and she hardly thought of George's absence.

"You should get yourself a fella," said Elliot.

Like George, thought Vivian. *Like beautiful, perfect George.* "Hah," she scoffed. "I don't exactly see a lot of prime candidates."

"Oh, I don't know," said Elliot. "A few of them aren't so bad." She and Quigley smiled dopily at one another, and Vivian ordered another round. Three drinks and Quigley and Elliot's flirting became nothing to her.

She took Elliot aside to remind her that Quigley had a fiancée.

Elliot laughed. "So? She isn't here, and he never talks about her. Don't worry about me, Shaw. I can take care of myself."

Sirens blared. Vivian rushed out of the barracks, the other women close behind her. A plume of oily smoke billowed up from the swamp south of camp. The pilots frantically accounted for one another—who was flying that afternoon?—until only Susan Patterson's whereabouts remained unknown. She'd been on a routine tracking flight. Vivian was shocked—in the secret and not-so-secret rankings they each kept, all agreed that Patterson was one of the best of them. Had been one of the best of them.

"Stephenson's saying pilot error," Elliot reported a few days later, her face twisted in disgust and anger.

Quigley, who'd been ordered away from inspecting the crumpled remains of the plane, looked gray and ill at ease. Vivian could get nothing out of him beyond, "She was a good person and a good pilot, and it's a damn shame is all I can say."

Vivian pressed for more—a persistent rumor about sugar in the gas tank had taken on an aura of truth—but Quigley kept mum. Someone must have talked to Cochran, though. She flew in with her own mechanics to investigate. While she was there, Vivian and the other women jostled for flying assignments, hoping for a chance to show Cochran how good they were. But Cochran never once looked up at the sky. The women got nothing from her—no pats on the back (*For what?* Cochran would have said. *For doing what's expected of you? Grow up, ladies.*), no questions regarding Patterson's abilities (assumed to have been exceptional), and not a single word on the results of the investigation.

George took up a collection—Vivian suspected most of the money came from her own pocket—for a coffin and train fare to Susan's hometown in Ohio. "I can't bear another funeral right now, Vivvy," she said. "Can you go?" *Couldn't bear a funeral or couldn't bear to be apart from Tom?* wondered Vivian. But she pressed her uniform, polished her pumps, and went.

Susan's mother was as dimpled and serious as Susan had been. Her father was ashen, his grip, when he shook Vivian's hand, trembling.

"Thank you for coming, Shaw," said Don Patterson. He looked ten years older than he had in Sweetwater. "I'm glad they sent you and not someone I don't know."

Vivian hadn't thought of that, but maybe George had. Maybe she wasn't as distracted by Tom as she seemed.

"Susan wrote me about Camp Davis. It's an outrage what you girls have had to put up with."

"Cochran came down," said Vivian. "They're investigating."

Patterson clutched her arm. "Listen, Shaw. I don't want this happening to any of the rest of you. Check your plane over three times before you go up. If anything looks off—even the slightest bit—stay on the ground."

Vivian returned to find O'Leary had been transferred.

"They claim it's unrelated to the incident," said Elliot.

"Quit calling it an incident," said Vivian. "She *died.*"

The transfer did nothing to mitigate the dark cloud of suspicion hanging over the airfield. *Had O'Leary tampered with Patterson's gas tank?* wondered the women. *Had O'Leary been framed?* wondered the men. As the weeks passed, the beach grew chilly, too chilly for walking. Not that it mattered, as George was rarely around to walk with. She spent her free time on R&R runs to meet Tom.

Vivian supposed she could have signed out a plane too. And flown . . . where? Ethel Blankenship was based in California, and there was no way she'd be allowed to take a plane that far. Home? Who in Hahira would want to see her? Elizabeth might make a show of welcoming her, but

Vivian knew she was more of an embarrassment—*Such an unusual girl,* Aunt Clelia would say—than a source of pride to her family.

Then one Saturday morning, rather than pressing a blouse and putting on lipstick, George threw on an old sweater and asked Vivian to walk on the beach with her.

"Aren't you off to meet Tom?" asked Vivian, unable to keep a tinge of hurt out of her voice.

"No, not today. I'm sorry, Vivvy. You must feel like I've abandoned you."

Vivian waited for the but. But we're in love. But you just don't understand. All the buts girls with boyfriends deployed when talking to girls without boyfriends.

"Well, I did abandon you. And I really am sorry. For what it's worth, I've really missed you."

She and Tom are through, thought Vivian, *and now she needs me again.* The sky and ocean were gray. February rain threatened. Waves roared past the tide line. It was far from a pleasant day for a walk on the beach, but Vivian was glad to be there, walking with her friend. She could feel George gathering herself to share her sad news. *I will be sympathetic,* thought Vivian. *I'll comfort and commiserate and be a good friend to her.*

"Vivian," started George, and Vivian arranged her face in an expression of care and concern. But George smiled her broad, sunny smile, sharing happy news, not sad. "We're going to do it here. At the O Club. I'm opening up the bar for the night—finally a good use for my Ector money. Will you be my maid of honor?"

How could Vivian not smile back and say, "Of course, George. You know I will."

They made a golden couple. George's eyes. Tom's hair. It was the flying. It had burnished all of them, thought Vivian. Made even the plainest among them beautiful and confident and strong. She felt somewhat golden herself.

The music was loud and the drinks, for once, were strong, and everyone was having a fine time guzzling George's Ector money. Even Mrs. Mellon was on her third drink and reminiscing about her days at Newcomb. "Sherry at five sharp on Fridays in the Kappa sitting room." Vivian slipped past just as she began extolling the virtues of *those Tulane boys.*

Elliot grabbed Vivian by the elbow. "Did you hear?"

"What?" Vivian kept her eyes on her destination: the bar.

"General Arnold wants to commission us."

"What?!"

"You know, make us official. Bring us into the actual USAAF."

"You really think so?" asked Vivian. Elliot tended to blurt out whatever she was thinking at any given moment, without much regard for whether it was true. And after the response to their presence at Camp Davis, Vivian doubted many of the brass would agree with General Arnold about commissioning women.

"Why not? Look, not every place is like this. I know girls who transferred to Liberty and girls out in California who say they don't have to deal with this stuff."

Quigley asked Elliot to dance. Other girls coupled off, dancing with pilots and Ack Ack guys. Vivian danced too. She felt loose and warm and easy in her body in a way she rarely did. For once, the atmosphere in the Officers' Club felt welcoming. She danced with one pilot and then another, and then heard a long-forgotten voice say, "Vivian."

It was Durham. In dress blues, captain's bars on his shoulders. He'd come far since their barnstorming days. They shook hands. Vivian, remembering how he'd pushed her in that hotel hallway, felt some of the looseness and warmth seep out of her at his touch. She asked the questions they all asked the men. "When are you shipping out? Where?"

"Two days. With Tom. Wherever they send us. So you're one of those fly girls."

"Yep."

"Huh."

Get used to us, she thought. *We're about to be serving in the same Army Air Force as you.*

George danced over to them, beaming, lightening Durham's scowl. "Who's your friend, Shaw?" She introduced Durham, who—Vivian wouldn't have guessed he had it in him—beamed back at George. "Tom's a great guy," he said. "And a great pilot. Congratulations." Even Vivian knew you weren't supposed to say "Congratulations." You were supposed to say "Best wishes." Why this was, she had no idea, but she liked knowing that Durham had gotten it wrong.

Tom joined them and made everyone laugh by ordering Durham to "stop consorting with my wife." Then he and George twirled away to the dance floor.

"What do you hear from Louis?" Vivian asked.

"You left him cold. What do you care?"

"He was ready for me to go, I'm pretty sure. I doubt he complained about it." *I know* you *didn't,* she didn't say.

As if he hadn't heard her, Durham went on. "I know about girls like you. Use men for what you want. Dump them when you've gotten it."

She couldn't deny the truth of this. She had used Louis—would have used any man in that moment—to learn how to fly. But it wasn't as if she hadn't cared for him. He was kind. He was fun. He'd been a good teacher in the air and in bed. And they'd been careful—she hadn't gotten in trouble, hadn't tied him down. He was probably relieved to find her gone. Angry about the cashbox and his lighter, perhaps, but she doubted she'd left him lonesome and pining. But here was Durham, seemingly angry at her departure, angry at how she'd hurt his friend. Had she been wrong all along? Had Louis cared more for her than she realized? Had she hurt a good man?

A good man who was somewhere overseas now. Flying bombers or fighters. Flying the same planes she'd flown, but flying them in a hail of ack-ack, dodging enemy planes. Did he think of her still? As the girl who'd left him cold?

"What's he flying these days?" she asked. You couldn't ask where they were stationed, not exactly, but sometimes you could guess by what they were flying. An F4F Wildcat would mean he was Navy. Launching off aircraft carriers. Threatened by Zeros. A P-51 Mustang might mean long legs to the Ruhr and back to Britain, hoping for cloud cover, hoping to drop payload before the German Luftwaffe caught up with him.

"Nothing."

That was ridiculous. If she knew anything about Louis, it was that he'd always fly. The only thing that could stop him was . . . "Oh," she whispered.

"Yeah. Oh."

"I didn't know," she said. "I'm sorry."

"Yeah, well, why would you know? Not like you bothered to keep in touch, right? Not like you needed anything else from him. And now you can play pretend, in your cute little uniform, up in the sky here at home, where it's nice and safe."

She could have told Durham about the ack-ack that caught the tail of her plane one night. She could have told him about the list they kept by the barracks phone of men to avoid. But he was right: it didn't compare, in the end.

"Don't hog the pretty ones for yourself, champ!" Another pilot—you could always tell: they swaggered even when standing still—reached past Durham to introduce himself to Vivian. What a relief to turn her back on Durham's scorn.

Taken on its own, her rescuer's face was farm-boy plain. He could have grown up down the road from Vivian. But his milk-fed confidence and grin made him handsome. He had something of George and Tom's golden glow about him.

He danced wonderfully. Vivian, never very graceful on the dance floor, felt light and beautiful moving with him. They talked of planes and the latest newsreels and how well George and Tom suited one another. The dancing and the talking made them thirsty, so they returned frequently to the bar. They talked about the beach. He'd love to see it sometime, he said. Maybe he could fly back in one weekend to see the ocean. And her. Vivian couldn't remember feeling so happy.

She drank and she danced and drank some more, and when George and Tom left the Officers' Club in a flurry of confetti, Vivian leaned against the pilot to stay upright. She leaned against him as he walked her to the barracks, deserted because the party at the club would continue until nearly dawn. She leaned against him to make it to her room, thanked him for a lovely evening, and then fell into bed and gratefully passed out.

When she woke, her first fear was not of the man and what he was doing to her. Her first fear was of someone else finding out and telling Cochran. Of being sent home. Of no longer being allowed to do her favorite thing in the world. Then she came to herself a little more. The pilot's weight pinned her to the bed. She pushed at him. Tried to roll out from under him. He punched her in the side of her ribs. The pain was paralyzing.

She should scream. No, if she screamed, they would come. They would see. They would throw her out. She would lose everything. *I'll tell Louis,* she thought. *Louis won't stand for this.* Then the pilot gave a triumphant grunt, and she remembered that Louis was dead.

Released from his weight, Vivian levered herself up off the mattress. Her head spun, her throat tasted sour. She barely had time to lean over the side of the bunk before she heaved. The contents of her stomach spattered over the plank floor. The pilot, buckling his belt, gagged. He pulled on his boots, grabbed his cap.

Then he was gone.

Two days after the wedding, Tom shipped out. "We knew it was coming," said George. "That's why the hurry to get married, though everyone probably thinks it was something else."

Vivian mustered some sort of reply. She should have been thrilled to have George back, to no longer be Quigley and Elliot's third wheel. But she felt better when George wasn't around. Then she didn't have to plunder her brain for the appropriate responses to whatever George said. She didn't have to come up with anything of her own to add to the conversation. The only moments she felt any peace were when she was flying, up away from people, distant from anything that could harm her.

But Quigley didn't want her in the air. "When was the last time you slept, Shaw? You look wrecked."

"Thanks," said Vivian. "That's just what every girl wants to hear."

"I'm serious. I can't let you up in one of these planes if you're not sleeping. Get yourself checked out by the flight surgeon. If he signs off, then up you go."

But Vivian had no intention of subjecting herself to any sort of medical exam. She knew Quigley was right—without sleep, she was unfit to fly, so she tried to sleep. She tried with earplugs from one of the Ack Ack guys, with an eye mask Helen had sent to George, and with far too much whiskey. On good nights she achieved a veneer of slumber—a tempting toe-in-the-water-of-sleep illusion of rest. Her eyes were closed. She was horizontal. At times, even dreaming. But her mind and body remained alert, vigilant. She despaired that she'd never be allowed to fly again.

Then Col. Stephenson convened the WASPs for a meeting. "Good news, ladies," he gloated. "You're all rotating out of Camp Davis." Half of them, including Vivian, would go to Liberty Field in Georgia, and the other half, including George, to Otis Field in Massachusetts.

George was distraught. "They can't separate us!"

"They can do whatever they want," said Vivian. She didn't have it in her to pretend to be sad. The truth was, she couldn't wait to go. To no longer be the shadow dodging George's relentless sun. To no longer enthuse over the arrival of letters from Tom.

"Vivian, are you okay?"

She was far from okay. But how could she explain the why of it to George? Where did the why of it even start? With herself, she concluded. She was a terrible judge of men. First Bobby Broussard, who just wanted sex. Then Louis, who must have found her lacking or he wouldn't have run around with all those other girls. Now this milk-fed pilot, the one she'd thought might be her Tom. Someone who would take her dancing, talk planes with her. But instead he'd—no, she refused to relive it.

Each of these men had detected something in her. Probably everyone else did too. Some damage she couldn't remedy. Her mother must have seen it the day Vivian was born. That she would never be quite right. She would never have—never deserve—what George had.

When she and George hugged goodbye, they both had tears in their eyes. Vivian hoped George couldn't tell that hers were tears of relief.

She'd ferry planes once she got to Liberty Field, and the USAAF saw no reason why she shouldn't begin immediately. They shuttled her to Ohio to pick up an A-24.

In the ready room at Wright Field, she smoothed her uniform. Jacqueline Cochran had recently outfitted them in what they called their Santiago Blues—a real uniform reflecting the real work they did, reflecting the promise that one day soon they'd be official members of the US Armed Forces. She found a metal folding chair, leaned her head against the wall, and closed her eyes. She'd be flying solo for the first time in weeks, with no Quigley to prevent her. She ought to get some rest first.

Probably the pilots who entered the ready room thought she was asleep. And once they started talking, whispering loudly to one another, she was afraid to open her eyes and catch them out.

"What do we have here?" asked the first.

"Looks like some victory girl got lost," said the second.

"Nah, that's that new WASP uniform. She must be a pilot."

"WASP, victory girl, doesn't matter. Once they take off the uniform."

"Not exactly heavy lifting, getting them out of their uniforms."

"Yeah, you hear about those WAACs they sent home from Africa?"

"Hey now, they were just serving their country. By servicing their countrymen." The joke reduced them to spasms of laughter.

"Looks like some of our countrymen wore this one out." Vivian, panicking, heard his boots approaching.

"Wouldn't touch her if I were you. Those girls are crawling with VD."

The boots retreated. The voices faded as the pilots walked away. "Such a shame," she heard. "I mean, they can't go back home afterward—not where I come from anyway." As they moved off, she caught the word "unwanted." She caught "no sister of mine."

She waited a few minutes and then cautiously opened her eyes. She'd heard all of it before and plenty more like it at Camp Davis. Except for the last bit, the bit about not being able to go home again. The word "unwanted" rang in the empty ready room. She was already unwanted at home. And if what she feared was true, she'd be doubly unwanted.

When she finally took off, lifting up away from Ohio, away from men who believed her diseased in body, soul, and mind, her gorge rose with the plane. Another sign—because she never suffered motion sickness—that there was something wrong with her body.

The CO at Liberty Field welcomed Vivian and the other transferred WASP pilots. The male pilots didn't seem bothered at all by sharing flight time. Some of the WASPs experimented with flying drones. Vivian and the rest mostly ferried planes. The ferrying meant she never had to stay in one spot too long; she could always plead the need for rest or an impending assignment to escape socializing.

George wrote Vivian regularly from Otis Field. Her letters were vague—George clearly didn't want the censors catching on to her predicament. But Vivian knew what she was driving at.

> I've never been so glad to be tall. I'm filling out around the middle—must be all that good Army food. Or something . . .

Vivian attempted several responses:

> I'm filling out around the middle myself. Because of something.

> So happy for your good news. I have similar news that you will find surprising. I know I did.

> What's done is done, and can't be helped, and I've decided to make the best of it.

She set a match to each of these letters. When the housemother yelled out that she had a phone call, "Long distance!" she hid in the john until the caller—it could only have been George—gave up.

Whenever her sister Elizabeth was pregnant, everyone coddled her, insisted that she take it easy. As if the womb were a precarious place, all too easily abandoned by its inhabitant.

Vivian did the opposite of taking it easy. She signed up for every flight possible. She took brisk walks in all weather. She swam in freezing ponds. She ate spicy peppers. Her inhabitant fluttered but held. Her belly swelled against her waistband. Every town had a woman who might help with "female troubles," but finding her meant admitting to having such troubles. An admission that would get her kicked out of the WASP if it reached her CO.

By October, the worst of the heat had passed. In the cooler weather, no one found it odd that she wore her flight jacket all the time. The jacket provided extra camouflage for what Vivian knew she couldn't camouflage much longer.

When the news came down that the WASP, despite the lobbying efforts of General Arnold and Jacqueline Cochran, would be deactivated in December, all Vivian wanted to do was talk to George.

Once the line for the barracks phone dwindled—one morose woman after another calling someone to say she'd be home soon—Vivian put the receiver to her own ear. "Otis Field," she said to the operator. The line clicked and buzzed, and as she waited, Vivian passed a hand over the swell of her abdomen. It was inadvertent, this maternal gesture. She found herself making it several times a day. If others were nearby, she quickly returned her hand to her side. If she was alone, she sometimes allowed her hand to linger there and tried to quell the revulsion she felt at what was happening—at what *had* happened—to her body. She always failed. She was as ashamed of this revulsion as she was by her condition. She didn't see how anyone, even George, could ever understand. By the time the operator said, "I have Otis Field for you," Vivian had hung up. A few days later there was a letter from George.

> Dear Vivian, what on earth is going on? This silence of yours is alarming. It's been months! Are you angry with me? Have you broken your right arm? Write me. Call me. Fly up here. But don't sit down there in Georgia making me wonder if you're grounded, or if you've gone home, or . . . worse. My CO won't let me near the planes anymore. I couldn't hide it any longer. Now that they've scuttled us, I'm keeping out of his way, but I'm guessing I've got about two weeks left before I'm out. So if I don't hear from you in a week, I'm taking a plane and flying down there, come hell or high water. What have I got to lose?

Vivian kept her hands firmly at her sides as she marched out to the hangar. She signed out an A-24 on the log sheet. "Are the tanks full?" she asked the mechanic.

"Yep. Going far today?"

"Yep," said Vivian. Officially, she was going as far as Washington, to deliver the latest reports on the drone research program. Then she was supposed to turn around and fly straight back to Liberty. They would be furious when she didn't show up. They would be more so when they learned she'd flown on to Otis Field. But, as George wrote, what did she have to lose? What could they do? Throw her out of a program they were shutting down?

"You're a long way from home," said the airman who took charge of the plane after Vivian landed at Otis. She shrugged and asked if he knew where she could find Georgeanne Ector.

"Ector?"

"I mean Rutledge." How long, she wondered, would it take for George's new name to stick in her head?

"Should have guessed. You her sister?"

"Well," he said as Vivian shook her head, "you might as well be. She's over at HQ. Filing, she says. But most days she stops by, says hello, tries to sweet-talk me into letting her take just a little bitty flight." He leaned toward Vivian and confided, "And I would, but the CO'd have my hide. Yours must not be so strict down at Liberty, letting you fly all the way up here in your condition."

This, along with George's startled blink when Vivian appeared before her, confirmed that, flight jacket or no, Vivian wasn't hiding anything from anyone.

Later, after they'd found a relatively private bench behind the exchange, and Vivian had explained, and they had dried their eyes, George said, "I remember him. He seemed like a nice man . . ."

This, Vivian thought, more than money, more than upbringing, was the primary difference between George and herself. George's life had been full of nice men.

CHAPTER 15

George hadn't flown in almost a month. Her CO never let his gaze fall below her neck, but he wouldn't let her anywhere near a plane. He cooked up desk work for her. Which, seeing as she couldn't type, meant sorting and filing the endless forms and memoranda the military spawned.

"He's a nice man," George wrote to Vivian. "I just wish he'd let me fly again. Maybe when the situation changes . . ." She didn't specify what the situation was. The censors read everything, and she didn't want anyone confirming what her CO must have already suspected. The longer she could stay a WASP, the stronger the possibility of a commission, of being able to fly once women were integrated into the USAAF.

It was a short-lived hope. When she learned that the WASP would be dissolved, that piloting jobs would be reserved for the men coming home from overseas, she wished she and Vivian were hearing it together. Months earlier, she'd felt relief when they parted ways. Vivian barely spoke to her anymore, barely even looked at her. Some friend, George had thought, turning on her just because she'd gotten married. After a few weeks of silence between Otis and Liberty, George decided to be the bigger person and send the first letter. Vivian hadn't responded. Not to that letter or any of the others that followed.

Serves me right, thought George after another fruitless mail call, thinking of Helen's letters piling up in her footlocker. She pulled out a fresh piece of stationery. "Dear Helen," she wrote. "I hope you and Frank Jr. are well. He might have a new little friend soon."

She filled a page with innocuous details about Otis Field, sealed it in an envelope, and walked across base to the mail room. She slowed as she passed the airfield. She couldn't fly, but she could still look at the planes. A tall woman in Santiago Blues—unmistakably a WASP—strode toward her. George hurried forward. It couldn't be. It was!

Her mirror image. Still mirroring her in every way. George put a hand to her own belly. Vivian did the same and then began to cry. Helen's letter fell to the ground. George wrapped her arms around her friend and did not let go for a long time.

After Vivian's renegade visit, George phoned her at Liberty at least twice a week. They didn't talk about the disbandment. Instead, they discussed the problem of Vivian's pregnancy.

"I can't bring it to Hahira," Vivian said. "They don't want me there as it is. Not that I even intend to go home."

"Not," she whispered so softly that George could barely hear her, "that I want to bring it anywhere."

George's eyes filled with tears as Vivian continued. "I don't think I can touch it. I don't think I can look at it. What am I going to do?"

She wouldn't hear of adoption. "A stranger? Would they love it? Could they?"

"Of course they could," said George. "I could."

"Could you? Really?"

"Yes," said George, the germ of a solution sprouting as she said it. "Vivian, I *know* I could. *Yes!*"

Another call, two weeks later: "Quigley has a cousin," Vivian whispered. "In New York. He's 4-F and works in the records office. It wouldn't be cheap, though."

"I've always wanted to go to New York," George said to Vivian.

"I've always wanted to go to New York," George said in her weekly call to Adele.

"I assumed you'd come home to have the baby, with Tom overseas and all." Every phone call with her mother devolved into the same conversation. George needed to come home. The sooner, the better. Why, now that the WASP had disbanded, was she still at Otis?

"Because they could change their minds," said George. "And you didn't raise me to be a quitter."

George needed the best possible care. She needed rest. Her mother's voice quavered with worry.

"The hospitals in New York are excellent, Mother. And I'll have Vivian with me. To help out."

CHAPTER 16

When George called to say she was getting married, Adele wondered if Frank Bridlemile had slipped the leashes of both the US Army and Helen. But it was that Tom fellow George had started seeing after Charles's funeral. A boy Adele had never even met.

"He's shipping out," said George.

Adele bit her tongue to keep from saying they should wait. She bit her tongue about them holding the wedding in North Carolina. She hid her hurt that George had flown so far from home, that she hadn't asked her mother to attend her wedding.

And now George was whispering on the phone from Otis Field, telling Adele she had big news. Hinting four different ways at pregnancy without ever actually saying the word expecting.

In an instant, Adele was standing in the rain, watching Pauline's casket disappear into a muddy hole. "Come home, Georgeanne. Come home right now," she urged.

"Nonsense, Mother. They'll kick me out if I do. I won't be commissioned."

Who cares? thought Adele. She wanted her daughter home where she could take care of her, protect her.

"I've never felt better. Not a bit ill, morning or night," said George. As if morning sickness were the worst of it.

When George told her they were disbanding the WASP, Adele tried again. But George stubbornly insisted on staying at Otis. If she believed they'd change their minds and give the few flying jobs that remained to women, she was delusional.

Then she went and moved to New York City with Vivian Shaw.

Adele spent a fortune on phone calls. She wrote letter after letter. Georgeanne, once such a malleable child, refused to listen to reason. "I'll come to you, then," said Adele.

"No!" The ferocity, the finality, of it brought Adele to tears.

"I mean," George continued, her voice calmer, "I'm fine. I'm healthy. I feel good. Barely even tired. And Vivian's with me. I'll come to you as soon as they're born, as soon as we can travel. That's when I'll need the help."

"They?"

A long pause before George spoke again. "Twins. The doctor says it's twins."

In the garage, Adele hurled every wrench and screwdriver, every pair of pliers, against the wall. Her face was wet with tears and snot. Twins meant twice the danger, she was sure of that. Her daughter was blind. Worse, her daughter didn't want her.

Panting hard, she collected the tools, one by one, and returned them to their rightful places. Then she did the only thing she could think of to help herself feel better: lifted the hood of Charles's car and began to disassemble the engine.

CHAPTER 17

Cochran summoned Vivian to DC. Vivian's CO had grounded her for her unauthorized flight to Otis Field, so she arrived as a passenger in someone else's plane. She could no longer button her uniform pants, so she'd purchased an enormous pair of slacks and attempted to take them in everywhere but the waist. The housemother took pity on Vivian's negligible sewing skills and stepped in to help. "Well, we've done our best," said the housemother, frowning at the crooked seams. "Press them and hope."

But Vivian knew better than to hope. Her only consolation for the discharge that she would surely receive was that the WASP was disbanding. Because Cochran would never have taken her into it, not now.

The housemother's frown was nothing compared to Cochran's when Vivian was ushered into her office.

"I don't know why I bothered to have them bring you up, Shaw," said Cochran. "When I could have just sent a telegram demobbing you."

Vivian, remembering when Cochran had let her north Florida accent slip in their first meeting, thought she might know why.

"I apologize for letting you down, ma'am. There were . . . extenuating circumstances."

"You're here, so you may as well explain yourself."

"There was nothing about this," she said, gesturing at her belly, "that I wanted or encouraged. Nothing."

Cochran tilted her head as if asking a question, and Vivian used every ounce of her willpower to keep from hanging her own head in answer to it.

"And did you somehow think that just because you are in the service of your country, the laws of your country no longer applied? Did you not avail yourself of the law, Miss Shaw?"

"It would have been my word against his."

"You haven't answered me. Did you not avail yourself of the law?"

"The same law that didn't apply to Susan Patterson? That law?"

They sat regarding each other for a long moment, and then Cochran said, "There will be a ceremony on December seventh. General Arnold will speak. The WASP will march together one final time. You will not be present. You will not be within fifty miles of Avenger Field. Do you understand?"

Vivian nodded.

"Until that day, you will serve on desk duty only in whatever capacity they can find for you at Liberty Field."

Vivian said nothing.

"Or, if you prefer, I could discharge you immediately."

"I'll take the desk duty," she whispered. Even if she couldn't fly, she needed to eat. She needed the paycheck.

"Speak up, Shaw."

"I'll take the desk duty, ma'am."

Cochran closed her file. "Dismissed."

In Manhattan, Quigley's cousin found them an apartment. George bought Vivian a brass ring. Now they looked like two war wives waiting for their husbands to return. The brass ring was just the beginning. George traipsed all over the city, her ankles as slender as ever, buying diapers, cotton blankets, glass bottles, a sterilizer, a double pram. Every purchase displayed for Vivian's approval and appreciation. She forced herself to smile, to say how sweet, how perfect.

But all she could think was, how long until it was over. How long until it was out of her and in George's arms, swaddled in George's blankets. How long until she could go.

She was grateful to George. She loved George. But she couldn't wait to put miles of distance between them. She felt trapped by the lack of sky in New York. And by her lumbering slowness, the constant kicking and turning of the child inside her. By the doctor who put his cold stethoscope to her heart and then to her stomach and cheerily told her she was shipshape.

She hated the liquid that gushed from her, puddling around her shoes. The cabbie who said, "Hang on, sweetheart, almost there." George squeezing her hand and whispering that everything would be just fine.

Her cheerful doctor put her under for the birth—a mercy that made Vivian hate him less. When she woke, the nurse wheeled the baby in and offered it to her. Vivian reluctantly accepted it. Its eyes were closed. She closed hers too. Then she handed it back to the nurse.

"Don't worry," said the nurse. "Once you get to know each other, you'll be just fine."

"I'll take her." George entered the room, her step graceful and easy, despite her enormous belly. "Oh, hello, sweetheart." She sniffed the baby's head, opened the blanket and inspected its tiny fingers and toes. "Vivian. She's beautiful. What's her name?"

Vivian pled fatigue to stay in the hospital as long as possible. The nurses tended to the baby. She lay in her bed, ignoring her aching breasts. Her fingers flicked Louis's lighter open and closed while her mind flicked through potential destinations. She couldn't stay in New York. She didn't want to be around other WASPs, who would wonder why she hadn't attended the final ceremony in Sweetwater. If she'd washed out like Fontana back in training, she could have been spared so much. Hmm. She wondered if Fontana still lived outside Philadelphia.

Philadelphia wasn't far from New York. But it was far enough away that she wouldn't be tempted to return. Vivian wrote Fontana that she'd be passing through, that she hoped to see her. Fontana wrote back: "We've got tons of room. Come and stay as long as you'd like."

1945–1957

CHAPTER 18

George lifted Ivy and Ruth from the pram—she had practiced this over and over, making sure she looked proficient at handling two babies—and then the porters whisked it away to some unknown part of the train. When they reached Chicago, pram and luggage appeared on the platform. Another porter took the suitcases, and George pushed the baby carriage to the train to Kansas City, where the process began all over again, until, traveling on a series of trains that diminished in size and amenities with each transfer, she arrived in Oklahoma City.

Along the way, she spoke only when necessary to other passengers, usually in answer to questions about her babies. "My twins," she practiced saying, over and over, until it sounded natural. "Three months old. Yes, both girls." Other women brought her sandwiches from the club car. They brought her hot wet towels. They held the babies, her twins, while she "freshened up." They told her to think nothing of it when she thanked them. The war was still on, and people had gotten used to helping one another out.

Like everyone else, she'd been elated when the Allies crossed the Rhine. Victory in Europe seemed likely now. But there was still the Pacific Theater: Bataan, kamikaze pilots. Tom was somewhere in the Pacific. *Over* the Pacific. Flying high enough, she hoped, to turn violence into an abstraction. Though she knew, from towing the targets for the ack-ack drills, that the sky was far from safe. Perhaps she should wish him grounded, far back from the front. Somewhere with warm food and dry socks and regular mail delivery. Somewhere he could learn that he now had two daughters.

Our *twins*, thought George as she restored the babies to the pram on the Oklahoma City platform. The air carried the scent of petroleum—just the creosote from the railway ties, but still, it smelled like home.

"You didn't waste any time, did you?" said Adele once they'd settled the babies in the nursery. The sight of two white cribs and two matching white dressers, pink-and-white curtains fluttering in the windows, her grandmother's rocking chair, spruced up with a pink cushion, had George blinking back tears. It was all so domestic, so sweet, so . . . unexpected. Adele bustled about, unpacking the babies' things. "It's this war. Children getting married, having babies, hardly knowing each other at all. Not that that matters. They won't know each other anyway once the soldiers come home, if the last war is any lesson. Still, all this rush. As if they'll cheat death because of it. Which one is this?" She lifted one of the infants from George's arms, and George's heart quickened. Her babies were so tiny, her mother such a force.

"Ivy. She has more hair."

"Must get it from Tom's side. You certainly didn't have much at this age." Ivy opened her eyes and batted a fist in the air.

"And this is Ruth," whispered George.

"Ruth and Ivy. Big for twins, aren't they?"

"Not really," said George. "Not that the doctor mentioned anyway."

"New York doctors don't know everything. I made you an appointment with Dr. Bristow."

Before George could protest that her babies were perfectly fine and didn't need to see a doctor, Ruth awoke and began wailing. George had lost track of time. The girls were overdue for a feeding. Ruth would cry until a bottle appeared, but not Ivy. Ivy would sleep and sleep and sleep. George had to wake her to feed her, and then she drank greedily, burped, closed her eyes, and slept some more.

George had waited to leave New York until her breasts had stopped leaking and throbbing. "Better go with formula," the pediatrician said, "if you plan to sleep the next few months." Not nursing them felt awful at first. Every time one of them—well, Ruth usually—cried, George's breasts ached and leaked. But now, they merely twinged. "Here," she said, handing Ruth to Adele, who sagged under the weight of both babies, "I'll fix a bottle."

She waited for her mother to condemn the use of formula, but Adele was bobbing and shushing and cooing, with a softness in her face that George didn't recall from her own childhood. Ruth squalled louder. George rushed to the kitchen, clasping her twinging breasts. She wondered where Vivian had gone and what she was doing.

"I should have brought you my baby books!" said Helen. "I have all the latest ones. There's a whole science to child-rearing that our parents— well, they just had no idea."

"Hmm," said George. She'd said little more than "hmm" since Helen arrived, with a plump, sticky-cheeked Frank Jr. in tow. Well, that wasn't entirely true. She had gushed about what a handsome boy Frank Jr. was, the spitting image of his father. It had been the wrong thing to say. Helen's eyes went flat, as they did any time George mentioned Frank. George changed the subject to the difficulties of handling infants. The idea of George having difficulties brightened Helen right up. To keep her from darkening again, George limited her responses to "Hmm." With an occasional "Oh yes?" thrown in for variety.

"You must miss Tom terribly," said Helen.

"Oh yes?" said George. "Oh. Yes. Yes, I do. Terribly." And she did. She feared for his safety. Just as Helen surely feared for Frank's, especially because Frank was being held as a POW in the Philippines.

Was it wrong that George feared for him too? That she could so easily call up their furtive moments in the back seat? "We'll all be so relieved when they come home, won't we?"

"I suppose you and Tom will head to Kansas?" The hope in Helen's voice told George those back-seat encounters hadn't been as furtive as she'd believed.

And then—it happened so suddenly, even though she'd received a letter telling her he was on his way—Tom was there. Standing in the doorway of her mother's house. Adele mentioned something vague about a lunch out, about errands, about not waiting for dinner on her account, and disappeared, leaving just Tom and George. And the girls.

Would he know? George wondered. Would he see right away that one of them wasn't his? By this time, both girls were so fully hers that she went days without remembering Vivian's role. She was prepared, in the event of Tom's knowing, to fall to her knees and beg, to remind him that when they'd first met, he'd spoken of chivalry. What could be more chivalrous than protecting and raising an innocent child?

But Tom had only marveled at his daughters, noting with awe the similar shapes of their ears and noses, the differences in their eyes, the way Ivy crawled like an infantryman, while Ruth scooted around the room on her bottom. Only when the girls went down for their nap did George think to marvel at her newly returned husband.

Tom pulled at his collar. Worry crept across his face. George took a deep breath, ready to launch into her speech, but he said, "So strange being in civvies again. Don't feel like myself."

"You must be exhausted," said George. "Naturally."

He chuckled. "Not *too* exhausted. I wouldn't mind lying down, Georgie. I wouldn't mind that one bit."

"God, I missed you," said Tom, after he and George rolled apart.

George giggled. "I could tell," she said, pressing herself back against him. She shook thoughts of Frank from her mind. She'd inflated those furtive back-seat moments in her imagination. Tom was home. Uncomfortable in his civvies, exhausted, but not *too* exhausted, and not at all suspicious, thank God.

"I wish I'd been there when they were born. I'm sorry you had to do it all by yourself."

"I had Vivian."

"Oh, I know. You always have Vivian."

"But I wish you'd been there too." Except, of course, she didn't. Because if Tom had been there, she might have only one of them. And she couldn't imagine a life without both her babies.

The girls stirred, and George rose to dress. "You rest," she said.

"No, I've got phone calls to make." He'd flown with a pilot who had an in at American Airlines. The pilot thought his in might extend to Tom, and Tom wanted to remind him of that before the pilot extended it to anyone else. There wouldn't be enough jobs for all of them—any fool could see that. Not with the munitions plants and the airplane and tank manufacturing lines shutting down. Not with more than fifteen million soldiers demobbed and needing to support their war brides. He couldn't sit around resting. He had his own war bride. He had two daughters. "And we'll want to get out of your mother's hair," he said. "Get a place of our own."

George envied him. No matter who she knew or how little she rested, TWA and Pan Am would never hire her to fly their planes. Adele had sacrificed George's own plane to the war effort years before. "Well, you weren't flying it anymore," said Adele. "And I could hardly justify just keeping it parked at the airfield, not when, as you always made such a point of saying, you were flying much bigger and better things."

Her mother was right. Her J-2 would have seemed puny and dull after her months of flying jets and bigger, more powerful planes. Flying wasn't in her future, and she decided not to let it color her present. She turned her focus to more suitable goals. Tom landed a job with American Airlines. He'd earn a good salary, buy them a house, keep up his end of the postwar bargain: to come home, pretend he'd never seen anything awful, and live a productive, middle-class life. George would keep up her end of that bargain, too, by taking superlative care of her husband and her daughters.

She was determined to be a more motherly, more *feminine*, example to her daughters than Adele had been to her. She learned to cook a roast and bake a soufflé. She browsed the shops for just the right throw pillows, for cute outfits for the girls. Helen sewed the most adorable things for Frank Jr., but George knew there was a limit to her own domestic abilities. That limit appeared to be the sewing machine—the one machine that refused to yield to her mechanical aptitude. This didn't escape Helen's notice. "I don't know how you manage to find such sweet things for the girls," Helen said. "The boys' clothes are just not quality. One touch and I can tell they won't hold up. But I suppose girls aren't so hard on their clothes."

"Hmm," said George, wondering where Vivian might be. Vivian had become itinerant. George never knew when to expect a call, or where it would come from. Only that she'd hear engines in the background. The roar of a takeoff, the falling pitch of a landing.

"Just a minute," Vivian would say, and then, when the plane had taxied farther away, or cut its engines entirely, she'd say, "Okay, I'm back." Vivian got to fly those planes. "Just Cubs, mostly," said Vivian. "Nothing like what we flew before."

"Hmm," said George.

CHAPTER 19

Outside the midtown bus station, George pressed a wad of bills into Vivian's hand. "Write to me in Enid," she said. "I'll be there in a month." Then she raced the pram away. When George disappeared around the corner, Vivian's stomach dropped as if she'd just hit an air pocket. She'd been so desperate to go, she hadn't once considered how glad George would be to get rid of her. Vivian had been useless, after all. The babies, sensing her lack of maternal instinct, fussed whenever she held them. Vivian swore, when she peered into the crib, that they looked past her, always seeking George. The person they could trust to take care of them.

After so many months of close living with other women, followed by weeks of close living with George and then the babies, she was on her own. She felt small, standing on the gritty sidewalk as people bustled past her. She felt better once she boarded the bus, but her shoulders didn't fully relax until it lurched out of the station.

George's cash meant Vivian could afford a taxi from the Haverford bus station to Marian Fontana's house. "Nice neighborhood," said the cabbie as he lifted her battered suitcase from the trunk. An emerald lawn stretched from the gray stone house to the street. A slate walkway, flanked by shrubs trimmed into perfect spheres, curved toward the wide stone steps of the house. The front door swung open, and Marian dashed out.

"Shaw! You made it!"

"I did!" She wished she'd worn her WASP uniform. The shabbiness of her civilian clothing looked all too apparent against the Fontanas' pristine lawn, next to Marian's sleek pencil skirt. Vivian shifted her cardboard suitcase behind her, but there was no hiding it.

"Jim!" called Fontana. "Vivian's here! Come help!"

"Oh, I don't need—"

Before she could finish, a man who had to be Marian's brother— same glint in his chestnut eyes, same cleft in his perfect jaw—bounded down the steps and took the suitcase from her hand. "The famous Vivian Shaw," he said. "Jim Fontana. A pleasure."

The Fontana parents were spending the winter in Florida. "Isn't that your neck of the woods, Vivvy?" Marian asked during dinner.

"Not quite," said Vivian, unable to imagine the people who owned this enormous house, who ate off such delicate china, anywhere near her neck of the woods.

"It's been just Jim and me since Christmas," said Marian. "And honestly, we're getting tired of each other, so I'm glad you wrote."

"Do you still fly?" asked Jim.

Vivian had been so consumed by getting out of New York, with solving the problem of the baby, that she hadn't thought of flying in weeks.

"Sorry about the WASP," said Fontana, in a tone that suggested she wasn't sorry at all.

"Forgive my sister," said Jim, glaring at Marian, who drained her wineglass in response. "She hasn't flown since she left Sweetwater. And forgive my question. That was insensitive of me. I only meant that, if you're interested, I could take you out to the airfield tomorrow."

"We still have the Fairchild," said Marian. Seeing Vivian's confused expression, she continued, "I don't fly anymore, but Jim was a bomber captain. He still likes to go up."

Jim's eyes went dead, as if he were trying not to see something. He blinked, topped off everyone's wine, and said, "We'll go first thing tomorrow."

"By which he means after lunch," Marian clarified.

"Well, we wouldn't want to miss the Scofields' party tonight, would we?" Jim said.

Marian lent Vivian a dress. "It's a tad short, but they'll all be looking at your gorgeous face, not your hemline. We'll have the housekeeper let it out tomorrow." They piled into Jim's Zephyr convertible and roared off to the Scofields', then roared back in the early hours of the morning. Vivian fell into bed and slept harder than she had in months.

After a late lunch, Jim drove her out to the airfield. "Let's see what you can do," he said, offering her the controls. Soaring high over the Delaware Valley, she felt like her old self again. "Nice!" said Jim as she banked into a chandelle. She did a few lazy eights for fun.

Jim applauded. "Those idiot generals don't know what they're missing."

When they returned to the house, Marian had laid out three dresses on the guest bed. "Marian, I couldn't."

"They're last year's," said Marian. "And Lottie already let them out. They're yours."

Vivian's days fell into a pattern: sleeping until noon, eating a decadent lunch, flying with Jim, rolling her hair and dressing for a more decadent dinner. Then driving off to this party or that, dancing and drinking the night away with Marian and Jim and their Main Line friends. One early morning, as Marian wove her way up the front steps, Jim took Vivian's hand, pulled her to him, kissed her. Her stomach dropped, then quickly righted. She wrapped her arms around his neck and kissed him back.

Waking long after daylight, she found herself in a boy's room. Model planes hung from the ceiling on fishing line. Posters of racing coupes covered the walls. A baseball mitt perched on the dresser alongside a bottle of cologne. Jim's clothes from the night before mingled with her own on the floor. She stretched until her leg met his and stirred him to life.

The next month felt magical. She ate the Fontanas' plentiful food, flew through the streets in the Zephyr, flew through the air in the Fairchild, flew through the night in Jim's arms. She studied the clothing that Marian and her friends wore. While shopping with Marian, she counted out George's cash and bought herself a few good pieces. George was in Enid now. She ought to write to her. To Elizabeth. To Aunt Clelia. But there was always another party, another flight, another kiss from Jim. Another chance to make love to him and erase that horrible night at Camp Davis.

"I'll be brought into the family business," said Jim when Vivian asked him if he had any career plans. "Mostly investing," he said when she asked him what the family business involved. He didn't seem to be in any hurry to start work. It was clear he didn't have to be. Vivian suspected George's Ector money paled in comparison to the Fontana fortune. She found herself thinking of George often, wondering how she was managing. She tried hard not to think about *what* George was managing.

Another month gone, and the novelty of Marian and Jim's life wore thin. The ease and impracticality of it wore her out. On rainy afternoons, she sat in the guest room window seat, flicking her lighter open and closed, telling herself to start making plans. Her welcome was bound to wear out. Better to leave before things turned.

She wrote to George, telling her about the Fontana house, about Jim and the parties and the flying. George wrote back asking for details about the plane, the airfield, the view from ten thousand feet up. Vivian wished she could tell George in person. Writing it all out in a letter took so long that she was late to dinner. She hurried down the grand staircase. The double doors to the dining room stood open—Jim and Marian were waiting for her. She heard the soft release of a cork from a wine bottle, the slip of liquid into crystal. She heard Jim say, "I'm going to ask Mother for Grandmother's ring."

"They'll never go for that," said Marian. "Look, I love Vivian, but who are her people?"

"I don't care who her people are."

"Neither do I. But Mother will. Don't look at me like that. You know I'm right."

Vivian trod heavily across the foyer. "There she is." Jim stood and filled her glass with wine. She took her seat at his elbow, across from Marian. Beneath the table, he put a hand on her thigh. "Finish your correspondence?" he asked. She hadn't once seen him pick up a pen, or a tool of any kind. He was a boy playing house, sitting in his father's chair. A tempting boy, but a boy all the same.

When she told him she was going, Jim lowered himself to one knee. "I was going to wait for a ring, but—"

Vivian took his hands and raised him from the ground. "No," she said. He dropped her hands. "I'm not the marrying kind, Jim."

"Every girl is the marrying kind. You just mean you don't want to marry me."

"Believe me," she said. "This is for the best." He sulked away to his room, refused to see her off.

"Marian, thank you. I'm going to miss you."

"I wish you wouldn't go," said Marian as Vivian's cab pulled up. But Vivian suspected they'd soon find a new toy to amuse themselves with.

Thanks to Marian, she knew what to wear. Thanks to Jim, she knew she could still fly, in the air and in bed. She traveled west, hopping from airfield to airfield.

Vivian entered the offices at these airfields with the attitude of a penitent. A worshipper come to pay her respects. She struck up conversations with the bishops of these cathedral-hangars. Over the course of the conversation, she let fall the names of certain aircraft, careful not to mention the most powerful ones, the ones the men in these churches were least likely to have flown themselves. She offered them the small and the middling. She complained knowledgably about sticky rudders and balky engines.

She returned, day after day, until she either wore them down or they took pity and let her repair an engine, file their disorganized paperwork, or attempt to balance their books, in exchange for some—never enough—flight time. Sometimes they paid her. Sometimes they let her sleep on the couch in the office. Sometimes she let one of them take her home.

When she had spare change, she called George. George could never talk for long—a pot was boiling over. A child was fussing. But she always asked the same question: What are you flying? Even though the planes weren't much, George sighed with envy when Vivian answered.

"I'm living pretty rough these days, George," she said, offering that up as compensation.

"Oh yes?" The wistfulness in her friend's voice nearly broke Vivian's heart. Even so, she kept the exact degree of roughness a secret.

She was horrible at bookkeeping. They always let her go. *So very sorry. Just no longer have a need. See how things are. Hand-to-mouth as it is around here.*

At an airfield in Michigan, every plane she saw was in excellent repair. The office looked as tidy as a ship—not a stray scrap of paper to be seen. "I could do your typing," she ventured, knowing that her typing would be a disaster. The man behind the desk—his bearing suggested he'd spent his war years as an officer—arched his brows. "Or your books," she said.

"You do books?" the man asked. Vivian gave a shrug that could have been read either way, and he laughed. "Come to dinner with me, and we'll figure something out." The offer had been made at other airfields by other men sitting behind desks or stooped over engine components. Occasionally—depending on the man, depending on the planes—Vivian accepted, knowing full well what they expected in return. But usually, she moved on.

"All right," she said.

She went to dinner with him. She went to bed with him. What she thought of as *the incident* hadn't put her off men. She refused to let it. She refused to let it take anything else from her—especially not sex.

The man had purchased the airfield with money his father had left him. It was a dream come true, he told her. A very expensive dream. In his waking life, he worked as an accountant. "It pays the bills," he said.

"So you don't need a bookkeeper," said Vivian.

"You're no bookkeeper."

"But I could be," she said.

He taught her single and double entry. He let her fly his Beechcraft. He took her to more restaurants. He took her to more hotels. And then his wife found out.

Vivian moved on, but with a marketable skill. No one wanted female pilots, but they liked a female bookkeeper. Especially one as ornamental as Vivian.

"Bookkeeping?" said her sister when Vivian called home. "You could do that right here in Hahira."

"You know I couldn't. Not really."

Elizabeth sighed. "You could at least call Mother. She'd sure appreciate it."

Vivian, dutiful, called her mother, who was so glad to hear her voice, who sure appreciated her calling, who couldn't talk now. A storm was blowing in and the roses needed to be tied to the trellis.

But Vivian knew it wasn't the roses, or even her mother's general lack of interest, that made her hurry the receiver back into its cradle. And it wasn't exasperation that kept Elizabeth from arguing with her about coming home. It was that they sensed that she'd done a terrible thing. But because they loved her (even her mother, in a distant sort of way), they were careful not to give her the slightest opportunity to reveal her secret.

CHAPTER 20

It was late and George was driving. Fast, out on the farm roads. Pointing the Dodge away from home until a T forced her to turn. She and Tom had fought. Again. The blush of joy that tinted Tom's first weeks back had faded. The airline had hired him almost immediately, thanks to his connection, but as a newbie, he got the dregs when it came to runs. The prop plane from Oklahoma City to Dallas and back. Never the jet to LA or New York, or even Saint Louis.

George understood how it must rankle. She herself had only the Dodge. Out on the farm roads, she opened it up on the long, straight stretches. At such a late hour, she didn't even need to stop at the intersections. It was as close to flying, as close to consolation, as she could get. After their fights, she lay in bed seething, stone still, pretending to sleep as she clung to the edge of the mattress, forcing her chest to rise and fall, her lungs to accept and release air. When she couldn't bear it any longer, she rose and dressed and grabbed the keys to the Dodge.

After driving an hour or so, she'd think back on the fight. What had it been about? Often, she couldn't recall. Some petty little something. Some feeling of being taken for granted. A sense of being wronged, in some vague way, that resulted in one of them lashing out, the other lashing back, all this lashing done in fierce whispers so as not to wake the girls. Though she suspected the girls knew. The very air of the house, the air that filled their precious little lungs, was toxic with the fumes of their parents' mutual disappointment. She would do better. She would be more patient. He'd had a hard war, after all. Her mother had warned her, "They come back different. So just remind yourself that at least he came back." A warning George had failed to take seriously. She and Tom were in love. They were golden. Their life would be golden too. Surely, now that the war had ended, everyone's lives would be a little more golden.

She retreated from the farm roads, nosed the Dodge through the nicer neighborhoods of Enid, turning, as she always did on these driving nights, not toward her own house but toward Helen's. Frank had returned home weeks before, but Helen had kept him under wraps. "He needs to rest. He's a skeleton, Georgeanne. It's criminal what they did to him."

Frank spent five months in a Japanese POW camp in the Philippines, then another month in an Army hospital, before being deemed parasite-free and healthy enough to go home. George couldn't say what she hoped to see when she drove by the Bridlemile house at 3 a.m. A light burning in one of the front rooms? Some sign of happiness or distress from the placid lawn, the porch with its pots of geraniums? This night, as on all the others she'd driven by (sometimes doubling back to look twice), the house and yard were dark, tidy, not a pine branch swaying in the breeze. Well, there was no breeze to sway them. But something swayed. She rolled down the window and squinted at the shadow beneath the live oak.

Someone sat in the glider, rocking it back and forth in the dark. She pulled the Dodge to the curb and crossed the lawn before she had formulated the words. What did you say to these men? These men who had been so terribly beaten up by war, who had seen and heard, and probably done, unspeakable things, who had come home to few jobs and to wives they no longer knew and children who were strangers to them.

What George said was, "You'll get eaten alive, sitting out here this time of night."

"Ah, Georgeanne," said Frank, stretching his arm across the back of the glider so that she could slide right up close beside him. "I sure missed you."

His clavicles were sharp through his thin cotton undershirt. They rocked the glider back and forth, not speaking, listening to the clank of the iron chains. George ran a hand over Frank's ribs. He gently removed it and held on to it. Eventually he brought it to his mouth and kissed it. "I think I made a mistake, Frank," she confessed.

"Well, then, what are you going to do about it?" he asked, laying her hand along his cheek.

"I was thinking I might make another one." She pulled him to his feet, began leading him to the Dodge.

"Oh, honey," said Frank, allowing himself to be led. "We were never the mistake."

The girls were nearly two when Vivian wrote to George and proposed a trip somewhere. "Just us girls—all four of us," Vivian wrote, provoking in George a fear that she might not know this current version of Vivian.

"Doesn't that just sound lovely?" George wrote back, thinking she didn't know this current version of herself either. Some friends of Adele's had a place in Port Arthur. It wouldn't be too bad a drive. Vivian wrote back that a friend would fly her to Houston. (She provided no details about the friend, and George made no mention of Frank Bridlemile.) From Houston, she'd take a bus. The arrangements fell easily into place.

George pressed the girls' prettiest outfits and trimmed their hair. She drew up menus that would showcase how well they ate and how well she cooked for them. She put aside favorite dolls and toys so that the girls would have something fresh to entertain themselves with on the drive. She considered their vocabularies. Not, according to Helen, particularly advanced, but "probably nothing to worry about." She reminded herself that Vivian's store of knowledge about two-year-olds wasn't exactly extensive. The important thing was to appear competent and calm. To show that she was as good a mother as she had been a pilot. To show that the girls were thriving and cheerful. But also, not to make it look too easy. Not to provide Vivian the slightest temptation to reclaim her daughter.

Salt air had rusted the lock to the house. George had to let Ivy pee behind a palmetto because she couldn't get the door open in time. This was such a novel and exciting adventure that Ruth demanded to pee behind a palmetto, too, even though by then they'd been inside for an hour. Finally, for the sake of preventing tearstained cheeks and puffy eyes, George had allowed it. Naturally the neighbor had seen, then stared hard at the Oklahoma plates on George's car and sniffed as if to say it all made sense to her now.

Just when she'd gotten the girls settled down and a chicken in the oven to roast, it was time to head to the bus station to pick up "Aunt Vivian." But Aunt Vivian's bus was an hour late. George hadn't brought any toddler provisions with her. She put this down to nerves; she certainly knew better than to leave home without at least a few graham crackers in her purse. An hour late was just late enough that the chicken would be dry, but not late enough for her to drive back to the house and then return to the station.

When the bus finally pulled in, she wiped the girls' noses and mouths, eliminating the traces of the candy bar she'd bought them. A stream of passengers disembarked. George wondered if Vivian had missed the bus, but then she stepped down, looking overheated but beautiful in silk and gabardine. She unwound her scarf as she strode toward them.

Why, thought George, *did I wear this frumpy old seersucker dress?* She wished she'd run a comb through her hair before leaving the house. How could this glamorous creature possibly want to spend a week with a dowdy housewife like herself? Ivy didn't help things by announcing, "I peed outside!"

Vivian burst out laughing, and George's chest eased. This was the Vivian she remembered. She glanced at her watch. The chicken should be charring nicely now. She imagined the smoke drifting through the open kitchen window and further enhancing her reputation with the neighbor. "Let's go home," she said.

Ruth cried out in the middle of the night. She'd vomited in her bed. She was pale and feverish, and George worked as quietly as she could to clean up the mess and settle her back down to sleep. Almost exactly twenty-four hours later, Ivy followed suit.

George and Vivian spooned chipped ice and JELL-O into Ruth's and Ivy's hot mouths. They placed cool cloths on their burning foreheads. They washed bed linens and towels. Then washed them again. Vivian found a roll of plastic sheeting in the shed and spread it over the carpet. George was exhausted. She and Vivian slept in shifts, but George tried to let Vivian sleep longer.

My God, George thought as she dipped her daughters into a cool bath to ease their fevers, *what if I catch it? How on earth would Vivian manage on her own?*

"My God, George," said Vivian as she mopped watery vomit off the plastic sheeting, "you'd better not catch this. How on earth would I manage on my own?"

And then Ruth's color returned. She kept down a few saltines and some flat Coke. A day later, Ivy followed suit. Their skin cooled. Their eyes brightened. At least, thought George, they could still have a couple of days of fun on the beach. They'd escape the cramped and now rather pungent Port Arthur cabin, build sandcastles, splash in the waves.

"Was that thunder?" asked Vivian.

It was. The first of a series of storms rolling up the Gulf Coast, bringing driving rain and piercing wind and not letting up until the time came to drive Vivian back to the bus station. "Next time," said George, "why not visit us in Enid?"

This was a long shot, she knew. After this awful week, Vivian was unlikely to want a next time. But their focus on the sick girls and the exhaustion that came from tending to them had erased the awkwardness between them. They had a job to do, and they'd done it. But she wished they'd had more time.

"We didn't get much chance to talk," said George. "I feel like we didn't catch up at all."

Vivian kissed Ivy and Ruth goodbye. She showed no signs of wanting to take one of them home with her. Then she hugged George tightly. "I'd love to visit you. I'll come soon. I promise."

CHAPTER 21

Vivian packed her best clothes for her trips to Enid. She had adopted Jacqueline Cochran's way of carrying herself. With her height and her jodhpurs and silk blouses and scarves, she looked, she knew, quite elegant. No hint of Hahira showed on her surface. George would never see her dingy garage apartment, her sofa with its sprung cushions, her cigarette-tanned curtains. She'd only see that Vivian was thriving, that she was keeping the faith, continuing what they'd started. She'd see that Vivian's decision had been for the best.

On this particular trip, she flew to Enid in a borrowed Beechcraft Bonanza. She wanted to see how the Beechcraft handled long distances. How it performed in climates other than the dry, high plains of Montana where she'd spent the last half year.

The first night of her visit, once they'd all finished their first cocktails and were each well into their second, she told them about the business she wanted to start in Billings. "The only books I want to keep are my own. Mostly teaching, but some transport—the Bonanza carries six, including me. Some small cargo runs here and there. Scenic tours over Yellowstone."

The second night, once they had finished two cocktails and were each well into their third, she asked George for the loan. "I've saved more than half," she said. This had required months of smoking two cigarettes for lunch and accepting dinner invitations from a broader range of men than she would have liked.

"I know you have expenses of your own," she said, gesturing at the pristine living room with its matching walnut tables and its spotless mohair cushions. She vividly recalled the Port Arthur trip and the speed with which two young children could destroy upholstery and carpeting. Secretly, she marveled that George managed to keep this one room, let alone the rest of the house, so orderly and clean. Probably she had a housekeeper. Probably George spent her Ector oil money on her own life and couldn't spare a dime of it for Vivian's dreams. Probably George would say no, that she'd have to figure out another way—maybe even accept that there wasn't a way. Why should George, who, Vivian knew, wished she could spend her days flying, guarantee Vivian's access to a plane? But George was kind. And, compared to Vivian and most of the people Vivian knew, George was rich. Why not take a chance and see what happened?

What happened was that George's head snapped back as if Vivian had slapped her. In the silence that followed, Tom said, "We'll have to discuss it."

George stared at Tom as if she weren't quite sure who he was.

"Of course," said Vivian. "Of course you should discuss it. Tell me about the girls. They're getting so tall. Ivy especially."

She should have blanked immediately into alcohol-fueled slumber, but George and Tom's fierce whispering carried through the air vents.

"It's my money," hissed George. "What is there to discuss?"

"It's your money, and you can do what you want with it," Tom hissed back. "I can support my own family! I'm not trying to live off my wife!"

"All of my friends have housekeepers—"

"Hire a housekeeper! Who's stopping you? It's your money."

"We agreed to save it."

"Save it. Spend it. I just said, do what you want."

"But you wouldn't say it in front of her. In front of her, you have to look like the big man."

"What I didn't want to say in front of her is that she's not stable! She flits around the country, she flits from man to man—"

"How dare—"

"Not to mention the drinking."

"You're no slouch at that yourself," said George.

The next morning, George wrote her a check. Vivian proposed a repayment schedule and a token amount of interest, George agreed to it, and Tom exhaled in a derisive snort and left for the airport. The next evening, he called. He wouldn't be home that night, George reported. He was stuck in Phoenix due to thunderstorms. Vivian didn't say a word when the weatherman on the evening news reported clear skies across the Southwest.

CHAPTER 22

Adele had never imagined she'd become one of those women whose world shifted completely with the arrival of grandbabies. But here she was, finding reasons at least twice a week to drop by George's and see her granddaughters.

Harriet Mayes had called and invited her to lunch, which gave Adele an excuse to drive into town. She liked to offer George a reason for stopping in, although George always insisted none was required.

Harriet Mayes no longer possessed a single opinion of her own. Whenever Adele ventured one of hers, Harriet cocked her head to one side and said, "Paul says . . ." Invariably, whatever Paul Mayes had to say on the matter was the exact opposite of what Adele had just said. "But," Harriet always finished, "it's certainly something to think about, isn't it?" Adele overlooked Harriet's absolute refusal to think for herself in exchange for a reason to be in dropping-by proximity to her granddaughters.

She was also cultivating Harriet as a future potential customer. She wanted to start her own car repair business. A place where women could get an oil change or have fan belts and spark plugs replaced without fearing some dishonest mechanic would take advantage of them. Men like Paul Mayes would never bring their cars to her. But men like Paul Mayes wouldn't live forever, and their widows might form a solid, reliable customer base.

She dragged out the lunch as long as she could, but it was still nap time when she exited the restaurant. She dropped into Herzberg's and was idly browsing a rack of shirtwaists when Helen appeared. "Oh, those girls," exclaimed Helen. Her delight in the twins meant Adele felt freer than usual to rattle on about Ruth and Ivy's latest milestones. Helen murmured, "So *sweet*," at appropriate intervals. And when Adele finally ran out of steam, Helen said, "Oh, they are the most darling things. And I really do think," she added, her face suddenly grave, "that little tic in Ivy's eye will clear up all in good time."

Adele had cataloged every inch of her granddaughters' bodies. She'd never noticed a tic in Ivy's eye and doubted that one actually existed outside Helen's imagination.

"Of course, Frank Jr.'s eyes are clear as a bell, so I'm no expert," finished Helen.

"And how is Frank Sr. doing?" asked Adele, poking at Helen's weak spot. "George told me about his troubles finding a position. It's been so difficult for our men coming home."

"Well, we're just delighted, absolutely delighted about it—he's gone to work for Plains Insurance."

"Your uncle Robert's company? How wonderful. I'm glad to hear it."

"Yes, Uncle Rob's been wanting Frank for months, but Frank was just being stubborn—he'd gotten some notion about real estate into his head. Not anymore, though. He loves it at Plains—I tried to get him to meet me for lunch out today, but he just has so much on his plate. Insurance is steady. And steady is best after all the turmoil of the war, don't you agree?"

Adele had never in her life agreed that steady was best.

This was one of the many ways in which she and George differed. George had been a placid child. "She doesn't have much rough-and-tumble in her," Adele had once said to Charles, who chuckled and said he thought Adele had enough rough-and-tumble in her for all of them. She missed Charles. Her chest still tightened when she thought of him. Even so, she would never have considered interrupting him in the middle of his workday and proposing they meet for lunch. (*Why didn't I?* she thought now.) But they had . . . reveled in each other. It was more than good conversation, company, or even sex. It was a special sort of ease, one she couldn't quite pin down. But she could see that George didn't have it with Tom, and that was a shame.

George, at nearly sixteen, had surprised her—in the best rough-and-tumble way—by asking for an airplane. Perhaps she was just a late bloomer, Adele had thought. And though it was a pinch—times being what they were—the Ectors had the means to provide a plane, when other families struggled to put a half-decent meal on the table every day. Then she'd gone off to fly for the WASP, and Adele had had to squelch her prideful impulse to mention it to everyone she met.

But since the decommissioning of the WASP, since taking on marriage and motherhood, George had veered back to her natural placidity. Adele worried her daughter might become like Harriet Mayes—a vessel for someone else's expectations and opinions, an attractive shell of a person. She resolved to stop by George's more often. She'd watch the girls and send George out. To do what, she didn't know. But there must be some way to nudge her daughter back to the rough-and-tumble side of herself.

She'd start today, she decided as she opened the front door to George's house. She never knocked, nor would she expect George to knock on her door. "Hello!" she called. She heard a scuffling sound from the direction of the kitchen. The twins must be having a postnap snack. "I was just downtown . . ."

In the kitchen she found George and Frank Bridlemile, both shoeless, Frank with his shirt open at the collar, though he appeared to be working on that.

"Mother," said George, cheeks flushed and her skirt askew, "I wasn't expecting you."

"Evidently not."

"You remember Frank Bridlemile. Frank, my mother, Adele Ector."

Frank gave up on his top button and nodded at her. "Oh yes," said Adele. "Yes, I remember Frank."

It was not the sort of rough-and-tumble Adele had had in mind— she would never admit to approving—but it was something.

CHAPTER 23

"You can't imagine how bad the nights are, Georgeanne. The nightmares he gets." This was Helen's way of staking out her territory, George understood. The wife got the hardship, the real meat of the marriage, not just the frivolous dessert. George would have taken the nightmares, too, but Frank never offered them to her. This was also Helen's way of letting George know she was no fool. For the sake of appearances, Helen would keep quiet, if, for the sake of appearances, Frank and George remained discreet.

Which they did. They kept their meetings sporadic, unpredictable. The girls in school, Tom up in the air somewhere. Adele surely knew, but she never said a word.

Helen and George still partnered at bridge. They attended the Women's Club together. They sat on the same Garden Club committees. Along with their husbands, they ate dinner at the club every other weekend, and if Tom was flying, they sometimes even went as a threesome. Though George often skipped those occasions, pleading fatigue or evidence of an impending cold for herself or one of the girls. "Those poor girls—always coming down with something," said Helen. "Frank Jr. never catches a thing. But then my father had the constitution of an ox." George would hang up with a pang of longing for her own father and try not to dwell on what he'd think of her now.

She didn't fault Helen for any of this. Helen behaved with remarkable decorum, considering. Maybe it was time to stop this nonsense. Her next "lunch" with Frank would be the last, she told herself sternly. More than once. Then he'd walk through the door, run a hand through his dark hair, turn his midnight eyes on her. Give her that smile that made her feel twenty again, with all her choices still arrayed before her. Her life not narrowed down to being a wife, a mother, a small-town matron.

How could anyone begrudge her this happiness? With Tom gone all the time and Helen still calling her up regularly to go shopping, she convinced herself she and Frank weren't hurting anyone.

She clung to this fiction even as the marital chill between herself and Tom deepened by the week. She was grateful for the flight assignments that kept him away for nights at a time. She had Frank, but then, she never fully had Frank. She had her daughters and her mother. She had Vivian, but she sometimes wondered, at what cost?

Vivian's request for a loan had hit her like a physical blow. Hadn't she known all along there would be a price? No one gave away a child without asking for something in return. Hadn't she always known she'd have to pay? She was utterly willing. She'd buy Vivian ten planes if it meant she could keep her daughter.

Vivian made sporadic payments on the loan. Every time one arrived, late and for less than the agreed-upon amount, Tom was ready with an "I told you so" smirk. The next time Vivian visited, bringing gifts for the girls, he said, "She's just buttering you up for the next ask."

Every visit, George prayed that Vivian wouldn't ask for a dime. She resisted her own "I told you so" smirk when Vivian departed without asking for a thing. But about once a year, a letter arrived. Landing fees had increased. Or the Beechcraft needed new wheels. Or Vivian wanted to advertise in the local paper, just to get her flight school off the ground. George opened her checkbook again and again, piled up more secrets to keep from Tom.

Their marriage worked better in the car. Maybe it had something to do with a shared focus—a destination. Maybe it had something to do with the compressed space—the confinement forced them to behave themselves. At home, when they argued, Ruth and Ivy faded away, silent ghosts drifting off to their bedroom.

So she and Tom and the girls went on lots of outings. They drove miles to peer over the edges of canyons, to swim in lakes, to float down rivers, to picnic at splintery tables alongside rusting playgrounds. George liked to think they were showing their girls the world. They were showing them that—regardless of how things sounded at home— the Rutledges were a happy family.

As they glided along the smooth new interstates, illusion became, at least temporarily, reality. George sometimes believed it herself. They stopped for burgers and milkshakes, for roadside flea markets. For the tallest tree here, the boulder that looked like Abraham Lincoln there, the waterfall just another mile downstream. For a caged bear in one county and the last known wolf, also caged, in the next. For anything that kept them all on the road another hour, that wore them all out a little more, made it that much more likely they'd make it until morning without hissing at each other.

Toward the end of one of these golden family-fun days, the girls drowsing in the back seat, Tom's hands tensing on the wheel, and George's shoulders hunching toward her ears as they neared Enid, she gazed toward the horizon in anticipation. As if she knew she was about to see something wonderful, a distraction from their impending homecoming.

Perhaps both of their brains detected the engine noise before they saw the planes. Perhaps that was why they knew where to look. Or maybe it was just luck. Lord knew they were due for some luck. In any case, when the planes coursed over the horizon line, flying wingtip to wingtip, she and Tom both gasped. Tom pulled to the side of the road. They got out of the car, leaned into the wind, toward the aircraft. Two Jennies. They flew one atop the other. Then they split off in beautiful chandelles before coming back together again, splitting, reuniting, splitting and shooting up-up-up, and then, stalling out, falling into breath-catching flat spins before righting themselves, then shooting back beyond the curve of the earth, out of sight.

George and Tom stared at the horizon until it was evident that the planes weren't returning. They stared a few minutes longer, just to make sure. They got back in the car, and Tom started the engine. "Barnstormers," he said, shaking his head with wonder. "First plane I ever saw was a Jenny."

"First plane I ever flew in. I paid three dollars for that ride, with a woman pilot, believe it or not."

Tom chuckled and said he believed her on both counts. Then he said, "George, you could fly, you know. Out at the airfield. I know you miss it."

She'd thought of this herself, and then dismissed it. Some nights she dreamed she had the controls of an A-24, or she was testing the limits of a BT-13. She could lease time in a Piper Cub, but she feared it wouldn't feel like enough.

"I know it wouldn't be the same," said Tom. "Trust me, what I fly now isn't anywhere near what either of us flew in the war. But it would be something."

Maybe, thought George. "But the girls," she said, and waited for Tom to point out that she had reliable babysitters, whom she ought to call more often than she did. Then she would point out the value of economizing, Tom would mention the loan to Vivian, and they'd hiss at each other until the girls stirred in the back seat.

But Tom didn't follow the script this time. "I've been thinking," he said. "Adele all alone in that old house. It needs a new roof. The chimney leans north. And don't say it always did. You know it's getting worse. She talks about having central air put in, but I don't even want to think about the state of the wiring. She should sell it before it falls down around her. She could move in with us, help you out a bit. You two could keep each other company."

And George, stunned by not one but two unexpected gifts from her husband in one afternoon, thought *maybe*, then *yes*. Yes, because in addition to the obvious benefits of having Adele around, she and Tom would have one more powerful reason (the girls not quite being powerful reasons enough) to behave themselves.

When his parents passed, the Bridlemile property went to Frank. His brother had died at Bastogne. His sister had left Enid for Dallas at eighteen and wanted nothing more to do with the Bridlemile land. It was worthless acreage. No oil. No good for wheat. Even cattle failed to thrive on it. But Enid was growing. Vance Air Force Base was expanding. Military families moved in, bringing merchants and tradesmen in their wake. The Bridlemile parcel was spitting distance from the base, and Frank wanted to build houses on it. "Nothing fancy," he told George. "Three-bedroom homes on midsize lots. Good for young couples with kids. I've sketched out floor plans myself." The next step was finding investors to fund the utility infrastructure, the street platting and paving, the finalization of the drawings.

"How much?" she asked, thinking of her Ector money, sitting cold and silent in the bank. Thinking of Frank's warm arms around her.

"No, Georgeanne. I couldn't. I wouldn't."

"Why not? You've got a sound plan. I see the way the town is growing. I'll make more money with you than by leaving it in the bank."

"Tom wouldn't go for it," said Frank, violating one of their rules: that in bed they never, ever mentioned Helen or Tom. Even the children were out of bounds.

"It's not Tom's money. It's mine."

Her father had insisted on this point, that George's inheritance would not be put under her future husband's name. That it would remain hers. "For two reasons," he told George when he explained his will, when his death (not to mention a future husband) seemed an impossibility and the discussion was, to George's mind, both theoretical and distressing. "First, you'll never have to worry about any man's intentions. If they find out they won't have charge of it—and it's a lot of money, Georgeanne, more than you may realize right now—and they run, well, better for you. Second, it'll give you more power in your marriage. You may not realize this, but your mother and I—ours is not the most conventional of marriages."

George had stifled a laugh. From the time she started school, she'd overheard numerous adults and even some of her childhood friends express bafflement at Charles Ector's abdication of his role as head of the household. Of Adele Ector's shocking independence and waywardness. "We aren't equal in all things, but we each rule ourselves, and we take turns ruling the other. It must sound odd, but it has"—and here her father's voice had trailed off wistfully—"been rather wonderful . . . Point is, George, we want the same for you. Money is power—you'll see someday. Money gives you leverage. I see what the world does, how it wants to tamp down women like your mother and make them something less than what they are. Even a good man can fall prey to that desire. Keeping it all in your name makes it less likely that the man you marry will be tempted to make less of you."

Once Tom started making noise about her loans to Vivian, George saw the wisdom of her father's plan. She stopped telling her husband about her financial arrangements with Vivian, and he was too proud to ask what she did with money that wasn't his to control. The problem hadn't exactly gone away—it had just laid itself low. Making room for a different set of problems.

"I wouldn't want to cause trouble, is all," said Frank, provoking George, who had just spent the last hour naked with him, to laugh until her stomach ached. When at last they pulled themselves together and she nestled back against him, she said, "Look, I want to do it. Even if I didn't know you, I'd want to do it. And if you're worried about how Tom will feel about it, well, as I said, I make my own decisions, some of which I don't even tell him about." Two months earlier she'd loaned Vivian another thousand. The only difference with investing in Frank, as far as George could see, was that she'd at least have a chance of earning a return on her investment.

"If it all goes south," said Frank, "you'll hate me."

"I could never hate you. But I will punish you by not sleeping with you ever again."

Frank pulled her on top of him. "You do know how to motivate a man."

"I knew it was only a matter of time," said Helen. "He just needed to get back on his feet." Frank's subdivision had gone up cheaply, thanks to the postwar glut of labor and building supplies, and the houses—three bedroom, two bath, with carports and nice big yards—sold easily. Frank's picture graced the business page of the *News & Eagle*, and Helen threw a party to celebrate. The Bridlemiles were shopping for a bigger house. "Something closer to the country club," said Helen. She'd taken up golf and tennis and badgered George to join her.

"To Frank." Tom raised his glass, and everyone else followed. "The man with the plan that paid off. Congrats, buddy." Neither Tom nor Helen knew yet that George had provided the capital for Frank's project. George never found the right moment to tell either of them. Mentioning it at this celebratory dinner felt like it would take something away from Frank.

"I was thinking," she said to Tom as they drove home, "I might put some of my Ector money into Frank's next project."

"You think there'll be a next one?" scoffed Tom. "Not if Helen can help it. She'd rather he spent Monday through Friday sitting in an insurance office and Saturday at the club."

George knew Frank was already drawing up plans for another development. "We could even build you an airfield," Frank said. "Bring Vivian down to run it."

But she liked having distance between herself and Vivian. Well, really between the girls and Vivian. Too much time spent with Vivian meant too much opportunity for Ruth and Ivy to compare their glamorous aunt with their boring mother. Too much time spent with the girls and Vivian might act on whatever regret she must harbor. Too much time spent with the girls and Vivian might bring George's carefully constructed family life crashing down. The irony of worrying about her family life disintegrating as she wrapped her bare legs around Frank's waist and pulled him toward her wasn't lost on her.

"I don't want an airfield," she murmured as she applied kittenish licks to his ear. "I think I'll start with just a plane."

CHAPTER 24

On a cargo run to Laredo, Vivian crossed the border to shop for the girls. At a tourist trap in Nuevo Laredo, she found just the right gifts: two nearly identical ceramic piggy banks, painted with festive swirls of color. She planned to stop in Enid on her way back to Kansas City and didn't want to show up empty handed.

Even though the ceramic banks were cheap, she knew she ought not to spend the money. The girls didn't need a thing. And while she hadn't asked George for a loan in over a year, she also hadn't sent her a payment in nearly that long.

But Aunt Vivian always brought gifts when she visited—the girls would expect something. And George had recently purchased her own plane—a brand-new Cessna Businessliner. She needed her loan repaid about as much as the girls needed the piggy banks.

Vivian had hoped the plane might make George happy in a way that her marriage clearly didn't. She hated causing strife between George and Tom. She'd hated to think George envied her flying life. Especially since her life was far from enviable. George had money and a house and a beautiful family. Everything a woman was supposed to want. All Vivian had was flying.

She did all right. Between the cargo runs and the lessons and her frugal habits (gifts for the girls notwithstanding), she covered her expenses. Her bookkeeping days were far behind her. She hadn't accepted a date just for the free meal in ages. But ask pretty much anyone and Vivian knew they'd say George had the better life. And yet, she sensed that for George it wasn't nearly enough.

Back on the US side of the border, she called George from a pay phone to let her know she'd arrive the following day. She looked forward to a home-cooked meal. To playing tag with the girls. If they still played games like tag. They were growing up. The way they spoke, the way they moved—they were George through and through. Vivian loved seeing her friend reflected in their young faces. She also loved it when they flung themselves at her in welcome, and when they argued about who got to sit next to her at dinner. She was their special aunt, the one who never arrived without something for them. And they were so thoroughly George's children, it was impossible to imagine that one of them had ever been hers at all.

CHAPTER 25

"I'm not that old," said Adele when George suggested she move into the Rutledge house.

"Of course you're not," agreed George, but Adele knew when she was being coddled. "But it's a big piece of property to take care of, and the house needs—"

"The house is fine," snapped Adele. She wasn't a helpless old lady, reduced to living with her child.

A few months later, her foot slipped off the edge of a stair tread. She landed at the bottom of the staircase, breathless and bruised. She watched with horror as her ankle ballooned. Not broken, thank goodness. Just a sprain. The doctor prescribed ice and elevation, which meant she had plenty of time to sit and think. What if she'd been seriously hurt? Could she have dragged herself to the telephone? Would she have had to wait for George to realize it had been too long since they'd spoken? Would she have had to yell when she heard the mailman? To hope he'd break down the front door and rescue her? The indignity of these scenarios was unthinkable. The better part of valor was knowing when to quit.

And there would be benefits. The biggest was spending time every day with Ruth and Ivy. And with George, who might need her if she tumbled off the high wire she walked with Frank Bridlemile. Plus, George lived in town. Widows in need of car repair wouldn't have to drive far to reach her.

She'd hoped, once George had her own plane, that Vivian's visits wouldn't stir her up so much. But, as always, as soon as Vivian announced she was coming, George jittered around the house, cleaning everything in sight, even the things no one would ever notice.

"I don't think she's going to care if the drapes don't get washed," Tom said. Adele raised her eyes to the ceiling. He should have known better.

George, who had already washed and was now ironing said drapes, looked like she might throw the iron at him.

"You would never understand," said George. "She's so . . . elegant now. So put together."

"She doesn't have a family to take care of," said Tom. "She has time for that sort of thing."

George glared at him, and he took a step backward. "I'll run to the liquor store," he said. "Always a good idea to stock up before Vivian gets here."

Tom had made Adele welcome, told her to make use of the garage and driveway. He was always pleasant to her, but she'd noticed that he and George didn't talk much. She often wondered if he knew about Frank Bridlemile, but either he didn't or he was exceptionally good at pretending.

On Vivian's first night in town, cocktail hour ran long and dinner ran late. Adele fed Ruth and Ivy early and put them to bed. George and Vivian, drunk, had wandered off to the kitchen. Tom, also drunk, sat alone and morose in the living room. Adele, not drunk, decided to call it a night. She patted Tom's shoulder and went to say good night to George and Vivian. From the hallway she heard them whispering, not as quietly as they imagined.

". . . what you must think of me, George. You never would have done it."

"Don't say that. We can't know that." George's voice sounded thick and sloppy.

"No, I know you. You'd never give up your child. Never. You're too good a person to do such a terrible thing."

"I'm not good. I'm not. And you did not do a terrible thing. Because I love her. We love her. I can't imagine my life without her."

Vivian let out a sob.

George's voice no longer sounded sloppy. It sounded desperate. "You were so brave. It was a *good* thing that you did. Because we love her. And you do, too, I know. But we love her. We *love* her. Don't you see?"

Adele thought back to George's insistence on delivering the girls in New York. She struggled to recall when George first announced she was having twins. Then realized that it didn't matter—the details of the con were beside the point. Vivian had given a child to George, and thus she had given a grandchild to Adele, who had absolutely no intention of relinquishing her. *Please don't say a name—I don't want to know which is which,* she prayed as she crept back down the hallway. This was one secret she hoped her daughter could keep forever.

CHAPTER 26

Ruth and a gaggle of neighborhood kids in swimsuits stood in a circle. In the center of that circle, Ivy perched atop a sprinkler, stopping the spray of water while Ruth and the other children hopped around in terrified anticipation. When would she rise? When would the water come back? Ruth knew the pressure was building up and that when Ivy stood, the water would shoot wild, far across the green lawn. Would she be too close? Or too cautious, too far away for the drops to reach her? Ivy rose with a shriek, the water spraying the bottom of her pink suit. The water flung outward, and Ruth and Ivy ran together, holding hands, shaking droplets from their hair. There was no one on earth she would rather run with than her sister.

At twelve, they were the oldest children on their street. For most of the summer, Ivy had acted like she was too big to play with little kids anymore. Some days she acted like she was too big to play with Ruth anymore. But on this particularly hot day, when they were both particularly bored, Ivy had relented. And Ruth could see, from the gleam in her twin's eyes as they skipped home, that Ivy had enjoyed it as much as she had.

"Aunt Vivian's coming tonight," said Ivy, doing a spin on the hot sidewalk.

How had her sister known this? No one had told Ruth. Probably no one had told Ivy either. But Ivy had ways of finding things out. Just last week she'd announced to Ruth that their mother and Uncle Frank were having an affair. Ruth was vague as to what having an affair entailed, but she knew it wasn't good. "How do you know?" she'd challenged her sister.

Ivy had shrugged. "I just know. Do you think they'll get divorced?"

Ruth had worried that her parents might get divorced ever since she'd learned what the word meant. Most of the time her parents ignored each other, their jaws set, their shoulders hiked up. They didn't yell—the Rutledge house was a quiet house—but that didn't mean there wasn't ugliness in the air. Until Ivy said the thing about the affair, Ruth had feared she'd caused this ugliness. She lay awake at night, wondering who'd she'd live with when her parents split up. Her mother, she supposed, because her father was always flying. But what if neither of them wanted her?

"What do you think she'll be wearing?" asked Ivy. She meant Aunt Vivian. She wore the most elegant outfits. She rolled her hair in a chignon. She carried a silver lighter with the mysterious initials *LK* on it. Even when she wasn't using it to light a cigarette, she flicked it open and then snapped it shut, flick-snap, flick-snap. Ivy had asked her once what the *LK* stood for. "Oh, just a pilot I used to know." A response both elegant and mysterious.

Their mother was nervous for days before Vivian's arrival. She planned fancy menus, even though anyone could see that Aunt Vivian didn't care about fancy food. She laid out matching outfits for Ruth and Ivy, even though Ivy argued they were too old for matching outfits. "Wear them for Vivian," said their mother.

When Aunt Vivian came, their grandmother grew uncharacteristically quiet. "You don't talk much when Aunt Vivian's here," Ivy said to her once. If Ruth had said it, Adele would have said, "Is that a question? I know you're much too well brought up to question your elders." But no one minded when Ivy said that sort of thing. No one minded anything that Ivy did, and Adele had replied, "If you don't have anything nice to say . . ." and then said no more.

CHAPTER 27

Ivy and Ruth crouched together at the bend in the stairs, listening. They were supposed to be in bed, but when Aunt Vivian came, certain rules were relaxed. When Aunt Vivian came, the conversations that took place after bedtime were much more interesting than the conversations that took place at the dinner table. Partly because all the grown-ups had been drinking since midafternoon. Sometimes even since lunchtime.

When Aunt Vivian came, their father stood at the sideboard stirring drinks, while Aunt Vivian stirred the household. Ivy never knew what she'd do or say next. Nothing was a given when Aunt Vivian came except that all the grown-ups would have headaches in the morning and that the house would seem strangely quiet when she left.

Ivy leaned toward the stair railing, straining to hear as her father and Vivian told their stories. They swapped tales of crosswinds and unbalanced loads. Of lightning and funnel clouds. Of unruly passengers and inept ground crews.

The best way to hear the truth was to listen when no one thought you were around. At the dinner table, Ivy heard only that flying was safer than automobile travel. "And I should know," said their father. His parents, Ivy's Nan and Pop-pop, had died in a car crash just last year.

Her father flew commercial airliners to Atlanta and Kansas City and sometimes even Los Angeles. The airlines never hired female pilots, though their father once announced, as if bestowing a precious gift not just upon Vivian but upon every female listening, that Vivian would have made a good one. Her mother flew, too, but just as a hobby. No one ever suggested that she might fly for a job. No one suggested she might do anything for a job.

Aunt Vivian and their father had had plenty of practice telling their stories. They knew just when to pause for her mother to laugh. But tonight, George didn't laugh much. She'd been snappish during dinner, and her mood only worsened as the evening went on. Perhaps she'd grown tired of the older stories. Ivy herself found the conversation less interesting than she'd anticipated.

Ice chimed against the sides of an empty glass. "I'll have another, Tom," said her mother.

Ivy had entertained herself throughout the afternoon and evening by privately tallying the number of drinks each grown-up had. (Grandma Adele was losing. Badly. But George was on track to set a record.) It had recently occurred to Ivy that she herself would be a grown-up someday, so she needed to know things like how many scotches on the rocks you could have before you couldn't stop giggling, or before it became necessary to lean against your friend in order to not topple over. And how many more you could down before your eyelids fluttered and all you could do was stagger off to bed. It was like a story problem. If four adults consume X cocktails between 3 p.m. and midnight, and Y equals the quantity of aspirin needed the following morning, solve for Y. Also: solve for the number of times you'd shush your daughters the next day, and whether they'd have to get their own breakfast.

"Another?" said Tom. "You've already—"

"I don't need you to tell me how many I've had. *I'm* not flying a plane tomorrow, am I? I'll have as many as I want."

Ivy heard the creak of chair leather as he stood. The plush carpet couldn't fully muffle his tread as he moved to the credenza.

"Don't skimp," ordered George.

Three plinks meant three ice cubes tonged into the glass, the sound ringing through the thick silence in the living room. Ivy held her breath and stared at Ruth, who pressed her own lips tightly together. Neither of them wanted their presence on the stairs to be detected.

"Here you go," said Tom. A pause, during which her mother was supposed to say thank you but didn't. Then the leather of her father's chair complained again, and he said, "Now where was I?" He took up his story, and Ivy and her sister breathed again.

"Let's count how many times they slur their words," said Ivy.

"Shh," hissed Ruth, widening her eyes.

"They can't hear a thing now. And even if they did—" She made a loose C with one hand and tilted it toward her mouth.

"Shhhhh!" insisted Ruth.

"Would've been different if Vivian'd been at the controls with me," said her father in the overly cheery voice he used when he and her mother had recently fought.

The thunk of a glass being set down on a wooden table. Someone wasn't using a coaster. "How?" insisted George. "How would it possibly have been different?"

"Georgie," said their father.

"You managed fine. What's his name, the copilot, Stevens. He managed fine too."

"Georgie, all I'm saying is she's a damn good pilot. You know that yourself."

"Yes, and I don't need to be reminded of it every goddamned night."

"Georgeanne," said Grandma Adele. "Language."

"One more, Tom."

"I just gave you—"

"A double this time." Ivy's shoulders jumped at her mother's tone. The one she used when she'd reached the absolute limit of her patience, when swift punishment was certain to follow any further nonsense from her daughters. A tone even Ivy knew better than to challenge. She'd never heard her mother use it with her father.

His lack of familiarity with it was probably why he dared to say, "I wouldn't if I were you. You'll regret it in the morning."

"Don't you lecture me. Especially about regret."

"George," said Aunt Vivian, her voice shrill and tight. "I need a cig. Join me outside?"

"And don't try to get me out of my house either. It's the one place I *belong*, after all."

"I just thought—"

"But that's just it. You don't think. Neither of you ever think. And I'm sick of hearing these stories. Over and over and over," said their mother. Her voice quavered. "You have no idea how sick of them I am."

"You're right, George," said Aunt Vivian. "We're sorry. We get carried away. We'll talk about something else now. Tell me what's going on with the girls." Ivy pressed up against the banister, eager to hear what her mother would say about her. Eager to compare it to her real life, and the increasing number of secrets she kept from her.

"You've seen them. You'll see them again tomorrow. You can ask them yourself." This was disappointing. Shouldn't her mother *want* to talk about her? Wasn't it actually her job?

"George, what's gotten into you?" It was a warning, not a question, not really, from her father.

"Not that you care about them," George said, ignoring Tom and talking to Aunt Vivian. "Not the way you care about your precious planes."

"If I were you," said Grandma Adele, "I'd take two aspirin and take myself to bed."

"That's not true," said Vivian. She said it so quietly Ivy almost didn't catch it. "You know that's not true. You know I love her—them."

"Easy to love from up so high," said George. "Easy to love from fifteen thousand feet. Where's my drink, Tom?"

"You've had enough," he said.

"I think we should talk about something else now, George." Ivy heard something new in Aunt Vivian's voice. After a beat, she recognized it as panic.

"Georgeanne," said Grandma Adele. "Bedtime."

"I'm raising her. As my very own. And you—you come into *my* house, and I *cook* for you, and I wait—I wait months for your letters, your calls, months for you to ask. Not about her—I know you care about her, I do. But you never ask about me. And I have to listen to all these stories. After I gave up *everything*."

Their mother was crying now, which was not unheard of, but still alarming. Aunt Vivian started crying too. "Oh God, George, I'm sorry. I'm so sorry, but stop. You have to stop now."

"What are you saying?" asked their father, panic in his voice.

"I love them both the same," said their mother. "Both exactly the same."

"Georgeanne! Hush right now!" said Grandma Adele.

"I can't imagine not having them. *Both* of them. But some days I wish you had taken them and I was—" Their mother had stopped crying. Her voice had become steady and bitter.

Ivy wanted to be alone. She wanted Ruth tucked safely in bed while she served as the only witness to the terrible thing happening in the living room. How much easier to be the one in sole possession of this story, the one reporting it to an innocent listener. How much easier to be the one filing off the sharp and dangerous edges, smoothing it down to something merely amusing.

"What the hell are you saying?" demanded their father. His voice was breaking, which was absolutely unheard of and terribly alarming. "Stop saying this! Stop it, now!"

The living room fell silent, and Ivy, in the dark, at the bend in the stairs, pretended Ruth wasn't there as she waited for someone to say something that would make everything right again.

"Adele," said their father, "what does she mean?"

Grandma Adele said nothing.

"Are you saying—which one is ours?"

"They're *both* ours," said their mother.

"Don't pretend you don't know what I mean, goddamn it. Twelve years. Twelve years, George? And this is how you tell me?"

"It doesn't change anything," said Grandma Adele. "Not a thing. And no one is to say one word, not one single word to those girls. Ever. It would break their hearts."

1957–1967

CHAPTER 28

Was her heart broken? Each night as she tried to fall asleep—impossible after what she had overheard on the stairs—Ruth pressed a hand against her chest, against the slight swelling that had, to her great relief, finally begun there. It had started first for Ivy, of course. Beneath Ruth's swelling, her heart went thud-thud-thud. Faster than usual. Meanwhile, Ivy breathed steadily in the next bed because, thought Ruth, she knew she was their parents' real daughter.

She prayed every night for her father to come home, but God had apparently chosen to ignore her, probably because they never went to church. She planned to ask about that in the morning, to see if they could start attending. Everyone else in Enid did, and she didn't like to stand out. But Ivy spoke first at breakfast the next day.

"Where's Dad?" Ivy wasn't shy about asking questions. The only surprising thing about her asking this one was how long she'd held off. Their father had been gone for nearly two weeks, when his usual run took four days.

"On an extended run," said Grandma Adele.

"Why?" Ivy's voice had a taunting edge, which her mother and grandmother ignored.

"Because the folks in charge asked him to, and he said yes," said Grandma Adele.

Their mother sipped her coffee and worked her crossword. After they left for school, Ruth knew she'd go fly her plane. Then she'd have lunch with Frank Bridlemile. ("Why," asked Ivy, shortly after she informed Ruth that her mother and Frank were having an affair, "are you and Uncle Frank always having lunch together?" "To talk business. Real estate. Investments," said their mother. Grandma Adele had cleared her throat and rattled the paper.) After her mother and Frank Bridlemile talked real estate and investments, she'd come home and cook them dinner. She'd ask Ruth and Ivy for a report on their days, and no one would mention their father or when he might return.

"Brush your hair, Ivy," said Grandma Adele.

"I already did!"

"Well, it needs brushing again. What are you brooding about, Ruth?"

"Nothing."

"Good. Stop moping, then. No one likes a moper."

Right. No one liked a moper. It was essential—now more than ever—to be a sunny, likable girl. She straightened her shoulders, brightened her expression. It didn't matter that her face didn't match up with how she felt on the inside.

After breakfast, she studied herself in the hallway mirror. From hairline to ankles, she compared her own face and body against her mother's. Everything was different. Her mother's skin was fair and rosy. Ruth's was sallow. Her mother was tall and lanky and carried herself with an easy grace. Ruth hadn't grown, it seemed, in three years, and was always bumping into table corners. They both had hazel eyes, but then, so did tons of people. George's hair was shinier than Ruth's. Her nose less prominent. Her chin stronger. Everything about her, in fact, was superior to everything about Ruth.

She didn't need a mirror to compare herself to Ivy. They weren't identical—Ruth had often wished they were—but she knew her twin through and through. Their constant togetherness meant she'd known, that night on the stairs, exactly what it meant when the muscle in Ivy's arm twitched as she pulled away from Ruth. That she was embarrassed for her. Because obviously, if one of them didn't belong, it was her.

One of them was Vivian's, and one of them was George's. One of them was Tom's, and the other was . . . whose? Ivy speculated about Frank Bridlemile. "That's ridiculous," said Ruth.

"You're right," said Ivy. "The math doesn't work. He would have been in the Far East. For the war."

Ruth had been too distraught to calculate conception dates. The fact that Ivy could calmly assess the possibilities only confirmed that Ruth was the one who didn't belong. To Ivy it was just a game—a mystery to solve. They were detectives—like Trixie Belden or Nancy Drew. They drew up lists of questions for their mother and father, for Adele and Aunt Vivian.

Their father had listened patiently to their inquiries. He seemed relieved to offer up the date and location of his wedding to their mother, reluctant to discuss anyone he had dated before meeting her. "No one important, no one that mattered." He grew defensive when asked why he wasn't there when they were born. "There was a war on, for God's sake. If every man whose wife had a baby had been sent home, we'd all be saluting Hitler now."

"So you never actually saw us be born?" pressed Ivy. "You never actually saw us as babies."

"You were still plenty babyish when I got back. Still are some days. Now, I've got to get ready to go."

Adele was a vault. Though she did agree to let them look through her picture album. There was their mustachioed grandfather, looking stern and old fashioned. "He was actually a very modern man," Adele corrected them. There was her mother as a baby, eyes wide, startled by the camera or perhaps the world in general. There she was again next to a pump jack, next to a ridiculous car. "Our good old Nash," said Adele. "What I wouldn't give to have it back." Their mother in her high school graduation robe. And then with Aunt Vivian, their arms around each other, beaming. "Their graduation. I went down to Sweetwater by myself. Your grandfather was not able." Was that a sniffle? Ruth looked up in alarm, but her grandmother blinked twice and returned to her normal self. Then, in a frustrating leap through time, their mother in a starched dress and pinafore (a pinafore!) holding the two of them on her lap.

"But what about the wedding?" asked Ivy.

"I wasn't there. Ask your mother—she's probably got a snapshot somewhere."

"Why weren't you there?"

"There was a war on, young lady. We couldn't all go gallivanting around the country."

"Or we'd all be saluting Hitler right now," said Ruth.

"Fat chance," said their grandmother.

They compared their own baby photos to George's, but babies looked boringly similar. Did Grandma Adele have any baby pictures of Aunt Vivian?

"Of course not," she said. "Why would I?"

Their mother was busy. Mostly with Frank Bridlemile. "Real estate is a time-intensive business," she said when they complained about her spending yet another evening out.

"Was Aunt Vivian at your wedding?" asked Ivy.

"Of course." Her mother snapped her compact shut and scooped up her keys.

"Did she already know Dad?"

"What? Oh yes. They'd met. There was a war on—we all got thrown together one way or another. I've got to run. You girls be good for your grandmother."

Vivian didn't return to Enid for a long time. Ivy wrote her a letter, which Ruth reluctantly cosigned, requesting childhood photos. They received no response. They wrote another. It was returned unopened, Addressee Unknown. No forwarding address.

Their mother shrugged. "You know your aunt Vivian. She's a nomad. We'll hear from her when she settles somewhere."

After their initial questioning, their father didn't come home for nearly two weeks. Ivy wanted to interrogate him again, but Ruth refused. "He doesn't like it. He'll stay away even longer if we keep at him like that."

"But—" Ivy began.

"I won't," said Ruth. Why was Ivy so determined to prove that they weren't sisters? "Don't you want to be twins anymore?"

"That's not the point," said Ivy. "The point—"

"I don't care what the point is. I just want to be sisters. If you don't, you can figure it out for yourself."

Ivy's eyes widened in the most gratifying way. *Why should she always be in charge?* thought Ruth. Just because their friends went along with every game Ivy suggested didn't mean Ruth had to. Why should she keep playing a game she could only lose?

She much preferred the research game that they'd started playing at sleepovers. Sandra, not Ivy, had initiated it. Over the course of seventh grade, Sandra went from a training bra to a C cup. Her authority grew right along with her boobs. Suddenly Sandra took charge of their group, and she had her own ideas about how they should spend their time.

In the research game, they practiced doing things boys would like. "So that when we're old enough to go on dates, we'll be ready," said

Sandra. She had a seventeen-year-old sister, who told her all about what boys liked.

"Pair off," commanded Sandra. Many of the games involved breaking their group of six into pairs. Sandra had called them each the day before to instruct them to wear something sleeveless. They needed access to each other's arms so that they could learn to give hickeys.

Ruth's partner was Cindy, a slender girl ("Flat as a board," sighed Sandra, the night they all tried the pencil test) with heavy glasses that kept sliding down her nose and a waterfall of coffee-colored hair. Sandra instructed each girl to give her partner a hickey on her upper arm. She turned out the lights. "So we won't be self-conscious." Cindy put her mouth on Ruth's arm and sucked. Ruth breathed in the strawberry scent of her hair. After a bit, she touched it. It felt silky. Cindy made a little noise as if to say, "Do that again." Ruth did that again. Cindy made the noise louder this time. Ruth put her own mouth to Cindy's shoulder. Cindy moved hers to Ruth's opposite shoulder. Then to Ruth's neck and up to her jaw, brushing her lips along Ruth's skin. Ruth's breath came faster. She pressed herself against Cindy, who sighed and pressed back. The lights blazed on, and Sandra yelled, "Freeze!" Ruth and Cindy bolted apart. But the other girls were too busy inspecting their arms to notice.

Four of them displayed fresh purplish-red bruises on their arms. "Ruth and Cindy, you didn't suck hard enough. It needs to leave a mark," said Sandra. When the lights went off again, they diligently suctioned each other's upper arms. Cindy put her hand on Ruth's breast, and Ruth, bold in the darkness, slipped her own beneath Cindy's sweater. Cindy gave a muffled moan. This time the floor creaked as Sandra moved toward the light switch, and they separated before the lights came on. "Much better," said Sandra when they displayed their arms for her approval.

Cindy hosted at least one sleepover a month. They ate popcorn, styled each other's hair, gossiped about which girls hadn't yet gotten their period, and who liked whom, until, at last, Sandra announced the night's research plan. Ruth always tried to station herself near Cindy. The other girls were boring partners. They stuck to the task at hand and never improvised.

It was okay to improvise, she told herself. She was just figuring out what boys might like by figuring out what she liked herself. At home, as Ivy breathed steadily in the next bed, Ruth sometimes imagined a boy touching her the way Cindy did. This required concentration, because Cindy's silky hair and smudged glasses kept floating into her thoughts. The only boy she could get to "stick" there was Frank Jr. He was blond like Aunt Helen and rangy like Uncle Frank. She and Ivy had known him since they were babies.

The three of them had spent mornings bickering over toys while their mothers sipped coffee and chatted. Evenings watching TV in their pajamas while their parents sipped martinis and played bridge. Summer afternoons running naked together through the sprinkler. "Only in the backyard," insisted Aunt Helen. "We're not trashy people."

When Ruth pictured herself with a boyfriend, she always imagined Frank Jr. She fantasized that he'd be her first real kiss—Cindy obviously didn't count. But Ivy, typically, got to him first.

A dinner party. Their father home for an extended stretch. Grandma Adele in Oklahoma City for an auto show. Apparent peace reigned between the Rutledges and Bridlemiles. George and Tom and Helen and Frank all dressed up. "We'll be at the Wilkinsons' until late," said her mother. "You children go on to bed when you get tired. The guest room's made up, Frank Jr."

"He can stretch out on the sofa if he's tired," said Uncle Frank. Aunt Helen said Frank Jr. was much too tall to stretch out on that dinky sofa—why, anyone could see it was more of a love seat—and he was growing so fast, he needed his sleep. Ruth mentally awarded her double points for managing to boast about Frank Jr.'s height and disparage the Rutledge sofa all in one go. Uncle Frank told Aunt Helen not to baby the boy, and Ruth's dad said they had all better get in the car or they'd be late.

"All the more fashionable," said Aunt Helen. "Frank Jr., you sleep in that bed, hear?"

"Yes, ma'am," said Frank Jr. Ruth was glad he didn't argue—anything to get their parents to leave already. She and Ivy were fourteen, and Frank Jr. was fifteen—all of them past needing a babysitter, though Aunt Helen still had to make some ridiculous point about Frank Jr. being in charge. Every minute their parents lingered at the door was pure torture. "The Wilkinsons' number is right by the phone," her mother said, for a third time, and then, finally, four car doors slammed, the engine turned over, and the tires hissed down the driveway. "Just to be clear," said Ivy, "we're each in charge of ourselves. No one's babysitting anybody else here." Frank Jr. cocked an eyebrow but didn't argue.

Earlier, Ivy had complained about Frank Jr. coming over. Why did the three of them have to hang out just because their parents did? They weren't friends with him at school. Now that he was a freshman, they didn't even go to the same school. "And Aunt Helen acts like he does us some big favor, gracing us with his presence," said Ivy.

Yet her sister had changed into her tightest sweater. The one that clung in all the right places and showed so clearly that Ivy's places were righter than Ruth's own. She couldn't compete with Ivy's sweater, but she did spend half an hour in the bathroom with her mother's hot rollers getting her hair to curl just right. George didn't allow makeup yet, so the field remained level there.

They made popcorn, pulled bottles of Coke from the fridge, then plopped down on the sofa. Frank Jr. held the bowl, so he sat in the middle. And perhaps the sofa really was more of a love seat, because there seemed to be very little space. And no way for Ruth to avoid brushing against Frank Jr.'s arm as she reached for the popcorn. He weighed down the middle of the cushion, which meant both girls pitched toward him, their legs coming to rest against his. None of them mentioned this unusual contact, and no one jostled the others for more space.

They watched *Wanted: Dead or Alive* and Lawrence Welk and *Gunsmoke*. Ivy went to get them more Cokes. Ruth had certainly been alone with Frank Jr. before. She had certainly been alone on this very sofa—love seat—with him before. The warmth of his leg against hers. The way her shoulder met his upper arm just so in the groove between his arm muscles. He shifted his arm out from under hers. She cringed, mortified that he must sense how much she liked leaning against him. She inched away, then felt a weight across her shoulders. He'd put his arm around her! It left a gap into which she could lean toward him, rest against his rib cage, and she was allowing her body to fill that gap, slowly, so that it would seem accidental, like something that just happened, when Frank Jr.'s arm retreated, just as Ivy returned with three more bottles of Coke.

After the second Coke, Ruth needed to pee, but she was determined to hold it in, to maintain physical contact with Frank Jr. It was warm on the love seat. The three of them drowsed in front of the set. Jack Paar was boring, and soon the national anthem would play and the screen would just be bars of color.

From the kitchen, the jangling complaint of the telephone stirred them all awake. "You get it," said Ivy. "I got the Cokes." Ruth had no argument for that. Plus, she could barely hold her pee anymore. "That'll be our mom," said Ivy to Frank Jr. "She thinks she has to check up on us." This was said in the world-weary, exasperated tone Ivy had taken to using lately and that Ruth hated. But Frank Jr. curled his lip in amusement.

After she'd assured her mother that everything was fine, yes, they'd had a snack, yes, they'd go to bed soon, yes, the parents should stay out as late as they liked, no problem; after she'd relieved herself, praying that Frank Jr. couldn't hear the thundering, unladylike stream; after she'd considered and then decided against spritzing herself with her mother's perfume—(a) she didn't want to seem like she was trying too hard, and (b) she didn't want Frank Jr. to think she smelled like her mother—she made her way back to the living room. No sound of laughter, no conversation, just Jack Paar saying, "I kid you not."

And there, on the sofa / love seat, Frank Jr. had one arm curved tight around Ivy's back and the other wedged between himself and the front of her tight sweater, where his hand was clearly getting a good sense of her rightness. They were kissing, and it was obvious tongues were involved.

At the next sleepover, they all sat in a circle, and Sandra proposed they each take turns saying which boy they liked. Sandra went first and named the cutest eighth-grade boy. Linda went next, then Diana, each picking a boy just a notch down in popularity from Sandra's choice. Then it was Ruth's turn. The only boy she liked was one her sister had gotten to first. She tried to think of which eighth-grade boy would rank fourth, but it was hard to focus with Cindy trembling beside her. "Earth to Ruth," said Sandra. "Hello?"

Ruth punted. "Well, I know who Ivy likes. Frank Bridlemile!"

Ivy glared at her. "Why jump ahead to me, Ruth? You and Cindy in a hurry to turn out the lights and start your *research*?"

Ruth stiffened. Cindy exhaled in a loud whoosh. The other girls goggled at them. "No!" Her voice had never sounded so shrill. "That's ridiculous!"

Ivy smirked, then opened her mouth as if she had more to say, and Ruth wished for once her sister could let something go. The wishing must have worked, because Ivy just shrugged. "Whatever you say, Ruth." Her tone implied she neither believed Ruth nor cared enough to argue. Cindy stared at the carpet. The other girls looked from Ruth to Ivy and back. Finally, Ivy rose and said she wanted more soda. Sandra, Linda, and Diana followed her to the kitchen. Cindy trotted after them, saying there was more out in the garage. She never hosted a sleepover again.

That fall they started high school, and slowly their group of six fractured. They each drifted off to new sets of friends and, especially, to boys. Even Cindy had a boyfriend. In the halls, she sometimes gave Ruth a shy smile or a half wave, but she never sat with her at lunch or sought her out. And Ivy, after they exited the school bus each morning, managed to avoid Ruth almost entirely. Ruth tried not to care. She made friends of her own. She tried to keep from looking for her sister, but her brain was like a radar she couldn't turn off—always sweeping her surroundings, searching for Ivy's ping. Was that her down the hallway? Up ahead in the lunch line? Getting into a car with that football player?

By sophomore year, Ivy had a date almost every weekend. Ruth heard from her friends—who heard from their brothers—that her sister was fast. She didn't want to believe it, but Ivy returned home seconds before curfew, her eyes bright, her cheeks flushed. Ruth didn't need a mirror to confirm that her own eyes and cheeks didn't look like that after a date. She didn't go out as often as Ivy did. But for school dances or other occasions that required an escort, she had Patrick Healy. Treasurer of the chess club, second clarinet in band. A boy she could rely upon to compliment her on her dress, dance with her and fetch her punch at socials, and never try any funny business in the car. A boy who required no research at all.

CHAPTER 29

"Have fun!" said George as she waved the girls off for the evening. Not a double date, because Ruth and Ivy ran in different social circles. This was a good thing, she told herself. They were separate people, each with her own taste. Still, she wished Ivy would go out with boys a little more like Patrick Healy, and that Ruth would find some who reminded her a little less of Mel Carson. Surely there must be some version of boy in between those two extremes.

The girls barely waved goodbye to each other, which made her sad. Not that they cared what she thought. To them, she was just a housewife. Well, she had only herself to blame for that. Wasn't a housewife exactly what she'd tried so hard to be when they were younger? She'd thought they might find her more interesting when she started flying again. But her daughters didn't take her flying seriously. Sometimes she felt like a child with a precocious hobby.

The phone rang—Tom's nightly check-in—and she hurried inside to answer. It was a quick call—he only had a minute—but it lifted her mood.

"Tom's coming home," she announced to her mother.

Adele lowered her *Popular Mechanics* and said, "Is that so?" in the bland voice she used whenever the subject of her son-in-law arose.

"For a month. Probably more," said George. Tom hadn't committed to any specific length of stay, but George had sensed from the sleepy way he said he missed her that this time things might be different.

The morning after Vivian's last awful visit, while the girls and Adele slept, while she listened to Vivian creeping out of the house and into a waiting cab, George had watched from the bed as Tom packed his satchel with more than the usual single change of clothes.

He'd turned, and seeing her awake, said, "Who else knows?"

Was he leaving her? Leaving them? What would she tell the girls?

"George. Who else?"

"Vivian."

"Of course Vivian. Because one of them *is* Vivian's—I figured that much out. But not which one. I know I asked last night, but don't you ever tell me. I mean it. Never."

She swore she wouldn't. But she didn't apologize. She would never apologize for having two daughters rather than one. She wasn't sorry. She would do it again a thousand times over.

"Who else?" he persisted.

"Probably Mother."

"Your mother never misses a trick. She's probably known since you brought them home."

George shook her head, remembering the pink curtains in the nursery windows. The rocking chair and cushion. Her mother's unexpected tenderness toward her granddaughters. Adele hadn't known. Not that day. George couldn't say for certain when she'd found out.

"Who else?"

"I wasn't trying to trick you. She was just a baby, and Vivian couldn't—if you knew, you'd understand why—"

"But I didn't know. And why not? Did you think you couldn't tell me? Did you think I'd say no?"

Yes, she thought. *I did.*

"You kept it from me. But other people know, don't they? Who else?"

George kept silent.

"Frank?"

George kept silent.

"Does Frank know?"

She closed her eyes.

"George."

"No. Why would he?"

"I'm not an idiot, Georgeanne."

He'd left the house and not returned for two months.

When he finally called her, he said, "I know it's not just real estate with you and Frank."

"Come home," said George. "Come home, and it will be. Just real estate. I swear."

She'd wanted her husband back. Wanted a father for her daughters. Wanted to move forward. To be the kind of wife and mother she was supposed to be. To have the family that she was supposed to have. So when Tom finally came home and unpacked, she'd been happy.

Frank Bridlemile had stayed away. They only saw the Bridlemiles as a quartet. Or on joint family outings. Because it was important to demonstrate—to others as well as themselves—that all was well. Nothing was compromised. The danger, the smoke, had cleared.

Tom never spoke of the girls' parentage again. That he hadn't demanded to know which girl was his allowed her to believe they could be a normal family. Because deep down he knew he was meant to be a father to both girls. That they were, in every respect except biology, really his twin daughters.

But normal only lasted so long. The two of them bickered about little things, then bigger things. Tom talked of nothing but work. Would he get the prime routes? The promotion? The bigger jets? Marrying him had been the smart choice, she reminded herself daily. He was a handsome man, a responsible man, a man with some solidity. And Frank was taken, after all.

Then, one afternoon, Frank showed up at her door. Tom was flying. Adele was out. The girls were at school. She hadn't heard from Vivian in ages. But there stood Frank, with his easy smile and his midnight eyes, and what was the harm of asking him in for coffee? Just coffee. Coffee and conversation with one of her oldest friends. As she scooped crystals from the Folgers can, he put his hands on her waist, and she didn't tense and she didn't say no. She dropped the scoop and turned to face him. They stood like that a long time, testing waters they already intended to swim in. Her blood raced, so fast and hot in her veins it dizzied her. She hadn't moved, yet her body somehow fitted itself against his. And everything began again.

For months at a time, Tom stayed away and George dreamed of someday—once the girls grew up and left—flying off with Frank. To . . . it didn't matter where. Someplace with an airfield. Someplace they could start the life they always should have had together.

Then Tom would come home and she'd plant her feet back on solid ground, do her best to make her marriage work. This was easier when Helen tugged hard on Frank's leash and he didn't come around for a while.

Tonight, with Ruth and Ivy out and Frank at home with Helen, George missed her husband. She flipped open her *Redbook*. Maybe she'd cool things off with Frank for good. Maybe things would go differently this time.

CHAPTER 30

Ivy didn't blame her father for disappearing. She wouldn't blame him if he didn't come back at all. If he flew far away and started up with a new house and a new wife and new children. Children he knew for sure were his own.

Why should she care if her father left her mother? Odds were, he wasn't her father anyway. This had been Ivy's first thought that night on the landing—that she was the one who wasn't theirs. Hearing that conversation fed the flame of something already smoldering inside her—the conviction that she wasn't part of them, that she didn't want to be part of them. That they would set themselves up as obstacles to all the things (things she couldn't yet even name) she was going to want in the next several years. Ivy hated obstacles.

Her second thought was that she was relieved not to be George's daughter. She felt a bit ashamed of that, but it wasn't her fault that her mother—Ruth's mother, George—was so boring. Yes, she had her little airplane. Her father had called it that once—"Your mother's little airplane"—and George had burst into tears. *Pathetic,* thought Ivy. Also pathetic: her mother and Uncle Frank making moony eyes at one another when they thought no one else was looking.

She didn't want a life anything like her mother's, which consisted mainly of flying her little plane (but always circling right back to Enid, never actually going anywhere exciting), planning meals and shopping, and going to her club luncheons. There was Garden Club and Literary

Guild and the Women's Club. None of which Grandma Adele attended. "Just an excuse for grown women to play dress-up," Adele had said when Ivy asked her why she didn't go. "Not my sort of thing." Not Ivy's sort of thing either. And now, no one else could reasonably expect it to become her sort of thing. Which left her free to consider exactly what her sort of thing was. Which left her free to be anything or anyone she wanted to be.

She didn't want to be like Ruth. Ruth had made her explain what they'd overheard, even though she knew perfectly well what it meant. Her supposed sister wasn't playing dumb. She just lacked imagination. She preferred not to see bad things. Ruth was on her way to being a very good grown-up. Pretending not to see what people didn't want you to see was a huge part of being an adult.

You had to pretend you didn't notice that Aunt Helen kept her body always between Uncle Frank and your mother. You had to pretend you didn't notice when Dad packed extra for what was supposed to be a one-nighter. You had to pretend you hadn't noticed he'd been gone when he came back weeks later. You had to pretend practically every boy in school was smarter than you were. And that you were just so impressed with everything they did or said. You had to pretend your parents were happy. You had to pretend you were sisters when you weren't.

Ruth was good at all this pretending. In fact, she seemed to prefer it. "I don't want to spy anymore," she said, a few months after their fateful night on the stairs. They'd spent the intervening weeks combing through the file cabinet and through desk drawers, scanning the photo albums on the living room bookshelf. In the file cabinet they found, neatly labeled in their mother's precise penmanship, a manila folder for each of them. In each, their immunization records, their report cards, their birth certificates with embossed seals on watermarked paper. "See," Ruth had said, "same day, same hospital, same parents."

"Haven't you heard of counterfeiting?" asked Ivy. "Or forgery?"

"It's got a seal on it," said Ruth, tracing her finger around the gold foil in the lower corner of her birth certificate. Ivy wasn't persuaded.

In the photo album, they found what they'd already seen many times. Photos of the two of them as tiny infants in matching caps, as larger infants in matching sunsuits, as toddlers, as elementary schoolers, losing and gaining teeth, hair shorter or longer. Smiling, always smiling. Pretending even before they knew they were pretending.

Ruth had stopped smiling at Ivy. She'd stopped the investigation. "We're only going to find out it's me. And, honestly, I'd rather not."

Ivy disagreed. She was positive she was the one who didn't belong. And she'd much rather know it for certain than suspect it. Than to have other people know what she didn't. When people knew what you didn't, it gave them a raw sort of power over you, a power you sensed even if you couldn't define it.

"Please," she begged.

But Ruth refused to do any more spying.

Fine for Ruth. She was good at pretending, but Ivy was terrible at it. Because she was terrible at it, she was always being told to mind her expression, to watch her tone, to *for goodness' sake, just behave, Ivy.*

She was terrible at behaving and pretending, but she was very good at other things. Kissing, for example.

At one of Cindy's sleepovers, Sandra, who'd recently kissed an actual boy, announced that she would now kiss each of them, a lips-on demonstration. Ivy was tired of Sandra's games. She didn't want to kiss Sandra, but the other girls seemed eager. Ivy missed the days when she could have said, *Sounds like a dumb idea*, and they all would have looked to her for a better one. But lately, if she didn't go along, they pestered and pleaded until she gave in.

When it was her turn, she closed her eyes, opened her mouth, and twirled her tongue around Sandra's for a bit until, thank God, it was over. After the final girl had a turn, Sandra announced that the best kisser of the night was Ivy. This was shocking, but also somehow reassuring. She was ready, she decided, to kiss an actual boy herself.

None of the boys in her class appealed to her. When her mother announced that the Rutledges were going to a party with the Bridlemiles and Frank Jr. would be coming over, she decided he'd be ideal. He was older, but not too old. He was good looking enough. And he didn't talk much, so he'd be unlikely to gossip about her later.

That night, as soon as Ruth left the room, Ivy slid closer to Frank Jr. He didn't scoot away. She had to act fast—Ruth could return at any moment. She leaned against him. After a second, he put his arm around her. She tilted her face up toward his, and that was all it took. They were kissing. And it was *much* better than kissing Sandra. He pulled her closer. She liked that. He kissed her harder. She liked that too. He slid his hand beneath her sweater. Research with other girls couldn't begin to compare. Then Ruth came stomping and coughing down the hallway. Ivy unwrapped herself from Frank Jr. but didn't move away. She sat snug against him, savoring the warmth of his leg alongside hers, until their parents got home.

She stuck close to the phone for the rest of the week, certain Frank would call to ask her out for a date, or at least ask if he could come over. But every call was some old lady wanting to talk to Grandma Adele about a pinging engine. With each day that passed, she grew antsier. By Saturday, she felt ridiculous. Was she going to mope around, waiting for a boy to call? No, she was not.

"Let's go to the movies," she said to Ruth. If there was any upside to being a twin, it was that she never had to venture out into the world alone.

Ruth wanted to see *Operation Petticoat*, which sounded like a stupid film, but the movie itself wasn't the point. Being away from the phone when Frank Jr. called was the point.

"Hey," said Ruth as they stepped away from the concession stand with their popcorn, "there's Frank Jr. You should say hello." Ivy noted the "you" as well as her sister's insinuating tone. "How'd you know he'd be here?"

"I didn't," said Ivy.

Ruth smirked at her, then sang out, "Hi, Frank!"

Frank, waiting in line with a crew of pimply high school boys, lifted his chin at them. Fine. She could play it cool too. "Hi, Frank," she said, not slowing her step as she walked past him. "Enjoy the show." She proceeded toward the theater entrance, not too fast in case he called out for them to wait, in case he wanted to introduce her to his friends. To ask if they could sit together.

"Who are those two?" asked a boy with a greasy ducktail.

"Nobody," said Frank Jr. "Just my parents' friends' kids. Just some little girls."

Ruth giggled all the way through the movie—something about a pink submarine with nurses on board—but Ivy barely paid attention. He'd called her a little girl. She'd been so stupid, assuming he liked her. Boys would kiss anyone—hadn't Sandra told them that?

If she couldn't tell—even when she was kissing one—how much he cared about her, then she'd make sure no boy ever knew whether she cared about him either. Better yet, she vowed as the lights came up, she'd never allow herself to care at all.

Freshman year, she made another vow: to put some social distance between herself and Ruth. They'd been defined as twins all their lives. And it wasn't even true! They looked enough alike, but they were different in any way that mattered. Ruth was obsessed with fitting in. Ivy wanted to be unconventional.

She cultivated an air of sophisticated detachment. Girls called her stuck up. Boys called her for dates. She never went out with any particular boy for long. She knew the kids at school whispered that she was fast. Better fast than dull, she thought. Even so, the cafeteria felt like a minefield. By junior year, she avoided it by spending her lunch hours in Mme Forrest's classroom, practicing her French conversation.

Carolyn Dasher

French came naturally to Ivy. Her teacher said she had an excellent ear and allowed her to run through four years of coursework in two. Mme Forrest had married an airman at the end of the war and then found herself in the middle of Oklahoma—a place so unlike France, she felt as though she'd traveled all the way to Mars—or so Madame claimed. The airman, like Ivy's father, had become a commercial pilot, and Madame had accepted a position teaching French at Enid High. She complained, in French, about the provincialism of Enid, the narrow-mindedness of Americans when it came to sex. Mme Forrest was elegant and sophisticated. Like Aunt Vivian. Ivy couldn't understand why she stayed in Enid. *"Amour,"* said Madame. Ivy rolled her eyes. She intended to be elegant and sophisticated somewhere far, far away from Enid, Oklahoma.

She already had a departure plan in place. She and Ruth and some other girls (more Ruth's friends than hers, but Ruth had been thrilled when Ivy asked to join them) were driving down to Dallas for a postgraduation shopping trip. Their parents had promised them money for it as a graduation gift. Ivy planned to use hers for a bus ticket out of Dallas. If she was careful, she could make it last for a while. She hadn't decided where she'd go and what she'd do, but these details would work themselves out. She'd go somewhere they'd never think to look. And she'd do something . . . unexpected.

CHAPTER 31

Billings hadn't lasted. Neither had Milwaukee or Denver, or any place in between. Eventually, Vivian settled near Houston. When she wanted male company but didn't want it under the watchful eye of her neighbors, she made her way to the truck stop out by the interstate. Not for the truckers, but for the other men who stopped there, on their way to somewhere else. Just something quick. Something light. Something that would carry her through the next couple of weeks, but nothing to get worked up about.

She wasn't looking for permanence. The men she met were in the oil business, mostly. They said things like, "A pilot? Well, I wouldn't want my wife doing something like that." And Vivian, flicking her lighter open and closed, would ask for another of whatever she was drinking. Not that she drank much at the truck stop. Not since that horrible night in George's living room had she allowed herself to get truly and utterly drunk. George's outburst had sobered her right up. She'd had no idea her friend was so unhappy.

One night at the truck stop, it wasn't an anonymous man, tie loose, footloose, morals (at least for the evening) loose, who sat down next to her and offered to get the next one. It was Don Patterson, rubbing the nape of his neck and grinning at her. It took her a minute to place him because of the beard, but he recognized her right away.

"Vivian Shaw. What are you doing back in Texas?"

She hadn't seen him since his wife's funeral. She recalled Susan's closed walnut casket. Heard the hymns, plaintive and off-key in that heart-wrenching quarter step that always took her back to a hard wooden pew in Hahira, Aunt Clelia pinching her arm, telling her to sit still. Don Patterson had been wreckage in a uniform, catatonic beside the Dubarrys. When the men lowered Susan's casket into the ground, he had emitted a great, gasping sob, and Mrs. Dubarry had taken his hand.

Now here he was, taking the barstool next to hers, ordering a double rye and saying, "Please tell me you're still flying, because hardly any of the rest of them are."

He was in town for only a few days. Working a contract job for Schlumberger. Inspecting or evaluating something or other. She barely feigned interest. What was the point if he'd be leaving town in a few days?

After he left Houston, she stayed away from the truck stop for weeks. Kept her feet warm on her own. Then, just when she'd managed to stop thinking about him, just when she thought she might perch on one of those barstools again and see what sort of company walked up, he phoned to say he was coming back.

"No more of this contract stuff," he said. "They're bringing me on staff. Looks like I'm moving to Houston."

She spent half a year after Don Patterson moved to Houston waiting for him to announce he was leaving. But he stayed. He called when he said he would and showed up at her door when he said he would, and always seemed happy to hear her voice and see her face. The ground beneath her feet steadied. She allowed herself to wonder, in this new steadiness, whether she'd be welcome again in Enid. A few years had passed since the horrible night in George's living room. Years of missing George desperately and fearing their friendship was ruined. Years spent trying to find the courage to ask if she could come back.

"If you and Tom will have me," she said to George on the phone.

"Well, it's mostly just me these days," said George.

Vivian was ready to fall on her sword at this, especially as she'd spent most of the phone call talking about Patterson and companionship and a recent feeling that came pretty close to happiness.

"Oh, don't," said George when Vivian started to apologize. "I'm the one who let the cat out. And we should have known it'd come out eventually. And Tom and I—well, it's always been up and down."

Vivian returned to Enid, visiting a few times a year. Tom, if he was living at home at the time, always managed to be flying when she arrived. Adele kept a wary eye on the level of alcohol in the bottles. During the first few visits, Ivy hovered close, eavesdropping, and Ruth kept her distance, avoiding. Vivian spoke only of the present and the future, careful never to poke the past and wake it.

In time, the girls settled down. They thanked her for the gifts she brought them. They asked politely how she'd been. They grew tall and luminous. They moved with George's easy stride, spoke with her inflections. When Vivian pointed this out to them, Ivy scoffed, "Right." Ruth looked pensive. Did they not see how amazing their mother was?

"Come with us today," said Vivian. "Your mom's going to take me up in her plane."

George often complained that the girls never flew with her. "Ivy thinks I'm silly," she told Vivian. "And Ruth might be scared." How absurd that George's daughters—Vivian couldn't possibly have given birth to one of these astonishing creatures—could be dismissive or frightened of flying. Vivian wouldn't stand for it.

"It'll be fun," she pleaded. "We'll fly along the Red River—you wouldn't believe how pretty it is from the air."

"No thanks," said Ivy.

"Your mother is an amazing pilot. You should both see how amazing. And it would mean a lot to me too. You girls are so grown up now. Soon you'll be off on your own, and I'll see you even less than I already do. I'll take you out to lunch beforehand. We can catch up."

Ruth glanced at Ivy as if to see which way her sister's wind was blowing. Ivy narrowed her eyes at Vivian, then said, "Okay. But only if we get to ask you questions too."

"Sure thing," she said, her voice steady. "I've got nothing to hide."

Adele decided to join them. George beamed. "This is going to be so nice," she said, and Vivian's heart soared. She had asked so much from her friend, and now she'd make something good happen for her. Only a small thing, but wasn't it the small things that mattered?

"A ladies' lunch out, and then up in the plane. You girls will love it—there's nothing at all to be afraid of."

"I'm not afraid," said Ivy. Ruth said nothing.

During lunch, Ivy asked about men she and George had known during the war. "Well, your dad, of course," said George.

"Besides him," said Ivy.

"And Quigley," said Vivian.

"And besides him. He was just a friend, right? I mean men you dated."

"We honestly didn't have a lot of time for that sort of thing," said George.

"But you and Dad found time," insisted Ivy. "Didn't Aunt Vivian have a boyfriend too?"

Vivian picked at her chicken salad. Maybe lunch had been a mistake. The girls hadn't pestered her with questions like this in years.

"Speaking of boyfriends," Adele chimed in. "Ivy, I hear you've been spending quite a bit of time with Slade Beckett these days."

"Who's Slade Beckett?" asked Vivian, grateful to change the subject.

"Varsity starting pitcher," said George.

Ivy waved a dismissive hand. "We're talking about Aunt Vivian."

"We're pestering Aunt Vivian," said Adele. "And it's verging on rude."

George signaled the waiter for the check. "I'd really like to get up in the air," she said. "The light is so nice right now."

"And the wind is low," agreed Vivian, eager to leave her chicken salad and this conversation behind.

"And we wouldn't want to get Ivy home late," said Adele. "In case Slade Beckett calls."

CHAPTER 32

Ivy's moodiness aside, George enjoyed the lunch. And the flight was beautiful. Clear skies. Not a single air pocket. Smooth sailing out and back and a textbook landing to boot. Maybe, she thought as the Cessna touched down, her daughters would fly with her again soon.

"Finally," muttered Ivy as they taxied toward the hangar. George glanced back at her passengers. Ruth looked a bit green. Maybe her tuna salad had been off. Ivy looked sour, but that was hardly unusual.

They disembarked, George climbing down last. The girls veered off, skirting a group gathered near another private plane, one George didn't recognize. She peered over, wondering who owned it.

In a low, tight voice, Vivian said, "I think that's Elliot."

"Oh, I recognize her from your graduation," said Adele. She started toward the group, calling out, "Hello!"

Ruth and Ivy glanced at one another in dismay. As if it would kill them to be pleasant for five minutes. "Come on, girls," said George.

She hugged Elliot, noting the expensive drape and cut of her suit, the cream-colored leather gloves that looked as if they'd been sewn specifically for her hands, the gin-scented cloud emanating from her.

"These are my girls, and maybe you remember my mother, Adele, from graduation," George said to Joyce. "Ruth and Ivy, this is Joyce Elliot. She flew with us in the WASP."

"Joyce Quigley now," said Joyce, and George's stomach dropped. Because Quigley knew everything, which meant Elliot knew at least some of everything, and Elliot had obviously been drinking since well before lunchtime.

"Bob transferred to Liberty not long after you left there, Viv. He always said you'd be fine, that I shouldn't worry. Even though you never sent a letter—not one!"

Vivian stammered, but Joyce wasn't done. "He explained everything," she said. *"Everything."* George grabbed both girls by the hand and pivoted away from the group, ready to run.

The movement drew Joyce's gaze. She eyed one girl and then the other. "Well! George and Viv always looked like twins, and so do you."

"Because they *are* twins," said George.

"Not a speck of their father in either of them, is there?" Joyce went on. She reached for Vivian's hand. "I know what George has been busy with all these years, but what about you, Viv?" Then the exuberance went out of her voice, and she said, "I have thought about you so often. Thank goodness for Bob, helping you out in your time of need. He always said you'd be fine. And here you are. And my, you do look fine. So elegant."

Vivian stood as if frozen, clutching Joyce's gloved hand. Her jaw worked, but she uttered no words.

"Maybe if I'd given up my boys—we have three!—I'd look as good as you do." Joyce cackled so hard, she wobbled on her kitten heels. Ivy stared at her with ferocious curiosity.

George tugged her girls away. "We have to head home. Mother can't be out long these days." This produced a snort from Ivy, but Adele obligingly slumped her shoulders.

"I'll say hello to Bob for you," Joyce shouted after them, but George, dragging Ruth and Ivy to the car, barely heard her.

Once they were safely locked in the sedan, she glanced to her right. Adele looked grim. She glanced in the rearview mirror. Vivian looked shell shocked—Ruth, queasy. But Ivy was on full alert. "What was she talking about?" asked Ivy.

"She was drunk," said George. "I can't stand being around drunk people."

"Well, that is just not true," said Ivy. "Especially when Vivian's here. Speaking of Vivian."

"Enough," snapped Adele. "Ivy, that's enough. No one wants to hear another word about Joyce. The poor woman. She has no idea what she's saying."

Ivy muttered that Joyce knew perfectly well what she was saying, and then fell silent. George fixed her eyes on the road ahead. There'd been a stretch, years ago, when the girls—Ivy leading, Ruth slouched behind her—had asked a lot of questions. The kind that made George fear they'd discovered something. But that was ridiculous. Neither she nor Vivian nor Tom had ever said a word to them. Eventually they'd stopped pestering, and George had assumed they'd gotten past whatever had stirred them up. She should have known better. Ivy never let anything go.

Back at the house, Vivian retreated to the guest room to pack. "Maybe they'll forget about it," she whispered as she hugged George goodbye.

"Not likely," George whispered back.

She steeled herself for more questions from Ivy. But Ivy never mentioned Joyce again. She stopped talking much at all.

She also stopped running around with boys. She appeared to be studying, and not just her French. She set and cleared the table and did her chores without complaint.

And then, one day, she disappeared.

CHAPTER 33

Ivy was nowhere to be seen after the final bell, which meant Ruth got to drive home solo. She liked driving, the smooth roadway slipping beneath the tires, the car leaning into the familiar curves of the route between school and home. A slice of her mother's apple cake waited. One single slice, and since Ivy wasn't with her, it was uncontested. As was the television. And the phone.

Lately, Ivy rolled her eyes at just about everything and sneered at the rest, and this had, Ruth thought, gone on long enough. Everyone was tired of it. It reflected badly on Ivy, and she didn't exactly need anything else reflecting badly on her. And, because they were twins and people considered them some sort of combined organism, it reflected badly on Ruth as well. Not that Ivy cared about that. Thinking of this, Ruth's good mood had already deflated when she opened the door to their room and found Ivy's pink sweater folded—with exquisite perfection—on her own pillow.

Bad enough having to share a room, but to have those closest to you—because who else but their mother or Grandma Adele would have put it there?—confuse a sweater for yours, when Ivy had worn it a hundred times. People always went on about how different she and Ivy were—how anyone who *really* knew them would never confuse one for the other. Except, thought Ruth as she wadded up the sweater and tossed it onto Ivy's bed, their very own mother and grandmother.

Only later did she realize what the sweater meant. After dinner had passed with no Ivy. After Red Skelton had passed with no Ivy. After George had called other mothers. "Oh, I'm sure it's just some misunderstanding," George said. "Probably a club meeting she forgot to tell me about. You know teenage girls." After Grandma Adele unpursed her lips and said, "Call Tom. And Vivian," and Ruth's mother replied that surely there was no need to alarm anyone. After *The Nurses* had concluded, and Adele said, "If you don't call Tom, I will," only then did Ruth—who up to that point had assumed Ivy's absence was just a bid for extra attention, as if Ivy never got enough of that—go to their bedroom and search through her sister's things. Nothing seemed out of place except the sweater she'd tossed on Ivy's bed. She turned to the curlicue-carved shelf their father had nailed up years ago. She and Ivy used it to display knickknacks and china figurines and the painted ceramic piggy banks that Vivian had brought them from Mexico.

First she shook Ivy's piggy. No jangle of coins, no rustle of paper. Empty. Her own piggy held $12.82. Or had held it. Ruth knew even before she picked it up that it no longer did. Sure enough. No jangle. Just a faint rustle. She pried the rubber stopper from the pig's belly. Maybe Ivy had left her a dollar. Nope. Just a scrap from the kitchen notepad. She unfolded it and read: *I'll pay you back.*

No *I'm sorry.* No *Goodbye.* Not even a signature. Though she could hear Ivy pointing out that a signature was unnecessary, because Ruth knew perfectly well who the note was from.

CHAPTER 34

She didn't need them to confirm what she knew to be true: she was Vivian's daughter. It was one thing for everyone to pretend when she was little, but she was eighteen now and done with pretending. She was tired of Enid, of the Rutledge house, of the boys she'd dated, of Ruth. She was tired of her lying, dull parents. She was even tired of Mme Forrest and her complaining. If Madame disliked Enid so much, she should convince her husband to take her somewhere else. And if he wouldn't, what was stopping Madame from going herself? More to the point, what was stopping Ivy?

Not a thing. She had a plan and it was simple. Step 1: get out of Oklahoma. Step 2: get to Dallas. Step 3: wait for things to settle down and then go to Vivian.

It would take a week, she calculated, for everyone to get over the shock of her leaving. She'd wait out that week in Dallas, which offered a degree of familiarity. Her mother had taken her and Ruth there once to shop for fancy dresses for the Spring Fling.

Sandra had recently learned about George's plane, and after Ivy mentioned the upcoming shopping trip, she said, "Wow. Your parents must be rich."

"No richer than yours," replied Ivy. But later she thought about it. No one else they knew had an airplane. Some families didn't even have two cars, while, if you counted Grandma Adele's, the Rutledges had three.

That night at dinner she asked, "Are we rich?"

"*We* are not," said Adele. "But your mother is."

This didn't make any sense. Their mother didn't have a job. Where had she gotten money?

"From your grandfather. And your mother invested it in your uncle Frank's company and made more. No, George"—Adele held up a hand to stop her from interrupting—"you should tell them. It'll be theirs someday, after all."

But Ivy didn't want it. Not if it came from a bunch of liars.

Liars who didn't even know how to spend it. They were rich, but she and Ruth had to share a bedroom. They had to wait for sales at Herzberg's to get new shoes. Their mother constantly hounded them about the length of their showers, the size of the water bill. Every now and then George did something expensive and unexpected—like taking them shopping in Dallas—and Ivy thought maybe she'd turned into someone more exciting. But then she went right back to being her predictable, motherly self.

Ivy ditched school at lunchtime and caught a bus to Oklahoma City. From there she headed south to Dallas. She'd planned to sleep during the bus ride, but her brain jittered with too much adrenaline. They reached Dallas just before midnight. Ivy deboarded and promptly locked herself in a stall in the ladies' room. She craved sleep, but it was too late for that now. She had to stay awake, in case a night watchman checked the bathroom. If she could remain hidden until daylight, she'd freshen up and find a boardinghouse—someplace cheap but clean.

In the morning she bought a doughnut at the station, then strolled through Dealey Plaza, then up Commerce Street. She spotted the Baker Hotel, where she'd stayed with George and Ruth on their shopping trip. The Baker was well beyond her means. *Someday,* she thought, remembering the plush carpeting and drapes, the soft bed she and Ruth had shared. She turned down one side street after another, searching for boardinghouse signs. She passed run-down, seedy hotels guarded by old men in webbed lawn chairs. The men smacked their toothless gums as she hurried by. At last, she spotted a house with a VACANCY sign in the front yard. The man who answered her knock leered at her with such open lasciviousness that she almost jumped back. "Sorry, wrong address."

When the sun dropped behind the skyscrapers, she retreated to the bus station. The woman in the information booth called out, "Need help, hon?" She probably kept a list of places that rented rooms. Ivy started to approach, then swerved off toward the ticket line. The lady probably also had a list of people to be on the lookout for. A list that might include Ivy. She waited in the ticket line until the information lady was occupied with someone else, then darted into the bathroom and locked herself in a stall for another night.

The next morning, she walked in the opposite direction. She'd done what she could to clean up at the bathroom sink, but she felt grimy. Her heels were blistered from walking. She'd packed light, but even so, the strap of her satchel bit into her shoulder. She didn't see any ROOM FOR RENT signs, and she couldn't face another night in a bathroom stall. She headed back to the bus station and bought a ticket to Houston.

While Vivian rattled and clanged in the cramped kitchen, Ivy examined the cramped, dimly lit living room. The shabby sofa smelled of cigarettes at one end. The cushion sagged at that end too. This must be where Vivian had her evening smoke-and-think. In Enid, she had it outside in the glider. Ivy sat in the smoke-and-think spot and inhaled deeply. Maybe she'd take up smoking. She'd tried it a few times and had felt neither here nor there about it. But then, she felt neither here nor there about many things.

What she felt strongly about was knowing who she was. She was Vivian's daughter. And if Vivian had given her up—handed her over to George and Tom—she must have had a reason. A reason Ivy deserved to know, even though she feared it.

Because maybe, right from the beginning, Vivian had sensed something . . . off about her. That Ivy wasn't like other people. Girls, especially. But then, neither was Vivian. Why did everyone refuse to admit the truth when they'd been so clearly caught out?

"Here you go." Vivian handed her a plate. She'd cut the grilled cheese sandwich horizontally, rather than diagonally, the way George and Adele always cut it. The pickle was a gherkin, not bread and butter slices. Every family, she reminded herself, did things differently.

"I know I'm not theirs," she said between bites of sandwich. It was undignified to have this conversation while eating, but she was ravenous.

"Don't be ridiculous," said Vivian. She picked up her cigarettes, then put them down again just as quickly. "Terrible habit," she said. "Don't you ever start."

"I'm the only one *not* being ridiculous. Everyone else just keeps lying, lying, lying. I thought you might be the brave one. The one willing to tell me the truth." Having delivered this eloquent and convincing argument, Ivy allowed herself the gherkin.

"This is nonsense, Ivy, and I don't know how it got into your head."

"Little pitchers have big ears. And grown-ups who drink don't watch what they say."

"I don't know what you're talking about." Vivian glanced longingly at her cigarettes, wrung her hands in her lap.

"Your friend at the airport? The one dressed up like Jackie Kennedy?"

"Elliot? She was drunk. And even when she isn't, she'll say just about anything for attention." She slid open the desk drawer, dropped the pack of cigarettes into it, and shoved it closed.

"I know they're not my real family. I'm not like them—not at all."

"Every teenager feels different from their parents. It doesn't make you special—it makes you normal."

"Liars," said Ivy, polishing off the sandwich. "Every single one of you."

The next day, while Vivian was at work, Ivy searched the apartment. In the desk drawer under the cigarettes, she found an envelope with her name on it and $200 inside. She fanned out the bills on the desk, then put them back in the envelope. She took a cigarette from the pack and put it between her index and middle fingers, pretended to take a drag. She tucked the cigarette into her rucksack and returned the envelope to the desk drawer. Vivian had assigned her some chores. It didn't take long to tidy up the apartment, to shop and prep for their dinner. If she worked carefully, Vivian might ask her to stay.

After dinner, Vivian flicked her lighter open and closed. She glanced at the phone, and Ivy understood it was only a matter of time before Vivian called her parents and told them she was there. That morning she'd tried to lure Ivy to the airfield. To get her into her plane. There was no way Ivy was falling for that.

She was about to try again to get her "aunt" to tell her the truth when the phone rang. Vivian lunged for it, and Ivy prayed it wasn't her mother. It was a man—Ivy recognized a boyfriend call when she heard one. While she talked to him, Vivian lit a cigarette as if she'd forgotten Ivy was there. She had a life. And she didn't want Ivy to be part of it. She wasn't going to claim her. Ivy's eyes filled with hot tears. She turned away from Vivian and swiped at them.

"Sorry," said Vivian as she hung up. She opened the window and swished the cigarette smoke with her hand. "I'll put it out."

Ivy waited until Vivian began snoring to slide open the desk drawer and take the envelope. She tiptoed out of the apartment and down the stairs. Out on the street, she walked fast, pretending she knew where she was going. In Enid the sidewalks were empty at night, but plenty of people were out and about in Houston. Most of them men. She felt their eyes following her as she strode along. She picked up her pace. Footsteps echoed in her wake, just well enough behind her that she couldn't tell if she ought to be worried. At the next corner, a cab stopped at a light. Ivy practically jumped in front of it, waving her hand to flag it down, just as she'd seen people do in movies.

"The bus station, please," said Ivy.

"You're almost there," said the driver. "Sure you wanna ride?" Looking back over her shoulder, she saw no sign of anyone trailing her, but she was certain she hadn't imagined it. "Yes."

The bus leaving the soonest was bound for New Orleans. All she knew about New Orleans was that it was in Louisiana and that Newcomb College was there. During Ivy and Ruth's junior year, Aunt Helen kept talking up Newcomb College, urging the girls to apply. But their mother hadn't gone to college, not for long anyway. Neither had Aunt Helen or Vivian or Grandma Adele. Girls who wanted to go to college, in Ivy's experience, were either squares or looking for a husband. Ivy wasn't the former and had no interest in the latter. Anyway, it didn't matter. You couldn't go to college if you never graduated from high school.

CHAPTER 35

After the call from George, Vivian looked around her dingy apartment and wondered where she'd put Ivy. Because it was only a matter of days, she was certain, before Ivy landed on her doorstep. Ivy, who had run away wearing a pleated skirt and a light-blue sweater. "Periwinkle," George had specified, as if the exact color of that sweater was the key detail that would lead them all to her daughter. Ivy, who was carrying only a school satchel, and, if Ruth's assessment of her finances was correct, less than twenty dollars. Twenty dollars wouldn't get a girl Ivy's age far, but there were other forms of payment that would, and thinking of that, Vivian had rushed to her tiny bathroom and been very sick.

When Ivy did appear, two days later, the pleats having fallen out of her skirt, her periwinkle sweater in need of a wash, but otherwise looking perfectly whole and healthy, Vivian already had a spare set of sheets waiting on the arm of the couch.

"Forty-eight hours," she said. "Because your mother and I have always spoken truthfully about things."

Ivy snorted. "She's not my mother."

Her eyes challenged Vivian, but Vivian only said, "You must be hungry," and retreated to the kitchen to make grilled cheese sandwiches. She'd laid in some Coca-Cola. And some graham crackers because she remembered the girls eating them when they were little. What did they eat now? She had no idea. She hadn't paid enough attention during her visits to Enid.

She felt terrible about not immediately calling George. But having run away herself, two years younger than Ivy and from a household with nothing like the Rutledge advantages, Vivian left the phone on the hook. After all, she'd returned to Hahira. Surely Ivy would find her way back to Enid. Vivian hoped to convince her to go sooner, rather than later. Not tonight, because Ivy seemed too petulant and exhausted to yield to any sort of persuasion. But tomorrow, after she'd rested, after she'd had another day to see that the world wasn't the marvelous, thrilling place she'd imagined. And that home was a better place than she'd realized.

Ivy needed to come to this realization herself. If George and Tom dragged her back to Enid, she'd be out the door again as soon as they looked the other way. And the next time, she wouldn't run to Vivian.

Vivian couldn't afford to skip out on a lesson, especially one with a new student, so she tried to persuade Ivy to come with her. "You can sit in the back and listen in. After, if you want to go up just the two of us, I'll give you a lesson."

Ivy leveled her glance at Vivian as if to say, "Do you think I'm stupid?"

Vivian tapped her appointment book. "Look. Right here. Chad Elkins at ten a.m."

"I'm not getting in your plane," said Ivy. "You'll just fly me back."

To be fair, Vivian had considered this option. She'd imagined George somehow knowing to be at the field to meet them, the gratitude on her friend's face when Vivian ushered Ivy out of the plane and back into her arms.

Ivy scanned the appointment book. "Ugh. *Chad.* All the worst ones are named Chad."

She lay curled up in a nest of blankets on the couch, wearing an old pair of Vivian's silk pajamas and sipping the orange juice that Vivian had delivered to her. It struck Vivian how accustomed the girl was to being waited upon. How she had reached up without even looking to take that glass of juice, to take the plate of eggs and toast, offering up a rote thank-you.

"What's that supposed to mean?" asked Vivian. "The worst ones how?"

"Never mind," said Ivy.

She's just a child, thought Vivian. *What could she possibly know about the Chads of the world?* "You'll be bored here," she insisted. "There's nothing to do."

"I'll manage."

"I really think you should come with me."

"I'll bet you do."

"It's just a lesson. I swear. Only a lesson. Then I'll show you around the field. We'll get lunch somewhere."

Ivy yawned and stretched. "No thanks."

Maybe tomorrow morning she'd dissolve a couple of sleeping pills into the orange juice. If this Chad was one of the worst ones, perhaps she could solicit his assistance in maneuvering an incapacitated teenage girl down the stairs, into the car, and then into Vivian's plane. But how did you even broach that idea? The rest of your lessons are free if you help me kidnap a girl? No, there would be no forcing Ivy onto a plane. No forcing Ivy home. Only the tedious process of convincing her to go herself.

"Okay, then," she said. "Wash up the breakfast dishes. When you're done, sweep the kitchen. I'm leaving some money right here. Go down to Oswalt's and get some chops and a vegetable for supper. I have two lessons after lunch, so I'll see you late afternoon."

Ivy didn't whine or resist the tasks assigned to her. When Vivian returned home, she found the vegetables washed, peeled, and diced, the table set, and the apartment as tidy as could be. Ivy had redonned her cleaned and pressed skirt and sweater. "How was your day?" she asked as Vivian walked through the door. It would be so easy to get used to this. Vivian made her heart stern against the possibility.

"Nothing special," she said. Though that was far from true, because Chad hadn't been one of the worst ones. He'd been attentive and respectful and had even asked questions, and her other lessons had gone well too. Patterson had taken her out for a burger at lunchtime and hadn't pressed her about Ivy. And Ivy was here. In her home. Smiling at her, asking her how her day had been. Which was the most special part of it all.

That night as she dabbed cold cream on her face and neck, Vivian mentally lectured herself about the necessity of enforcing her deadline. In the morning, she'd fix Ivy breakfast, take her to the bus station, and give her some money. She'd prepared a speech. "You can buy a ticket home. And if you don't buy a ticket home, you're to at least call your mother and let her know you're okay. Tell her you love her." After spending two days with the girl, she recognized in Ivy the look of someone who wasn't going back home—who didn't believe she had a home. And honestly, she'd expected Ivy to have that look. That was why she had already stashed $200—all she could spare—in an envelope for her.

But when Vivian woke the next morning, the sheets were folded on the arm of the couch and the envelope with the $200 was gone. Ivy had left a note propped against the percolator. "Thanks, and please don't tell I was here. I'll be fine. Maybe next time I see you, we can speak more truthfully. About things."

CHAPTER 36

"Get up," said Adele, sweeping open the curtains. George rolled over and pressed her face into the pillow to escape the sunlight. She had to pee, but that could wait until her mother left the room. Then she'd tiptoe to the bathroom and back to her bed before anyone realized she'd been up at all. But her mother wasn't leaving.

Adele flapped the chenille bedspread. "Time for a shower," she said.

George moaned a no into her pillow.

"You can't go out smelling the way you do."

Who cared? She was never going out again.

"Ruth graduates today. You'll hate yourself if you miss it."

She hated herself already. What kind of a mother must she be for one of her daughters to run away?

As if Adele could read her mind, she said, "What sort of mother misses her daughter's graduation?"

Showered, powdered, and dressed in a clean skirt and blouse, she sat propped between her mother and Tom. He kept a protective arm around her. Adele held her hand. George's chest felt simultaneously heavy and empty as Ruth followed Carl Rutherford across the stage. She clapped for her daughter, singular, and willed herself not to cry. She sensed people in the crowd staring at her, but when she looked around, no one met her eyes.

Ivy's name was not called. Nor was her disappearance mentioned by any of the staff or the families of other graduates of Enid High. George felt this erasure of her daughter like a physical illness. Her trembling hands fumbled with the program. She doubted she'd ever be able to fly again. It didn't matter. Once this ceremony was over, she'd go back home and never leave. She had to be there when Ivy returned.

The police had assured her they were looking. ("But she is over eighteen, ma'am. Legally allowed to go where she pleases.") Tom had assured her Ivy was a smart girl—she'd be all right. But his hair had gone from blond to gray virtually overnight, which told George he didn't buy what he was selling. Frank had held her but said nothing because what could anyone possibly say? No one wanted to speak Ivy's name. No one wanted to hear Ivy's name spoken. Not Adele. Not even Ruth.

Ruth had gone with her friends, stubbornly smiling down the other girls' concern, on their shopping trip to Dallas. George barely slept, imagining all the reasons she wouldn't come home. Imagining losing both of them. But Ruth had returned. She'd lazed in front of the television set for two weeks, which suited George just fine. If her daughter wanted to sit at home and watch television all day, George wasn't going to complain; she'd always know exactly where she was. But Adele wasn't having it. "A grown woman now," she said. "Time to get out in the world. *Do* something."

So Ruth went to work in Frank Bridlemile's office. Filing and fetching coffee and looking decorative at the front desk when customers came in. "If her typing speed picks up, if she learns shorthand, we'll put her in the steno pool and give her a raise." Frank said this to George one afternoon as they unwrapped themselves from the sheets. He said it as if it were the greatest compliment he could give to a young woman. *I flew planes,* she wanted to say to him. *I flew planes, when they wouldn't let you do that.* Instead, she said, "I'm busy the rest of the week," and nudged him out the back door.

"Now," George said to Ruth as they sat down to dinner that night, "do you want this steno pool promotion? Because if you do, we'll get you a shorthand class. I mean, if that's what you want, that's fine with me."

Ruth set down her fork and scowled. "It's not flying airplanes, I know, but it's not lunching with the Women's Club every other Thursday either."

"Sweetheart, you misunderstand me. I'm only trying to help you have what you want. But to do that, I need to know what that is."

George regretted this conversation for months because Ruth doggedly stuck with her filing job at Bridlemile Properties. George believed she stayed there out of spite, but she began treating Ruth the way she used to treat Ivy. Don't say no outright. Don't make demands. Bide one's time, wait for the right moment, then obliquely propose or provide what seemed appropriate.

She waited more than a year before Ruth, one night at dinner, suggested that she wanted to go into nursing.

"Nursing?" said Adele, unable to keep the disdain from her voice.

"Leave her alone, Mother," said George. She understood Ruth's desire to be a normal girl. To fit in. To do what the world expected of her. Part of George—a part her mother would never understand—applauded Ruth's instinctive conformity. It would make things easier for her in the long run. And Ruth deserved some ease.

Not long after Ivy left, Tom had stopped pretending to live at home. He'd transformed from a family man into something more exciting—a pilot with an apartment in Oklahoma City. A pilot with a dashing air that his evident grief about Ivy only enhanced. A pilot who—she wondered exactly when—had stopped wearing his wedding ring, though they never spoke of divorce.

He surfaced on occasion. George would arrive home from the store and find him sitting at the kitchen table reading the newspaper. "Hi, sweetheart," he'd say, as if he'd been there all the time. She allowed this.

She even allowed him to share her bed. She told herself that by allowing this she allowed Ruth some sense of normalcy.

"Normalcy," said Adele, "is overrated."

But George disagreed. Normal, at her age, meant a husband in one's bed at night and the knowledge of where all of one's children were during the day. Ivy had been gone for more than a year. "Missing," everyone said, as if Ivy herself had no choice in the matter. George, knowing her daughter, didn't believe that for a moment.

And now Ruth would leave too. This was healthy, George told herself. This was good. And she was only going as far as Oklahoma City.

"Nursing," said Adele again.

George wondered what choice her mother would prefer Ruth to make. "Exactly what doors do you think are open to young women these days?"

"She could at least go farther away," said Adele. Then she placed a placatory hand on George's arm. "I'm sorry, but you know what I mean."

"We're lucky she's willing to go anywhere at all," said George, pulling her arm away and ignoring her mother's apology, refusing to confirm her mother's suspicion that she wanted to keep Ruth as close to home as possible.

CHAPTER 37

The principal told Ruth that he'd understand if she decided not to return to school. Her grades were solid. She could cross the graduation stage and accept her diploma. Her friends told her they'd understand if she didn't join them for their trip to Dallas. Patrick told her he'd understand if she skipped prom. They all wanted nothing to do with her. As if some Rutledge taint might rub off on all of them.

She went to class. In the hallways, other students scurried past her as if she weren't there.

She went to prom. In the car after the dance, she took Patrick's hand and put it on her breast. He yanked it back. "We shouldn't."

"If not now, when?" she asked, placing her hand on his thigh. He flinched from her touch and mumbled something about curfew. About waiting. "Never mind," said Ruth. "Just take me home."

She went to Dallas and forced herself to trill over dresses and pedal pushers and shoes. To appear fascinated by her friends' accounts of their own post-prom adventures.

Patrick never called her again. Her friends called occasionally, but Ruth declined their invitations. She was tired of them all. She was tired of everything.

She lazed around the house, ignoring her grandmother's disapproving glare. She'd mope if she wanted to.

Her father called her regularly. He came by the house to see her. He had an apartment in Oklahoma City, "convenient to the airport," he said, as if that were the only reason. No one mentioned divorce, and her parents no longer seemed angry with each other. As if Ivy's disappearance had freed them from caring about their marriage. Ruth wondered if she were to disappear, too, whether they'd talk at all.

She took the job at Bridlemile Properties so that she could stop taking an allowance from her mother. Ivy, wherever she was, wasn't collecting an allowance. She was living on her own, independently, without help from anyone. Well, Ruth was perfectly capable of doing the same.

She was perfectly capable of making coffee, and filing, and answering phones. The next step up, if she wanted that, was the steno pool. She observed the ranks of typists, seated at their identical desks, wearing nearly identical skirts and blouses, deploying their identical bottles of whiteout and sheets of carbon paper. She thought of Ivy, out in the world having all kinds of adventures. She felt poky, sitting in Enid, still living in her mother's house, working at her mother's boyfriend's company, still tethered to her childhood.

Then one morning, outside the five-and-dime, a red, white, and blue flyer caught her eye. The Army wanted nurses and would pay for their training. Nursing sounded much more exciting than filing and fetching coffee. The flyer didn't mention Vietnam, but Ruth watched the nightly news. She knew where the Army needed nurses.

"And would you be willing to go overseas?" asked the woman who looked over her application.

Overseas was the whole point. She slept in her childhood bed. She dithered away her days filing and fetching at Uncle Frank's office. Meanwhile, Ivy was out in the world, wings spread, soaring, having adventures Ruth couldn't even imagine. Never once looking back, never once missing them, missing her. Ivy wouldn't find any aspect of

Ruth's life surprising. Ruth's life was unfolding exactly as Ivy would have predicted, minus, perhaps, an engagement ring and wedding plans.

"Would you be willing to go to Vietnam?" asked the woman, her tone indicating that the answer was usually no.

"Yes," said Ruth. "Yes, I would really like to go to Vietnam." Because Ivy would certainly never imagine her doing that. Not even in peacetime.

The woman raised her eyebrows.

"Really," said Ruth.

"We'll let you know when your application has been approved. Shouldn't take long."

"A scholarship?" said her mother when Ruth explained that she didn't have to pay tuition. "Oh, sweetheart, I'm so proud of you."

Ruth had never been an exceptional student, so she was surprised to find herself near the top of her class in nursing school. The bio and anatomy material just . . . stuck. When they trained with actual patients, the teaching nurse complimented her bedside manner. Ruth loved the sensation of placing her hands on another human body, assessing its well-being and providing comfort. What a powerful feeling—probably Ivy had always had it—to know you were good at something, to feel so confident in your abilities. She was eager to get to Vietnam, to charge into a new adventure with her newfound confidence.

But first, she wanted an adventure closer to home. She wasn't going to travel halfway around the world with her virginity still intact. She let her classmates know she was interested in dating, and then accepted every offer that came her way. If a man didn't seem right for her purposes—not attractive enough, not kind enough, not un-Patrick enough—she declined a second date. At last, she winnowed the pool to an acceptable candidate. He was more than willing, once he understood what she had in mind. She combed her memory for Sandra's advice from their sleepover days, but came up with only images of Cindy. Besides, they'd been only fourteen. None of them—not even Sandra— had known a thing.

Naked in his bed, she liked the roughness of his skin against hers. She'd expected the pain, but she hadn't expected the undertaking to wrap up so quickly. Surely there must be more to it. But he levered himself up off her and said, "You can stay if you want." In the morning they tried again. The result was the same, except that this time he said, "I'll drive you home."

"Oh, him," said one of her classmates when Ruth hinted at her experience. "He doesn't know anything." Which suggested that there were men who did know something. The trick was to figure out who they were. If she kept hunting, she was bound to find one. Eventually she did: a dark-haired, serious resident. Even before he'd gotten her clothes completely off, she knew it would be different. The way he ran his fingers down her sternum, the way his lips brushed her jawline, made her think of Cindy. *So that's what all the fuss is about,* she thought when it was over.

Even so, when he called for another date, she told him she was too busy studying. Really, she was busy wondering what had become of Cindy. Besides, she didn't want a boyfriend. Men had opinions about women going to Vietnam. They had opinions about women working, period. Ruth wasn't about to let anyone stand in her way. Not when she was so close to the finish line. In just a matter of weeks, she'd don her dress uniform and board a flight to Travis AFB. En route to Tan Son Nhut.

CHAPTER 38

Ivy kept her face hidden behind a day-old *Houston Chronicle* until the bus rumbled out of the station. The early-morning sky lightened as they crossed into Louisiana. She lowered the paper and gazed out the window, listened to the conversation of the couple seated in front of her. They made no attempt to keep their voices low, apparently trusting their unusual French to maintain their privacy as they argued about a dog. She was getting too fat, said the man. She was overfed.

He would starve her, complained the woman. Just like he had starved the last one.

What fantasyland did she live in, asked the man. Their last one had been thick as a sausage and keeled over from heart failure.

Heart failure brought on by malnutrition, the woman insisted.

Ivy laughed. Then put a hand to her mouth. She didn't want to draw any attention, but it was too late. A man across the aisle stared at her. He wore a gray linen suit, shapeless and wrinkled. She shook open her newspaper, raised it to cover her face once again.

"You speak Cajun?" the linen suit man inquired. When Ivy didn't answer, he asked again, more loudly. "Excuse me, do you speak Cajun?"

So that explained the strangeness of their French. The man cleared his throat, about to ask again, no doubt in an even louder voice. Nearby, passengers raised their heads from their magazines or stirred from their naps to look. If she didn't answer him, they'd soon glare at her with disapproval. Not at him. She knew from experience that boys were allowed to call attention to themselves. And ignoring them only aggravated them. It was probably worse with grown men.

"French," she said.

"Not from Louisiana." It was a statement, not a question, so Ivy let it lie. She pretended to read. He allowed this for a bit, then pressed: "The accents don't trouble you?"

The couple with the fat, starving dog had shut up. Ivy wondered if the man's question offended them.

She shrugged. "I don't really notice the accents." Mme Forrest said her French was excellent. She'd learned a lot from Madame, not all of it language related. Like how to choose the correct shade of lipstick, how to walk in a pencil skirt, how to twist her hair into a chignon. Madame gave Ivy French novels to read, made her discuss the plots in French, made her discuss everything in French. She did not let pass any errors in grammar or pronunciation. Ivy had repeated and repeated Madame until her sentences were perfect.

"That's a pretty strong accent not to notice," said the linen suit man. Ivy shrugged again. The Cajun man turned and glared at them both.

"Maybe I could pay you to be my translator for some business I have in New Orleans. If that's your final destination."

The Cajun woman muttered something about the morals of today's young women, and the man across the aisle smirked.

"You don't need a translator," said Ivy. "You speak French yourself."

He chuckled. "Smart girl," he said. "Smart girl. Speaks French. I wonder if she needs a job."

Ivy raised her *Chronicle* again, and the two didn't speak for the rest of the trip. But as the bus pulled into the New Orleans station, he leaned across the aisle and offered her his card. "This is a family occasion for me," he said, waving his hand to encompass, she supposed, the city of New Orleans. "I'm headed to Arizona from here. To pick up some linguists. For some work in California."

Ivy took the nondescript beige card. On the front, shiny raised letters spelled out SAM BENSON, ASSOCIATED INTERNATIONAL CONSULTANTS, above a phone number and a PO Box address.

"Work for people who aren't bothered by accents. If you decide you need a job, give me a call."

It was shocking how quickly New Orleans depleted her money. Ivy spent her days walking. In a café window she saw a WAITRESS WANTED sign. She didn't want to pour coffee for the sad men sitting inside, hunched over their racing forms, but beggars couldn't be choosers. Checking her reflection in the glass, she put a hand in her skirt pocket to fish out her lipstick. Her fingers brushed the business card. She ran her thumb over the raised print of Sam Benson's name, then walked on. By the end of the week, she had just enough money left for four more nights at her boardinghouse, and that was only if she got by on cigarettes and coffee most of the day.

In the phone booth, she counted out her change and stared at Sam Benson's card. She was tired and hungry. Worse, she was lonely. She missed Ruth. Ruth would like New Orleans—the moss-choked live oaks, the intricate wrought-iron balconies. Ivy imagined showing her around, telling her where to buy the best pastries, where to hear the best blues, not that Ivy could afford either of those things yet. She'd never spent more than a day or two apart from Ruth, and the absence of her sister (of Ruth, she instructed herself sternly) made her chest ache. New Orleans would be so much better if she were there—even if they were both tired and hungry.

But being with Ruth meant calling home. And if she did that, her mother and father (Georgeanne and Tom, she instructed herself) would swoop down to get her. They'd hug her too tightly, fuss over her, insist that she was theirs, that they were hers. And if she got hungry enough and tired enough, she'd be desperate to believe them. She'd return to Enid, and they'd all pretend she'd never left.

She lifted the receiver and dialed the number on the card, but Sam Benson didn't answer. A crisp-voiced woman said, "This is his answering service. Leave a number, and we'll have him call you back."

She touched the phone to its cradle, but she'd already paid for the call. And she didn't want to wear a pastel uniform and serve coffee to despondent men in cafés. She put the phone back to her ear. "I don't have a number. He said he had a job for me."

The woman was silent.

"Translating."

Still nothing.

"In California?" She was being ridiculous. He was just a man who wanted a quick lay in New Orleans. How many girls did he meet on buses and try to pick up with this line about a job in California? She was such a fool.

"No address, either, I suppose," said the woman.

"Well, just for a few more days. It's temporary."

"Tell me the address. If there's a job for you, we'll deliver a train ticket tomorrow. You must be there to sign for it. Do you understand?"

"Yes," said Ivy.

"Tomorrow," repeated the woman. "If you're not there to sign, don't bother calling again."

In California, Ivy was surrounded by recent Ivy League graduates who spent their breaks discussing their deferment potential. They snickered at her accent, both her French (it seemed Madame's pronunciation hadn't been quite so refined after all) and her English. But she had no trouble translating the French of the Viet and Lao speakers, while some of the Ivy Leaguers, with their perfect accents, were shuffled into other jobs. "Something more consonant with their abilities," said Sam Benson.

She learned to keep a weather eye on the fullness of the ashtrays, on the emptiness of the coffeepot. Whenever either approached its extreme, she made herself scarce. She was the only woman there, and in her presence, the college boys became incompetent. I will not be my mother, she vowed, picturing George trailing Tom as he dropped his travel case, his hat, his tie—gathering them up, brushing off the imaginary dust, tucking them away in their respective places. But one afternoon she was so captivated by a conversation on the tapes, she neglected to pay attention. Carlyle, who wore his Princeton tie every day, despite how incredibly square that looked even in their staid government office building, thrust the percolator under her nose. She jumped. Then took her time stopping the tape.

"Oh, no thank you," she said, indicating her half-full cup. "I have plenty still."

Carlyle had pale, almost translucent skin that pinked up when he was excited or upset, and rabbity little eyes that narrowed at her. "No, dummy," he said. "Pot's empty."

Usually the "dummy" remained unspoken. Though she knew it was how they thought of her. Her accent, her education, her three skirts and three blouses that she mixed and matched in as many combinations as possible (which never disguised the fact that she had only three skirts and three blouses), and, more than anything, her being female, all pegged her as not quite a person in their eyes. She was their dancing bear, their horse that could count. If he hadn't called her a dummy, she might have accepted the pot from him, rinsed it out, and set it up to perk again.

But he had said it out loud. And everyone in the room had heard. She felt them assuming her submission, their smug confidence that she'd do their bidding.

"Oh," she replied, putting a hand to her throat. "Oh." She allowed herself a giggle. "Oh, you wouldn't want me to do that. I'm completely hopeless at that sort of thing." She giggled again, just to watch his face turn vermilion.

Ivy shared a two-bedroom apartment with three other young women, all stenos. Each one pleasant, pretty, and hoping to catch the eye of some young executive. Trade up to a wedding ring and starter home. Ivy told them she was a lowly girl Friday, filer of papers and fetcher of coffee and sandwiches. Not in one of the glossy downtown high-rises where her roommates worked, but in a dowdy, low-slung stucco shoebox at the edge of the military base. Whenever one of them asked about her job, she made it sound as bland as possible. Soon enough they stopped asking, but they never lost interest in what she planned to do with herself on the weekends. The stenos fretted about Ivy's days off. They spent theirs at home with their families, doing laundry, seeing high school friends, eating home-cooked meals. "You must miss your family, being so far away," said one. "Did you say they live in Dallas?"

"Houston," said Ivy. To make the stenos feel better, she lied and told them how excited she was to go home for Thanksgiving. Her chest still ached for Ruth, but more sporadically now. Sometimes she allowed herself to imagine how impressed her family would be to learn that she earned her own keep by serving her country, even if the purpose of her work wasn't exactly clear to her. On lonelier days she was tempted to call. Until she remembered: she wasn't really theirs. She was just a burden George had carried for Vivian. A burden Vivian had refused to pick up. A burden that George obviously didn't want returned, because Vivian hadn't exactly tried to send Ivy back home. They were all relieved she was gone. She trained herself to squash thoughts of her family. To focus her attention elsewhere.

Usually listening to the voices did the trick. She wasn't sure what the Ivy League boys were listening to, but on Ivy's tapes, people spoke of this general or that colonel, evaluated their potential allies, their potential good faith. Ivy supposed that someone whose good faith was unquestionable secretly recorded these voices. She was grateful to this person, not for patriotic reasons—the necessity of the recordings was, at this point, still opaque to her—but because the voices became her new family. One she pictured vividly as she listened to them bicker, come to some temporary accord, then set to bickering all over again.

Today she heard a familiar voice on the tape. The people on the recordings—usually men, but occasionally a woman—didn't use their real names. There were lots of Viets and Nguyens. Which she had learned mirrored the population at large. Some were savvy enough not to use any name at all. But she got to know certain voices. This one, familiar, belonged to one of the savvy no-named men. It had a rich timbre that made Ivy wish she could hear him sing. Privately, she thought of him as Sinatra.

It wasn't only his voice that was familiar, but the words he spoke. "We must prepare to welcome our friends from across Asia," intoned Sinatra. His French was beautiful. He'd had better teachers than Mme Forrest. But what intrigued her was "friends from across Asia." She stopped the tape, rewound, and listened again. She'd heard that phrase almost two weeks earlier, the day of what she now thought of as the coffeepot incident. And he'd said it prior to that, she was certain. She just couldn't remember when.

"This is probably nothing," she said to Sam Benson.

"Never start with 'This is probably nothing.' People already want to think it—don't let them imagine that you agree."

"Okay. I noticed something strange. Sinatra—"

She winced at Sam's puzzled look—here she was revealing how frivolous she was, undercutting herself yet again. "I give some of them nicknames when I listen. The ones who don't go by fake names."

His smile was encouraging. "Go on."

"This one man—he has a nice voice, so I call him Sinatra—he keeps using the same phrase. He's used it at least three times on tapes I've listened to. 'Our friends across Asia.' No one else in these conversations ever mentions any friends in Asia. And he always uses those exact words: 'our friends across Asia.'"

"That's very interesting, Miss Shaw. Thank you for letting me know."

Two days later she was escorted to a different office where she started a new job. Something more consonant with her abilities. Now, in addition to translating the words, she analyzed the intent behind them. She attended briefings on competing South Vietnamese factions and feuds. No one asked her to make coffee.

Each morning as she slipped her headphones on, she looked around for Sam. He was rarely there, and when he was, he mostly ignored her. *Stop it,* she told herself. He was nothing special—a thirtysomething-ish man of nondescript features who wore a wrinkled suit. His smile was kind, but he deployed it freely to everyone, not just her. He probably never thought of her at all, which meant she shouldn't think so much about him either.

She listened to the tapes for months. Then one day he perched on the edge of her desk.

"Miss Shaw. What would you say to some work in the field?"

1968–1969

CHAPTER 39

After the flight from Travis to Hickam, the nurses deplaned to stretch their legs and breathe the island air. Ruth felt like she'd been flying for days, but they still had eighteen hours left to go. She'd been told Honolulu would smell like flowers, but all she could smell was jet fuel.

"Don't you wish we had time to see the beaches?" said one.

"Even just one beach," said another.

There were four of them—nurses—traveling to Vietnam as a group. Once in Saigon, they'd split up and head to their individual assignments. But for the flight over, they bunched together, even Ruth. Her opinion on the beaches was not solicited, a fact she noted with resignation. They'd quickly pegged her as the quiet one. Nice enough, but not much to say. It was her own fault. She'd held back too much in the initial womanly give-and-take. Hadn't revealed anything intimate enough to let them in.

Her dad was a pilot and her mom was in real estate, she said when asked about her parents. She didn't mention her dad's separate apartment or her mom's investment—business and otherwise—in Frank Bridlemile.

Yes, she supposed it was interesting that her mother had a career (could Frank Bridlemile himself be considered a career?), but it wasn't as if she spent all day at an office, and besides, her grandmother lived with them, so, no, Ruth had never felt neglected. "Oh, how sweet," cooed one of the other nurses, and Ruth decided not to try to explain Adele.

No, she didn't have any brothers and sisters. "There's just me, I'm afraid." This was easier than explaining Ivy's disappearance. She supposed the marathon flight time from Travis to Tan Son Nhut was good practice for all the introductions and small talk she'd have to make once she reached her base. She didn't yet know precisely where she was going. Two of the nurses on board were Navy and already had their assignments. "Ruth and I will find out *in country*," Kimberly, who was Army, like Ruth, told the Navy nurses. Kimberly was fond of the phrase "in country" and deployed it at every opportunity. Ruth tried to catch the eyes of the Navy nurses the third time Kimberly said it, but they didn't seem to mind. They were discussing why they had each signed up.

"For me," said one of the Navy nurses, "it was all those protesters. I can't stand how dirty and raggedy they look. Why they imagine anyone wants to listen to their opinions when they look like that, I'm sure I don't know." Ruth nearly broke her silence to suggest that, wardrobe aside, the protesters had a point, but the other Navy nurse spoke first.

"My brothers were both over there. One of them's home now. The other has two months left. It just doesn't seem fair that I wouldn't go and do my part too."

"My dad was a soldier," said Kimberly. The rest of them nodded. Their fathers had all fought in the war. "He was there when they emptied out the camps. The things they saw. Well, when he got back, he planted a flagpole in the front yard, and every day we kids were responsible for running up the flag, and every night we had to take it down, fold it proper, make sure it never touched the ground, you know?" The rest of them nodded. They knew. "So I just thought, easy to be a patriot in my safe little hometown, but a real patriot would go where the fighting is. Even if I can't fight myself. I can be there for the soldiers."

Ruth wished her own motivations were as selfless. Trying to one-up an adventurous sister you hadn't seen in years wouldn't cut it. She murmured something about just wanting to do her part, but the other women had already moved on to new subjects.

Kimberly made a retching sound in the back of her throat as they descended the metal staircase to the tarmac. It took Ruth considerable effort not to do the same. After their long hours trapped inside the stale plane, the sopping heat of Saigon felt like the worst summer day in Enid, times ten. Then there was the smell. A seemingly impossible mix of jet fuel, burning trash, and overripe vegetation. Neither she nor Kimberly discussed it. They'd be traveling to Long Binh together. If Kimberly made it. She looked close to passing out. Ruth forced herself to take a few deep breaths. It was like swimming in a cold lake: you had to just dive in. Other women, harder women, filed past in the opposite direction, tugging at the collars of their dress uniforms. Ruth guessed they were headed home. Stateside, as Kimberly would say. None of them spared Ruth and Kimberly a glance, let alone a greeting.

Kimberly's shoulders sagged. Ruth took her elbow. "They're just tired," she said. "We're going to be fine." Kimberly, her lips leached to gray, barely nodded. Ruth sussed out the ladies' room so they could freshen up before they found their bus to Long Binh. If Kimberly was going to throw up, Ruth didn't want it to happen on the bus. Not in this heat. But after Kimberly washed her face and combed her hair and brushed down her uniform, she looked brighter.

The airport swarmed with men in olive drab. "Bus to Long Binh?" Ruth asked as she made her way through the crowd, one hand clutching Kimberly's wrist, pulling her along. Fingers pointed, Ruth followed, and at last they found themselves in front of a camouflage-painted bus with metal grilles screwed over its windows. "Long Binh?" she asked the driver.

"Hop on," he said. "You two must be new." Kimberly had perked up considerably, and now here was someone she could talk to. While she chattered away to the driver, Ruth peered through the metal grille at the crowded, bustling city. At long, beautiful avenues, stately colonial buildings, the stumps of trees that once shaded graceful streets. Cut down for fuel, she learned later. She saw beggars and hawkers and children and bicycles and cars moving in all directions, like a flock of birds, somehow all merging and separating and merging again without mishap. And then they were out of the city, the bus jolting down a rutted road. Dense green jungle loomed in the distance, but for yards on either side of them, there was nothing but dirt. "They naped it," the driver said. "Keeps the VC back from the main arteries." The road and jungle blurred to darkness as Ruth dropped into a doze. At Long Binh, Kimberly nudged her awake. They each smoothed their hair and reapplied their lipstick.

"Well, good luck," said Kimberly.

"You too," said Ruth.

Long Binh was packed dirt topped with regiments of identical prefab buildings. A WAC led them to one of the Quonset huts, where another WAC gestured for them to take a seat. She dealt with Kimberly first. "Quy Nhon," said the WAC. "You'll like it. There's a great beach nearby. Ask for Sergeant Posen at the airfield. He'll get you on a transport."

"Cu Chi," she said to Ruth. No mention was made of Ruth liking it or of there being any beach. "You can take your bag and wait outside. They're sending someone for you."

She flattened her body into the insufficient strip of shade in front of the Quonset hut and waited. Now, so close to her destination, she jittered with impatience and exhaustion. She hadn't slept on the plane, and her nap on the bus to Long Binh couldn't have lasted more than twenty minutes. She hoped she'd be assigned her quarters soon after she arrived. "Picture spartan," her mother had said, "and subtract from there." She smiled to remember it—her mother hadn't done much joking since she'd learned the truth about Ruth attending nursing school on the Army's dime.

"We'll pay them back," her mother had said at the time. "Every cent. Because you can't seriously intend to go over there. Frank knows people. Your father does too. It would only take a few phone calls."

"Georgeanne," said Grandma Adele. "Can't you see she *wants* to go?"

"Only because she has no idea what that means. No earthly idea."

"She watches the same news you and I do," said Adele.

By the time Ruth left, her mother had come around. "It's very brave," George had said as she kissed Ruth before the flight to Travis. Ruth tried to summon some of that bravery now amid the utterly strange sights and sounds of the base. She was hungry and tired. She was about to go back inside and ask the WAC how much longer until her ride arrived, when a jeep careened around the corner and braked in front of her.

She tossed her bag in the back and turned to greet the driver, a WAC in faded fatigues and mirrored sunglasses. Ruth envied the fatigues. They looked so soft and much more comfortable than the skirt, blouse, pantyhose, and pumps she'd been wearing for close to two days now. She was sweaty and itchy and dying to get out of her dress uniform. The WAC removed her mirrored sunglasses, turned her head, and grinned. And Ruth burst into tears.

Looking back, she wished she'd responded with more nonchalance—with any nonchalance at all—to the first sight of her sister in four years. She wished it had played out this way:

She smiled back at Ivy, but only with her mouth, not her eyes, and said, "You owe me $12.82."

And then Ivy said, "I'll round it up to thirteen. Interest."

And then they chuckled, and somehow, that was it. They moved past it. The mystery and the abandonment and the pain no longer mattered. They were together again, and just as thoroughly sisters as ever. Happy to be in each other's company.

What really happened was this:

"What are you doing here?" asked Ruth once she'd climbed into the passenger seat and caught her breath.

"I should ask you the same question," said Ivy, zipping the jeep past the Quonset huts, toward the main road. "Mom must have had fits."

The mention of their mother started Ruth's tears again, and several minutes passed before she could carry on a normal conversation. Which gave her time to think about the questions she most wanted to ask, because Ivy wasn't volunteering anything, that was for sure. While Ruth gathered herself, Ivy simply drove. She offered no explanation, no excuse. She was unchanged, thought Ruth. No apology would be offered because Ivy didn't believe one was owed.

Ruth could spend this drive attempting—and no doubt failing—to extract one. Or she could go a different way. "So you're a WAC?" she said at last.

Ivy shook her head. "Nope. Look at the sleeves. You need to learn the insignia if you want to know who can do what for you while you're here. Not that it's always about rank, but rank never hurts." Ivy tugged at the unadorned olive drab fabric covering her upper arm. "No rank, no unit, see? I picked these up in Saigon to wear on my off days. They're comfortable and hardly show dirt at all. Unlike my Donut Dolly uniform."

"Your what?"

"My Donut Dolly uniform. We wear these cute little powder-blue dresses. They're comfortable, but you stand out more than I . . . well, you stand out. Which is the point, I suppose. We're here with the Red Cross, keeping up troop morale. You know, songs and games and lemonade and snacks and conversation with a real live American girl."

"You came to Vietnam to boost troop morale?"

"Something like that. It would take too long to explain."

"Oh, I think I've got time."

"Time is one thing nurses here never have. Listen, you're going to see some stuff here, Ruth. It's going to be pretty awful."

"You haven't changed a bit," Ruth said. "So you think I haven't either. But you're wrong. I keep up with the casualty counts. I know it's terrible here. I *chose* to come because it's terrible here." *And,* she thought, *because you weren't supposed to be here.* But maybe Ivy's presence meant that she had made the right choice. They were reunited. *In country,* as Kimberly would have said.

"You know I have to tell them that you're here. I'm not going to lie for you," said Ruth.

"Tell them whatever you want. I'm blown anyway. I ran into Frank Jr. last week. Me in my powder-blue dress with my stack of board games and him with his face covered in mud—keeps the mosquitoes off—cleaning his M16."

Ruth wondered what seeing Frank Jr. had entailed, exactly. Her face must have shown it, because Ivy said, "That was a long time ago. If I could take it back, I would. Him and most of the others. I would have left him for you, Ruthie."

"Well, I don't want him now."

"Me neither. Why didn't he get a deferral? He could have stayed in college. Only son. All that." Ivy waved her hand dismissively at *all that.* "At least gone the National Guard route."

"That's what Aunt Helen wanted. She and Uncle Frank argued about it for months. Grandma Adele thinks he signed up just so he didn't have to hear them fight anymore. Aren't you worried he'll write his parents?" Who would, naturally—Aunt Helen with considerable delight—then inform their mother that Ivy was in Vietnam too.

"He didn't strike me as the letter-writing type. Maybe a postcard every six weeks or so. *Things are fine here. Hope this finds you well.*"

Ivy slowed the jeep. "We're almost there," she said.

"Good, I'm beat. I can't wait to get out of these clothes. Maybe take a shower."

"Don't get your hopes up," said Ivy. She named two units that had gone out just before she left the base. There had been signs of a new VC supply line pushing through toward the Iron Triangle. Ivy suspected there'd be fighting. And that meant medevacs of wounded coming out, with Cu Chi the closest hospital to receive them. "You're going to hit the ground running, Ruth. They'll let you change, but it may be a long time before you shower or sleep."

Ruth had anticipated a leisurely tour of the base, a forced but amiable hour of conversation with her new colleagues, a disappointing meal in the mess, and a full night's rest before she even changed a bandage. But this was what she'd signed up for. "Okay," she said.

"Look. I could probably get you out. We could turn around right now. Drive back to Long Binh and ask to see the paperwork. There's almost always something you can point to in the paperwork. And I know some people. I could make a couple of phone calls, get you on a plane home, but only if we turn around now."

"God, you sound just like Mom. Knowing all the right people to call. Forget it, Ivy. Look, you don't have to take care of me. I didn't come here looking for you. I never expected to see you again at all. So don't worry about me. Go play games and sing songs with the GIs and let me do what I came here to do."

"Fair enough," said Ivy as the base came into view. "Just one thing you should know. I go by Shaw now, not Rutledge."

As Ruth pulled on her stiff newly issued fatigues, disappointment pierced her relief and shock at seeing Ivy. Vietnam was supposed to be her own adventure, one that would top whatever Ivy was up to. Yet once again, Ivy had beaten her out. Once again, Ivy knew more than she did. *"Nyeh nyeh nyeh, you have to learn the insignia,"* thought Ruth. Her ribs began to vibrate with the drumming of propellers. The nurses in her hooch took off running to the airfield. Ruth followed and found herself in the midst of what at first appeared to be chaos, but which, once she focused on Captain Stanich, the nurse in charge, resolved itself into a pattern. A stretcher was pulled off a helicopter, or, more rarely, a GI climbed out on his own. Two nurses looked him over, asked him questions if he was conscious, took his vitals, and pointed to the area where they wanted the medics to take him.

"Rutledge, let's go," ordered Stanich. Ruth moved to her commanding officer's side. "This one looks easy. The medics can stitch him up, give him antibiotics," Stanich said, indicating the gash on the soldier's forearm. "You hurt anywhere else? Turn around so I can see if you're bleeding anywhere. Sometimes they're in shock and they don't feel it even when they've got a bullet in them. But this one's clean."

They moved on to the next stretcher. "He's dead," said Ruth.

"Not yet." Stanich pressed her fingers against the man's bloody neck. "Thready pulse." She tugged his dog tags from under his fatigues. "O negative," she shouted, and in seconds a medic arrived with a bag of blood. "OR," she said, and the medics carried the soldier to the operating tent.

The third one she barely glanced at. A large chunk of his skull appeared to be missing, yet he still struggled to breathe. "Morphine," said Stanich. "Put him over there."

The worst cases got sent Over There, where only one nurse was on duty, mostly administering morphine and speaking soothingly to the soldiers in her care, all of whom appeared to be beyond listening. Before Ruth could suggest that perhaps Over There needed staffing up, Stanich moved to the next stretcher. Ruth strained to catch her voice over the sound of the Hueys.

"I said, grab that boot." Stanich scowled at having to repeat herself. She was petite—Ruth had to stoop to hear her—and the softness of her looks wasn't reflected in her stern manner. The soldier on the stretcher clutched his boot to his chest.

"No," he said when Ruth attempted to take it. "No, I need it."

"Don't worry. I'll keep it safe for you," said Ruth. Stanich took his pulse and examined his pupils, looking him over for bullet wounds.

"We need it out of the way so we can see where you're hurt," said Ruth, gently tugging the boot. The soldier held firm. She tugged harder.

"It's his foot," said Stanich. Ruth waited for her to send him off with the medics for bandaging and crutches. But when the soldier released his boot, repeating, "I need it," the weight of it shocked her. How did they march in such heavy footwear? Glancing down, she glimpsed the field tourniquet on the soldier's leg, saw the bony, ragged stump protruding from the boot's opening. "Sew it back on," he pleaded. "I need it."

"We'll see what we can do," soothed Stanich. To Ruth she murmured, "Get rid of that."

How? she wondered. *Where?* It was all she could do not to drop the thing and bend over and vomit where she stood. Only her desire to make a good impression on Stanich and to avoid frightening the soldier kept her upright.

Stanich moved on to the next stretcher, and a medic gently took the boot from Ruth's hands. "It gets easier," he said. But she didn't see how it could ever get easy enough.

Hours later, she collapsed on her cot. When she woke, she was already late for her first shift in the hospital. She'd lost track of how many days she'd gone without a shower, but already she knew it didn't matter. She glanced around for Ivy as she jogged to the latrine and then to the hospital. The Donut Dollies' hooch was near hers—the women were corralled together in their own pocket of the base—and she glimpsed several women in powder-blue uniforms, not one of them her sister.

She rarely saw Ivy in her Donut Dolly uniform. Mostly she dressed in fatigues. Perhaps, thought Ruth, the Donut Dollies received a surprising number of days off. Maybe they needed it, because how could you keep up the soldiers' morale if you didn't tend to your own? She could tell already that tending to one's own morale *in country* would be tough.

She also never saw Ivy drive a jeep again. Like the other Donut Dollies, Ivy was driven or choppered where she needed to go. It occurred to Ruth only much later that Ivy's appearance at Long Binh had been no accident. That Ivy, by driving that jeep to pick her up, was telling her something.

She'd known Ruth would arrive at Long Binh that day, and she'd known—maybe she had even arranged it—that Ruth would be stationed at Cu Chi.

Over the next few weeks, though Ruth saw little of her sister, it became clear that Ivy knew things. And people. She had access to resources. The nurses would let Ivy know when they ran low on IV tubing or compression bandages or even tampons, which the soldiers often requisitioned to clean their weapons. And in a few days, those things would appear. Not delivered by Ivy, but, everyone knew, thanks to her ability to speak the right words to the right people.

Occasionally, Ruth spotted her sister wearing her pale-blue dress, boarding a Huey with the other Donut Dollies—heading out into the field or to another base with their board games and their Autoharp, with their bright smiles and their conversational aptitude.

Once she saw her in a ruby-red cocktail dress, picking her way toward a Huey in a pair of strappy high heels. Ruth's curiosity got the better of her, and she went and rapped on the door of the Donut Dollies' hooch. "Anyone seen Shaw?"

"Based on her wardrobe," Patty Dubroski offered, "I'm guessing Saigon." Patty's thick eyeliner had smeared. No, Ruth realized, those were just dark circles beneath her eyes.

"Embassy party," confirmed Jean Poltraine. She, too, looked exhausted. They all did.

"Guess that's why she wasn't with us in the field today," said Patty. "All that primping takes time."

Ruth fought the urge to defend her sister. But Ivy lived with these women. She could fight her own battles.

Jean explained that their group had come under fire as they lifted off. When they looked down, the soldiers, who had been joking and telling stories moments before, now grim faced, picked up their guns. Ruth had been on duty when the medevac copter came in that afternoon. Two of those GIs had died, and a third looked likely to follow. How could you justify a red cocktail dress, strappy heels, and an embassy party in the face of all that?

"She'll get us some booze at least," said Jean. "She always comes home from these things with some booze. Booze and tampons."

"Did you want us to give her a message? She's usually not back for a couple of days when she goes down to Saigon."

"Yeah, if you're low on supplies, you should have caught her earlier."

"No message. No need to even tell her I stopped by." Though they would, naturally. Then Ivy would know Ruth had been curious. And Ruth didn't want Ivy thinking she was curious. Here they were, living in hooches not twenty-five yards from one another, and there might as well have been half a world between them still. She felt just as disconnected from her sister as she had after Ivy ran away. The only difference was the occasional glimpse Ruth got of her, the occasional snatch of conversation. Otherwise, Ivy remained opaque, impenetrable.

The nurses protected Ivy. Everyone, it seemed, protected her. "Shaw?" said Stanich the one time Ruth dared to probe. "I don't know who she is, but I know this: she's no Donut Dolly. She told me she's your sister." Stanich cocked an eyebrow, waiting for Ruth's denial. Ruth felt her cheeks pinking with warmth.

"That's true," she admitted. "Yes. We're sisters."

"I see the resemblance. Why does she go by Shaw? She doesn't wear a ring. Is she married?"

It would be just like Ivy to get married and not tell anyone about it. "Not that I know of," she said, hoping Stanich didn't probe any further. But Stanich apparently knew a wall when presented with one, and let it go.

Ruth had intended to write her mother and father and grandmother and tell them the exciting news that she'd found Ivy. They'd worried for so long, and she had the power to relieve them of that worry. But if she told them and Ivy found out, she might disappear again. And if that happened, Ruth doubted there'd be a second serendipitous reunion. If keeping her sister close meant keeping Ivy to herself, she could do that, for now. She would tell them about her someday. Just not yet.

CHAPTER 40

It had taken months, but George had—mostly—taped up her shattered heart and reentered the world. She flew, attended club meetings, went shopping with Helen. But every time she returned home, she went straight to the kitchen. Maybe this would be the day she'd find Ivy there, sitting in her accustomed chair, flipping through a magazine and sipping a Coke. "Hi, sweetie," George would whisper to her phantom daughter. It was like pressing a bruise. The pain just sweet enough that she wanted to touch it again and again, to keep the wound of Ivy's absence from healing over.

Now Ruth was gone, too, and she had a second bruise to press. She watched the news every night, hoping for a sight of a nurse. She saw soldiers, tanks, jeeps, helicopters. She saw explosions and bloody bandages and crutches, but she never saw Ruth. And she never heard any reports of women dying in Vietnam. She hoped that meant they kept the nurses well behind the lines. Safe.

Unlike poor Frank Jr. He'd tripped a Claymore mine along the Ben Cat River eight days after Ruth left for Cu Chi.

When George heard the news, she drove straight to the Bridlemile house and let herself in without knocking. She found Helen sitting still as a statue in the sunroom with a pad of paper in her hand. A pen lay on the floor.

"Helen, I'm so sorry."

Helen accepted her hug and said, "Frank's not here."

"I'm not here for Frank. I'm here for you."

Helen blinked and bent to pick up the pen. George lunged to grab it first and handed it to her. She glanced at the notepad. Helen was making a list that said things like, *Casket, Notice for paper, Luncheon after service.*

"Let me help, Helen. You need to rest."

Helen ignored this and added another item to her list. George wanted to take the pen from her hand. She wanted to tell her it was okay to cry. To collapse. To go to bed and not get up for days. She wanted to tell her that after enough time passed, she, too, could tape up her splintered heart.

"When I lost Ivy," George began, then stopped herself. Because it wasn't the same. Ivy wasn't dead. George knew that as certainly as she knew her own name.

Helen smiled bitterly. "But Ivy's not lost anymore, is she?"

"What?" Her friend was just overcome with grief, thought George. She understood all too well how loss could addle a person.

Helen fished in the box at her side, the one labeled PERSONAL EFFECTS–BRIDLEMILE, F. She pulled out a smudged airmail sheet and handed it to George.

> Dear Folks, Things are fine here. Hot as heck still (sorry, Mother), and you never saw so many bugs. But I eat my three squares and keep my boots dry, just like Dad says. Ran into Ivy Rutledge at Cu Chi. She goes by Shaw now, but I didn't see a wedding ring. She's a Donut Dolly, if you can believe it. Not sure what I think about women being over here, but they are a sight for sore eyes. Hope this finds you well.
>
> Your loving son,
> Frank Jr.

"We assumed you'd heard it from Ruth." Helen stressed the "we." Frank had known this, and he hadn't told her? For how long? He's just lost his son, George reminded herself, trying to douse the flame of anger that flared in her chest. "We assumed you had your reasons for keeping it to yourself, but maybe you didn't know," said Helen. That "we" again. That victorious pinch in Helen's expression. And then the news sank in. Helen could have all the "we" she wanted. Frank Jr. had found Ivy!

George handed back the letter. "Well," she said, "I'm just relieved to know she's alive." Words she immediately wanted to bite back, because Frank Jr. was dead, and Helen, having rallied to fire her single round of ammunition, slumped over on the wicker sofa and sobbed.

George wrote letter after letter to Ivy. She tore up each one, threw the pieces in the garbage. "I can't send them," she told Tom. "They all say the wrong thing."

"Try a postcard," said Tom. "That's what I did."

"What did you say?"

"I said, 'Dear Ivy, I'm so relieved that you're alive. I miss you and love you, Dad.'"

George hung up and went outside to find her mother. Adele rolled out from underneath a Buick sedan. "That Tom," she said when George told her about his postcard. "He gets right to the heart of it, doesn't he?" Then she rolled back beneath the car.

No, thought George. *No, he didn't. Not quite.*

Adele had sent a letter too. Now it was only George who hadn't written. She couldn't write to Ruth either. The betrayal. Knowing where Ivy was and not telling. Keeping Ivy all to herself.

And neither Tom nor Adele getting to the heart of it, which was all the questions George needed answered: Why did Ivy go? Where did she go? How had she ended up in Vietnam? And when was she coming back?

As much as George needed the answers to these questions, she dreaded hearing them. Because she suspected Ivy would say, "I left because of you. I went as far away as I could get. From you. And I am never, ever coming back." Answers that threatened to splinter her heart all over again. She couldn't bring herself to put those questions in a letter. And without them, what was the point of sending any letters at all?

CHAPTER 41

"Thank God," said Vivian when George called to tell her Ivy was in Vietnam. "She's safe. I can't imagine how relieved you must feel."

"Hmm," said George. Vivian tightened her grip on the phone and held her breath. She could have eased George's worry and fear years ago, but she'd kept mum about Ivy's visit, about giving her the money to run even farther from home. And look how far she'd gotten.

Long ago Vivian had run away from home herself. And then gone back. She'd been waiting, all these years, for Ivy to do the same. Why wouldn't she? Ivy had run from a much better home than the one Vivian left. But as months and then years passed with no reappearance, no word from Ivy, Vivian's heart filled with regret. She knew nothing about teenagers, just as she'd known nothing about babies. And because of that, she'd failed her friend yet again.

George finally spoke. "I wouldn't call Vietnam safe. But at least we know she's alive."

"And she's with Ruth," Vivian managed. "I'm glad they're together."

"Hmm," said George.

George hadn't wanted Ruth to go to Vietnam, but Vivian had thought it sounded like a grand adventure. Like something she and George would have done when they were young. Until she remembered Camp Davis. George feared the war itself, but Vivian feared the men who fought it.

After George's call, Vivian wrote to each of the girls. A few weeks later she received two cramped pages from Ruth, describing her hoochmates, the hospital, the GIs. No mention of Ivy. And no reply from Ivy herself. Maybe she'd never gotten Vivian's letter. Vietnam was a long way for such a flimsy envelope to travel. Maybe it got torn or lost. Vivian sat down at her desk and wrote to each girl again.

Weeks later she received another chatty response from Ruth. Nothing from Ivy. She pulled out two sheets of stationery and flicked her lighter open and closed, thinking about what to write this time. Patterson rested his warm hands on her shoulders. How she loved the weight of them. He began kneading. "Mmmm." She closed her eyes and set down the lighter.

"Keeping up with your correspondence?" he asked.

"Writing to Ruth and Ivy." He lightly rested the point of his chin atop her head and peered at the letters. She hadn't gotten far. One sheet read, "Dear Ruth, thanks for your letter." The other read, "Dear Ivy, I hope you received . . ." She should ball that one up and start over. She didn't want to sound like a scold.

"The famous twins." She stiffened at the forced lightness of his tone. He massaged her shoulders again, and she willed herself to relax.

"You're very close to them."

"Well, they're George's, and I'm very close to her." She eased out from under his hands and stood, gathered the pages, and slid them into the desk drawer.

"It's probably nothing," said Patterson, and Vivian closed her eyes again, waiting for the nothing that would almost certainly be something. "But there was a rumor, near the end of the war. That you were . . . expecting."

She tapped a Winston from her pack. He picked up the lighter and lit it for her. "Were you?" he asked.

She inhaled, turned away from him, and blew out a long blue ribbon of smoke. "Obviously not," she said.

He lit one for himself. "That's what I thought." He picked up the newspaper and settled into his chair. Two chairs—one for him and one for her, with a table between them to hold the ashtray. An arrangement of furniture that meant they had a life together. He ashed his cigarette, shook open the paper. "For the record," he said, "I wouldn't have minded."

Easy to say, she thought, taking another drag, *when you think there's nothing to mind.*

CHAPTER 42

The warning sirens wailed. Ruth groaned and pulled her helmet from beneath her cot. She didn't put it on, just held it, eyeing her hoochmates. At the first blare of the siren, they were supposed to immediately rush to the bunkers. The first time she'd heard the warning, she'd made it halfway to the sandbagged entrance, helmet snug on her head, before she realized no one else had made any move toward safety.

"Back so soon?" asked a laughing Terrence when Ruth sheepishly reentered the hooch.

Today none of them moved. The perfume bottles in Lewis's footlocker tinkled against one another, a light, musical trill punctuating each boom. Lewis was the most beautiful of all the nurses. Men on leave often brought her back a little something from Tokyo or Clark. (Ruth had no idea whether the gifts got them anywhere; the nurses and soldiers weren't supposed to fraternize.) She wanted to steady the bottles, but no one else in the hooch seemed to notice.

"Once the dust clouds look close, we go," said Terrence, noticing the helmet in Ruth's hands. She didn't define close.

"And you don't want to be first in," Lewis added. "First in stirs up the rats before they've had time to hide."

What did they do? Stand around outside the entrance waiting for someone—someone new like her, someone who hadn't been warned—to chase out the rats? Sometimes she wondered how anyone could survive this place.

And yet, she loved it. She felt vital. Nurses had power here. Not just Stanich, who decided who went to the operating tent, who went to a medic, and who got put Over There, but all of them. There were never enough doctors. No one had time for questions and requests for approval. If you saw something that needed to be done, you did it, or you told a medic to do it. And the medics, all men, jumped when she issued instructions.

She'd done a few months in a stateside hospital before starting her tour, months during which she'd been forbidden to do more than check a patient's vitals without a doctor's orders. So many times she knew what a patient needed, knew that the patient needed it quickly, and yet she'd had to wait for a doctor's approval. If she offered her own opinion, the doctor might be tempted to dispute it. They had to be handled delicately, sometimes more delicately than the patients, those stateside doctors. In Vietnam, delicacy was an unaffordable luxury. She was expected to think and act for herself. And if she was wrong, well, there would be another wounded soldier in front of her shortly, and no time to dwell on mistakes.

Another reason, she suspected, no one wanted to shelter in the bunker. Sitting in the dark with no distractions other than the boom of shells echoing in their throats gave everybody too much time to think.

"Up and at 'em, ladies. This one's for real."

Ivy, wearing civvies, swung her helmet by its strap, whapping it against the wooden doorjamb of the hooch. A clutch of Donut Dollies hovered behind her. The nurses groaned, and Terrence ventured, "No dust, Shaw."

"There will be. Let's go."

They strapped on their helmets as they ran. Ruth stumbled across the trembling ground. Puffs of dust rose beyond the perimeter of the base, dimming the afternoon sun. *Ah*, she thought, *so this is* close. When they reached the sandbags, no one dithered. Certainly not Ruth. Being the first one to meet the rats seemed a small price to pay for shelter.

Mail call. The other women in her tent received care packages and thick letters. "Oooh! Hershey's!" crowed Terrence, who wasted no time tearing open her box. "And new underwear. God bless my mother!"

"Another postcard, Rutledge?" asked Lewis as Ruth plucked at the corner of her paltry mail haul.

"That's my dad. King of the postcard." *But at least he sends me something,* she thought. *Him and Aunt Vivian.* Her mother hadn't written in weeks. Ruth flipped the card over, expecting her father's usual upbeat report. In tiny, precise penmanship, he gave her the latest weather in Enid. "Hot, but nothing compared to the heat over there, I'm sure." This he followed with cheerful advice about dry socks, eating properly, sleeping when she could. "Keep your strength up. Those boys need you well." And his usual closing: "I'm so proud of you, sweetheart. All my love, Dad." What she hadn't expected was the print scaled down to squeeze in an extra two sentences. "Understand Ivy is there. Glad you two are together again."

She felt like a child who had been caught out. No wonder her mother hadn't written her. How long had they known? How had they known? Had Ivy written to them without warning her? Then she remembered Frank Jr. Naturally he'd written his parents and told them he'd crossed paths with Ivy. Aunt Helen would have wasted no time letting their mother know. She'd better write all of them and explain. But what explanation would get past the censors? Ruth suspected her sister's name would get redacted regardless of the words around it. She'd send postcards herself, she decided. Each with the simple confirmation: "She's here. She's safe. More later." They'd all know what it meant. And if the censors got suspicious and redacted even that? Well, at least she'd tried. Better late than never. She rummaged in her footlocker for stationery.

A surprisingly refreshing breeze blew through the hooch. She didn't go on duty for another two hours. After she got her postcards written, she planned to lie on her cot and listen to the birds calling and the jeeps whirring around the base and the other women in her tent talking. She did this sometimes. I hear this, she would think (usually engines). I smell this (usually garbage and fuel). I feel this (usually sticky and hot, but today, thanks to the breeze, a little less so). And it restored her, more than any nap ever did. But before she even picked up her pen, her rib cage vibrated with the rhythmic thrumming of Hueys. *I hear helicopters,* she thought. So much for postcards or restoration. She pulled on her boots, tied up her hair, and ran.

Deep in the middle of the night, after she'd sutured and bandaged and soothed the wounded, she made her way out of the hospital. Passing Over There, she heard a familiar voice and peeked behind the screens. None of the nurses had been able to spare much time for the lost souls Over There on this particularly bloody day. Ruth's boots were sticky; blood had soaked through the cloth covers. She planned to wipe them down in the latrine because bloody boots would only upset the wounded soldiers when they woke up. Funny how after the terrible things these men had seen, something like a woman in bloody boots just felled them.

She peeked behind the screen and saw Ivy sitting beside a man—odd age for a soldier, late twenties, Ruth guessed, rather than the more typical nineteen. Ivy held his hand through the rattle of his final breaths. When his chest no longer rose, she kissed his forehead. Then, starting with the breast pockets and moving systematically downward, she removed every single item he carried. The photo of a woman, the money, she put back. But a few odd bits that Ruth couldn't identify, Ivy pocketed herself.

Ruth stepped outside and waited. Moments later, Ivy joined her.

"Someone you knew?" asked Ruth.

She expected her sister to deny it, but Ivy nodded. "I'll write his wife," she said.

"Will that be a comfort to her?" asked Ruth.

"I can be comforting. When I want to be."

"Well, it may be time for that," said Ruth. "They know you're here."

"I know. I got a postcard from Dad. And a letter from Adele."

"But not Mom?"

"No, nothing from Mom."

"Me neither. Not in weeks. Guess I can't blame her," said Ruth.

"I suppose you want me to write them."

"Only if you can find it in you to be comforting."

CHAPTER 43

Adele had advised Harriet to buy the Impala, not the Bel Air. But Harriet's husband had always bought Bel Airs, and Harriet didn't want to dishonor Paul's memory. This meant Harriet's inferior Bel Air was frequently parked in the Rutledge driveway, with Adele half-hidden beneath its open hood.

Harriet, from her lawn chair in the shade, called out, "See anything?"

"Oil and brake fluid look good. Battery's fine. A couple of hoses starting to crack—we should replace those. I'll take a look at the filter next."

She didn't like having an audience, but Harriet stuck close to her vehicle, as if Paul Mayes's spirit resided somewhere inside it. And maybe it did, thought Adele. Paul had grown crotchety and demanding toward the end of his life, not unlike Harriet's Bel Air.

Harriet sipped her iced tea. George had offered her a magazine too. As if Adele ran a hair salon.

"I had the hardest time choosing between Grotto Blue and Grecian Green, but I think the green was the right choice, don't you?"

Harriet had asked her this question so often that Adele wondered whether she ought to be driving anything at all. She had the air filter out now. Harriet might be interested to see how much debris was stuck in it. She might consider parking someplace other than beneath her crape myrtle. Adele ducked out from under the hood, straightened to her full height.

The world spun. The Bel Air and the trees and the grass turned orange and fuzzy. She dropped the air filter and crouched down. Her ears buzzed. She lowered her rear end to the concrete and put her head between her bent knees.

"Adele, are you all right? Georgeanne! Georgeanne, come quick!"

George fanned her with a magazine. Harriet pressed the sweating glass of iced tea into her hand. Adele obediently sipped. She raised her head. The pecan tree remained in focus. So did George and Harriet. The cicada buzz in her ears faded. Slowly, ignoring George's extended hands, Adele pushed herself to standing. "I'm fine," she said. "I just straightened up too quickly, that's all." George and Harriet cut their eyes at one another. "Really," she insisted. "I'm perfectly well."

George hovered around her for the rest of the week, pestering her with questions. How did she feel? When had she last eaten? Didn't she think she ought to call Dr. Fleming?

"It was just an isolated incident. A hot day and I stood up too quickly." But George kept hovering and asking until Adele snapped at her to stop fussing.

Since she'd learned that Ivy was alive and well, the dark shadows had disappeared from beneath her daughter's eyes. The household felt lighter, airier. Adele didn't want to change that. George deserved a long worry-free stretch.

A week later, the cicadas buzzed in her ears again. Her heart went fluttery. She pressed a hand to her sternum and breathed slowly, in and out, until the buzzing and fluttering subsided. When it happened later that evening, she did the same. Her heart misbehaved again the next morning as she brushed her teeth.

This was ridiculous. She'd watched Harriet and Bess Cramer and other women her age grow too fat or too scrawny. She'd listened to them moan about their blood sugar and their arthritis. She'd murmured sympathetic responses, all the while taking pride in her own reliable body. Yes, she'd thickened around the middle, she had the occasional twinge in her right knee, but nothing worth remarking on. Until now.

Suddenly, walking from her car to a store entrance left her winded. And her ankles! She'd always taken pride in her slim ankles—even when she was pregnant, they'd kept their well-turned shape. Now they puffed like bread dough, rising over the sides of her shoes. It was the ankles that did it. Charles had suffered from them too. Without saying anything to George, she went to see Dr. Fleming.

Her blood pressure was high, he confirmed. Just a little. He'd give her something for that.

"What about my heart?" she asked.

He listened to it again and told her she was likely just overtired. He prescribed rest. Adele obediently lay down for a nap that afternoon at two. Not half an hour later, she was up. She had three cars parked in the driveway and customers who expected a quick turnaround. She didn't have time for napping. She put on her coverall and walked down the stairs—taking them slowly, trying to trick her body into behaving itself—and felt the flutter again.

The next week, she nearly passed out after sitting up from the creeper. Thankfully, George was out flying. And Harriet wasn't there to watch her put her head between her knees until the world righted itself. Time to get a second opinion, she decided.

"Rest is the best medicine," said the doctor in Oklahoma City, "for a woman your age."

"My late husband had heart trouble," said Adele. "They gave him digitalis, but there's probably something better now."

He patted her knee as if she were a child. "Just rest. Soon you'll be right as rain."

She forced herself to nap daily, limited her business to a handful of loyal customers. One season passed into another, and settling down for a nap grew easier—she felt so tired.

She wrote to Ruth and Ivy. Her brave, beautiful granddaughters who'd traveled halfway around the world to a place filled with violence. Adele had never gone farther from home than the Grand Canyon. Every afternoon as she drifted off, she thought back to her honeymoon journey with Charles, revisiting those blissful days. When she woke, she caught the faint dried-cherry hint of his cologne. As if he'd been in the room with her, watching over her as she slept.

And then one night she dreamed of him. Silhouetted against the purples and reds and golds of the canyon walls. He took her hand and led her up the trail. Higher and higher they climbed. The sun rose hot above them. The colors shimmered and shifted. The reds lightening to pink. The purples deepening to black. Adele's chest heaved and ached. "Almost there," Charles said, urging her on. Until at last she crested the rim with a bursting, heart-rending gasp.

CHAPTER 44

Whether or not Ivy wrote their parents, Ruth didn't know, but at the next mail call she received a thin letter—a single airmail sheet—addressed to Ruth and Ivy Rutledge.

> Dear Girls,
>   I hope you are reading this together.

They weren't. But Ruth hadn't seen Ivy in days and she wasn't going to wait around for her to find out what her mother had to say.

> I wish I didn't have to write this letter.

Laying the guilt on rather thick, thought Ruth. Not that they didn't deserve it.

> Your grandmother passed away two nights ago in her sleep. The doctors believe it was her heart. They say she never felt a thing, but I don't entirely believe them. I hate to think she was lying there in the dark, needing me, and unable to call. Her service will be this weekend. I wish you girls could be there.
>   There's more to be said, but I just don't have it in me right now.

Ruth had no time to cry. Hueys were descending with a beautiful delicacy that belied their horrible racket and cargo. Ruth put the letter in her pocket and jogged out to meet them. Hours later, when she stepped out of the hospital, she found Ivy waiting for her.

"Where have you been?" asked Ruth. Ivy's only response was a hardening of her jawline.

"Forget it," said Ruth. "Honestly, I don't care where you go and what you do. Whatever it is, it just brings in more business." Ruth jerked her head at the hospital behind them.

"Is that what you want?" asked Ivy. "To know what I do?"

"I think I know what you do."

Ivy's laugh was low. "I put on a pretty pastel dress and smile for the GIs."

"Okay, Ivy. Good night, then." Ruth turned to go.

"Fine. Here's what I do. I watch. I listen. Mostly to find out where people are and where they aren't. *And* I put on a pretty pastel dress and smile for the GIs. Sometimes I do all of that at once."

Ivy slouched against the frame of the tent. Ruth wondered if she'd been drinking. But no, she didn't smell like she'd been drinking, and her eyes were clear. She recognized a gleam in them that meant Ivy wanted something. Ruth didn't know what she wanted, but no doubt it was the reason she spoke so freely.

"I'll give you an example," said Ivy. "A village might be there one day, and then we move them out."

"Meaning you burn them out."

"But come back two weeks later, and it's there again. Or it's there, but the residents are VC—fresh down from the trail."

"Not if it's been naped," said Ruth, thinking of the blistered lesions she'd seen on the locals she'd treated recently. Horrible wounds that could never possibly heal enough to make their sufferers whole again.

"I keep tabs on who's moving where, mostly," said Ivy. "That's it in a nutshell."

"I don't know how you can stand it," said Ruth. "Working to keep all this going." She'd had a bad week—first the nape victims, and then more Hueys, disgorging one wounded man after another. They lifted them onto the operating tables and repaired them and then sent them back out to the jungle. Where the insatiable maw of the war devoured them. The lucky ones were injured enough to be sent home to a fractured existence. Ruth was disgusted.

"I don't want to keep this going any more than you do," said Ivy. "I'm working to make it end. As fast as possible. So they can all go home."

And what about you? wondered Ruth. Because her sister seemed oddly content in Cu Chi. Would Ivy go home? It was difficult to picture her back in Enid. Difficult to picture her in anything but her fatigues or the occasional cocktail dress. The Donut Dolly uniform didn't count—it was so patently a costume.

Ruth had been on her feet for ten hours, and the news of Adele's death, submerged beneath her focus on the wounded, suddenly shot to the surface. She pulled the letter from her pocket and handed it to her sister.

Ivy scanned it and said, "Oh, Ruth. I'm so sorry."

Ruth turned and strode toward the hooches. Ivy had been waiting for her. She wanted something. To get it, she'd have to do better than that.

Ivy caught her arm. "Really, I am. She was . . . she was a great lady, wasn't she?"

Ruth yanked her arm away. "For God's sake, Ivy, what do you want?"

"I've found someone. Someone who knows everything. Come with me. You'll see."

"I go back on duty in four hours. I'm not going anywhere except to bed."

"I already worked it out with Stanich. She put you on a later shift."

"Screw you, Ivy. You don't get to work things out with my boss. I'm not going anywhere. *Our grandmother just died.*"

"I doubt she's *my* grandmother."

"How can you be so stupid?!"

"Stupid is letting people fool you with lies. I want the truth. I want to know who I am."

"You're Ivy Rutledge. You're my sister. That's who you are." Ruth stopped herself from adding: Why isn't that enough? She blinked rapidly, determined not to cry. Why was she always the weak one? Where did Ivy get the strength to remain so . . . unmoved?

But maybe she wasn't. Ivy's own eyes looked damp. She brushed her sleeve across them.

"Why can't you see that that's true?" pleaded Ruth.

"Why are you so afraid?" asked Ivy. "Why are you so afraid to hear what's real? I'm the one who should be afraid."

"You know we're sisters," insisted Ruth. "Maybe not by blood, but you know it all the same. Same with Adele. She's *our* grandmother, and you know it."

"Come with me," begged Ivy. "Come with me, and we'll find out for sure. It took me forever, but I found someone who knows."

Maybe it was the exhaustion. Maybe it was the grief. Or the novelty of seeing Ivy cry. Or just her lifelong habit of giving in to her sister. But for whatever reason, Ruth went.

Ivy led them to the Officers' Club. Ruth wasn't much of a drinker, but some days obliterating the images of the preceding hours was absolutely necessary if she was ever going to set foot inside the hospital again. And there had been nights when she'd been so lonely, when she'd needed someone's arms around her, and given the unbalanced gender ratio and the fact that pretty much everyone in Cu Chi at one time or another needed someone else's arms around them, sitting alone at the O Club bar was an invitation that never went unaccepted.

Ivy's quarry wore civvies. He was stationed at a table near the back with the camp CO and a visiting officer whose bearing (Ruth couldn't make out the insignia in the dark) suggested a rank of colonel at minimum. The civvies—clean and well pressed and seemingly unaffected by the damp heat—caught Ruth's attention right away. The man wearing them saw Ruth and Ivy almost as soon as they saw him. He blanched and then recovered himself. Ruth's stomach dropped.

"We'll get something to drink first," said Ivy. "On me."

"Who is he?" asked Ruth. Before Ivy could answer, the man had joined them at the bar.

"Ladies," he said, touching an imaginary hat brim. "May I get you anything?"

"As a matter of fact," said Ivy, "you may."

Without asking what they preferred, the man ordered three scotches with rocks from the bartender. "If you're not the Rutledge girls," he said, "I'll eat my hat." Ruth giggled. Exhaustion, the man's insistence on his imaginary hat, the fact that she was in Vietnam at all—the scotch couldn't come soon enough.

"I go by Shaw now," said Ivy. The man's face revealed nothing. "Ruth, this is Mr. Quigley. He was with our . . . with Georgeanne and Vivian at Camp Davis. He's at Lockheed now. Corner office, or so I hear."

"My wife warned me that you girls were the spitting image of your mother." He raised his glass to them. "How is she? Besides worried sick about you two."

"If you mean Georgeanne, she's been better," said Ivy. "Her own mother just passed."

He mumbled apologetic sounds into his drink. Ruth struggled to keep up. Who was this man, and how would his wife know what she and Ivy looked like?

Ivy went on: "If you mean Vivian, who knows? She writes, but I don't read her letters. Ruth probably does. She's good about things like that."

Mr. Quigley signaled the bartender for another round. His glass was empty. Ruth's was close behind. Ivy hadn't touched hers. *What the hell,* thought Ruth, and tossed back the rest of her drink.

"Attagirl." Mr. Quigley pushed another glass toward her. "Fancy running into the Rutledge girls halfway around the world. Although, in the aviation business, you do tend to run into people where you least expect it. Saw your dad at Travis on my way over. Dropping off a transport. Looked sharp in that American Airlines uniform."

Halfway through her second scotch, it hit her. "You're married to Joyce Elliot," she said.

"Oh, bravo, Ruth." Ivy scowled.

"Guilty as charged," said Quigley. He asked if she wanted another drink. Ruth declined. "Suit yourself. I should get back to the brass. Bad for business to leave 'em hanging. But what a treat. Wait till I tell Joyce. She won't believe it. Give my best to your mom."

"Mr. Quigley," said Ivy. He was someone who gave orders rather than took them now—anyone could see that. But Ivy's tone rooted him to the spot, his hands clutching a bouquet of scotches for the brass, his eyes suddenly wary and tired. "Which one of us is whose?"

"Sweetheart," he said, "I have no idea what you mean."

"Yes, you do. Your wife said you helped them. In their time of need. Which was exactly when they would have been pregnant with us. We already know that much. So: Which one of us is whose?"

He stood there, the ice in the drinks melting, watering down the booze. Then he nodded as if he'd made a decision and that decision was final—one to be lived with, regardless of where it led. "Does it matter," he asked at last, "at this point?"

"Facts always matter," said Ivy.

Quigley emitted a harsh laugh. "Oh, sweetheart. If facts mattered, none of us would be anywhere near this place."

"They matter to me," Ivy insisted softly. "They matter to us." Ruth shook her head no, thinking, *Not to me,* thinking, *Please, please, please, whatever secrets you have, please keep them.*

Perhaps Quigley understood, because after another pause, he said, "Sorry, sweetheart. I don't know. And I'm not sure I'd tell you if I did." And then, without seeming to move at all, he was back with the brass, passing the drinks around, saying, "Daughters of a pilot I knew at Camp Davis. Spitting image. Now the fuel capacity in these new models . . ."

Lewis—the beautiful one—was the first nurse in Ruth's hooch to rotate out. They went through two bottles of gin celebrating her departure. Then another nurse left, and another—more empty gin bottles, more miserable hangovers, more grousing from the ones left behind about how much longer they had to go. But Ruth never groused. She thrived on the adrenaline rush of it all. Yes, she saw awful things. Yes, she was exhausted. But none of this made her long for home. Home wouldn't quite be home with no Adele there.

New nurses rotated in. Ruth was now the one with the patinated, worn-in fatigues. The one they looked to for reassurance and advice and comfort. She gave it when she had it in her to give. Which was why it was right to leave when your time was up, she knew, because at some point you wouldn't have a shred of reassurance or comfort left in you. Stanich rotated out, replaced by a woman who was her exact mental replica encased in a different physical form. This one tall and rangy where Stanich had been short and all curves.

The Donut Dollies went home and were replaced too. All of them except Ivy.

Ivy never pestered Ruth again about their parentage. On the occasional evening when they had a drink together, they spoke of other things entirely. Usually the present, sometimes the future, rarely the past. No longer on the defensive, Ruth sometimes allowed herself to wonder, Was she her mother's daughter? Was she Vivian's? Unwanted by one? Wanted—was she?—by the other? Could she trust herself not to demand the truth from them when she saw them again?

When the paperwork came through for her return, she tore it in half and signed up for another tour.

CHAPTER 45

George's separation from Tom had never culminated in actual divorce. While they rarely spent time together, one tangible thread of their marriage remained: a weekly conversation. Always on Sunday, because he didn't fly on Sundays anymore. He had the seniority now to pick up the flights he wanted when he wanted them, and he'd declared Sunday his "day of rest."

It wasn't a religious thing. They had never been churchy. Which was just one more thing, George knew, to feed the gossip mill at the country club. Even Helen and Frank made regular appearances at First Methodist.

"That club," her mother had scoffed, when she was still around to scoff. "As if anyone should care what those spoiled know-nothings think about anything." The house felt empty and enormous without her mother in it. She'd considered selling it and getting an apartment for herself—something small and easy to care for. But that wouldn't do, because someday the girls would come home. She liked to picture them walking in the front door. To imagine them in their childhood beds, giggling at some private joke as she listened from the hallway. How could they have grown up so fast and flown so far away from her?

"I'm still here," said Tom. He'd been so good to her after Adele's passing. Calling almost every day. Bringing a bag of what, for him, constituted groceries: a six-pack of Coke and a Styrofoam tray of cube steak and ten pounds of potatoes. She even woke one morning to find him mowing her lawn, which didn't need mowing.

"I have a yard man for that," she told him.

But she understood. He'd liked Adele. And he knew how it felt to lose a parent, to lose both parents. To feel like you were the last remaining bulwark against the mysterious force that gave and took life. He wanted to help, and, like almost everyone else, he didn't know how, so he came over and mowed her already-cut lawn.

He never said anything about Frank, and George believed this was his way of allowing her room to come back, to do the right thing. It wasn't too late. Sometimes she was tempted. No more guilt. No more sneaking around. But then Frank would trace a finger down her neck, and suddenly neither of them had wrinkles or stiff knees or to-do lists, let alone grief or disappointment. They were young and beautiful and the world and all its possibilities lay before them, theirs for the taking, and they hadn't yet chosen the wrong possibilities, made the wrong turns.

"You still there?" asked Tom.

"Sorry. Yes. What were you saying?"

"Any mail this week?" Sometimes one of them received a letter. The one who hadn't tried their best to sound pleased for the one who had. And the one who had tried to ease the disappointment of the one who hadn't by reading theirs aloud over the phone.

"No, but I talked to Vivian, and she got a letter last week." George didn't need to specify that it was from Ruth.

Ivy had written to her and to Tom each once and never again, and the text of those two letters—they'd read them to one another, naturally—had been identical. Ivy was in Vietnam. She didn't want them to think she was ungrateful for the comfortable childhood they had provided her, because she wasn't. Though she didn't, George reflected, say that she was grateful for it either. She was well, and she hoped they were too. And they didn't need to worry about Ruth, because Ivy kept a close eye on her.

George had found that reassuring, though she wasn't certain why she should.

CHAPTER 46

From the start, Vietnam enchanted Ivy. The moisture, the heat, the green, the flat diamond light held her in thrall, and she thought, *So this is what home feels like.* Home felt like freedom. Freedom from handling others so delicately. All those brittle porcelain men in California—now she was free of them. Free of Sam Benson, too, apparently. Though Benson seemed impervious to any sort of damage. She didn't have to be delicate with him. "Where did you go to school?" she asked him once. His mouth twitched as if he were stifling a laugh and he said, "Not Yale."

"But where, then?"

"Louisiana State. Baton Rouge."

Ivy must have looked surprised. "Now, Miss Enid, Oklahoma, you of all people should know talent doesn't only exit through the doors of the Ivy League. Talent can be found in Baton Rouge, Louisiana. It can be found on buses to New Orleans."

Ivy no longer had to handle anyone delicately except sources and potential sources. Because she couldn't always be certain, at first, who those were, she often kept quiet. Many of the stateside rules that had chafed and fettered her didn't exist in her new enchanting home. And she could usually work around the rules that did.

On the face of it, she knew she shouldn't have been good at the job. She stood out. She was female. She was tall. Her hair, like Vivian's, caught the sun at any angle, lighting up like a halo around her face.

She intentionally carried herself with a calm certainty that made people look. But it also steadied the people she talked to, relaxed them, loosed their minds and then their tongues, so that they told her things without realizing or remembering it. The sources she recruited trusted her. The radiomen especially liked her. They kept her up to date on troop movements, skirmishes, supply communications, anything they thought she might like to hear.

Her French had taken on a Viet inflection. And she had taken classes back in California, getting the basics of Viet and Lao. "I don't need you to speak them," Sam Benson told her before she left. "Might be better if you don't. But it can't hurt you to understand them, even if it's just a little."

After she arrived in Vietnam, she rarely heard from Sam. He'd passed her along to Ned Pennywell—quiet, steady, not at all fragile despite his Princeton tie. Ned kept an office in a newsroom in Saigon, where he wielded an editor's pencil. He invited her to embassy parties, where he mostly ignored her presence. He suggested a tailor just off Tu Do Street. She went in and came out with coded messages slipped into her pocket by Mr. Anh as he measured her for yet another dress. That's how she'd learned, nearly two years ago now, that Ruth was on her way to Vietnam. One of these messages—not in code and signed SB—said, "Your sister's coming."

Which had set Ivy's heart cantering around in her rib cage. She knew Sam had backgrounded her before she started working with him. But somehow, she'd imagined that he would leave it at that—just background, just history—not continue watching her family. What did he know about her mother and father? About Vivian? About Adele? About Ruth? What did he know, she'd wondered for the first time, about who she really was?

And what would bring Ruth to Vietnam? Had Sam approached her? Recruited her? Lured her to California? But why would he? Ruth had no facility for languages. And she lacked the essential unobtrusive curiosity to do what Ivy did. No, there must be another reason.

Ivy's heart had settled to a trot. There weren't many American women in Vietnam. But when you looked closely, you did see them around. And why were those women in Ivy's enchanting country? She knew of four possibilities: Ruth was a WAC, Ruth was a journo, Ruth was a nurse, or Ruth, like Ivy herself (ostensibly), was a Donut Dolly. Her heart had slowed to a walk now, ambling through untroubling pastures. She'd begin with the most likely possibility (Donut Dolly) and finish with the least (journo and nurse). Ruth's preference for not knowing—her natural inclination to mind her own business— made her unsuited to a journalism career. And Ivy suspected she lacked the stomach for nursing. Especially the sort of nursing required in a combat zone.

Ned Pennywell's office had three desks and three phones. One for Ned and only Ned. Two for a rotating cast of journos, both of which were currently in use. Ivy sat on a window ledge, smoking, waiting for Ned to acknowledge her presence. Which, after much scribbling with his blue pencil, much head shaking and sighing, at last he did. "Shaw. You are here and yet I did not summon you."

"Hello, Ned. Just popped in to do some research."

"Will I be interested in this research? Will it in any way assist me with filling my requisite copy needs?"

"No."

Ned pulled another sheaf of paper from his inbox, raised the blue pencil and his eyes to heaven.

Ivy lit another cigarette. "I was wondering," she said, provoking a mournful sigh from Ned, "how one might go about finding a list of all the journalists working in or on their way to Vietnam."

"That's a rather wide net, Shaw."

"Well, I do have a specific name."

"Let's hear it, then."

Ivy had found herself suddenly reluctant to reveal Ruth's name to Ned. As if he would care, she'd told herself. As if he would concern himself with Ruth's identity at all.

"Rutledge. Ruth Rutledge."

"Never heard of her." Ned returned to his papers and his blue pencil.

"That's it? You've never heard of her, so she's not here? And not coming?"

Ned released a sigh of Shakespearean proportions. "There aren't that many females in this profession. And especially not in this country. So no, she's not here. Or I would have heard of her. And if she were good enough to be here, I would have heard of her too."

She may very well not be good enough, thought Ivy as she dove for the now-free phone. In two quick calls, she'd eliminated Ruth as a WAC or a Donut Dolly. With one more call, during which she smoked two cigarettes while on hold, she learned that Ruth Rutledge, RN, would report for duty at Pleiku in less than a month.

Ivy could have easily steered clear of Pleiku. Ruth never would have known they were in the same country. Which, the more Ivy thought about it, was unacceptable. Here was Ruth doing something utterly un-Ruth-like, taking her by surprise. She wanted to spring the same surprise on her sister. It would mean exposing herself. As soon as Ruth got a letter out, the whole family would know where she was. But what did it matter? They couldn't exactly come get her. She was an adult. She made her own choices now. If they wanted her to come home, they could tell her the truth.

Ivy ignored the journo hovering behind her. She picked up the receiver and made another call.

Ivy hung back from the airfield. She liked watching Ruth during triage. She was efficient. Competent. The nurse in charge kept an eye on some of the other women, but never Ruth. Ivy had been watching Ruth more often of late. Spying on her—she should just admit it. Soaking her in, as if that would make things any easier when Ruth went back to Enid.

Just the other night, she'd watched Ruth stumble out of the O Club in the arms of a surgeon. They headed toward the motor pool, no doubt looking for a back seat and some privacy. Everyone needed an occasional distraction.

For a time, Ivy had had a distraction of her own. A USAID worker (officially). Married, which was how she preferred them. (Was Sam Benson married? She'd never noticed a ring.) She and the AID worker had often crossed paths in Saigon. In hotels with crisply pressed sheets. A pitcher of water on the bedside table. The ceiling fan revolving slowly above them.

But a year ago, he'd come too close to a tripped land mine. The soldier five feet behind him was only nicked by shrapnel, but her AID worker wasn't as fortunate. Ivy had found him in the hospital—in the curtained-off section where the nurses put the ones who weren't going to make it. She held his hand until he stopped breathing. She kissed him one last time and then took everything unrelated to his USAID work or his family out of his pockets and burned it to ashes in a coffee can.

She was doing just fine without distractions for now. At least until Ruth left or Sam Benson found a reason to make an appearance.

Down at the airfield, Ruth shouted, "Go! Go!" as she jogged alongside a stretcher to the hospital. Maybe Ruth would re-up again. *Don't be greedy,* Ivy chided herself. Ruth had already stayed for an extra year. Who in their right mind would stay for a third?

Besides me, thought Ivy.

1970–1976

CHAPTER 47

When she lost the first five pounds, George, gleeful, invited Helen to meet for lunch at the country club. It was a chance to wear a dress she'd bought last spring, knowing even in the fitting room that it was slightly too tight and bound to get tighter. "Well, I think you look nice," Helen had said that day in the fitting room when George mentioned the snug waist. "And anyway, it's a wonder what a week of cottage cheese and lettuce will do for a girl. I wouldn't worry."

George hadn't worried. She wasn't fat. It was just that things had begun . . . shifting. And while her height accommodated more shifting than some women's, still, things were changing, and not for the better. Her week of cottage cheese and lettuce hadn't had the slightest effect. But now she'd lost five pounds, and George could think of nothing she'd done to give them a reason to leave. She wore the dress, met Helen at the club, saw Helen's eyes pass over her slimmer waist and her mouth tighten. George returned home pleased.

Two weeks later, she stepped on the scale again to find that five more pounds had disappeared. The mirror revealed no difference. Her stomach still pooched a bit, as did her inner thighs. Most likely she'd purchased a bum scale. Maybe she'd get herself a new one for Christmas. Or give up on scales altogether.

But now she was intrigued. Rather than weighing herself every seven to ten days, she stepped on the scale—skeptically, as it was clearly not to be trusted—every day just before dinner. Her weight held steady for three days, and then another pound was gone. And two days later, another.

George, ignoring the voice in the back of her mind that said *doctor*, in increasingly urgent tones, tossed the scale in the trash and didn't weigh herself again for months. Adele wasn't there to say anything. There was only Helen, who marveled at how slender George had become and pleaded with her to share her secret, pretty please. And Frank, whose pleasure in her body seemed connected to something so deep within her that he never seemed to notice how it had changed.

George let the phone ring twice before picking it up. "Hello, Tom." There was a companionable pause while he sipped from his glass. His Sunday night tumbler with two fingers of rye and three lumps of ice. They hadn't had much news for one another lately. But this past week they'd each received a letter from Ruth. At last she was coming home. "I still can't believe she stayed for a second year," said George. "You never hear of anyone wanting to stay longer."

"Come on, George. Remember how devastated you were to leave the WASP? Maybe that's how she feels."

"Maybe. But I was flying airplanes. Not stitching up wounded teenagers."

"Maybe stitching up wounded teenagers feels like flying to Ruth."

"I think she stayed because of Ivy," said George.

Tom sighed. "I don't think we can blame Ivy for this."

"Oh, I know Ivy didn't ask her to stay. When did Ivy ever ask anyone for anything unless it was to stay out past curfew or something like that? But I think Ruth didn't want to leave her. I think she's afraid Ivy will disappear again."

The sound of Tom taking another sip. And another. He often reverted to silence when she brought up Ivy. But Ivy was a mystery she couldn't help but probe. Ruth had sent them letters announcing her

DEROS date, but Ivy would never tell them her own return date, let alone where she was going. They'd found her—sort of—but it wasn't as if they could jet over to Vietnam and see her. "And it's not like Ivy's going to come home to Enid," said George.

No, Tom agreed, that was probably true. But Ruth was coming, and that was something. And when she was back, she could tell them all about Ivy. "And maybe," said Tom, "Ivy'll tell Ruth when she's coming back to the States."

"Maybe," said George. She wanted both of her daughters to come home, but she was also terrified to see them.

She still had the letter from Quigley in the drawer of her nightstand: "Met your daughters in Cu Chi. Spitting image. Understand one of them goes by Shaw now."

Quigley swore he hadn't told them a thing, but the fact that they had asked him meant Ruth and Ivy had never bought the explanation that Joyce was just a drunk spouting nonsense. Which meant the whole thing was blowing up. And George, who'd had years to prepare for the day they demanded the truth, who had laid out explanation after explanation in her mind, and found none of them sufficient, knew that time was nearly up.

CHAPTER 48

Maybe it was just that she was leaving, but on her flight home, tucked into a window seat, Ruth finally understood her mother's affinity for airplanes. There was something appealing about being on board. Not in Cu Chi anymore, but not home (whatever that meant) either. A peaceful in-between nothingness. A not quite of this earth–ness.

That feeling deserted her the instant the plane touched down at Travis. By the time she reached Chicago, she was trembling. It was just exhaustion, she told herself. It wasn't the civilian hair and clothing and ways of talking and moving, which seemed in some subtle, undefinable way different from how everyone had talked and moved in Vietnam.

Life had kept on, as it was perfectly entitled to do. Everything seemed changed, yet just enough the same to be jarring. She felt passed by, unmissed. It was partly her own fault. Her father had wanted to pick her up at Travis. "I'll bid a flight—bring you home from there myself," he'd written. Her mother had offered to meet her anywhere along her route home and fly her back in the Cessna. But Ruth had told them both no. She didn't want to spend her first hours back fielding questions about Ivy.

While changing planes in Chicago, she had to detour around a group of teenagers. They sat in a ring, like they were about to play duck duck goose, blocking the concourse. All of them—even the boys—wore their hair long. Everyone had longer hair now. Or maybe that was just a Chicago thing. Ruth didn't mind the hair. The protesting didn't bother

her either. More people ought to protest, as far as she was concerned. What she hated was that so many of them wore field jackets, painted and embroidered with peace signs and flowers. Had the boys who'd been issued those jackets made it home? Had Ruth bandaged them up and topped them off with fresh blood and sent them back to the jungle to be shot up again? What did these kids, sneering at her dress blues, know about the young men whose jackets they'd defaced? She hurried past them, swallowed her bile.

She was going to be just fine, she told herself as she gulped deep breaths of air on the flight to Oklahoma City.

The stewardess slipped her a gin and tonic. "My sister was a nurse over there," she said.

Ruth was about to ask where, but the passenger next to her cut in. "What's that?"

"Just 7UP," said the stewardess as she faded up the aisle.

The drink was heavy on the gin, and it helped. Ruth's breathing slowed, and her hands stopped shaking. She took the last swallow and began, to her seatmate's evident irritation, to crunch her ice while gazing out the window. Cloud cities reared up over sweeping white plains. Ruth imagined angels gliding back and forth among them. Her father wouldn't find the view remarkable at all—he must see this all the time. Had her mother flown this high during the war? Ruth had never asked. She and Ivy had been almost malicious in their lack of interest about their mother's WASP days. It was one thing to listen to Aunt Vivian and their father talk about flying, but another thing entirely to hear about George's love of planes, her nostalgia for a time before her daughters existed. The note of longing in her mother's voice when she spoke about her WASP days suggested regret. For not choosing a life more like Vivian's. A life without daughters. Especially the one who wasn't really hers.

Her parents might not want to hear about her war either. But they'd want to hear about Ivy. Her sister hadn't answered when Ruth asked when she planned to return. "Not home, necessarily," said Ruth. "Stateside." Ivy merely lifted her shoulders, as if she didn't care whether she ever saw any of them again. But just before Ruth stepped into the jeep that would take her to Tan Son Nhut, Ivy had rushed up and hugged her fiercely. She'd pecked Ruth's cheek and said, "Be good, Ruthie," then melted back into the crowd of farewell wishers.

The landing gear shuddered down, and Ruth spooked.

"Nothing to worry about, hon," said the man next to her. "Just means we're about to land."

She considered informing him that both her parents were pilots. That she knew what landing gears sounded like, thank you very much, but she didn't want to encourage any further conversation. Instead, she smiled softly at him, pretended she was grateful for his reassurance.

She thought of her mother and father again. "It's not that I don't want to see you," she'd written them. "I'm just going to need some time." Time to think about whether she wanted to ask the questions, to seek the answers Ivy had long wanted. To decide whether she wanted to hear those answers herself. She knew so little about her parents, not even whether they were actually her parents. "Time to settle in," she wrote.

She met her father first, because he was easier. He, too, had been deceived. He broiled her a steak and set a wedge of iceberg lettuce with Thousand Island dressing, her favorite, on the plate beside it. "Iced tea?" he asked. Ruth shook her head. "Whiskey, then."

"I know you want to ask about her," Ruth said. "It's okay to ask about her."

He took his time chewing a bite of steak before he answered. "Let's start with you," he said. "Hard to come home?"

She couldn't answer, as if the very question swelled her throat shut.

"Yeah. That's not gonna change for a while, just so you know."

She sipped her drink. Tom swallowed another bite of steak, then said, "War makes people do stupid things—I don't just mean the fighting. You didn't get married, did you?"

She nearly choked on her whiskey.

"People do. Your mother and I did. Frank and Helen . . . Well, like I said, people do stupid things when there's a war on. No one's quite in their right minds. But I'm sure I don't have to tell you that."

She set down her glass and started to speak, but he interrupted. "I know what you want to ask—I'd want to ask it too. So I'll just say right off, I don't know. I made your mother swear not to tell me, and she never has. And whatever you and Ivy manage to find out, I'll thank you both to keep it to yourselves. I have two girls. That's just that, Ruth. That's just that."

She tried Vivian next. Not in person but with a long-distance call. Vivian had moved to Oregon. She hadn't mentioned this move in her letters, but George had written Ruth about it just before she came home.

> I thought she was following a man we knew from the war. But it was the other way around. She wanted to move and he went along. I wish she'd picked somewhere closer. Oregon is so far away.

It certainly was. And the timing of Vivian's move was . . . interesting. It wasn't a short trip from Enid to Houston, but it was nothing compared to Enid to Oregon.

Vivian's phone rang for a long time before a man—the follower, Ruth assumed—answered. No, he said, Vivian wasn't in.

"Do you know when she'll be back?"

"I couldn't say."

"Couldn't or won't?"

"Who is this?"

"This is Ruth Rutledge. Her . . ." Her what? They'd grown up referring to Vivian as their aunt, though she wasn't—not really. Their only real aunt, their father's sister, had died of complications from polio, long before they were born. Ruth and Ivy never referred to themselves as Vivian's nieces. And almost certainly one of them was her daughter.

"Ah, one of George's girls," said the follower. "I knew your mother in The War." His voice supplied the capital letters. As if her own war were lowercase, less than.

"You're a couple of wars behind," said Ruth. Then she hung up.

CHAPTER 49

Her daughter had been back for more than a week. She'd insisted on arriving alone. And, once in Enid, had refused to come to the house. Refused to even tell George where she was staying. Helen claimed to have glimpsed her in the parking lot of a motel out on Route 60.

"Alone," stressed Helen. As if that fretted George: the idea that her daughter, who had just returned from a war zone, was bunking up with a man. No, it was the shame of Ruth not coming home to *her*, not settling into her old bedroom—her and Ivy's bedroom. Of the fact that when friends said, "Oh, you must be so glad to have Ruth home. How is she?" George had to lie and say Ruth was doing as well as could be expected. Because her daughter had refused to see her. Until this morning. She'd called early, saying she wanted to come over and talk.

Now she was striding up the walk, expecting an explanation. George, spying through a gap in the curtains, clocked the determined set of her daughter's jaw. Her cheeks had shed their babyish fullness. She looked like she'd seen and done hard things, and George wished, as she had so often, for the power to protect her children from life's hardness. Ruth wore one of those long, flowing skirts girls favored now—George saw them in magazines and on television more than she did around Enid. The skirt didn't suit Ruth's seen-hard-things-done-hard-things face. She had earned a more severe sort of fashion. Perhaps one of those tailored 1940s utility suits with padded shoulders and darts and a cinched waist.

George herself wore a loose shirtdress. Nice, but not dressy—she didn't want to look as if she made too much of the occasion of her daughter—at last—agreeing to visit her. After being in town a week.

Ruth reached the door, and if she noticed George twitch the curtains closed, her face didn't betray it. Would she knock? Or just come in? Either choice would send a message of some sort, a denial or acceptance of "home." George filled a glass from the tap and gulped down half of it. Her hand shook. The rim of the glass rattled against her teeth. Water splashed onto her sleeve. She wore long sleeves all the time now. She was always cold these days. And she didn't like anyone to see how scrawny her arms had become.

Ruth turned away from the house. She appeared to be staring at the driveway. "Honestly," muttered George, "this is ridiculous." She'd have to open the door, an admission that she'd been watching, which was the least of the admissions Ruth was looking for. Well, done was done, as Adele would have said.

How have you been hurt? George thought. *Really, how? Because we raised you with all the comforts we could. We gave you love and a good home (well, minus the fighting and separation), we gave you a sister, we fed you and clothed you, and . . .*

Deceived us, Ruth would say. Deceived us every day of our lives. Robbed us of the truth. And now it's time to give it back.

George feared that if she waited any longer, Ruth might walk away. She opened the door and opened her arms to her daughter, hoping, praying, that Ruth would walk into them.

CHAPTER 50

Her mother, her maybe-mother, Georgeanne, was the hardest to face, and so Ruth had left her for last, but it was past time to go home. To see if home was still home. Her father had warned her that it wouldn't feel like it. "Nothing," he said, "is going to feel like home for a while. So just go easy, okay?"

Ruth had taken his instructions as another excuse to avoid meeting her mother. Until not seeing her became more difficult, heavier to bear. She put on a new skirt and top. Even if she didn't feel like she belonged back home, she could at least look as if she did. She phoned and told George she was coming over and then hung up, cutting off her mother's enthusiastic response.

Some of the cars were newer, but otherwise, the street looked the same. The pecan tree was gone, but otherwise, the house looked the same. As she came up the walk, Ruth's heart racketed around in her chest. Maybe she *was* George's daughter, and thus, Adele's granddaughter. Maybe whatever had been wrong with Grandma Adele's heart was wrong with hers, too, and she'd die of a heart attack at age twenty-five, right here on the front lawn where she and Ivy used to play in the sprinkler. She concentrated on the oil stains on the driveway—another reminder of her grandmother. She offered up a silent greeting to Adele, wishing she were there, about to roll out from underneath a car. When the door latch clicked, she straightened her spine, ready for the painful conversation ahead.

She wasn't Ivy, but she was braver than she used to be. Brave enough, she thought, to learn she wasn't really her mother's daughter. No matter how badly she wanted to be.

The door swung open to reveal a haggard, drawn, aged woman.

"Hello, sweetie. I'm so glad you're home."

Ruth stepped into the woman's outstretched arms. They were too bony, but just as comforting as they'd always been. "Mom," said Ruth. She held on, not bothering about the tears that flowed freely down her face. Because her grandmother wasn't there, her mother wasn't herself, and they were about to have an entirely different conversation than the one she'd prepared for.

Before an hour had passed, they'd secured an appointment. Before a month had passed, they'd secured a diagnosis. The oncologist lifted his hands in apology.

"But her mother died just a year ago," said Ruth, as if to demonstrate the wrongness of this. The impossibility of it.

She hadn't planned to stay in Enid, but her mother was ill, and St. Mary's had an opening for an ER nurse. From the start, she hated it. She had to run every decision by a doctor. Any suggestions she made were ignored. Except for a couple of doctors who'd been over there, too, she'd treated more difficult cases than most of the St. Mary's ER staff could even imagine. After a few weeks, she asked to transfer to another department.

"Don't worry," soothed one of the older nurses. "A lot of people find the ER too difficult. There's no shame in requesting a transfer." Ruth refrained from explaining that it wasn't the trauma she couldn't tolerate, but the stubborn placidity of the staff. Of this nurse, with her bright, singsongy voice and her old-fashioned white cap, in particular.

The hospital reassigned her to pediatrics. She knew nothing about children, held no preconceived opinions about how they should be handled. At least in the pediatric ward, she could start with the assumption that the doctors and nurses knew what they were talking about.

"Because no one stateside seems to," said Ruth that evening, not to anyone in particular. The bartender had long since stopped listening to her.

"Well, hon, neither do you," said a man on the barstool next to hers. He patted her knee and left his hand on it. "Neither does anyone who hasn't been over there."

"But I was over there."

"Better cut this little lady off," the man barked. The bartender chuckled. The man next to her was paying, after all, for Ruth's drinks and for the hope that they might lead to something more. Every now and then—more frequently as her mother's treatments proceeded—the drinks did lead to something more. Not that the drinks made the decision for her; she knew when to switch to seltzer. It was loneliness. Since leaving Vietnam, it stalked her, waited for her to find herself at loose ends, pounced whenever she lacked distraction.

Without distractions, thoughts of Cu Chi flooded her mind. But whenever the subject of her time in Vietnam arose, people shifted uncomfortably, turned the topic to something—anything—else. Many of them, like the man on the next barstool, his hand now creeping up her thigh, openly disbelieved her. Even those high school and nursing school friends who had written to her, professing to miss her, didn't want to know what she'd seen, what she'd done, what it was like. She slid off the barstool. "Thanks for the drink."

"Oh, hey, don't go!"

But she was already at the door.

"It was the same for us," her mother said when Ruth complained about no one believing her. They sat in yet another waiting room—Ruth went to every appointment she could—listening to the hum of the HVAC system, the ding of elevators coming and going, the vending machine in the corner spitting five-cent orange soda into paper cups.

Ruth looked forward to these intervals in waiting rooms. Her mother filled them with stories about her days as a WASP. "People still don't believe it," said George.

Ruth winced. For years, she'd been no better than the man at the bar. She'd never really believed her mother had towed artillery targets while men on the ground shot live ammunition at her. And she didn't even have ignorance as an excuse. She'd seen photos of her mother in uniform. She'd flown with her in the Cessna. But it was easier to picture Vivian doing these things. Ruth had preferred to imagine her mother safely at home, taking care of her and Ivy, waiting for their father to return from overseas.

"I'd like to hear about it," she said. This, she decided, was the sort of truth she was interested in. Her mother's past. Every story George told her linked them more closely together, allowed Ruth to believe, at least until the tale ended, that she belonged to this woman.

But George looked suddenly tired. "Another time, sweetie."

CHAPTER 51

"This wouldn't have anything to do with Ruth coming home?" asked Patterson when Vivian proposed moving to Oregon.

"Of course not." She hadn't stayed in one place this long since she'd left home, she explained. Houston seemed a little tired, didn't he think? And she'd passed through Oregon years before. The emerald landscape, those forests of towering fir trees. Wouldn't it make a nice change?

"I know someone at Bonneville," said Patterson. "I could see if there's anything there for me."

There was. They sent their furniture off in a van and flew to western Oregon. A fairy-tale land where giant trees dripped with rain and enormous toadstools sprouted overnight. A magical place to hide out. Until Tom called and told her the news.

"It can't be true," she said to Patterson. George was one of the healthiest people she knew. All those balanced meals. All that exercise at that ridiculous country club.

"You should go," said Patterson.

"To Enid? I'd just be in the way."

But he insisted. "I was supposed to visit Susan before she . . ." He could never bring himself to say crashed. "But I didn't get my request in on time. They pushed my leave back a week, and by then—" By then, Vivian remembered, he'd needed that leave to attend his wife's funeral.

"Besides," he continued. "You should be there for Ruth." He said the name lightly. Weeks ago, he'd told her Ruth had telephoned. A call she still hadn't returned, because she didn't want to face Ruth's questions.

She'd saved all of Ruth's letters in her desk drawer, tied with a ribbon, like letters from a sweetheart. She wished she had a similar stack from Ivy. Now that Ruth was back home, they no longer wrote one another. Vivian still sent an occasional letter to Ivy. She doubted they ever reached her. That was easier than imagining Ivy receiving them and not replying.

Patterson took her by the shoulders. "Vivian, you're her best friend."

In Enid, she found Helen in George's kitchen, drying a stack of casserole dishes. "We're getting three or four a week. She can't possibly eat it all," said Helen. "I've frozen whatever will freeze. That one," she said, indicating a lasagna on the counter, "you all can eat tonight. I'll heat it up before I go home. There's a list on the counter of people who need thank-you notes. You can handle some of those while you're here."

"Of course," said Vivian, grateful to be taken charge of, and even more grateful that Ruth was at work.

George reclined against a mountain of pillows on the living room couch. When Vivian walked in, she snatched up a silk scarf and draped it over her head, then pulled it off again. "I'm not going to hide it from you," she said. Her hair was cropped short, patches of it missing. Vivian hadn't realized that someone's skin could look so ashen. She hung back, afraid to approach this fragile creature.

"Oh, get over here," said George. "You aren't really going to come all the way from Oregon and not hug me."

Vivian put her arms gently around her friend, but George pulled her close, her touch as peaceful and soothing as it always had been. "Now," said George when they released one another, "I have a few things to say about this Oregon business."

Vivian laughed, relieved. George was still herself. Surely that meant she'd be okay.

Ruth joined them later for lasagna. She didn't mention anything about Vivian not returning her phone call. Conversation at the table dragged. Ruth kept asking George how she felt. George kept saying, "Fine, sweetheart." Vivian couldn't seem to find her own tongue. As soon as they finished eating, George pleaded exhaustion and went to bed.

"Thank you for all your letters," said Ruth as she and Vivian cleared the table. "Mail meant a lot over there."

"Not at all," said Vivian. "I looked forward to yours too." Ruth swiped at the table. She hadn't met Vivian's eyes all evening. Which had left Vivian free to stare at this tall, striking young woman. This Ruth carried herself with such authority—not like the shy child Vivian remembered. This Ruth looked as if she'd have no qualms at all about asking questions. What better time than now, when it was just the two of them. Vivian was prepared to dodge and deflect, admit nothing at all.

"Would you mind washing up?" asked Ruth, stretching her arms above her head and yawning. "I'm beat, and I have an early shift tomorrow."

"Not at all," Vivian repeated. Moving to Oregon now seemed silly. Ruth didn't even want to talk to her. Vivian washed up, wiped down the counters. Then she went outside and rocked and smoked in the glider, trying to think about something besides Ruth's disappointing lack of interest.

Helen arrived at eight sharp the next morning. "We have a full day today," she said, looking askance at Vivian's robe. Vivian hurried to get dressed. When she returned to the kitchen, Helen had a list of dishes that needed returning, of thank-you notes to write, of prescriptions to pick up.

"Helen," said George, startling them both from the kitchen doorway. "Oh, don't worry, I'll go back to my couch. And I'm perfectly capable of getting myself there, thank you, Vivian." Vivian stepped back and dropped her arms. No one liked to be treated like an invalid—not even an invalid. "As I was saying," George continued, "Helen, I'd love to spend a little time with Vivian while she's here. Couldn't she be spared some of the errands? For today anyway?"

Helen clicked her tongue against the roof of her mouth but didn't argue. A moment later she was out the door. George giggled. "I feel like a teenager with the house to myself when she goes."

"I could call up some boys," joked Vivian.

They spent the morning sipping coffee and catching up until Vivian noticed the skin beneath George's eyes darkening. "I'm exhausting you," she said.

"No. Well, yes. But I like it."

"I'll let you rest. We can talk more later."

George burrowed lower into her nest of pillows. As Vivian unfolded a blanket to drape over her, she said, "I think it's time we tell the girls."

Vivian froze. The blanket hung still in her hands.

"They're old enough to know," insisted George. She raised herself from the mound of pillows, and Vivian quickly spread the blanket over her, tucked it around her shoulders.

"Shhh," she said. "We can talk about it later." George relaxed back into her nest.

Once her friend's breath steadied, Vivian tiptoed to the kitchen to call Patterson and let him know she'd be home sooner than expected.

CHAPTER 52

The doctors advised surgery. Then chemotherapy. Then a course of radiation. The treatments seemed endless. Her mother was a good soldier, following one doctor after another into battle. Never complaining. Ruth admired her courage. But each treatment left George weaker. Loopier. "Ivy," she said, when Ruth, who had taken to sleeping in her old bedroom some nights, came in to check on her.

"No, Mom. It's Ruth. Ivy's still overseas, remember?"

"Yes. Yes, that's right. Sorry, sweetie."

She knew George wrote to Ivy. Longed to have her real daughter by her side. Ruth occasionally wrote Ivy herself, detailing the treatments (extensive), the prognosis (uncertain). Suggesting that her sister try to find it in herself to write to George. "She did raise you, after all," wrote Ruth. "No matter who you think you are."

Months later, Ivy replied. She wrote that she'd been transferred into the Army Special Services. "It's not as impressive as it sounds," read the terse postcard that made no mention of George's illness. "Really, it's just a fancy new way of saying Donut Dolly." As this wasn't exactly news, Ruth didn't bother to share it with her parents.

"I've been thinking," said her mother on one of her better days. "I want to tell you the truth." They were strolling around the block, slowly.

Once, twice, three times, if George felt up to it. The fresh air put color in her mother's face.

"What do you mean? The truth about what?"

"Come on, sweetie. The truth about you girls."

Ruth's stomach lurched. She concentrated on putting one foot in front of the other. "Mom, you don't have to tell us anything." *Oh, please, God, don't tell me anything.*

"I was going to tell you when you first got home, but then . . ." She stopped and passed a hand down the length of her torso. "Well, here we are. And I want to tell you." Ruth's head swung violently from side to side—*no, no, no*—seemingly of its own accord. She'd been angry when she came home. Home hadn't felt like home, which was a betrayal, a robbery, especially after so much else had been taken from her—faith in her country, faith in her family, for starters. She'd come back ready to demand answers. To demand payment for those losses.

But then George's illness had confirmed how desperately she didn't want to lose her mother. She'd walked out of the doctor's office holding the maximum amount of truth she could manage. And now her mother wanted to hand her more. "But only when I can tell both of you," said George. Ruth took her arm as they stepped over a break in the sidewalk. "That's fair, I think. As fair as I can manage at this point anyway. I've written Ivy to let her know—more than once. I made a promise to her, and now I'm making it to you. When Ivy comes home, we'll talk about it. All of it."

Ruth stopped walking. "Have you heard from her? Did she say she's coming home?" She'd recently received another postcard. Ivy was in Laos. "Doing fine. Vientiane is beautiful. Will write more soon." No mention of any letters received, no questions about how their mother was doing. No hint that she even thought of home. Ruth hadn't shared this one with her parents, either, but Ivy might have sent them one herself.

"Someday. She's coming home someday." Her mother shrank in Ruth's silence. "Don't you think?"

After that conversation, Ruth stopped writing to Ivy. She wanted Ivy to be safe. She wanted her family all on the same patch of earth. But Ivy coming home meant losing her mother. Maybe if they weren't all in the same place, they had a better shot at staying a family.

After her shift, she found a table in the back of the Jet Way. She circled help wanted ads while she drank.

An airman hovered next to Ruth's table. "Not interested," said Ruth.

"You were interested last week." She glanced up, took in his sharp, feral features. He was the type she occasionally allowed herself to take an interest in. Was it last week she'd taken one of the airmen home with her? Or two weeks ago? These men were interchangeable. And always temporary.

"Guess that was then, this is now."

"Can't I even buy you a drink?"

"Suit yourself. But it won't get you anywhere."

They never believed this. Because of that, she received a fair number of free drinks. She kept careful count of them. Aunt Vivian used to tell her and Ivy: "Know your limit. And stick to it, no matter how much fun you're having, no matter who you're with."

"This doesn't seem like the most appropriate conversation for young girls," Grandma Adele had said.

"The really useful conversations often aren't," argued Vivian.

Now that she was stateside, Ruth's limit was four if she was alone. Three if she was with someone. She planned to sip this drink and then head home. Alone. Leaving a disappointed airman behind.

She circled another ad.

"You looking for a job?"

"I have a job."

"Why you circling those, then?"

Why indeed? wondered Ruth, when she never, ever applied for any of them. The plan had been to end up in a bigger city. The plan had not been Enid. Ivy had suggested, one particularly revealing evening, that she wasn't sure she herself could get any closer to home than Guam. Perhaps that's where she was now. Because she certainly wasn't responding to the letters their mother sent. Ruth hadn't told George about Ivy moving to Laos, but the letters probably reached her eventually. Ruth inspected the incoming mail, checked the trash for powder-blue airmail envelopes. Not that she needed to. A letter from Ivy would be the first thing George announced.

"You wouldn't want to go home?" she'd asked Ivy, that night—a night that seemed a century ago—back in Cu Chi.

"Maybe home is somewhere else for me," said Ivy.

"Where?"

In the pause, Ruth heard the faint sound of tracer fire off in the distance. Then Ivy said, "Maybe it's here."

"Here?!"

Ivy waved to the bartender for another. "Maybe it's someplace I'm still figuring out."

Ruth drained her glass and folded up her newspaper. "Thanks for the drink," she said to the airman. She headed out into the twilight . . . and found herself still in Enid, still rooted to the place she'd grown up. The place she lived. Not home. Not exactly, anyway. Because home was someplace she was still figuring out.

In line in the hospital cafeteria, waiting for her grilled cheese sandwich and pickle, Ruth stiffened as a helicopter flew low over the building, rattling the windows. She could tell who had been *in country* by whose white-coated shoulders tensed, who raised up on the balls of their feet, ready to run for the Hueys. A nurse a bit farther up the line was one of them. Ruth wondered where she'd been stationed. The woman shook the tension from her shoulders, then smoothed her hair. Something about the gesture tugged at Ruth's memory. Kimberly smoothing her hair in the lavatory at Tan Son Nhut. What was Kimberly doing in Enid, Oklahoma?

"My husband—we got engaged over there—he's from a tiny little town over in the panhandle. And I mean little. There's not much of a hospital near there, so when he came back, we moved here."

She said "here" with such disdain that Ruth knew she had to immediately make clear that here was where she started from. Then she interrupted Kimberly's stricken "I didn't mean—" with her own qualifier. "My mother's been sick. She's getting better, but I want to be close."

Some days this wasn't true. Some days she wished she were as far away as she could get—wished she was back in the hospital tent in Cu Chi. She felt listless—lifeless—in Enid. Too listless and lifeless to leave.

They carried their trays to an empty table, but Kimberly refused to sit down.

"I'm sorry," she whispered, "but I just cannot sit anywhere near *that*."

She tipped her head toward a long-haired young man wearing a field jacket, flared jeans, and strands of wooden beads. It wasn't a popular look in Enid, and Ruth suspected it wasn't making his life easy.

"I know what you mean," said Ruth, steering them across the room to another table. "I try to remind myself that some of them were actually over there. You can't always tell by looking.

"And honestly, I'm not sure this is much better." Ruth nodded at a nearby table where a couple their age, he in chinos and a button-down and she in a Peter Pan blouse and earrings that matched her necklace, picked at their lunches. "It's the spitting that really gets me," the man in chinos fumed, glaring across the room at the long-haired man.

Ruth knew what he meant—the spitting got her too. She hadn't yet seen any evidence of protesters spitting on soldiers—not a single photograph or news clip—but you heard about it everywhere these days. It was inexcusable. As if the GIs were nothing, not worth even a minimal degree of respect. Plenty of people in Enid these days complained about the spitting. And while Ruth didn't disagree with them, she wasn't sure why that was what got them so fired up, when they didn't say a thing about the napalm, about the naked children on fire, about My Lai, about the surge of damaged veterans stumbling among them. It wasn't the spitting that had broken those soldiers, after all. They'd endured far worse than that.

"Yeah," said Kimberly. "I have to admit I'm not sure where I belong these days. Do you ever wish you were back there?"

"Almost every day. And I didn't exactly have a premium posting."

Kimberly confessed that the beach where she was stationed was beautiful, but the nurses rarely had time to swim. "And it seemed so frivolous, you know. Putting on a swimsuit and tanning oil and all that. Though we did. When we weren't too exhausted. We weren't saints by any means."

"No one over there could afford to be a saint," said Ruth. She told Kimberly about running into Ivy, about not being an only child as she'd told her on the trip over. She left out the part about her sister not really being her sister.

Kimberly told Ruth her husband hated her working. "He wants me to quit. We can afford it. But I can't do it. I just can't. I feel like if I stop working, if I stay home and have babies, I'll go out of my mind. We fight about it all the time," said Kimberly. "I was glad when they switched him to night shifts. If we don't see each other so much, we get along better. Are you seeing anyone? Engaged or anything like that?"

Ruth knew she had ventured into old maid territory as far as most of Enid was concerned. Aunt Helen was always trying to set her up with someone from the club. She seemed to believe Ruth just hadn't found a good enough athlete to strike her fancy. "His serve is technical perfection," Aunt Helen would say, or, "He's a scratch golfer." As if Ruth even knew what that meant. Usually she agreed to a date, because after all, who knew. If she played her cards right, perhaps someday she'd have a husband of her own to argue with all the time.

"Don't rush," said her mother. Ruth had begun to understand that while George looked the part of a middle-aged, upper-middle-class Enid matron (at least before the ravages of the chemo, and if—as everyone did—you ignored her whatever-it-was with Frank Bridlemile), she didn't fit in with the country club crowd. This would surprise Ivy, she thought. Her sister probably assumed their mother was the sort who'd pester them for grandchildren, urge them to flirt with single doctors and lawyers, remind them they weren't getting any younger.

Ruth gamely went on the dates Helen set up. She smiled and nodded and said the right things. *"You're so funny." "You're so smart." "Thank you for a lovely evening."* She allowed the men to gloss over her time in Vietnam, to assume that her job was exactly as it was portrayed on television. She allowed them a demure kiss at the end of the evening. She told them she was so sorry, when they called to ask for a second date, but she was seeing somebody else. And yes, it was serious, but no, she hadn't known that when she said yes to the first date. The men accepted this excuse without question. Everyone knew that by the time a woman reached her midtwenties, whether it was serious or not was the man's call.

"No boyfriend, no fiancé," she said in answer to Kimberly's question. "Can't say I really like the options." She nodded at the man with the long hair and then at the man in chinos, who had moved on to explaining that he certainly believed in equal rights for all races. He just wished "the coloreds didn't have to get so loud about it."

Kimberly sighed. "I try to remind myself that pretty much everyone in this place who's not on the payroll is here for a sad reason. But it doesn't always help."

"You probably have to head straight home after your shift," said Ruth as they hurriedly cleared their table. They'd lost track of time.

"Not really," said Kimberly. "In fact, I'd rather not."

"She's much better, thank you," was Ruth's standard response when anyone asked her about George. And since her mother *was* better, there was not, theoretically, anything keeping her in Enid anymore. She could go someplace glamorous—Los Angeles, Honolulu, even. Nursing was a portable profession. She could get a job anywhere she wanted. All she had to do was pick.

But although George had improved, she wasn't the same as she had been. "Oh, I'm hanging in," she said whenever anyone asked how she was doing. Ruth suspected she was being less than up-front with her doctors about her condition. Anyone could see she was tired and frail.

The doctors themselves were cagey about George's remission. "How long can we expect it to last?" Ruth asked—because no one else would. George was being a good patient, acting grateful for the healing and time she'd been given, not wanting to seem greedy by asking for more.

The oncologist hadn't looked at Ruth, had pivoted his shoulders away from her when he spoke—Ruth was persona non grata at George's appointments. She asked too many direct questions, pressed for substantive responses, refused to be patted on the head and told not to worry, that her mother was in good hands. George's doctors acted as if they'd had quite enough of Ruth. "We don't have a crystal ball," one of them snapped. "It's best not to worry about things. You're better now," he said to George. (Not *well*, Ruth noted, not *cured*, just "better.") "That's what matters. See your friends, enjoy your hobbies." He didn't say *while you can*, but Ruth felt he might as well have.

She wrote to Ivy. Not apologizing for her lengthy silence, just telling her it was time to come home. If George got sick again, she deserved to have her real daughter with her. Not a stand-in.

Stop moping, Ruth, she heard Adele say. *No one likes a moper.*

How could she leave Enid when her mother was enjoying life *while she could*? How could she leave Enid when Kimberly had only just arrived?

Kimberly worked in cardiology, in a different wing of the hospital. They tried to coordinate their shifts so they could eat lunch together in the cafeteria and go out together after work. Usually to the Jet Way.

Ruth explained her three-to-four drinks rule to Kimberly. "But look at me," said Kimberly, who was all of five one. "I'd better make it two or three, don't you think?" And Ruth, who often went home with one of the airmen, leaving Kimberly to make her way home to her husband, found herself in adamant agreement. Yes, Kimberly should keep her wits about her. It was upsetting enough to think of Kimberly heading home to her husband. To Lloyd. Worse to think of her going home with one of the airmen.

Ruth and Lloyd had met only once, when Kimberly insisted that Ruth come to dinner. "He wants to see who I'm spending so much time with. He wants to get to know you." Ruth didn't reciprocate Lloyd's interest, but she went. For Kimberly. Lloyd hadn't invited her again, and she assumed she'd either passed or failed some sort of test. She didn't care which, so long as she could still see her friend.

The two of them drank. They flirted and danced with men. They left Vietnam, hard days at the hospital, sick parents, and irritable husbands behind. Just for a few hours, in a dark, musty bar, they let everything go and felt, if they didn't have that one drink too many, themselves again. Ruth watched Kimberly dance. During slow dances, Kimberly closed her eyes and rested her head against the chest of her dance partner, and Ruth imagined what it would feel like to have Kimberly's head resting on her own chest. Then she'd find an airman of her own to dance with, to distract herself from thoughts of Kimberly.

One night, when the Jet Way looked too rough, they went down the road to the Control Tower instead. "It'll be less crowded there," said Ruth.

"You sure do know your bars," said Kimberly. Which sent them both into fits of laughter. "Never would have pegged you for a bar hopper when we were on our way to Tan Son Nhut."

"Oh God," said Ruth. "I remember practically dragging you through that airport. I thought I was going to have to scrape you up off the pavement and haul you to that bus." She could have too. Kimberly was tiny, pixieish—her little hands, her little nose, her little ears, even her elfin hairstyle. Get yourself together, Ruth told herself. No need to enumerate Kimberly's every perfect feature. (Her delicate elbows, her nipped waist, her child's feet.)

"What about you? Those flights lasted hours—more than a day! And you hardly said two words to any of us. I thought you might be like my cousin—he's a touch off when it comes to other people. I didn't see how you'd possibly last."

"But I did," said Ruth.

"Here's to lasting," said Kimberly.

"To lasting."

They clinked glasses and turned to look for a table. Across the room, through the cigarette murk, Ruth spied a woman whispering in a man's ear. She felt a prickle of longing for someone to whisper in her own ear. She wasn't quite ready to admit that she wanted that someone to be Kimberly.

Three drinks later, Ruth clung to an anonymous airman who whispered in her ear that he had a truck out back, and did she want to head somewhere else. She was about to say yes, when she felt a tug on her arm. Kimberly.

"Can you excuse us for a sec?" Kimberly deployed her sweetest voice, and the airman relinquished Ruth.

"Don't leave with him," whispered Kimberly, her lips soft and ticklish against Ruth's earlobe.

"Why not?" She glanced over at the airman, who watched them closely from across the room. He didn't seem any different from the others she went home with. She couldn't fathom why Kimberly objected to this one.

"Because." Kimberly ran her hand down Ruth's arm, and Ruth shivered. "Because," she whispered, "I thought we might go home together."

CHAPTER 53

By the end—after all of the excisions and infusions—George felt as though she'd washed up on a beach after being battered by a monthslong storm. The doctors celebrated this "outcome." She couldn't pretend to join them. She lay on the figurative sand, spent. Wishing some days that the tide would pull her back out and take her. Knowing, regardless of the cheer in the oncology department, that another wave would come—bigger and stronger than the last. That she could never make it far enough from the tide line to stay safe.

She was weak, she was slow, her brain felt like it was filled with mud. Food tasted like metal, but she ate anyway. Ivy couldn't stay in Vietnam forever, and George intended to be well and strong when her daughter returned. At which point, she would tell both girls the truth. Tell them together. Regardless of what Vivian or Tom or anyone else wanted. She wrote to Ivy, repeatedly, promising to tell her everything, but only if she came home. Only if they could see each other.

Every time she mentioned Ivy to Ruth, Ruth either left or changed the subject. When George asked if they'd had a falling-out, Ruth said, "Of what?"

Better not to press, thought George. She didn't know how she'd have survived her treatments without Ruth by her side. She worried that once she recovered, her daughter might leave. There were so many more interesting places in the world than Enid. But Ruth seemed happy these days. She'd made a good friend at the hospital.

After a few months, Ruth's increasingly frequent mentions of Kimberly gathered enough weight to pull the cord of the light bulb in her mind: her daughter and Kimberly were something more than friends. Once she recovered from the surprise of it, the notion didn't trouble her. Some of the WASPs and WAACs she'd known had preferred women. What troubled her was how she'd been blind to her daughter's true self. Ruth had taken such good care of her, had stood by her side during every one of her worst days, and George had never really seen her. One more maternal failing—this one unforgivably huge—to add to the ever-lengthening list. Would she never get better at being a mother?

She pulled out the plat of the latest Bridlemile Properties subdivision and traced a finger through the maze of streets until she found the lot she wanted.

The Avonlea was the smallest model in the Bridlemile portfolio, and it was still, Ruth insisted when George handed her the deed, too much.

"But you deserve it," said George. "For taking care of me. For taking care of all those boys overseas. And those children at St. Mary's."

"I'm happy where I am."

"In that little room in Mrs. Cannady's house? You can barely turn around."

George didn't mention that Mrs. Cannady had called her twice in the past month to say she thought something might be wrong with Ruth. "She wakes up yelling. Something about *over there* and something about a foot. It's waking up my other boarders. And the room is a single. But lately there's always another girl here."

"It's plenty for me," insisted Ruth.

"Sure," said George. "But it might not always just be you. Someday you might have a . . . roommate."

CHAPTER 54

After the peace of '73 (Cessation of Overt Hostility, Ned Pennywell called it, though plenty of hostility remained as far as Ivy could see), Ned shipped her off to Vientiane. "No troops, no Donut Dollies, no stories here," he said, meaning Vietnam. "Or so it is felt." Ned, she knew, was sensitive to feelings. On her first day in Vietnam, he'd explained that there was "some feeling" (he didn't say whose) that Defense was less than forthcoming, what with their myopic obsession with casualty rates, about the nature and location of many "encounters." Ned favored words like feeling and encounter over the more explicit suspicion and fight.

No more powder-blue uniform. No more fatigues either. She missed both. In Vientiane, she was supposedly a stringer. "You'll sell mostly to Henry Weldon. He's a stickler. I'm afraid you'll actually have to file a story now and then," said Ned. Ivy didn't mind. She slapped some words together, and Henry fixed them up and wired them out. If a byline of hers ever appeared anywhere, no doubt it was due to Henry calling in favors, as she intentionally put nothing of substance on paper. Unlike Ned, Henry wasn't a stickler about language, didn't dwell in the linguistic shelter of *feeling* and *encounters*. "Spreading that fucking mess into Laos now," he said. "Wasn't enough to go tits up in Vietnam. Now we'll give it a go in Phnom Penh and Vientiane."

Vientiane was quieter than Saigon. The boulevards were lined with plane trees that hadn't been cut down for fuel. Yet. There was electricity, at least most mornings, then ink-dark nights with no power. She loitered in hotel bars—the sort favored by internationals—where she allowed a narrow selection of traveling businessmen and the occasional Pathet Lao higher-up to buy her drinks. She paid the bartender to keep the gin minimal in hers and heavy in theirs. She made encouraging sounds and memorized details about shipments and contracts and meetings and contacts. "Oh, not at all," she assured the few who worried (correctly) that they bored her. "I mean, they wouldn't send just anybody all this way for such important work, would they?"

She rested her chin on her fist, gazed up at them, wide eyed and rapt. And they talked on—telling her about deals past and future, connections fortuitously missed or barely made, fortunes won and lost in a matter of hours.

For the first several months, she kept an oblique reference to a story ready. But this was unnecessary; none of them ever asked about her work.

A year of this, and then one afternoon, Sam Benson appeared at the bar. "Not looking good in Cambodia," he said. Which wasn't exactly news to Ivy. He bent close, mouth brushing her ear as he whispered, "Time to come home, Shaw."

"No," she pleaded.

"Not right away. Back to Saigon first. A few loose ends to tie up." She flinched, remembering her sources and recruits back in Vietnam—the nationals who had begged her for papers before she left, any sort of paper, anything that might get them out. She'd done what she could. It hadn't been nearly enough.

"There'll be something else after this," he said. "We're not cutting you loose. But everyone goes home eventually."

How to explain that she already *was* home? She could distinguish the sound of an M16 from an AK, of outgoing from incoming. She loved the sweet aroma of opium smoke that drifted from her neighbor's apartment, the melted gold hue of the rice fields at harvesttime. She could name the makes and models of the jets and copters that buzzed overhead, and knew who they belonged to. All of this was part of her, and, here, it was even useful. What could she possibly do with this sort of knowledge stateside?

"Maybe a diplomatic posting," said Sam. When she grimaced, he added, "You'd like it more than you expect."

"I never like things more than I expect."

"You could try Hong Kong. Veddy British, but plenty of opportunity for a woman who wants to work—in and out of the field."

"Sure. As someone's secretary."

"There are secretaries and secretaries, as you well know. And there are other options in Southeast Asia if HK's not your cuppa. Malaysia. People tend to like Malaysia. Easy to get you in as an aid worker, what with all the refugees. Ah, you like that idea. And you're well suited. But home first, Shaw. That's the way it plays."

"Okay, but I want something."

The grooves in his forehead deepened. "This isn't a trade."

"It shouldn't be difficult. Not for you. I want you to find out whether Vivian Shaw is my mother."

"Shaw." His eyes had the same wary cast that Ruth's used to get when Ivy pressed their parents for answers.

She signaled the bartender for another round and then leaned toward Sam, allowing her bare shoulder to rest against his. He didn't pull away, but he didn't move closer either. He smelled of cinnamon and aftershave and caution. "Don't," she said as she straightened back up. "Don't tell me not to ask questions I might not want to know the answers to. Just find out. Please."

Once she had the proof, she would write home. Tell them what she knew. Demand that they acknowledge the truth. She'd received a flurry of letters from each of them after they learned she was in Vietnam. She kept them wrapped in a silk scarf the USAID worker had given her. Letters they must have sent out of obligation, because she hadn't received any more since Ruth left Cu Chi. Another release of her, now that they had Ruth, their real daughter, home. The relief they must feel being free of her. Well, *she* would be relieved—once Sam came through—to be free of them too.

A week later, back in Saigon, she was being measured for a phantom dress by the tailor off Tu Do Street. Mr. Anh waited until his assistant left the room, then tucked a slip of paper into her pocket and whispered in Viet, "Can you get me papers? If you get me out, I will make you a real dress. A beautiful dress."

Her throat tightened as she recalled an earlier slip of paper he'd given her—the one telling her Ruth was coming. A different Ruth, it turned out, than the one she'd left behind in Enid. A Ruth she'd wanted more of—so much more that she'd forced herself to keep her distance from her sister. She'd stepped away from their last hug, on the day Ruth left Vietnam, maintaining that distance to the end. She'd had to in order not to cry.

A tear burned a track down her cheek now. Mr. Anh sighed. "Never mind. There are others I can ask." The assistant returned and Ivy, hating the note of empty promise in her voice, said, "If I hear of any incoming cloth shipments, I'll let you know."

Later, back at her flat, she decoded the message:

V.C.S. dismissed from AAFFTD service October 17, 1944. Basis: Pregnancy and unpermitted use of military aircraft. G.E.R. dismissed from AAFFTD service November 5, 1944. Basis: Pregnancy. No record of live birth for V.C.S. Record of twins born to G.E.R. on January 23, 1945, Bellevue Hospital, New York City.

She crumpled the paper into a ball and hurled it across her flat. "Useless," she fumed as she retrieved it. She read it once more, then, following protocol, set a match to it.

The party at the American villa was one of those last-gasp affairs. The liquor uncut. The guest list paltry—hardly anyone was left in Saigon, but those who remained soldiered on. They filed their reports and sipped their citron pressé and showed up when invited, even as they shipped their valuables stateside and wrote discreet letters home, sussing out job listings and apartments for rent. The parties had a fatalistic air about them now—no one was in the mood for gaiety. Not that Ned Pennywell ever had been.

"You're back," he said—not with any enthusiasm—as Ivy slipped into the room in her red party dress.

"For now. Got any assignments for me?"

Ned shrugged as if to ask, Would it matter if he did? What good would her little assignments do anyone now?

"Nothing?" asked Ivy. "I can write for you—something real."

Ned wrinkled his nose at the notion of her writing anything real. He put a hand to his breast pocket, sighed, and proceeded to pat down each of his pockets, one by one. "I'm glad you're here," he said. Oh God, he wasn't chatting her up, was he? He wasn't thinking she might end up in his bed? She retreated a step. He continued massaging his various pockets. She balanced an unlit cigarette loosely between her fingers, her go-to party prop; she could always turn away from one person to ask another for a light. Maybe he was looking for a lighter. The pickings were sparse, and, she supposed, about to get sparser, but she wasn't down to the Ned Pennywell dregs yet.

She'd assumed Sam would rush her out of Saigon as soon as he could, but she hadn't heard from him in weeks. She'd taken care of the "loose ends." Then she'd spent her days attempting to track down her contacts. Most of whom she couldn't find. Maybe they'd gotten out. She hoped so. She didn't have much to offer the ones she did find. Cigarettes. However many dollars she had in her pockets. A gold bracelet that her parents had given her years ago and that, despite everything, she'd worn all these years.

She'd given the bracelet to the cigarette boy outside the Caravelle Hotel. He'd always had perfect recall of who had come and gone that day (or any day before), and at what times, and often, even which direction they arrived from or departed to. Would it be enough to buy his way onto a transport? Doubtful. But she'd done what she could.

That ought to be the tagline for this entire enterprise, she thought, still waiting for Ned to fish out his lighter. *We did what we could. Sorry it wasn't enough.* Did good intentions count? Again, she doubted it.

"Ah, here we go." Ned produced a creased and smudged postcard that read GREETINGS FROM OKLAHOMA! on its front. "Came months ago. I nearly threw it away, but everyone comes back through eventually."

The return address was in Enid. Adele Avenue. A throb in her chest, a sudden longing for her grandmother. The street name evidence that George and Frank continued expanding the bounds of their small city. She thanked Ned, whose attention had already drifted. Who clearly had as little interest in her body as he did in her writing.

She drained her first drink and took the second and the postcard down to the foyer where she could read without interruption. The message was brief, its tone impatient, implying that Ivy had ignored a slew of correspondence. Ruth, comfortably stateside, had apparently forgotten how certain things, such as timely mail delivery—the postmark said 1972, for God's sake—tended to lapse in a war zone.

> Mom is done with her treatments. Thank God, because I'm not sure she could take much more. The doctors seem pleased. But sometimes I see a look on her face, and it takes me back to triage. How sometimes you could tell, before you even examined a soldier, before you even tallied the damage. Just by the look on their faces, you could tell that one wasn't going to make it.

So I'm begging you, Ivy. Again. Write her a goddamn
letter.

Two martinis—large gins really, as there was no longer much
vermouth to be had—and she was stone sober, sitting in the foyer of
the American villa in her red evening gown, fighting tears, fighting a
surge of longing for George. For her mother. As if a drilling rig had at
last hit oil, sending it spouting up out of barren-looking ground.

Back at her apartment, she tossed the red dress out the window.
Some prostitute would love it. Some mother with hungry children
could trade it for food. That at this point these two women were likely
to be the same person was a thought she tried hard not to think. She
pared her belongings—never much to begin with—down further. Only
the essentials. Only a single easy-to-carry satchel.

In the morning, she headed to Tu Do Street. She needed to get
word to Sam Benson, to tell him to bring her home. Who knew how
much time her mother had left? But the tailor's shop was shuttered
and dark. She drew a metal nail file from her pocket. The lock yielded
so easily that the file may as well have been a key. Inside, the sewing
machines and bolts of fabric were gone. Two empty wooden spools lay
in a far corner. She told herself he had sold everything (but to whom?),
used the money to buy his way out. She hoped it was true.

At the press office, Ned Pennywell did not look pleased to see her.
"Ned, I need to get out. I need to go home."

"Get in line, Shaw. Get in line."

"Isn't there anyone you can call?"

"I call the same people you call. If they're not answering you, they
won't do otherwise for me. Keep a steady head, Shaw. I very much
doubt they'll leave us behind."

CHAPTER 55

The pain took root deep in her sternum. A couple of months later, it radiated, traveling to the middle of her spine. Aspirin, ice packs, hot soaks in the tub all did nothing for it. But if she concentrated hard enough, if she really focused, George could manage lunch out with Helen or a quick interlude with Frank (sex was out of the question, but the pain eased when he held her). Ruth had invited her to dinner, and George believed she could manage that too.

"Kimberly will probably do most of the cooking," admitted Ruth. "She's better at it than I am."

George had taken advantage of a better-than-usual morning earlier in the week to pick up a bottle of champagne. Ruth's house sat well back from the curb. With two cars already in the drive, George had to park on the street. The champagne was a lead weight, slowing her progress to the door. She paused halfway up the walk to catch her breath. She felt pathetic, ridiculous. She rested the sweating bottle against her breastbone, hoping it would cool her aching chest. Three breaths, she commanded herself, and then you move. Once she was inside, she could sit down, count to one hundred, a trick that sometimes outwitted the pain. The victory she felt at making it to the front door was cut short when Ruth opened it.

"Mom!"

"I'm fine, Ruth."

"You're breathing like you just ran a mile."

"I just need to sit down for a sec."

Ruth took her arm and led her to a new armchair. "This is so nice," George managed to gasp.

"Mom. Have you been to the doctor recently?"

"The curtains are just perfect."

"Mom."

A pretty, petite woman peeked her head around the kitchen door. She'd looked forward to meeting Kimberly, and already she'd ruined the occasion. She tried to smile but must not have managed it, because Kimberly's eyebrows flew up in alarm. "Hello. Whatever you're cooking smells delicious," said George. But the girl had ducked back into the kitchen.

"Mom. Stop." Ruth's eyes shimmered. "We need to get you in."

George shook her head, then stopped because the motion made her chest hurt worse. "I won't go through it again, Ruth," she whispered. "I can't."

"It's probably nothing," said Ruth. "But that's the reason to go. To make sure. Then you won't have to worry."

Then you *won't have to worry,* thought George. But her daughter had done so much for her—scheduling the appointments, watching over her after every treatment, staying in Enid when she could have gone anywhere.

"I won't go through it again," George said, this time to the doctor who'd just given her the bad news.

"No," said the doctor. "We don't recommend another course of treatment."

CHAPTER 56

Tom told Vivian to come soon and stay as long as possible. He was calling her himself, he said, because he feared George might not convey the seriousness of the current circumstances. "Current circumstances" being a phrase he fell back on repeatedly during their phone conversation. If George had called—she hadn't, confirmed Vivian—he wanted to stress that she may not have given Vivian the full picture.

"Of the current circumstances," she finished.

"Right," said Tom.

"She's worse," Vivian told Patterson that night. "Tom thinks this is it. He thinks I should come soon."

"Then you should," said Patterson.

She was about to ask him to come with her, when he reached across the table and took her hand. "It makes you think, Viv. I mean, she's not old."

"No," said Vivian. "She's only fifty-two."

"We're not getting any younger, either, are we?"

They'd been together for years, Don said. And he didn't want to be with anyone else. He hoped she felt that way about him too. So how about it? Why not tie the knot? Make it official? "It would make me so happy," he said, finishing up, "if you would be my wife." Then he held out a velvet box with a ring that was just right: elegant, not flashy, a single emerald flanked by two tiny diamonds. She loved it. She loved him. Her heart seized up and her breath went shallow and Don sounded far away when he spoke her name again.

She dropped her head to her knees and tried to breathe. She heard him slip the box back in his pocket, felt the steady warmth of his hand on her back, thought in time with her rapidly beating heart: *I do not deserve this. I do not deserve this.*

"Will you at least give it some thought?" asked Don, once she managed to raise her head again without everything turning orange.

"I will. I really will. I'm so sorry," said Vivian as he massaged the nape of his neck. "I don't know why I get like this." A lie—she knew exactly why she got like that. And Don must never, ever know. Or maybe he ought to know. Either option seemed unbearable. If she didn't tell, well, that was the same as lying about who she was, deceiving a good man, tricking him into loving her. If she did tell, odds were he'd no longer love her at all. He'd try, she knew. He'd say it didn't matter, but something would change between them. Distrust and shame would sidle up right next to them and never leave, always underfoot and in the way. And who would live like that for any longer than they had to?

"I'll think about it the whole time I'm in Enid," she promised.

"I hope you're not planning on moving in," said George. "Because I won't have it."

"Georgeanne Ector!" Even after all these years, Vivian forgot the Rutledge. "I am a very busy woman with many, many commitments," she said in her best imitation of Helen. "I can barely spare a week."

George laughed, then groaned.

"Really, George. I can stay however long you like. I'm commitment-free for the time being." She winced as she said it, thinking of Don.

"Lucky you. I have doctors' appointments from now till kingdom come," George said brightly, as if having a slew of doctors' appointments was a great source of amusement.

In times of crisis—when a relationship ended, when money ran low, when she couldn't stand to live inside her own skin another day, Vivian had scraped together enough money for fuel and flown to George. Because with George, she felt like a person again. Like what she did mattered, like everything would work out. It wasn't exactly clear to her how George made her feel these things. She didn't do it by saying, *It'll be okay*, or *Let's calm down*, but by some subtle, undetectable mechanism. This talent must have made her an excellent mother. A far better mother than Vivian herself ever would have been. At this point, Vivian could claim to be the better pilot, if only because she logged the hours for it. But from any objective standpoint, she thought, George had won everywhere else.

She had the well-appointed house. She had her country club friends. It might be unconventional, but she had a marriage. She was a successful businesswoman who'd parlayed her luck, her Ector inheritance, into multiples more. She had her own plane—a better one than Vivian's. And she'd raised the girls to be smart and funny and, Vivian had thought until Ivy ran away, happy.

And through it all, she'd worked her special magic, making everyone feel better. Vivian could see her working it even now, turning the macabre into the amusing, getting Vivian to buck up.

They spent a couple of days reminiscing. Then George asked her to take them up in the Cessna. "I can't fly it myself anymore, but I'd like one more ride." Once they reached altitude, high above the red-and-green patchwork below, Vivian said, "Clear skies and no one in sight, if you want to take the controls for a bit."

"I never know when the pain will come, or how strong it will be. I'd better not, Viv. But I'm happy just to be up here."

Vivian had pretended not to notice when her friend's eyes closed, when she turned inward, battling for composure.

Vivian's throat tightened. She fiddled unnecessarily with the controls and then glided into a lazy chandelle.

"How about a flat spin?" asked George, working her magic once again.

"You sure?"

"You have to ask?"

She could see for miles, and they weren't carrying any cargo. "Ready?" She took them up, up, up and forced them into the spin. She hoped George's eyes were open, that she was spellbound by the spinning world and sky, that hanging face down wasn't hurting her. Vivian, counting the rotations, couldn't afford a glance at her friend, couldn't get lost in the mesmerizing view. But she needn't have worried. George let out a joyous whoop and said, "That's seven!" Vivian allowed one more rotation before pulling out of the spin and looking at her passenger. George closed her eyes. Vivian took that as permission to head for home.

For the rest of the week, she complied with anything George asked. Everything except her final demand.

"I want to tell them," said George. "The girls. Tom. They all deserve to know."

"George, no."

"It's the right thing to do. And we should have done it years ago. Maybe if we had . . ."

"No," insisted Vivian. Not just because she disagreed, but because she needed to keep George from finishing that sentence, from saying that if they had told the girls years before, Ivy never would have run so far. That she wouldn't have run at all. "Please, George. Don't do this. They'll hate me."

"I'm pretty sure Ivy already suspects. I think that's why she left. Ruth probably knows too. Whether she wants to admit it to herself or not."

Vivian felt the world pitch beneath her. "George. Please. We promised each other."

"But we were wrong. Besides, I'm not going to be here anymore. It's your turn now."

Vivian's cheeks were wet with tears. "I don't think it works that way," she sobbed. "You know it doesn't work that way."

"They're going to need you."

"Then don't set them up to hate me. I'll do everything I can for them, I swear. Please don't tell them."

CHAPTER 57

"What if you give me some time? To think about how to frame it. How to explain," Vivian begged.

Don't you see what a gift this is? George wanted to say. *Two daughters, when you had none?* The nearly constant pain made her impatient, allowed her to see clearly how much nonsense cluttered up everyone's lives. Vivian, she realized, didn't believe herself worthy of forgiveness. Well, George was too tired to try to persuade her that there was nothing to forgive. Each day, she found herself less capable of resistance. In the end, all the nonsense would win. Why waste her strength fighting it?

"All right. Take some time. But don't take too long, because I don't have long."

She woke the next morning to find Vivian sitting on the side of her bed, her suitcase at her feet. "I've got a taxi waiting," she said. "To take me to the airfield."

George started to protest.

"You're being very generous," said Vivian, not meeting George's gaze. "Giving me time . . . I'll think better somewhere else, though. The girls feel too close to me here. I just need a little distance."

"Will you call me?" asked George. "I won't pester you—I promise. But just—it will help me to hear your voice."

"Of course. I love you, Georgeanne. Take care." Vivian leaned down for a hug, and George clung to her, holding on until her friend gently pulled away.

The matrons of Enid passed through George's living room. Friends of Adele's at first. That older generation had seen enough death that they weren't skittish about it. Though it was such a shame, she heard them whisper. A woman her age. Just getting started, really. Golden years and all that. *Such* a shame. But who could fathom God's will?

George certainly couldn't.

Next came her own generation. A second wave of casseroles and cakes surged through George's living room.

Tom was often there. She refused to let him move back in, but he was always dropping by.

Whenever Tom left, Frank appeared. "This is it," he said. "I'm leaving Helen. Let's stop pretending we're all fine with—whatever this has been. Let's do what we should have done all along."

"You're going to need Helen," she said. "Don't you dare leave her."

"This isn't entirely up to you, George."

They were infuriating. She was dying, and nothing was up to her anymore.

The day was coming—it wouldn't be long now, she realized—when she'd need to stay in the hospital full time. She called Helen and asked her to come by. Tom was on a two-day trip out west, Frank had meetings with his design team, and Ruth had a morning shift. George wanted to apologize to Helen before she no longer could.

Helen didn't want to hear it. "I don't know what you're sorry for. Everything is just fine, Georgeanne."

Even after Frank Jr. died, Helen had clung to the safety of Just Fine. As in, *"Of course it's terrible, but we'll be Just Fine"* and *"As soon as I get his clothing off to the Salvation Army, I'll be Just Fine."* George knew she'd been anything but. She was, despite her polished surface, anything but Just Fine now.

I could have stayed in New York, thought George. The lady downstairs might have helped me out occasionally. I could have managed. But I came home. Where Just Fine is what everyone aspires to. Scratch that—it's what everyone *is.* Tom had probably told his copilot just that morning that she was Just Fine. It was the equilibrium everyone sought. Because the alternatives, Not Fine or Very Fine, were either pitiable or boastful.

"Helen, I'm trying to be honest with you. I was selfish. Terribly selfish. It was wrong, and I knew it every moment. I was a horrible friend to you, and you deserve so much better. I'm sorry, Helen. You don't have to forgive me, but please hear me, that's all I'm asking."

Helen stood at the credenza with her back to George, plucking dead stems from various flower arrangements and fluffing up the remainder. She said nothing for so long that George stopped expecting her to speak. She resisted performing any conversational CPR. If Helen wanted to change the subject, that was up to her. Or maybe Helen would pick up her pocketbook and walk out the door, and the two of them would never exchange another word. It was exactly what she deserved.

Helen moved away from the credenza, ran a finger along one of the end tables, inspected it for dust, brushed it on her skirt, and, finally, spoke. "I wasn't going to be one of those divorcées. I wasn't. He wanted to, you know. Even though you and Tom didn't, which, believe me, I did point out. But I said absolutely not. Till death do us part. And he always came home. Every night in my bed. Even if . . ." She broke off and turned to face George.

"Maybe you think I'm stupid. Worrying about how it all looks. But I don't know how to fly airplanes, and I don't have investments to manage, and I don't want to go out to roast beef dinners with balding, paunchy middle-aged men. I want my house and my husband in it. And you two were reasonably discreet. I know it looked weak and stupid to you."

"No. Never, Helen." Though it had at times.

"Doesn't matter in the long run, does it? In the long run, none of us decides who's left to come home to."

George wanted Ivy to come home. She had written letter after letter, promising to tell her everything, but Ivy had never replied. She wanted Vivian to come back, but Vivian had gone AWOL.

She called Patterson, but even he didn't know where she was. "I spooked her, George. I proposed to her—she probably told you." George didn't admit that Vivian had not.

"I think I may have spooked her too," she said.

"I can't think where she's gone to," said Patterson. "If you hear from her—"

"You'll be the first to know, Don. I swear it." She could sense Ivy and Vivian, floating just beyond her reach, just when she needed and wanted them most.

CHAPTER 58

Ivy had begun to think Ned Pennywell was wrong, that she *had* been forgotten. So many people were. Sam Benson had a great deal of cargo, human and otherwise, to extract from Vietnam. Just because he was so often at the top of her mind didn't mean she was on his.

This Saigon wasn't her Saigon anymore. The boy selling cigarettes outside the Caravelle hadn't been seen in weeks. The empty tailor's shop off Tu Do Street had been torched. A message? If so, to whom, exactly? Because wasn't the dire state of the entire city of Saigon a message at this point? One her country had been particularly obtuse in decoding. She unwrapped the silk scarf and scanned the old letters from her family. Their professions about missing her and longing to see her, their pleas for her to stay safe no longer read like words of obligation. Maybe they were still writing to her. Maybe they had been all along. Letters that sat at the bottom of some censor's inbox, that clogged file cabinets in San Diego or Saigon. Letters charred to ashes in a burn pile near Tan Son Nhut.

She replied to this phantom correspondence, writing her sister, her mother, her father, Vivian. Imagining the censor's black marker hovering over her words. Careful not to mention things like the vanished cigarette boy, the torched shop. Not to write anything of any relevance at all except for variations of: *I'm sorry. I'm coming. As soon as I can.* She doubted her letters made it out. Probably the mail clerks checked them for cash, then tossed them in the burn piles, atop the contents of the embassy file cabinets. She wrote them anyway.

She stopped by the press office daily, but Ned had no pale-blue envelopes for her, no assignments, no instructions.

She began chatting up American pilots, doling out marijuana cigarettes—packaged just like regular cigarettes—to anyone with a flight license. Anyone who might be able to get her to a ship. To Manila. To Tokyo.

Because that spring, everyone who could was bugging out. The Sam Bensons of the war effort were bringing out the interpreters, the scouts, the people with the right credentials, and also plenty of people with no credentials at all (the call girls, the supposed orphans, the cigarette boys and tailors). There hadn't been any parties in weeks—nothing she considered a party anyway. Just hotel rooms full of increasingly despondent journos and diplomats moping over their increasingly watered-down drinks. Ivy showed up anyway. If you wanted to be remembered, you had to make yourself seen. Finally, one night Ned caught her by the elbow and murmured, "It's time, Shaw."

She strapped one child after another into the cargo hold of the C-5. Then she fastened herself in and waited for the plane to take off. Outside, palms clacked in the wind, and men shouted over the engines, and the gut-punch miasma of defeat drove everyone into a nauseated panic. Ivy took a deep breath and thought maybe, after she saw her family (she couldn't think about her mother dying—there was no way it could be true), she'd turn around and head to Hawaii. Or Malaysia. They'd want her to stay home, but Enid wasn't home. She no longer allowed herself to think of Vietnam as home, because how would she ever return to it?

She placed a soothing hand on the frightened toddler beside her, recalled the touch of her mother's steady, cool hand. She remembered being little and feeling that steadiness transmit itself deep within her, soothing whatever troubled her. She remembered being older and dodging her mother's hand, shaking off her touch. When she reached Enid, she would let that hand linger for as long as her mother wanted. Maybe, just maybe, that touch was home.

The engines fired, and the plane began its slow taxi. She wished she had a window, regretted volunteering for the cargo hold over the passenger bay. For her there would be no last long look, between liftoff and the moment the plane punctured the clouds, at the beautiful, wrecked country below.

She wasn't particularly worried about what would come next. When she left Enid, she'd never imagined she'd end up in Vietnam. Her life had been spontaneous, not planned. Not by her, anyway. Now people would expect her to have a plan. They'd start by asking, *Where have you been?* The bolder ones might add, *Why did you go?* And everyone would want to know, *What will you do now?*

The plane tipped. The child beside her fussed. "Don't worry. It's okay," she murmured in Vietnamese. The plane tipped some more. The smaller children cried out. The older ones' eyes steeled over with resignation. The other adults in the cargo hold clutched their harness straps.

"Shhh," soothed Ivy, keeping her hand on the child beside her. "Everything's going to be all right."

She closed her eyes and felt her mother's cool, steady touch.

And then the plane tipped one last time.

CHAPTER 59

Vivian paced the front yard of her childhood home, picking up windfall pine cones and chucking them in a wheelbarrow. Aunt Clelia would want them for kindling, Elizabeth said. That Aunt Clelia, at nearly ninety, still lived on her own—Rosemary had been laid to rest nearly a decade ago—and that she was still both able and allowed to light her own fires, mystified Vivian.

"Well, who's going to stop her?" said Elizabeth. "I can't be over there all the time. I already take her shopping twice a week and drive her to church on Sunday, and let me tell you, the congregation would dwindle if I didn't. She'd put them in the ground one by one, the way she drives."

"I'm just surprised she still lives on her own, that's all."

"She has an open door here," said Elizabeth. "One she refuses to walk through. But you see if you can convince her. Go right ahead."

All of Vivian's conversations with her sister had gone something like this. Vivian expressed surprise at something in Hahira that either remained the same or had changed dramatically. Then Elizabeth put up a stirring defense of her inability to prevent either the stasis or the transformation.

The house in Hahira—Elizabeth had inherited it when Clara Shaw passed away—had been sited to catch whatever scant sea breezes found their way so far inland. Its deep eaves covered a porch that circled the entire house. Elizabeth's husband had screened its large windows to keep out the bugs.

Vivian loved the contrast between the dark, cool interior and the baking heat of the yard. She loved the tall pines and the glossy camellias and the Lady Banks roses that frothed over the water tank behind the house. She had decided, despite the heat, to tidy up the yard and to take a break from her sister, who liked to preface every other sentence with "Well, of course, you weren't here . . ."

She'd go over to Aunt Clelia's later, she decided, and see what needed doing there, away from Elizabeth's watchful eye. Whatever she did she'd do wrong, but effort ought to count for something. She lobbed more pine cones into the rusting wheelbarrow, enjoying the clank of each one landing. She was tempted to make a game of it. See how many she could get in from various distances in the yard, but Elizabeth was probably watching.

The hiss of a car pulling up to the curb made her look up. The latest Thunderbird, so new the whitewalls still gleamed. She knew who it was before he even stepped out.

"Well, if it isn't Bobby Broussard. You come here straight from the dealer?"

"I remember how much you appreciate a good car, so I thought you'd like to see this one."

Vivian gave him her southern-lady embrace. A hug that wasn't actually a hug—none of one's own body parts made contact with the recipient's body parts. It was a disconcerting sort of hug if you hadn't grown up with it. Vivian had had to unlearn it living out west, where people seemed put off—baffled—by it. Here, though, they understood. You finessed the impression of an embrace, without any actual physical contact, thus preserving the drape of someone's blouse, the fresh hairdo, the pressed powder on a cheek. The southern-lady embrace also served as a compliment: the woman on the receiving end was too fragile, too delicate, to be subjected to a true hug. She was a lady, after all. Bobby Broussard wasn't a woman, but he was—Vivian checked his left hand as he approached and noted the groove where a wedding ring had recently resided—most likely a married man. In Hahira, those didn't bear touching either.

"Vivian Shaw. It is still Shaw, isn't it? I heard you were in town." Bobby received the faux embrace without a hint of offense. He'd been raised right, after all.

"Just for a bit. My," she said, taking in the suit and the shoes, "don't you look prosperous. Elizabeth tells me you're with the bank now."

Bobby laughed. "Who would have guessed, right?"

Not Vivian. She led him up to the porch and sat him in the best rocker while she went in to pour them some iced tea.

"You never married?" he asked as she handed him his glass.

"No." She blanched, thinking of Don, of his proposal, of his patience, which surely must have an end. She hadn't spoken to him in two weeks. She hadn't told him she was in Hahira. She could only suppose he'd been in touch with George, who also didn't know where she was. She'd never had anything nice to say about her hometown, so who would think of looking for her here? It was the perfect place to hide out.

She'd hoped Hahira would feel like a splash of cold water, that returning would wake her up, clear her thoughts. Help her see how best to help George. Because it was impossible that George was dying.

The best way to help George, she decided, was to keep her distance. She lacked the caretaking ability that came so naturally to other women. Women like Helen. And Ruth. Vivian would only make things worse. Offer ice chips when broth was called for, tuck the blankets too tightly or too loosely, say and do everything wrong. She would stay away a little longer. Give George time to rally.

"Very modern of you," said Bobby. "But then, I always knew you would be. A modern gal, that is."

"And you," she said, nodding at his left hand, the indentation circling his ring finger. "Looks like if you're not married, it's a recent development."

"Ah, that. It was just feeling a little tight today, I guess. The heat, you know."

Right, thought Vivian. The new car, the too-tight ring, a visit to a modern gal. It all added up to one thing in Bobby's mind. Some things never changed.

"And how is Mrs. Broussard?"

"Mrs. Broussard, my mother, is just the same as she ever was."

Vivian was sorry to hear it.

"Mrs. Broussard, my wife, Sandy, is—well, we're expecting an addition to the family in a few weeks, so she's not feeling entirely herself."

"Congratulations. How wonderful for you both."

Bobby looked as if it were not, at the moment, quite such a wonderful development, but he sipped his tea and recovered himself. He was just leaning forward with a gleam in his eye, saying, "Remember when we . . ." when Elizabeth stepped out onto the porch.

"Hello, Bobby. How is Sandy doing? His wife," she said to Vivian. "Second wife, that is. Has she turned twenty-five yet, Bobby? The first one ran off to Waycross."

Elizabeth cut the poison of her words by smiling a sweet southern-lady smile. Bobby turned a brilliant shade of pink.

Elizabeth continued: "Saw her the other day at Winn-Dixie, and she looked about ready to pop." Vivian's jaw dropped. No one referred with such directness to a woman's—a lady's—pregnancy. Elizabeth did not want Bobby Broussard on her porch.

Bobby knew it too. He rose from the good rocker. "Just turned twenty-seven. I'd better check in on her before I head back to the office."

"Give her my best," said Elizabeth.

"I'll do that. Certainly will. And Vivian, maybe I'll drop by later so we can catch up properly."

"Oh," said Vivian. "I'm over at Aunt Clelia's tonight. Giving her a hand with a few things."

"News to me," muttered Elizabeth.

Aunt Clelia still stored her sweet potatoes layered in pine straw in a wooden bin on the shady side of the house. Vivian fished out two and baked them with the chicken legs that Elizabeth had sent over with her. Elizabeth had also insisted that she bring a congealed salad and part of a peach cobbler, and Vivian, being a modern gal who left most of the cooking to Don, had happily complied.

Aunt Clelia complained that Elizabeth's offerings took up all the space in her icebox, that she had no room for her own food anymore. But all Vivian found on the shelves was a jar of pickles and a ham slice long past its prime. When Clelia wasn't looking, she took the ham slice and tossed it into the bushes for the raccoons.

"You're taller than I even remembered," said Aunt Clelia. It wasn't a compliment. "Still flying those airplanes?"

"Yes," mumbled Vivian.

"What?"

"Yes, ma'am. I have my own plane now," she shouted.

"Nonsense," said Aunt Clelia. She went back to picking at her food but not actually eating much. Vivian, on the other hand, had devoured her serving and looked forward to polishing off whatever her aunt didn't finish.

They dined in the living room, in front of the blaring television. Aunt Clelia insisted she had perfect hearing. The volume of the television suggested otherwise. Vivian had a headache. Not just from the noise but from the space heater pumping out waves of kerosene-fumed heat next to Aunt Clelia's chair. It was over eighty degrees outside, and Vivian had suggested they eat on the porch. Clelia had snugged her cardigan closed and sniffed that it was much too chilly for a picnic.

After dinner, Vivian scraped the remaining cobbler straight from the dish into her mouth—a reward for washing up. She must remember to tell Elizabeth what a good cook she was. And she wouldn't say one word about the kerosene heater. She wondered if she could manage to turn it off while Aunt Clelia snored in front of the television. It seemed dangerous to leave her aunt alone with it in an old wooden house. Though Vivian supposed Clelia and the space heater had lived happily together without incident for years.

Back in the living room, she shooed the tabby cat off the sofa, thinking she'd doze a bit herself before heading back to Elizabeth's. But an image on the television caught her attention. The nose cone of a plane—it looked like a C-5—lay on its side in a rice paddy. Funny, thought Vivian, how everyone in America knew what a rice paddy looked like now. And far too many people recognized a C-5 when they saw one too.

The camera panned. Yards away lay the upper deck of the plane, and then the tail. The cargo deck. Smoke still billowing. A track gouged into the paddy where the plane had bellied down. Another set of tracks, farther back, where it had first touched down before losing its landing gear and then getting a bounce that lifted it back into the sky.

"One hundred and thirty-eight dead," intoned the anchorman. "More than seventy of them children. While almost everyone on the passenger level was saved, few on the cargo level survived."

The camera panned across the segments of the C-5, and Vivian thought how neatly it had fractured into its assembly line components. She shivered in Aunt Clelia's stuffy parlor. "Oh God," she whispered. "Ivy."

The young men drove out from Moody two days later. Their shoes gleamed like Bobby Broussard's tires. They'd spotted her sitting on the porch and had carefully arranged their faces into solemnity before they emerged from the sedan.

Was this how they were spending their war? wondered Vivian. Or had they drawn the short straw today and been rousted from their desks to deliver news that there was no good way to deliver?

"Miss Shaw?" one of them asked.

"Yes?"

"Miss Shaw, I'm afraid we have some sad news about your daughter."

Elizabeth stepped out, wiping her hands on her apron. "What on earth are you talking about?" she said. "Vivian doesn't have any children."

One of the men—so young he looked as if he shaved maybe every other week—consulted his clipboard. "Ivy Shaw. Stationed in Saigon with the US Army Special Services. She lists you, Miss Shaw, as her next of kin. As her person to be notified in the event . . ."

Oh, Ivy, thought Vivian. And then, *Oh, Georgeanne.*

"This must be a mistake," said Elizabeth. Her youngest son had come back from Vietnam three years before. He wasn't himself, but at least he was home. Well, he was in Macon, which was close enough. Closer than Quang Tri, that was for sure. And Elizabeth had expressed relief that her days of dreading the arrival of solemn-faced men from Moody had passed. She scowled and made a shooing gesture at them. "Vivian, tell them this is a mistake."

"This is a mistake," said Vivian. "This has all been a horrible mistake."

CHAPTER 60

George was trying to speak to her daughter, but the nurse Ruth didn't like, the one who wore the old-fashioned white dress and cap, sidled between them. She pressed her cold fingers to the inside of George's wrist. What was the point of these nurses taking her vital signs anymore? She had so little time left, and she had so many things to say to Ruth. Maybe she'd already said them. Her memories scattered. She was too tired to corral them. Completing a thought or a sentence, raising her voice above a whispery rasp took so much strength. She closed her eyes. She'd rest for a moment, then try again.

She woke to the torment of the mattress, plank-hard beneath her spine. She yearned for and dreaded the morphine. The drug stretched and contracted time, made it elastic, untrackable. Was it day or night? In the glare of the yellow hospital lights, always day. Every time she opened her eyes, there was Ruth. Often Tom. Sometimes Frank. Never Vivian. Nor Ivy. She'd stopped expecting Ivy. But always, always Ruth.

"Not for another hour," said the nurse, to something Ruth asked her. Then she was gone. "My daughter," said George, and Ruth took her hand, which hurt. Everything hurt. Even the sheets against her skin. But she endured it. "My daughter," she said again. "Love." She had hoped to get out "you," but another wave of pain crested within her.

There had been a day—maybe it was yesterday, impossible to be sure. A day of so little pain, and she'd been alert. Ruth had been there, and Tom and Frank, and they had all laughed together, even Tom and

Frank. And she'd thought, Why wasn't it like this all the time? Why weren't *we* like this all the time? Why only now? Oh, right. Because of the dying.

The dying meant it was time to say everything that needed saying. To tell Ruth all of it. She couldn't leave that task to Vivian. Where *was* Vivian? George pushed her mind to the surface. "Ruth," she rasped, and her beautiful daughter turned toward her. "Ruth, you were born on January eleventh. I suppose that's your real birthday. There's so much interest in what's 'real.' I have to say, I don't necessarily agree that 'real' is what matters."

Ruth shushed her and stroked her arm.

"What's she saying?" asked Tom, looming over Ruth's shoulder.

"I'm not sure. Something about a birthday."

She tried again. "We were wrong to keep it from you. Not wrong to do it. You were mine before you were even born, regardless of what's 'real.' You were mine. You are mine. Should have told you both," said George. "You and Ivy. When you were young."

"I think she's asking for Ivy," said Ruth. "She's coming, Mom. She'll be here soon." But George still knew a lie when she heard one. She fought to stay awake, to keep speaking, to tell Ruth everything.

"Ivy," she'd said, when the nurse brought in the forms and asked the baby's name. "Ivy Amelia Rutledge."

"Ivy's a nice name," mumbled Vivian. She'd entered the hospital room bearing Ruth before her like an offering, holding her as far from her body as it was possible to hold a baby and still carry oneself somewhat comfortably. This, along with Vivian's flat response to the name Ivy, irritated George. At least she'd picked a cheerful name for her daughter, and not something old fashioned. Though George had praised the name Ruth when Vivian proposed it. "Lovely," she'd said, not just *nice*. "Ruth is just lovely." And if her tone had sounded overenthusiastic, it was only because Vivian had added, "You can change it. Anything you like is fine with me."

Under different circumstances, she would have named her daughter after Vivian. But that was impossible now. Ivy had a hint of Vivian about it, though. And that would have to be enough.

Ivy slept in the nursery down the hall. The nurses brought her in every four hours for a feeding. She nursed, burped, tolerated having her diaper changed, gazed at George for a few moments, then drifted back to sleep. At which point a nurse magically appeared and whisked her away again. "So that you can sleep." George, having grown up in Adele's energetic household, had never realized a person could sleep so much. After two days in the hospital, she felt as though she'd built up a lifetime reserve of rest. She couldn't imagine ever needing more.

"Then tell them you want to come home," said Vivian. She was unencumbered now, having trundled Ruth into George's eager arms. Ruth stared up at her with wide blue eyes, then nuzzled against her. George had missed her terribly in the day they'd been apart. "There's my good girl," she murmured. Vivian turned and walked to the window.

"Do you think they'll let me?" George asked.

"Let you what?"

"Go home." She supposed it was only natural that Vivian would be upset, distracted.

"You're not under arrest."

No, but she should be. Both of them should be, for what they were about to do.

"If they say no, just become a more difficult patient. They'll kick you out in a flash."

George inhaled the powdery scent of Ruth's nearly bald head. She'd never liked being difficult.

"Look, George, if you're going to do this, you're going to have to take charge. Otherwise, I don't see how you'll manage it."

"You're right."

"I know I am. Now, Quigley's cousin is coming tomorrow. He'll handle the paperwork." Vivian quoted a scandalous price for the handling of the paperwork.

"Okay," said George. She would have paid double if she'd had to.

"Good. I'd better go. Come home soon, George. Promise?" Vivian, pinch faced, reached for Ruth, and George reluctantly surrendered the sweet weight of her. Vivian's dress hung loosely on her too-thin frame. The delicate skin beneath her eyes looked bruised. George wanted to trade places with her, tuck her into a hospital bed and go home with Ruth herself.

"Promise."

"Should have told you both," said George. Her ribs were an edifice constructed purely of pain, but she forced air up through her lungs, determined to be heard. "Should have told you both when you were young."

"Sounds like someone has a secret to share," said the white-capped nurse, materializing next to Ruth. "Not uncommon at this stage."

"Just give her the morphine," said Ruth. "Just do your goddamn job."

The room fuzzed and dimmed, and she floated away from the pain, Ruth's warm hand enclosing hers.

Sleep.

Voices.

Tom and Ruth talking. Too far away for her to catch the words. Her hand still in Ruth's. She drifted between sleep and wakefulness, lulled by the sound of their voices until the current bore her out of earshot.

A comforting hum struck up in the center of her heart. It strengthened and spread outward. Warming her to her fingertips, her toes, her scalp. It revved, rocketed forward, the accelerating force of it pressing her against the mattress. No pain now. Just that miraculous bursting instant when thrust overcame drag and she was released, aloft. Rising. Up through a gray furze, escaping the cloud cover. Ahead of her the golden ball of the sun. Around her pure azure sky. So bright, but she kept her eyes wide open. No need to squint. Such perfect blue. Such beautiful streaks of light rippling through it. She picked up speed, soaring higher, racing straight toward the brilliant sun.

CHAPTER 61

"Ivy," her mother said.

"She's coming, Mom. She'll be here soon." Truth didn't matter anymore. Only her mother's comfort mattered.

George grimaced, and Ruth pushed the button—again—to call the nurse.

"Tell Ruth," her mother murmured.

"I'm right here," she said. Her mother's hand felt like ice, the fingers—once so strong and nimble, capable of fixing everything: bandaging knees, mending hems, repairing engines, soothing sorrows—clenched, rigid against the pain. Ruth gave up on the button and yelled toward the hallway. "She needs morphine! Now!"

"Ivy," George said again. Then uttered a jumbled string of syllables.

The nurse didn't look at Ruth when she entered the room. She walked slowly to George's bedside and spent a long time taking her pulse. Ruth wanted to strangle her.

"Just give her the morphine," she said. "Just do your goddamn job."

The nurse glared at her, then injected the drug into her mother's IV. In less than a second, George's fingers unclenched. Her breathing leveled out.

"I can't give her any more—I *won't* give her any more—this has to last until the next shift," said the nurse. "So you can quit yelling down the hall at me." She pivoted on her crepe-soled heel and stalked out.

By the next shift change, Ruth's mother was gone.

"I thought white roses for the casket," said Helen.

"That sounds fine," said Ruth.

"I had them put a navy dress aside for you at Herzberg's. I do recommend navy. It won't wash you out the way black does."

"That sounds fine."

"And I made an appointment for you at Lois's."

"I'm not getting my hair cut." She was grateful to Helen, but there was a limit.

"She's completely booked, but I convinced her to squeeze you in. Maybe she can just do a wash and set. Though I think it would look so pretty if you let her cut it. Lois is a genius."

After Helen left, Ruth called Lois to cancel the appointment.

"But Helen insisted I fit you in," argued Lois. "For your mother's funeral."

"My mother knows how I look. She never once suggested I look any other way."

"It kills them," said Kimberly when Ruth recounted these conversations. "Simply kills them that we keep our hair long. That we don't do the weekly wash and set thing."

There had been a time—well, that time had been most of her life—when what Ruth wanted most of all was to fit in. Before she left for Vietnam, she'd assumed her future held weekly appointments with Lois. Marriage to a man with a good job and a good handicap. Membership in the Junior League, then the Garden Club and the Literary Guild. Having babies and doing everything that everyone expected of her. The things Ivy would never do in a million years. She had planned, she explained to Kimberly, to do it all well enough for both of them.

"I know what you mean," said Kimberly. "I wanted all of that too."

"Maybe we can still have it—the parts that matter, anyway," said Ruth. "Together."

Something that looked like doubt flickered across Kimberly's face. But she leaned in and kissed Ruth, who kissed her back like she was making a vow.

The service was beautiful. Helen had handled everything: convincing the minister, reluctant because he hadn't known George, to speak, ordering the roses for the casket, arranging the impressive regiment of wreaths flanking it. The minister spoke about George's close relationship with her mother, the talented daughters she'd raised, her long marriage to Tom, her service during the war, her contributions to the Enid community. He left the details rather vague and made no mention of her partnership—business or otherwise—with Frank.

The Quigleys had flown in. Bob eyed Ruth warily as Joyce clasped her hand and slurred her condolences.

Don Patterson flew in. "This isn't the time," he said, "and I apologize for that. But have you heard from Vivian? Is she here?"

Ruth hadn't and she wasn't.

Adele's friends (those who remained) claimed seats near the front of the church. Tom's pilot friends filled the back pews, alongside club members and an assortment of aviation types. Kimberly fidgeted beside Ruth, flipped through the hymnal, fussed with the clasp of her purse, swiveled her head to look at anything other than the casket beneath its blanket of white roses. Ruth scooted closer to her on the hard pew. Kimberly scooted away, apparently determined to keep a good half foot between them.

The ladies' auxiliary laid out a luncheon in the annex—another coup spearheaded by Helen. Ruth poked at her Waldorf salad and chicken casserole. Kimberly had crossed the room to say hello to a table of fellow nurses and fallen so deep into their conversation that Ruth couldn't catch her eye.

Over near the buffet, Joyce Quigley swayed a bit on her kitten heels, and her husband steadied her. Don Patterson cornered Tom near the pitchers of iced tea. Her father shook his head, no doubt saying he didn't know where Vivian was either. From somewhere behind her, she heard Helen say, "They're in no shape to handle the thank-you notes. I'll probably take care of those too."

She must remember to thank Helen. For the dress she'd picked out, for the roses and the minister and the luncheon. And the thank-you notes. For doing all of that despite her husband's ashen face. Frank, still whip thin, had turned stoop shouldered overnight. He stumbled a bit when Joyce Quigley brushed past him, and Bob caught his arm to right him. He looked old and lonely. Ruth abandoned her plate and went to stand beside him.

He patted her shoulder. "Come by the office this week, Ruth," he said. "I'll walk you through your mom's portfolio. Give you the lay of the land."

Frank's secretary—and then Frank—called her house repeatedly, trying to set up a meeting. She decided to hide out at her mother's and tackle the thank-you notes instead. She bought a few boxes of black-edged Crane's and drove over. Tom had been sleeping in the guest room. His name was on the deed; the house was his. She'd tried to convince him to move back in, but he'd been noncommittal. He was George's executor, and he kept trying to talk to her about the will. She didn't want to talk about any of it. "Let's deal with these letters first," she told her father.

They sat in the kitchen, a fifth of rye on the table between them, and began. But they made better headway with the bottle than the correspondence. Ruth, eager for any distraction, jumped up at the sound of a car pulling up outside and went to the window. Two young men with gleaming shoes and baby faces stepped out of an olive-green sedan.

"Dad?"

In an instant, he was at her shoulder. "No," he said, taking in the uniformed men as they came slowly up the walk. "No, no, no."

She hadn't yet written to Ivy. Couldn't bear the possibility—the likelihood—that she wouldn't respond. Now, she understood, there was no point in writing her sister at all.

"No," he repeated when Ruth moved to the door, "don't let them in." As if keeping them outside, preventing them from speaking, would make it untrue.

"Dad, we have to let them in." She shifted him gently out of the way so that they could enter, led him to the couch. The young men followed a respectful distance behind.

They were well practiced. Serious, sympathetic, straight to the point. "We're sorry for the delay in telling you," the shorter one said. "But her paperwork contained some inaccurate information."

Ruth snorted, and he startled. "Sorry," she said, "it's just that, if you knew Ivy, the inaccurate paperwork wouldn't come as a surprise."

He continued as if she hadn't spoken. "They sent the file to Moody AFB first. It didn't reach us at Vance until yesterday, I'm afraid."

"But Moody's in—"

"Yes, sir. South Georgia, sir."

"Vivian," Tom said, and dropped his head into his hands. "So that's where she went." Ruth put her arms around him.

The taller one glanced at his clipboard. "Miss Vivian Shaw. That's correct, sir."

"She didn't call," said Tom, shaking in Ruth's arms. "Why didn't she call?"

But Ruth had a different question. "That plane," she said. "That plane was bringing Ivy home?"

"Yes, ma'am. Well, as far as California, anyway."

She would have taken California. Or Hawaii, or Guam. She would have taken Ivy remaining safely in Saigon, though she supposed *safe* and *Saigon* should no longer appear in the same sentence.

"I never realized she had so much," said Ruth. Tom had refused to put off discussing the will any longer. "She could have lived in a mansion. She could have—" But she found herself at a loss as to what else rich people might do with their money. Which was a shame, because now it was her money. It shouldn't be. She didn't deserve it, had no idea what to do with it. Maybe Kimberly would know. Maybe this bit of news would be just the thing to capture her attention and focus it back in Ruth's direction. She'd barely seen Kimberly since the funeral.

"Your mother could have done whatever she wanted," agreed Tom. "Well, she mostly did." Ruth detected no anger in his voice as he said this. "Now you can do whatever *you* want."

"I don't know what I want," said Ruth. Not true. She wanted Kimberly to stop dodging her at the hospital, to return to her bed.

"That's okay, sweetheart. You don't have to change a thing. Just go to work. Spend time with your . . . friend."

If only, thought Ruth. Kimberly had made herself scarce since the funeral. Always too tired from work or too busy with Lloyd to see her. "What about you, Dad?"

"I'll be here. You can see me too."

"No. I mean, shouldn't most of it go to you?"

"She left me a bit. And some to Helen and Vivian. But she wanted most of it to go to you and Ivy. Except for the plane. The plane she left just to you."

"What? Why?"

"It's a good plane. You can easily sell it. I know someone who might be interested."

"Cardiology is just swamped these days," said Kimberly when Ruth caught up with her in the hospital parking lot one morning. "I can barely find time to pour myself a cup of coffee."

Ruth feigned understanding. "What about tonight?" she asked. "It's been a while. I miss you." She reached out to touch Kimberly's arm, but Kimberly stepped just out of reach.

"Maybe. I might have to stay late."

"Come late, then. You know I don't mind."

"Okay."

"I'll cook something," said Ruth. Her cooking had improved. All it took was practice. Pork roast, she decided. With chopped iceberg salad and twice-baked potatoes on the side. Her mother's recipes. Dishes that made her nostalgic for the days when the five of them, Ivy and Tom and George and Adele and herself, sat down together. Now it was just herself and her father, and he bid every flight he could, keeping himself up in the air.

The roast was dry and the potatoes long cold when Kimberly finally called and said she couldn't make it after all.

"It's okay," said Ruth, trying her hardest to mean it. "Maybe tomorrow."

But the next day Lloyd was home sick and Kimberly couldn't come. The day after that, Kimberly announced that she and Lloyd had decided to freshen up their kitchen and she'd have to spend all her free time painting.

"I could help," said Ruth.

"Oh, sweetie," said Kimberly, and Ruth's heart swelled, "I couldn't possibly let you help. Not with everything you're going through right now. I just wouldn't feel right about that at all."

No one likes a moper, thought Ruth. She kept busy, kept it together. At work, during meetings with Frank Bridlemile to review her mother's investments, while listening as Helen tried to interest her in an excellent serve-and-volleyer from the club.

She kept it together—if only barely—when she spotted Kimberly across the parking lot. Kimberly waved, then pointed at the watch on her delicate wrist and darted into the hospital.

She kept it together when at last Kimberly called and asked if she could come over. "There's something I need to tell you," she said.

Ruth played it cool. Not much in the fridge, no dinner on the stove. She wouldn't chase or beg. She wanted Kimberly to understand this the moment she walked into the house.

"I wanted you to hear it from me," said Kimberly as she perched on the edge of the armchair, "and I think some of the other nurses in cardiology are starting to suspect. You know how everyone gossips at the hospital."

Ruth was ready to plead extra caution. Separate cars, staggered arrival and departure times from work. Whatever it took.

"And in a couple of months, there won't be any hiding it anyway, I suppose."

Ruth was ready to argue that she could be discreet for years on end.

"I'm pregnant."

She was ready for anything but that.

"You're what?"

"I'm going to have a baby."

"But—"

"I know I said I didn't want to have babies. I know I said that."

"You did."

"And Lloyd and I don't always get along."

"You don't."

"But your mom's service made me realize, I want to make a family with someone."

430

"I want that too," said Ruth. "More than anything in the world." More than anything in the world she wanted that with Kimberly.

"But we couldn't really, you and I," said Kimberly. "You know that, right?"

"No," said Ruth. "I don't." Ivy had been bringing children out of Vietnam when she died. An impossible number of orphans had been shipped to the United States. The supply and demand ratio surely tilted in their favor.

Come on, Ruth, she heard Ivy say. *You saw it yourself, what those kids went through. Now they get doled out to nice, upstanding American families. Little spoils of war. And you want in on this?*

Ruth ignored her sister. "We'd be good parents," she insisted.

Kimberly's brow squinched up the way it did when she was exasperated. "You're delusional. I can't keep living a delusional life, Ruth."

"You *will* be living a delusional life if you stay with Lloyd."

"He's not so bad," said Kimberly, her voice soft. "And we're having a baby together. So there's that."

There was also the Jet Way. The Control Tower. Ruth hadn't gone in months, but she felt right at home returning. There were airmen, stationed far from their hometowns, who were just as lonely as she was. She no longer saw the point in counting her drinks and knowing her limit.

At work, she argued with the doctors and the head nurses. She was reprimanded twice for tardiness—because sleep only descended in the hour before her alarm rang—and once for unkemptness—because her hair had escaped from its pins and she hadn't worn lipstick. The previous night had bled into morning, and she was still too drunk to apply it within its proper bounds, so she simply hadn't.

Now here she was, late again, bare lipped, her hair escaping its pins. She batted strands of it out of her eyes as she raced through the hospital lobby.

Kimberly caught her arm before she reached the elevators. She hauled Ruth into the restroom and made her splash water on her face. Then she repinned her hair, swiped a coat of lipstick on Ruth's lips, and handed her a tissue. "Blot," she commanded. Ruth blotted. "Now get some coffee and stay clear of your supervisor. You don't smell so great, to be honest."

"Gee, thanks," said Ruth.

"I'm trying to help you. But you could do a little more to help yourself these days."

"What do you care?"

"Don't do that, Ruth. Don't make me regret helping you keep your job."

No one likes a moper, thought Ruth.

She hid out in the cafeteria, sipping her coffee, wondering whether she'd be fired when the head nurse discovered her malingering again. A man approached her table. He wore civilian clothes—a crumpled linen suit—but Ruth recognized a military bearing when she saw one.

"Miss Rutledge?"

She nodded and gestured to the empty seat across from her.

"My name's Sam Benson. I worked with Ivy."

She leaned forward in her chair, pushed her coffee aside. She didn't need it now; she was bolt awake. "You were in Vietnam."

"Back and forth. As the situation dictated. I understand you're in the pediatric unit here—they say it's a good one."

Did they? Well, the children weren't dropping like flies, she supposed. The majority of them made it home, minus their tonsils or appendixes or adenoids. There was no Over There in pediatrics. Thank God.

"I spoke with Claire Stanich about you. She says you're wasted in pediatrics. That you should be in trauma."

"Mr. Benson, I can't see any reason why you'd need to talk with anyone about me. And so far, I can't even see a reason why you need to talk *to* me."

"I apologize. Professional habit." He placed a small box on the table between them. "A few things Ivy left behind in her apartment. She was in a hurry to get home. I'm sorry about your mother. And your sister."

"We weren't actually sisters," said Ruth. "But you already knew that."

"That's what she claimed. Even though she called in some favors to transfer you to Cu Chi. But then, I may not put as much stock in biology as someone in your profession does."

"And there's this," he added, sliding a pale-blue envelope across the table. A letter from her to Ivy. One of the later, pleading ones. Begging Ivy to take pity on their mother and come home, claiming that Ruth had found out everything and would only tell once Ivy got home.

"I'm afraid this didn't make it to her. I thought you might want it back."

"It's been opened."

"Yes. We kept a close eye on correspondence of our employees."

Ruth snorted. "The Donut Dollies knew so much."

"Let's not play games, Miss Rutledge."

"No, let's not. Is it the truth, that she never saw this letter?"

"It's the truth. There's one in the box that she did receive."

Ruth lifted the lid of the box. A postcard offering GREETINGS FROM OKLAHOMA! sat right on top. On its reverse: one of her nagging messages to Ivy, updating her on their mother's illness, pleading with her to write.

She was coming home because she loved us, thought Ruth. She loved us after all.

"I have a question for you, Miss Rutledge."

Ruth suspected that his question, rather than the return of Ivy's paltry effects, was the real reason for Benson's visit. She gestured for him to ask it.

He pointed at the blue airmail letter he'd brought her. "You told her you knew who her mother was. I had my best researchers on this. And unless you learned something from your mother or from Vivian Shaw—which strikes me as unlikely—I'd like to know what they missed and how you found out."

"I was lying," said Ruth. "Saying what I needed to say to get her to come home."

The corners of his eyes crinkled. He seemed pleased by her answer. He pushed back from the table, ready to stand, then paused. "Do you have any questions for me?"

So many questions. What had Ivy been doing in Vietnam? (What had any of them been doing in Vietnam?) How did Ivy get there to begin with? What was Sam Benson going to do now; what were all the Ivys and Bensons going to do, now that it was over? Where was he headed next, and what terrible price would everyone have to pay for it?

"Nothing you could answer. Not truthfully anyway."

The chrome-and-canary Cessna, so vivid in Ruth's memory, was clouded with pollen dust. Her father had found a buyer and she decided to take a last look at the plane before accepting the offer. She circled it, wishing her mother would talk to her the way Adele sometimes did. But Ivy's voice came to her instead, taunting her to open the door and climb inside. *Don't tell me you're chicken. I know you're not chicken. I watched you in Cu Chi.*

Ruth ran her hand along the top of a sun-warmed wing. Her fingers came away gray.

The plane was beautiful with its yellow swoops of paint. Voluptuous right down to its fenders. (Were they called fenders on planes? She wished she'd paid more attention.) But it looked lonesome alongside the planes tethered nearby. Planes whose owners kept the tires filled, the fuselage polished, the props oiled. She'd bring some towels out tomorrow and clean off the Cessna. Buff it until it shone. It would do her good to get out in the sunshine. Then reward herself with an early start at the bar.

Ivy's voice again, exasperated: *Come on, Ruth. Last one standing wins. And that's* you.

They'd only flown with their mother that one time. Now she was gone. Adele and Ivy too. She traced their names on the plane's dusty flank. A manifest of missing passengers and crew. Only she and Vivian remained, and Ruth wondered if she'd ever see Vivian again. But here was this plane. Her prize for winning. For lasting. No, she would not sell it.

CHAPTER 62

Cardinals calling from the pecan tree. Heavy, turpentine-tinged air. Towering pines and baked blue sky. Bermuda grass struggling for purchase in the sandy lawn. Crickets. Yellow flies. Spanish moss draping the live oak. Ant lions dimpling the sand driveway. Vivian had been away for years, and yet it felt as if she'd never left. As if she never fully could. But even now, that familiar adolescent desperation to get out, escape, go somewhere, anywhere but here, plagued her. Hahira wasn't home. Was Oregon?

She rocked on the porch, hoping to catch a breeze. Elizabeth joined her, must have sensed her restlessness. "It's not the same without Mama, I know," she said as she sat down.

"She wasn't the same for me as she was for you," said Vivian. There was no resentment in her voice, no resentment in her heart. At this point it was simply her accepted truth. Her mother hadn't been a real mother to her. Oh, Clara Shaw had fed her and clothed her, but she hadn't really taken an interest. She'd left that to Elizabeth and Clelia. They'd done their best, Vivian supposed, but they'd never filled the mother-shaped hole in Vivian's heart.

Elizabeth snapped her fingers. "Vivian!"

"Sorry. Daydreaming, I guess."

"Vivian, do you have a daughter?"

"That was a paperwork error, Elizabeth. The military makes them daily."

"A man called while you were out at Clelia's. Someone named Patterson. Looking for you. You sure you don't have a family you haven't told me about?"

He had tracked her down. She dipped her head to hide her smile, surprised by how pleased she was.

"He said your friend Georgeanne had passed and you weren't at the funeral."

Vivian stifled a cry. She'd imagined that by some magic her friend would win out, because didn't George always win out? And that if she didn't—if she was right about not having much time left—Vivian would somehow sense this and return to her in time to say a final goodbye and hold George's hand. Not that Vivian deserved that honor.

If only she'd told Ivy the truth the night she arrived at Vivian's door wearing that periwinkle sweater, everyone might have been spared years of heartache and loss. Maybe Ivy would have allowed Vivian to fly her home. Maybe, at the very least, she wouldn't have flown so far away from all of them.

George had been right, and Vivian had been wrong. And she'd made everything worse by hiding from George at the end. Running away when she should have been at her friend's side, fighting for her. With her. Another unforgivable thing she'd done to Ruth.

Motherless, sisterless Ruth. She deserved more than a mother-shaped hole in her heart. She deserved the truth. And if she couldn't forgive that truth, well, Vivian would have to live with that.

"Elizabeth, I need to go to Oklahoma."

"Your friend's funeral was days ago."

"I know, but there's someone there I need to talk to."

"I'm pretty sure he's gone back to Oregon. He said to tell you that's where he'd be. He said, 'You tell her I'm waiting.' A man waiting for you in Oregon, but you want to go to Oklahoma. I will never understand you, Viv."

"I know," said Vivian. "I won't even begin to try to make you."

George's house was curtained and dark. Vivian ran a hand along the underside of the porch glider but found no spare key taped there now. George and Tom had argued about that. Now George was gone, and Tom had his way.

In the stuffy phone booth at the airfield, she found a number but no address listed for R. Rutledge. She considered just calling. She wouldn't even have to admit she was in Enid. She could pretend she was checking in, ask how Ruth was doing, listen to her say that given the circumstances she was doing okay. They could make all the correct noises at one another across the phone lines, and then Vivian could carry on with her life and leave Ruth to hers.

Because how could Ruth possibly understand? What kind of mother abandons her baby? *If you had seen your parents on their wedding day,* she imagined telling Ruth, *how golden and perfect they were, you would have wanted to give them all the babies in the world to raise. You would have thought to yourself,* I could never measure up to that.

She set the receiver back in its cradle, then lifted it again and called a taxi to take her to the country club. If anyone would give her an honest accounting of George's last days, it would be Helen, who'd never approved of her and must like her even less now. Because Helen had been there, and Vivian had not.

Helen strode into the club with her racket propped on one shoulder. She looked remarkably fresh for someone who'd just finished bounding around the court. Vivian had watched her play a few points, admiring Helen's sure ground strokes, the way she announced the score in a firm voice before each serve. When she'd caught sight of Vivian, Helen had extended her racket toward her like a queen pointing a scepter and said, "I'm almost done out here. We can have lunch in the bar afterward. The tuna salad is surprisingly good."

The tuna salad *was* excellent. It provided some comfort while Helen described George's last days. And Ruth's troubles. Helen had a friend in administration at the hospital, and this friend had confided that Ruth skated on thin ice in her department. Not to mention, Helen had set Ruth up with a nice man—in insurance and doing *very* well. "I mean, he could have his pick! Well, he went to collect her at the time they had arranged, and Ruth's door was answered by—oh, I can't even talk about it, it's so upsetting.

"And I've offered to take her shopping, and to take her to get her hair done, and she always says maybe another time, but I know when I'm being put off."

Eventually Helen wound down, and Vivian extracted Ruth's address.

"Maybe you can do something with her, because she won't listen to me. More like her sister by the day. Rest her soul," added Helen. "Thank God George was already gone when they heard—that was a blessing. By the way, there was a man at the funeral asking about you."

"I know," said Vivian. Under Helen's persistent stare, she added, "Don Patterson. He's . . . We're . . . I think we're engaged."

"Congratulations. You might give him a call. He seemed quite worried about you, your fiancé."

Vivian reminded herself that she had once been a brave person. She'd tinkered with cars when no one thought she should. She'd run off with a barnstormer. She'd learned how to fly airplanes, and earned a living by continuing to fly them. All of this had taken courage and a fair dose of obstinance.

In her room at the Holiday Inn, she waited while the operator dialed her number in Oregon. She was going to do two brave things today. The first would be telling Patterson what he needed to know about her, that if he wanted to back out, she'd understand. Because she couldn't protect him from what had happened. Trying to do that was wearing her out. She didn't think he'd leave because she'd been raped—he was too solid, too good a man for that. But he might leave because she'd hidden it from him all these years. And that secrecy had kept him at a distance. He'd have every right to view it as a type of lie.

"Collect call from Vivian Shaw," said the operator.

"Vivian. Thank God."

By the end of it, she was sobbing, and he was silent. Stricken speechless, she supposed. She took one ragged breath after another, trying to get control of herself. When she could speak again, she said he could take what he wanted from the apartment, anything at all. But he interrupted.

"Just come home, Viv. Please. I wish to God that hadn't happened to you. But it doesn't change how I feel. I know who you are. You're exactly what I want—all of you. Come home."

Two hours later, she stood on Ruth's doorstep. The call to Don hadn't taken long. But recovering from it had required a shower and a change of clothes. Fresh lipstick and powder. The car she'd borrowed from Helen hadn't needed gas, but she'd stopped and topped it off anyway.

She'd hoped it might feel easier, once she told Don, to tell Ruth. But the call had left her jittery and drained and fearful of Ruth's response. Because Ruth would want to know how Vivian could have handed her to George and stepped onto that Greyhound bus. Five hundred dollars in her purse. Cash George had pressed into her hand at the last moment. Blood money. Child money. Don't-come-back money? Vivian had always wondered.

That day at the bus depot, she'd assumed it would be as easy to leave George as it had been to leave Hahira and her family. But George, it turned out, was firmly planted in the sandy soil of her heart. Their continued relationship hadn't been about Ruth. Vivian rarely thought about the baby—she couldn't allow herself to. Ruth and Ivy were a unit.

"The babies." George's daughters. And Tom's. Never hers. How could she possibly explain this to Ruth?

Vivian knocked. Then knocked again, louder. No one answered. She peeked through the front window and noticed that the apple hadn't fallen far from the tree when it came to housekeeping, when someone behind her said, "May I help you?"

She turned, and the young woman jumped. "Oh! I thought I'd seen a ghost for a minute. You look so much like Ruth's mother."

Vivian held out her hand. "Vivian Shaw," she said. And wanted desperately, for the first time in her life, to add, *I am Ruth's mother.*

"Kimberly Peale. I work at St. Mary's. With Ruth. I heard she called in sick today, so I came to check on her."

"She's not answering," said Vivian.

"I was afraid of that. She's probably at the Jet Way. Maybe the Control Tower."

"I see," said Vivian. "Helen mentioned something about her spending a lot of time in bars. To Helen that could mean five minutes, so I took it with a grain of salt."

"Well, much as I hate to agree with Helen about anything . . ."

"I see," said Vivian again.

"I hauled her home twice last week, and to be honest, I'm not sure I have a third in me. My husband doesn't like it. And if she doesn't start showing up at work soon, she won't have a job anymore. Not that she seems to care."

"I'll do it," said Vivian. "I'll make sure she gets home tonight. I'll talk to her." *For all the good it'll do,* she thought.

"Try the Jet Way first," said Kimberly. "That's where she usually starts."

CHAPTER 63

Ruth had been at the Jet Way since it opened. She'd stopped counting her drinks weeks ago. It hadn't taken long for her to become known as that easy nurse. The one who'd go home with just about anyone.

She didn't care what people thought or said. She only cared about erasing everything. And some nights—more nights than not—that meant doing just about anything with just about anyone.

The anyone at present was an airman who'd laid out a chunk of his fresh paycheck on Stoli for Ruth. She liked to insist on a top-shelf brand. Making them spend more, making them earn it. Earn her. He was half leading, half dragging her out to the parking lot. "Got my own truck," he was saying. "We'll get you home nice and safe now."

Ruth snorted. "You're not safe."

The airman laughed. "No," he admitted. "I'm not. But that's what you like, isn't it." He gave her a push and she staggered, started to topple to the pavement. But he caught her. Gave her a shake. She giggled. She liked it when they got rough. "Yeah, I thought so," he said. She hoped his truck wasn't too close. She wanted him to push her again. Let her fall. Skin up her elbows and knees. Maybe she'd be too heavy to pick up. Maybe he'd have to drag her a little. And that would hurt even more. Enough to drown out the real hurt.

Someone else tugged at her arm. Someone who called her by name. "Ruth, it's me."

"No way," said Ruth. "Let go." She'd stopped counting her drinks, but she still had rules. One of them was only one guy at a time. This one was persistent, though. He yanked her arm again.

"Hey, get off," said the airman.

Maybe they'd fight. That would be fun to watch. "Yeah, get off," she shouted.

"Ruth! Wait!"

"Jeez, lady. Back off," said the airman. He pulled her one way, and the lady pulled her the other. Lady? The voice *was* a little high. Ruth didn't object to the idea. A lady might remind her, in a good way, of Kimberly. But she was surprised anyone in Enid would openly propose it. Especially anyone who knew her name. She blinked, trying to clear her vision. Her mother's face loomed before her. Ruth screamed. Her mother screamed back.

"Shut up!" said the airman. "Both of you! Shut up!"

But the lady wasn't shutting up. She was shrieking, "Let her go! Let her go! Let my daughter go!"

Ruth screamed back, "Mom! Stop!" Headlights swept across the parking lot, temporarily blinding her. A car swung past. Passengers hung out the windows, gawping. The airman gave Ruth a final shake and let her fall.

"Look what you did!" whined Ruth as he bolted for a pickup at the end of the row. "Now what am I supposed to do?"

"Oh, honey," said the lady. It was Aunt Vivian. Aunt Vivian who had skipped the funeral. Who hadn't called even though she knew about Ivy. "Oh, honey," she repeated as she helped Ruth up from the pavement, "anything but that."

Ruth woke to the familiar flick-snap of a lighter coming from the direction of her kitchen. Her head hurt. Her mouth was Saharan. Her entire body felt wrong. None of this was unexpected—she felt this way most mornings. The physical wrongness was so familiar, it was easy to overlook. The new feeling—though Ruth suspected it wasn't new at all, only showing itself clearly for the first time in a while—was misery.

The drinking and the men had made her feel better for a while. And then they had allowed her to feel nothing, which was almost just as good. But now she just felt miserable and ashamed.

Oh, poor you, she chastised herself.

No one likes a moper.

She closed her eyes and willed her grandmother's voice away. *Why shouldn't I mope?* she thought. *Why shouldn't I say poor me? I'm motherless.*

Maybe not, her grandmother replied.

Another flick, the hiss of the cigarette catching, the snap of the lighter closing. By the time a hint of smoke reached her bedroom, she'd levered herself upright. She inhaled the comforting aroma of burnt tobacco. It reminded her of Ivy. The thought of Vivian in her kitchen was also comforting. It meant Ruth wasn't alone.

CHAPTER 64

Vivian spent the night on Ruth's couch. Not sleeping, as the couch was somewhat shorter than she was. But it had seemed imperative to stay, even after Ruth began snoring in the other room. As soon as the mourning doves called, she gave up on sleep. She rose and washed the pile of dirty dishes, wiped down the sticky countertops, swept the floor. All the things she never thought to help other women with, she did on this beautiful morning for Ruth.

She sensed George's hand in the design of the house. The rooms were small but well laid out. Windows and doors placed just right. The window over Ruth's kitchen sink looked out on a flowering shrub. Elizabeth would know what it was. George and Adele would have known. Wasn't that the sort of thing real mothers knew?

A wave of longing for her friend swamped her. She had been selfish. She had been weak. Too weak to stay at George's side. Too weak to call after Ivy died. Far too selfish and weak for far too long.

She brewed a pot of coffee and lit a cigarette. Ruth didn't have much food in the house. She'd go to the store later and take care of that. An image of George writing out her daily shopping list rose before her, and she had to sit down and put her head in her hands. When she looked up, Ruth stood in the kitchen doorway.

Vivian ashed her Winston and dabbed her eyes with her sleeve. "Sorry. I was just thinking of George."

Ruth shot her a look that said, "Better late than never," and went to pour herself a cup of coffee. The percolator shook in her hands. Coffee splattered on the countertop. She looked thin and tired and older than her years. Vivian wanted to fetch her some aspirin. But that was exactly what a mother would do. She didn't have the right.

"It was unforgivable," she said. "Me not being here with her at the end."

Ruth leaned against the counter, silent. Sipped from her cup.

"Unforgivable that I didn't call about Ivy."

Ruth sipped again.

"I am so sorry, Ruth. For all of it."

Ruth pushed away from the counter and joined her at the table, nudged the ashtray toward her. Vivian glanced at her cig, caught sight of the slump of ash just in time, and quickly stubbed it out. "And I'm sorry about last night—it wasn't my place to interfere. I have no right."

Still nothing from Ruth. Vivian reminded herself that she wasn't entitled to anything. Not forgiveness. Not a single word of speech. She forged on. "I gave up all my rights. For a long time, I thought that was the best thing. Because I couldn't have done half as good a job as your mom did. I still can't."

Ruth stared into her now-empty cup.

"I'm not strong like she was, and I'm sorry for that too. But I did what I thought would be best. I gave you two good parents—not perfect, I know—and a sister. I'm *not* sorry for that. George wanted to tell you all about it. That's why I left when she . . . I couldn't face it. I was sure you'd both hate me. Maybe you do. You should. I'm a coward."

A blue jay complained from a nearby oak tree. Locusts tuned up their late-morning static. A breeze stirred the flowering shrub. The sun beat against the window and brightened the kitchen.

Ruth's voice, when she finally spoke, was soft, almost a whisper. "I think she tried to tell me, near the end. But she was too far gone."

"She was waiting, hoping to tell both of you. I wish Ivy were here too. That's the way your mom wanted it." Vivian took a deep breath.

"But you're here. And I'm ready to tell you the whole thing. If you're ready to hear it."

Ruth stood and refilled her coffee cup, then topped off Vivian's. "Okay," she said.

Vivian fixed her gaze on the wall just over Ruth's shoulder and began.

When she finished, she said, "You probably have questions. Go ahead. You can ask anything." Now that she had said it, she could look directly at her daughter.

Ruth's eyes were wet. Her voice trembled when she spoke. "Did you hate me?"

"Never." Vivian removed the coffee cup from Ruth's hands—capable, womanly hands she wished she'd held more often while they still belonged to a child—and clutched them in her own. "Not once. But I was a mess. I couldn't . . . It was the best thing I could think to do. I couldn't bear to give you to a stranger."

The blue jay filled the silence with its shrieking. "What else?" asked Vivian. "Ask me anything."

Ruth pulled her hands away and stared at the windowpaned sun patch on the kitchen floor. Then looked up at Vivian with a defiant glint in her eye. Vivian braced herself. This was the moment Ruth would send her away, tell her to never come back. She'd never hated Ruth, but Ruth had every right to hate her.

This time Ruth's voice was steady and sure. "She left me the Cessna. Could you teach me to fly it?"

Vivian startled, and Ruth folded her arms across her chest. "You probably think I should sell it," she said. "Everyone else does. Dad keeps offering to talk to his pilot friends. Helen says someone at the club wants it."

"No," said Vivian. It was a beautiful plane. Curves and swagger, comfort and power in just the right measure. Vivian remembered stalling it into George's last flat spin, the final time she'd heard George really laugh. "I'm glad you want to keep it. Of course I'll teach you. If you feel up to it, we can start today. But you need to eat something first."

"Do you think she realized I hated that she flew?" asked Ruth as she buckled into the seat beside Vivian.

George had suspected, but what did it matter now? "Why didn't you want her to fly?" Vivian asked.

"It's not that I didn't want her to. Well, maybe I didn't. I mean, it never felt safe to me. Even though Dad flew all the time. It never felt like something a mom was supposed to do."

"Well, she wasn't like most moms."

"No, she wasn't. I resented it sometimes. And it scared me. Especially after Dad left."

"Because you worried she'd leave too?"

"She could have. She and Frank. We had Grandma Adele. We would have been fine. Not really, but in theory."

"She never would have done that. Not in a million years." *I am never going to leave you again, not in a million years,* Vivian thought.

"Yeah, I know that now, but when you're a kid . . ."

Ruth's hands trembled as she placed them on the controls.

"Don't be nervous," said Vivian. "This is going to be easy as pie today." She smiled, because easy as pie sounded like something George would say. "We have a clear sky. We've got low wind. And I've taught tons of people how to fly—people far less capable than you."

"Okay," said Ruth.

"Ready, then?"

"Ready."

Vivian launched into her intro of the dash and controls. She talked through the takeoff. Once they reached altitude, she demonstrated steering, climbing, descending, narrating everything she did, keeping it simple and clear. After a while she asked, "See anyone else around up here?" When Ruth, leaning forward to check the blind spot on the right, confirmed that the sky was clear, Vivian said, "Okay, you take her."

Ruth kept the plane pointed straight ahead. After a while, she nudged it to the south and grinned. Then to the west, and whooped. Vivian whooped too. She relished the moment when a student fell in love with flying, with the power of the plane and their sense of authority over it. "Remember your blind spot," she said, and Ruth steered beautifully into an S turn to open up her view. She was a natural. Vivian hated to reclaim the controls when it was time to land. She wanted to stay aloft forever, watching Ruth navigate the vast American sky.

"Can we go up again tomorrow?" Ruth asked as they taxied in. Her eyes sparkled, and the color was up in her cheeks.

Vivian, thinking back to her first flight, said, "That's how I felt after my first lesson with Louis."

"Who's Louis?"

"Louis was a barnstormer. He taught me how to fly." Ruth listened intently as Vivian told her about Louis and the barnstorming circuit, about running away from home to learn to fly.

"You must miss him," she said when Vivian finished.

Vivian set the brakes and locked the controls. "Now and then. But I have someone I miss much more now."

"Oh. You probably need to get home," said Ruth.

It was true. Don had waited for her for so, so long. Even before she'd left Oregon, he'd been waiting for her. But hadn't Ruth waited even longer? "I'll call him," said Vivian. "And sure, we can go up again tomorrow." Then, remembering the nurse who'd found her on Ruth's doorstep, she added, "That is, if you don't have to work."

She hoped Ruth didn't. She wanted to remain in the Cessna, talking with her daughter, telling her stories. She dreaded the moment Ruth climbed back through the cabin and out of the plane. Because then Vivian would return to her lonely room at the Holiday Inn. And she still had so much to tell Ruth. About meeting George. About Sweetwater and Camp Davis and all the places that came after.

"I think I'm about to get fired," said Ruth.

"Your friend—Kimberly—she said she was worried about that."

"You met Kimberly?"

Vivian described their doorstep encounter. "She seems very concerned about you."

"Hah," scoffed Ruth. Her jaw worked, and her cheeks reddened. She nodded to herself as if committing to a dare, then faced Vivian and said, "I don't really like my job. But it's a way to stay close to her, to still see her now and then. Kimberly was my girlfriend."

It took Vivian a moment to realize Ruth meant more than someone to go shopping with. She wondered if George had known. Then wondered if this was some sort of test. The look in Ruth's eyes suggested it might be. Well, she was determined to pass it. "My aunt, Clelia. She had a girlfriend." It was the wrong word, but it was the best one Vivian had. "Her name was Rosemary."

"And people knew?"

"I knew. If other people did, they kept it to themselves." One more item on the too-long list of things no one talked about. "You can tell me about her. Kimberly. I'd like to hear."

Ruth fiddled with her seat belt. "There's not much to tell anymore. She's married. And she's having a baby."

"I'm sorry, Ruth."

She felt furious with that tiny nurse. Standing on Ruth's doorstep, pretending concern, when she was just assuaging her own guilt over abandoning her. Vivian knew all about that kind of guilt. "I know it's not the same, but Louis—the pilot I told you about—he didn't really love me. He was . . . keeping me and leaving me all at the same time. I finally realized he wasn't strong enough to call it quits. I had to be the one to go."

"You think I should quit?"

Vivian was too tired and angry to bite her tongue, to refrain from offering advice she hadn't earned the right to give. "Only you can decide that, but if you're just staying at that hospital for her, what's the point?"

CHAPTER 65

Ruth called in sick the rest of the week, claiming a bad flu. Each morning, Vivian took her up in the Cessna, and every day the plane and the sky felt more her own. Vivian's stories were becoming hers too. When she learned Don had proposed and Vivian hadn't seen him since, Ruth accidentally let the nose dip.

"You have to go home!" she said as she quickly brought it back up.

"I will. But I can't just leave you, Ruth."

"That's ridiculous. I'm not a baby. I'm perfectly capable of taking care of myself." Was she? "I'll be just fine." Would she? "And you'll come back soon." *Would* she? "I hope."

"I will. Absolutely. As soon as I can. And once you get your license, you can come to us too."

The next morning, Ruth donned her white dress and shoes. She pinned up her hair and did her makeup. On her way to the hospital, she stopped at the airfield to see Vivian off. "I'll be back soon," said Vivian. Her forehead pinched with worry. *I'm not always such a mess,* Ruth wanted to say. *I had a bad season, but it's over now.* Out at the edges of the airfield, the leaves of the pecan trees were just turning. Ruth felt something turning inside her too. She trusted herself to hold steady while Vivian was in Oregon.

"What will you do while I'm gone?" asked Vivian, failing to hide her concern behind her artificially bright voice.

Ruth gazed down at her white shoes. They were still a bit damp at the toes from the polish she'd sponged over the scuffs that morning. She'd tried to look her best. A defense against all the things the other nurses would whisper while she did rounds. *She's sick all right, but it's not the flu. Did you hear she goes home with a different guy every night? Do you think she'll argue with the doc again today?* To armor herself against their sympathetic superiority.

"I think I'm going to quit my job," she said. "No, I don't think it. I'm really going to do it."

Vivian's face broke into a grin that was anything but artificial. "I can't wait to hear all about that."

The personnel office waiting room held two rows of candy-colored molded plastic chairs facing a large steel desk. Behind the desk, guarding a wall of matching steel file cabinets, an attractive young woman sat typing. "How can I help you today?" she shouted over the clatter of her IBM Selectric. She hit return with a flourish, spun her chair to face forward. She had apple-pink cheeks and curls like a cherub, a spark in her eyes that touched something inside Ruth and set it smoldering.

"I'm giving my notice."

The receptionist turned off the typewriter. Ruth wanted to lean across the desk and sniff her, to see if she smelled like the apples she evoked. "Please take a seat," she said, gesturing to the hard-candy chairs. "I'm Frieda, by the way."

"Ruth. Ruth Rutledge."

Frieda rose from the steel desk and pivoted like a dancer to the cabinets behind her. She slid open a drawer and riffled through it, pulled out what Ruth could only assume was her file. "Someone will be right with you, but I'll get the paperwork started. May I ask why you're leaving us? Not moving away, I hope."

"No." It had been a long time since Ruth had considered leaving Enid. She couldn't think where she'd go if she left now. She hadn't expected to have to give a reason for quitting, wasn't sure how forthcoming she ought to be. Frieda flipped open Ruth's file and began to read. Ruth's heart sank. All of her tardiness and unkemptness and general argumentativeness was no doubt recorded there. Frieda's eyes, when she raised them at last, held a question. Ruth's cheeks burned.

"You were in Vietnam? I'd love to hear about that." She closed the file, glided out from behind the desk, and sat down beside Ruth.

There was no one else around, and Frieda seemed to mean it, so Ruth told her about Cu Chi. About the hospital and hooches, the wounded GIs and the nape victims and Over There. About staying for a second tour of duty. But not about Ivy. *Not yet,* she thought.

"Sorry," she said at last. "I'm blabbing away, and you must have work to do."

"Oh, not at all." Frieda tucked her chin and said, "I have a confession to make. Someone will not be right with you, and there isn't any paperwork to get started. All you need to do is sign this form here. So, Ruth—I like that name, by the way—what do you plan to do next?"

"I'm not sure," said Ruth. Frieda's fingers brushed hers as Ruth accepted the pen she offered. "But I'm learning to fly." It felt like bragging to say it out loud. Even more so to say, "I have a plane."

"Wow! And date here," said Frieda. "When can I get a ride?" Again, Frieda's fingers lingered on hers as she took the pen back.

"Oh, I've only just started learning."

"I guess it's not something you pick up overnight. How long do you think it will take?"

It was embarrassing to admit she had no idea. "I'm not sure. I'll ask my . . ." And even more embarrassing to realize she had no idea what to call Vivian now. "Teacher," she finished.

"Well, you know where to find me. When you're ready."

Elizabeth looked like a smaller, older version of Vivian. That plus her evident nervousness about the plane made Ruth tender toward her. She helped her buckle in, made sure the straps weren't too tight. Elizabeth kept up a stream of anxious patter as Ruth prepared for takeoff.

"I never thought I'd see the day," said Elizabeth. Her husband, Henry, wasn't coming to Vivian's wedding. "Maybe if there'd been enough notice for him to drive. And what's the rush after all these years? As I said, I never thought I'd see the day. Though, of course—oh, here we go! My, you're doing very well at this."

"Thank you." Ruth grinned. She'd been flying solo for a year now, but she never tired of impressing a passenger. "Do you fly often, Mrs. Carroll?"

"Aunt Elizabeth, dear. And no, I do not. Once to Miami for a conference with Henry's work. Nice of them to invite the wives along. But I prefer to keep my feet on the ground, thank you, ma'am."

"I used to say that too," said Ruth. "So you never know . . ."

"Oh, not me. I could never. I'll leave that to the men. Although I just read somewhere that the big airlines are bringing on lady pilots now. But it's still *mostly* men. I always thought Vivian would have married sooner if she'd spent her time doing more ladylike things. Men don't like women competing with them."

"That's for sure," agreed Ruth.

"And she was so pretty. It's a shame about how tall she is. Oh, dear, you're tall, too, aren't you?"

"I am."

"I don't mean any offense. It's just a fact that men prefer more petite women, that's all. But you got her looks, at least. That's something. That's from Mother. Even when she got older, folks always said how pretty she was. Even at the end when she was failing. Daddy married up, in more than one way. He was a bit of a renegade, Daddy was. But I suppose Vivian has told you all about them."

Vivian hadn't. Ruth, suspecting Elizabeth might take offense at Vivian's reticence on the subject of her parents, made an agreeable sound. Not that she needed to. Elizabeth was already speaking again.

"I guess it's no surprise she taught you to fly. She loves it so much herself. And that's what we do, after all."

Ruth found this confusing. "Wait . . . You fly too?"

"Oh, dear Lord, no. I already told you I don't. I mean that's what mothers do. Teach their daughters the things they love themselves.

"Take me," Elizabeth went on. "I love to quilt. And I'm not half-bad at it. I taught Rebecca—that's your cousin, my second oldest—when she was only eight. And she just finished up a Wedding Star. Just wait until you meet her. Oh, I am sorry none of your cousins could come."

Elizabeth went on to tell Ruth all about her cousins. Ruth listened avidly. Cousins were a novelty. She'd grown up with none, and now, according to Elizabeth, she had seven. Possibly eight, depending on which ones her uncle Walter claimed on any given day.

Elizabeth fell briefly silent during the landing, then started right up again as Ruth helped her out of the plane and escorted her to the car. The airfield was jammed with private planes. Plenty of Vivian's and Don's war friends still flew. Those who didn't own planes had begged rides from friends. Vivian and Don had shuttled others in themselves. Elizabeth had waited until the last possible minute to accept the offer of a flight. Ruth had agreed to get her so that Vivian could take care of the final wedding details.

At the church, Ruth peeked into the chapel. She scanned the pews until she found Frieda. Her *special friend*, as Helen liked to say. As in, "Make sure your special friend has a nice dress for the wedding. Not one of those long skirts she likes to swan around in. Think church dress."

"Frieda's been to weddings before, Helen. She knows what to wear."

"Well, she doesn't know what to wear to dinner at the club, so I felt I ought to say something."

Her father escorted Helen to a good seat near the front. Frank Bridlemile had succumbed to a massive myocardial infarction not long after Frieda moved in with Ruth. Helen had buried Frank on the opposite side of the cemetery from George, mourned for a respectable interval, and then struck up a tasteful flirtation with Tom. He didn't seem to mind. What would Ivy and Frank Jr. have made of it? Ruth wondered.

She felt suddenly lonely. Ivy and Frank Jr. were gone. Some days she felt like the only remaining child of her generation. And far from childhood too. She hurried to the annex to change into her dress.

"Everything all right out there?" asked Vivian as Ruth entered the dressing room.

"The Quigleys just sat down," said Ruth.

"Ah, good. I was hoping they'd make it."

"I wish . . ." Ruth trailed off. Ivy and George and Adele had shadowed her all day, all the way to Hahira and back.

"I wish they were here, too, sweetheart. It's my biggest regret about not doing it sooner."

Ruth quickly changed into the sea-green dress Helen had advised her to buy. ("Brings out the flecks in your eyes," said Helen. "Mm-hmm, sure does," agreed Frieda.) Vivian looked elegant in a slate-blue suit of shantung silk. Soignée. A word Ruth associated with Ivy, the two of them getting ready for Spring Fling in their shared bedroom, each in a new tea-length dress. Ivy had been in a good mood—perhaps she hadn't yet tired of the boy who was taking her. Ruth pictured her sister so clearly, swishing the skirt of her dress and saying, *Très soignée.*

"Très soignée," Ruth said as she fastened George's pearls around Vivian's neck and smoothed the shoulders of the suit.

"I have no idea what that means," said Vivian, "but I like the way it sounds."

"Just something Ivy used to say."

Vivian ran a finger along the pearls.

"Mom's parents gave her these," said Ruth, grazing the smooth pearls with her own fingers. "For her seventeenth birthday. She would have gotten them at sixteen, Adele always said, but that was the year she asked for the plane."

"A plane at sixteen and pearls at seventeen. George had it okay, didn't she?"

"She did," agreed Ruth. "You look beautiful."

"So do you." Vivian turned and placed her hands on Ruth's shoulders. "You sure you're okay with all of this?"

A gentle tap at the door and Frieda, in a flowered dress with butterfly sleeves, poked her head in. "The preacher says ready when you are."

"Don't you look lovely," said Vivian.

"Thank you. Helen nodded at me, so I knew I looked okay."

"Better than okay," said Ruth, delighting at the pink that rose in Frieda's cheeks.

"See you at the reception," said Frieda. "Break a leg, Miss Shaw!"

"It's Vivian, and you know it." Vivian smiled. It was impossible to scold Frieda.

Frieda would struggle with that directive, Ruth knew. She'd been raised better than to call anyone from a previous generation by their first name. But at least she had options. Vivian had stopped being Ruth's "aunt" the day she told Ruth everything. If Ruth had to introduce her to someone, she said, "This is Vivian Shaw." If an explanation was required, she added, "My mother's friend." She found it remarkably easy to get by without labeling their relationship. And since no label seemed quite right for the woman standing before her, Ruth usually avoided using one at all.

"You asked if I was okay with it all," said Ruth. "And I am. I'm happy you're getting married, and I'm really happy that you'll be close by."

Initially, she'd been thrown by Vivian and Don's plan to move to Enid. Did that mean she had to stay? What if she felt drawn to someplace more exciting? "Then you'll go," Vivian had said. "We'll still see each other. We both own airplanes, after all." But for now, Ruth had decided, Enid was home. Not because she grew up there. Not because of the comfort of a known landscape or familiar voices. Enid was home because Frieda was there.

At the back of the chapel, Ruth took Vivian's hand. "Ready?"

"Ready."

The organ sounded. "All right. Let's go." She almost added *Mom*, but stopped herself.

The guests stood. The past reared up within her. Ivy and George and Adele pressed close, urging her forward. Maybe another day she would call Vivian Mom. For today it was enough to take slow, deliberate steps as she preceded her up the aisle.

The reception. Smoked salmon canapés, mushroom vol-au-vents, and pineapple chicken at the country club. The catering arranged by Helen. The champagne paid for by Ruth. Every direction she turned, another waiter bearing a tray of the stuff. Tongues and ties loose with it. Vivian and Don dancing. Guests knotting up and then untangling, so much to say, so many years gone by. Quiet corners sought and abandoned. Ruth, keeping company with Ivy and George and Adele, stalked the perimeter, observing, listening.

To her father telling Helen he had to fly to LA in the morning. Would she mind if he phoned her during the turnaround?

To Joyce ordering "just soda" at the bar.

To Frieda telling Elizabeth she hoped to get married herself someday.

"Oh, I'm sure the right one will come along," said Elizabeth.

"She already has," said Frieda. Elizabeth's mouth hung open for a beat. Then Frieda clinked her champagne glass against the older woman's and they both drank.

To Don telling the Quigleys about the honeymoon. He planned to show Vivian Memphis, his hometown, take her to hear blues and eat ribs, to meet the relatives who couldn't travel to the wedding.

She declined another glass of champagne from a passing waiter and snuck off to the sitting room, a frilly parlor that served as a buffer between the rest of the club and the women's bathroom. The walls were papered in a rose pattern, barely visible beneath numerous gilt-framed mirrors and watercolors of Edwardian ladies strolling beneath parasols. The furniture was old fashioned and deep. Ruth sank into the crushed-velvet sofa. She'd woken up before dawn to collect Elizabeth and had been on her feet ever since arriving back in Enid. She slipped off her heels and savored the quiet. But not for long.

Two pilots' wives rushed in. "Pardon us!" said the first. "Nature calls," sang the second as they stumbled into the restroom.

Hoping to forestall any conversation when they came back through, she picked up a newsmagazine from the side table and flipped through it, not really reading, just pretending absorption. Halfway through, a photo of a 737 caught her eye. Female Pilots Take to the Skies read the headline, over a shot of a woman wearing a captain's uniform like her dad's. This must be the article Aunt Elizabeth had mentioned. Ruth scanned the pages. It was true. Several big airlines wanted, or at least allowed, female pilots now.

The door swung open again. "There you are!" said Frieda. "We wondered where you'd run off to." Vivian followed her in.

"Look," said Ruth, passing the magazine to Frieda.

She scanned it quickly and handed it to Vivian. "Babe, you've got to do it!"

Vivian's eyes shone. "Oh, Ruth, it would be perfect for you!"

"I don't know. I've only ever flown the Cessna."

"No one starts with 737s," said Vivian. "And there's a whole crowd of aviation people right outside who could get you access to bigger planes. Your dad. Quigley! Especially him. You could do this, Ruth."

Yes, whispered Ivy, whispered George, whispered Adele. *Yes, yes, yes.*

Back in the ballroom. Back in her shoes. Vivian and Don fed one another cake. The band struck up one last song. Did she dare to dance with Frieda? Yes, she did.

A final toast from Tom to the newlyweds. Helen catching the bouquet. Guests collecting their coats. Did she dare to ask Quigley if he could arrange for training in some larger aircraft? Yes, she did.

Rice and confetti showering the couple as they dashed to the car. Ruth and Frieda in the front seat, waiting. Vivian and Don giggling like children as Frieda revved the engine, put the car into gear, and sped them away.

By the time they reached the airfield, the sky had turned from blue to violet. Far out on the horizon, the orange-gold sun rested. Crickets sang. Swifts dipped and wheeled over the grass, acrobats hunting. Dew dampened Ruth's shoes as she hugged Don goodbye, then Vivian.

Vivian kissed Ruth's cheek, brushed stray grains of rice from her hair. They didn't say goodbye, just looked long at one another.

Then Ruth and Frieda showered the couple with a final handful of confetti as they climbed into the plane.

The Bonanza's position lights flicked on, then the taxi lights. The engine sputtered awake and warmed to an easy idle. Vivian and Don waved from the cockpit. The Beechcraft hummed down the runway, picked up speed, lifted into the air. It cleared the tree line, rising, and banked east, Memphis bound, its lights growing small in the darkening sky. Ruth held Frieda's hand as the plane bore her mother away, and knew that it would bring her back.

AUTHOR'S NOTE

Years ago, I heard a *Radio Diaries* episode about the Women Airforce Service Pilots program. I was immediately struck by the amazing women who stepped up to serve their country, and, as soon as the war was over, were expected to step right back down (without complaint) and transfer their talent and energy to home and family life.

American Sky is historical fiction due to its time frame and subject matter, but, really, it's a story about family and friendship. Even casual students of World War II and the Vietnam War will notice that I've emphasized *fiction* at the expense of *historical*. That said, I couldn't have written this book without considerable research. See below for a partial list of sources I found helpful.

The WASP program was born in August 1943, when the Women's Flying Training Detachment (WFTD), led by Jacqueline Cochran, and the Women's Auxiliary Ferrying Squadron (WAFS), led by Nancy Harkness Love, officially merged into a single organization. For the sake of narrative simplicity, I've ignored distinctions among these programs and treated them as a single entity called the WASP. For instance, I use WASP to refer to Georgeanne and Vivian and their early 1943 training cohort, even though these women actually would have been WFTD pilots at that time. Ethel Blankenship, the WASP who visits Vivian at Avenger Field, actually would have been a WAFS pilot at the time of her visit.

I've also conflated certain events and places. For instance, WASP training took place in two locations, but Georgeanne and Vivian's class trains only at Avenger Field.

With the exception of the inimitable Jacqueline Cochran and the WASP's CO at Camp Davis, the characters in *American Sky* are entirely fictional and do not represent any actual pilots, military personnel, Red Cross workers, combat nurses, or civilians. The "real" characters who do appear are fictionalized versions of themselves.

I'm indebted to many excellent books, articles, podcasts, and documentary film sources. Any and all errors in my interpretation and/or presentation of places, events, processes, and people are my own.

If you'd like to learn more about the WASP, I recommend:

- *A WASP Among Eagles: A Woman Military Test Pilot in World War II* by Ann B. Carl
- *Flying for Her Country: The American and Soviet Women Military Pilots of World War II* by Amy Goodpaster Strebe
- *Women in the Wild Blue: Target-Towing WASP at Camp Davis* by David A. Stallman
- *Greetings from Camp Davis: The History of a WWII Army Base* by Clifford Tyndall
- *Our Mothers' War: American Women at Home and at the Front during World War II* by Emily Yellin
- *Fly Girls: Breaking Barriers in the Skies* (documentary film) produced and directed by Laurel Ladevich for PBS *American Experience*
- *The WASPs: Women Pilots of WWII* produced by *Radio Diaries*

If you'd like to learn more about American women who served and worked in Vietnam, check out:

- *War Torn: The Personal Experiences of Women Reporters in the Vietnam War* by Tad Bartimus

- *Women at War: The Story of Fifty Military Nurses Who Served in Vietnam* by Elizabeth Norman
- *Women in Vietnam* by Ron Steinman
- *Home Before Morning: The Story of an Army Nurse in Vietnam* by Lynda Van Devanter

ACKNOWLEDGMENTS

I offer heartfelt thanks to the intrepid women who, when our country needed them, stepped up to serve in the WASP, WFTD, WAFS, WACS, WAVES, SPAR, WARD, medical units, USO, Red Cross, and other military and military-adjacent organizations. And also my immense gratitude to those who serve and have served in today's armed forces. I *see* you and the sacrifices you and your families make, and I salute you.

Victoria Sanders has been a tireless and visionary champion of this book. I'm thankful for her creative direction and full-throttle support, and for Benee Knauer's wise, skillful editing. I couldn't ask for a better group of wingwomen than Victoria, Benee, Bernadette Baker-Baughman, and the rest of the VSA team.

Chantelle Aimée Osman's dedication to publishing books about women in places they aren't supposed to be made her the perfect editor for this book. Working with her, Jodi Warshaw, Jen Bentham and her brilliant copyeditors, and the talented, thoughtful team at Lake Union Publishing has been an absolute pleasure.

Thank you to the amazing writers who have been so generous with their time, intelligence, and friendship. Leigh Anne Kranz (BGE, girl!), Jackie Shannon Hollis, and Ella Crabtree read early drafts of *American Sky* and pointed me in new and better directions. Sarah Bailey, Janie Mae Cohen, Kate Rubick, Helen Sinoradzki, and writing genius Joanna Rose helped me elevate key scenes. Jennie Shortridge believed in me before I dared to believe in myself.

Thank you to Steve and Sally Dasher for raising me to love books, to Ken and Mike Dasher for enduring and forgiving my bossy big sister–ness, and to all four of them for making the transitions that come with military family life as easy as possible. When your home is an ever-shifting location, the people who share it make all the difference.

Thank you to Owen and Ella Crabtree for teaching me new ways to look at the world, for cheering me on, for conversations—silly and deep—about life and books. And for their excitement about this book in particular.

My first reader is always Peter Crabtree, which means he sees my writing at its worst. And even so, he reads the next version, and the one after that. For this, for the time and space to write, for believing in me, for reminding me to dance, for the love and laughter and everything else that makes up our life together: Thank you.

ABOUT THE AUTHOR

Photo © 2024 BMAC Studio

After a nomadic military-brat childhood, Carolyn Dasher set down roots in Portland, Oregon. *American Sky* is her first novel.